# The
# HISTORY
## of
# MISCHIEF

Winner
2019 Fogarty Literary Award

# The HISTORY of MISCHIEF

## Rebecca Higgie

*For Marye and Mum*

# Jessie

There's an old lady outside vacuuming her driveway.

I've seen old ladies do many things, but I've never seen an old lady do this.

It's 3 am. She's across the road at Number 61. She drags a round vacuum cleaner on wheels, sucking up the sand in the cracks of her driveway as a fluffy white cat watches her from the veranda. It's loud, like how a plane sounds as it's taking off. I've been on six planes so I know.

I wonder why Kay hasn't woken up. Maybe she's ignoring it. Maybe the old lady does this often and the other adults on the street have decided to pretend it doesn't happen. Adults do that a lot. Maybe I'm the only one who's ever seen her.

She turns the vacuum off, takes out a pair of glasses from the pocket of her nightie, and inspects her work. She turns the vacuum on again and shuffles back and forth, going over any spots she missed. Once she reaches the front door, she turns it off and pushes it inside. The cat flicks its tail and goes inside too.

From the doorway, the old lady looks out at the street. She can't see me though. There's lace over the window so I can peek out without people seeing me. I smile at her just in case. She doesn't smile back. She just looks, as if she's waiting for someone, and then goes inside. The lights go off at Number 61. The street is quiet again.

I go back to bed. Kay will be angry tomorrow if I'm tired. She's always angry these days. She used to be silly and fun. She used to tell stories about weird old ladies like the one from Number 61. Now she just goes to work and snaps at me and won't let me eat ice-cream, except on weekends. If I'm good.

My name is Jessie and I'm nine years old. I'm good at many things. Like counting. I can count lots of things without losing where I'm up to. I counted all the names on the giant gravestone in the park. There are two hundred and ninety-eight on the stone spike in the middle: one hundred and two on one side, one hundred and two on another, and ninety-four on the third side. They are men from Guildford who died in the war. On the fourth side, there's a sign that reads 'THEIR NAME LIVETH FOR EVERMORE'.

Kay says it's a memorial not a grave, but I don't believe they buried all those men in other places and put their gravestone here. I like to guess where they are lying under my feet. I count out every one, taking a big step so they have lots of room between them. There are way too many to be buried under the gravestone itself. I have to go past the footpath and into the park to count out all of them.

Kay won't let me go to the park by myself. She says it's not safe because you need to cross two roads and train tracks. Also, there are strangers around, especially near Alfred's which is a burger place that has a fire outside and ladies who yell numbers at the customers. But I like to go to the park. When it rains, I imagine the ground being eaten away, leaving all the coffins out in the open. Everyone walks past like all those men aren't there. Sometimes I worry I'm being rude by stepping on them. I say, 'I'm sorry, Allan A.M. I'm sorry, Allan G.T. …' I use their names so I hope they forgive me.

I wish Mum and Dad had a gravestone but Kay said they

didn't want to be buried. I want a tomb for them like we saw in Europe, where people are buried in mini temples called mausoleums. Others are in big marble coffins above the ground with angels, skeletons and Jesuses all around them. In Venice, there's a whole island graveyard. They have plastic lights on the graves that never go out and a huge stone lady in long robes. She looks down and has one hand on a coffin. I wasn't supposed to, but I took a photo of her. Mum said she looked like sorrow. I wanted to remember what sorrow looked like. I want something like that for Mum and Dad. I want everyone to feel sorrow for them too.

## *Jessie*

'Time to get up, Jessie.'

The first wake-up call. I pull the covers over my face.
Kay leaves for five minutes, then comes back and opens the
curtains.

'Come on!'

The light can't get through my doona but I know what's
coming next. I grip the covers.

'Get up, Jessie!'

She yanks the doona out of my hands. Bundles it up and
leaves. It's cold and bright. I'm so *so* tired.

Kay's at the kitchen table, sitting on my doona. I glare at her.
She smiles at me, not a proper smile, a fake one. She takes her
earphones out of her ears.

'Morning,' she says.

I sit down. She pushes a bowl of cornflakes towards me.

'Eat.'

I nudge the cornflakes with my spoon. They bob up and
down in the milk. Some sink when I poke them.

'You need to stay at school today. I can't keep leaving work
because you decide to go home without telling anyone.'

I fill my spoon with milk and let it slowly drip back into the
bowl.

'Jessie, please,' Kay says. She looks tired. I wonder if the old
lady from Number 61 woke her up with her vacuuming.

I put the spoon in my mouth. 'It's soggy.'

Kay snaps. 'Well, don't let it sit then!'

She snatches the bowl and dumps the cornflakes in the sink. She fills it again and shoves it back in front of me. My eyes go blurry with tears. Kay sighs.

'At least half in the next ten minutes. Please.'

I eat half a bowl. Then she walks me to the bathroom, turns the shower on, checks the water and waits until I get undressed. I don't like her watching me but this is the rule now because yesterday I sat on the bathmat in my jammies and let the water run for ten minutes. I smile when I remember how angry she was, how she screamed and shut off the shower and said I could go to school smelling like shit. That made her even angrier because she doesn't swear anymore now that she's supposed to be a real adult.

So I take off my jammies and get in the shower. I know I'm being annoying but I don't care. I hate Kay the most in the mornings, when she makes me do the things Mum used to make me do. Since the accident, Kay's stopped putting on makeup and doing her hair. She doesn't wear nice clothes or put on nail polish anymore. She wears button shirts she never irons and ties her hair up in a boring ponytail. She looks more like Mum now. She has Mum's thin brown hair that flops about when she moves. She's soft and has big cheeks that Dad called puppy fat, even though Kay is twenty now.

Me, I look like Dad. I have his nose. That's what Grandma said at the funeral. She touched my nose and said 'Dear Harry' and cried a lot. I used to have his hair. Dad and I were the only ones with black hair, and we had lots of it. It was thick and a little wavy, not like Mum and Kay with their limp straight hair. Dad called theirs boring hair. Me and him: we were the funky hair gang.

But my funky hair is gone now. The doctors shaved it off.

When I woke up it was gone and everything hurt and there were staples in my head. I have a big scar there now. It runs from the top of my head to my right ear. It goes red in the shower, like it's angry. The hair is growing back a little, but it stays away from the scar. Kay bought me a wig but I lit it on fire in the backyard at our old house.

I get out and Kay helps me dry off and get dressed. My school uniform is red and blue, but Kay lets me wear a pink beanie with sparkly cat ears even though it's not really allowed. I glance in the mirror, seeing the uniform and cat ears. I start to cry again.

'I'm tired.'

'I know,' Kay says softly, and puts my backpack on my shoulders. I let it slip off. She picks it up.

'I'm hungry.'

'There's an extra banana in your bag.'

She takes my hand and leads me to the door. She gets the big umbrella 'just in case'. As we walk to school, I glance at Number 61 and imagine the old lady in there, sleeping with her fluffy cat on the bed, warm and happy and dreaming about vacuum cleaners that can suck up all the sand in the world.

Kay leaves me at school. She puts her earphones in and walks away. I know she can feel me glaring at her.

I hate Wednesdays because Wednesdays are dance days. The dance teacher, Mrs Lornazak, dresses like she stole the craziest things she could find out of the kindy costume box. Today, she's wearing chunky red glasses and a poufy pink skirt with black roses on it. Her shoes are sparkly and red, like Dorothy in *The Wizard of Oz*, and she has hundreds of jangly bracelets.

We go to the undercover area. She makes the boys get in one line and the girls in another. I sit on the concrete in the far corner, leaning against the wooden bench.

'Not today, Jessie?'

She says it every lesson and then touches my arm. I shake my head.

'Maybe next time.'

One of the boys asks why he can't sit out too and she snaps at him to get in line. There are whispers, getting louder as the weeks go by.

*It's only cuz her parents are dead.*

Miss Sparrow, our normal teacher, isn't at dance. I don't know what she does. Maybe she has lunch. There's another lady in the class who isn't a teacher, and she's always here. Her name is Mrs Armstrong and she does things for the teacher, like photocopying, reading stories, and taking the autistic kid outside when he yells. At dance, she sips her coffee and sits on the bench next to me. Sometimes she asks if I've seen a new movie and then tells me not to because it's 'garbage'. Sometimes she tells me knock-knock jokes that make fun of teachers. But most of the time, she doesn't say anything.

A boy skips over to us at the end of the first dance. I don't know his name, but he's the weirdest boy in class. He's skinny and short. He has a grin that takes up his whole face. He does strange things, singing and dancing on his own in the mornings when he's dropped off. He has a tiny square iPod like Kay's and he sings pop songs in another language. If anyone teases him about it, he asks if he can teach them the words. He doesn't notice when people are annoyed or mean or don't want him around. When I first started at the school, he yelled that my head had a cool line on it and I was bald like his dad. The whole class laughed and Miss Sparrow told him off. He didn't think he did anything wrong. At recess, he asked if we could be friends. I said no. He still bothers me. He bothers everyone.

'You should dance with us!' he says.

I ignore him.

'Mrs Lornazak doesn't mind if you don't do it right.'

I ignore him.

'Dancing is good for you because dancing is exercise. When you exercise, your brain gets full of happy chemicals called dolphins.'

'I don't want dolphins in my brain,' I tell him.

'They aren't like normal dolphins. They're happy dolphins. Everyone has them!'

I put my head down. All my happy dolphins are dead. Dancing can't bring them back.

'Get back to your cha-chas, mister,' Mrs Armstrong says. 'How else will you become the next Justin Bieber?'

He explodes with laughter. 'Justin *Bieber*!'

'I would have said Fred Astaire, but you don't know who he is, do you?'

He laughs again and runs back to class.

'I think he could do with a few less happy dolphins,' Mrs Armstrong says.

I blink the tears away.

Kay's not here. The bell went twenty-three minutes ago and she's not here.

I stand by the gate between the school courtyard and the out-of-bounds area. The principal, Mrs Fraser, tells me to come wait in the office.

I watch the clock. 3:26. Kay's only been late once before and that was only by three minutes. Normally she arrives before the bell goes. She stands off to the side and doesn't talk to any of the parents. She always has her earphones in, only taking them out when I come. She asks if I have everything – 'Is your lunchbox in there? Where's your jumper?' – and then we leave. She smiles at anyone who says hello but never stops. She shrugs her shoulders like she's apologising.

But she's not here now. The office lady tries to call her but she doesn't answer.

I hate that Kay drives to work. We don't need a car. We have the train near our house. It goes right to her work in the city. She doesn't have far to walk. Too many people use cars and it's dangerous and bad for the environment anyway.

I try not to think about cars so I look at the pictures on the wall, of all the faded faces from Guildford. I wonder if my picture will be there one day. Maybe girls one hundred years from now will wonder what I was like.

Everything is old here. Even the new things look like they came from a black-and-white movie. The school is the oldest in Western Australia. I think that's why the heating isn't good in the classrooms. Grandma told me that many of the houses in Guildford are from colonial times. They have fireplaces that work and little signs that say they're 'heritage listed'. The busy road near our house doesn't have normal shops. There's a place that sells rusty metal things and broken chairs, and a hotel that was burnt years ago but just got fixed. I went in there last week when I shouldn't have. There are still burnt bits sticking out of the roof. There's a bakery too where sometimes Kay will buy me a jam donut, but only if I hold her hand when we cross the road.

Our house is old too. It was Grandma's place before she went to the nursing home. She went a long time ago, before I was born. We didn't even know about the house till Kay met with the lawyers. We always just saw Grandma at the nursing home. I think Dad was supposed to sell her house but he never did. When we first arrived, it was covered in dust and the plants were dead except for the ivy, which still covers the veranda and blocks the drains. Small sculptures hide between the weeds. Some are like the statues in Europe with their blank eyes. But there are tiny dragons and jousting knights too. Some are painted messily, like maybe a kid painted them.

I didn't want to move here but I didn't want to be at home anymore, where we all used to live. Everyone knew about the accident. At school, kids I didn't even know cried like *their* parents had died. They came to the funeral and sobbed and hugged each other. I hated them for it. For weeks, parents from school would drop by without calling and give us big pots of food. It was always the same: 'I made way too much and thought you might like some. It's my kids' favourite, you know. But how are you, Kay? We all miss Jessie at school, she's such a lovely girl. You tell me if you need anything, okay?' Kay started ignoring the doorbell. Then we moved.

The house is surrounded by a fence made of tall iron bars and a gate covered in metal roses, some in full bloom and others just little buds. You need a big key, like the ones you see in movies with castles, to open it. When we moved in, Kay gave me one of the keys. It has a small copper rose on top, its petals only half open. On the handle, there are the strangest words: *Property of A. Mischief.*

'Huh,' Kay said when I first showed her. 'I didn't notice that.'

'What's A. Mischief?'

'I dunno.'

Maybe Kay's locked out because she forgot her key. Why wouldn't she just come to school and pick me up? We could open the gate together, like we do every day. She makes me put my key in the gate and then puts her hand on mine and we turn it together. I have to do it even if I'm angry with her. I wonder if she's home yet or if she's still on the road in her stupid car.

'Jessie?'

I turn to the office lady. She's on the phone.

'Kay's at home but she's had a little problem. One of your neighbours is going to come get you.'

We don't know any of our neighbours.

'I'm not allowed to go with strangers.'

'Kay says it's okay because Mrs Moran has been helping her.'

'Why can't Kay come and get the neighbour to fix whatever it is?'

The office lady pauses. She purses her lips together like she's trying to decide whether to tell me something bad. 'Kay needs to be the one to fix it. Everything's fine, there are just people she needs to wait for.'

I glare at the office lady and her lie. The best thing to do when adults lie is to be quiet and stare as angrily as you can. She goes back to the phone.

'She's not keen to go with your neighbour.'

Kay says something LOUD because I can just hear her down the phone. The office lady nods a lot and mutters, 'Of course, don't worry, I'll talk to her, don't worry,' and then hangs up.

'Kay says it's very important. She says Mrs Moran is not a stranger, so you can go with her.'

I glare at her until she looks away. Then I look at the clock. 3:41.

At 3:46, I hear a meow. A big one. *MOWW*! The lady from Number 61 comes into the office. Her fluffy cat trots in beside her on a bright pink lead.

'You're Jessie then, are you, dear?'

I nod.

'I'm Mrs Moran,' she says. 'This is Cornelius. Be polite, Cornelius.'

The cat meows and lifts its paw.

'Be a good girl and shake Cornelius' paw.'

I shake the cat's paw. It meows at me again.

'Cornelius says it's very nice to meet you.'

This lady's weird.

'Be a good girl and say "it's nice to meet you too".'

I look at the lady from Number 61. 'It's nice to meet you too.'

'No, to Cornelius, dear. Say "it's nice to meet you too, Cornelius"'

I look at the cat. 'It's nice to meet you too, Cornelius.'

The cat meows again.

'Good, good. Let's go then.'

The old lady from Number 61 leads me out of the office. We walk towards home, with Cornelius trotting in front of us on his lead. He has a pink harness too, and swishes his fluffy tail at us. It looks like a feather duster dancing.

'Now, I bet you've never seen a cat on a lead before.'

I shake my head.

'He's a very clever puss, aren't you, Cornelius?'

The cat meows.

I wait for a moment and then ask, 'Is Cornelius a boy?'

'Of course. A most fine gentleman.'

'Why does he have a pink lead?'

'Pink suits him, dear.'

I don't know what to say to that.

'Where's Kay?'

'Well now, dear, your house has been burgled. It looks like nothing was taken, but your sister arrived as it was happening. She scared the little bugger away but she's a bit upset so you need to be nice to her, alright? She's talking to the police now.'

Suddenly I feel sad and angry that we're here in this strange old place where the locks are no good and people try to rob you.

A police car leaves just as we arrive, but there's still a white van with blue writing that says BRIGGS AND SONS' LOCKSMITHS – 24/7 RELIABLE SERVICE. YOUR FAMILY'S SECURITY IS OUR FAMILY'S TOP PRIORITY. Kay is talking with a man who holds a toolbox on his hip.

'Don't get me wrong, we can change every lock, but I don't want to cost you a fortune for nothing. The little shit probably found it under the mat or something. We don't even need to change the backdoor lock; he left the key in there.'

'I don't care how much –'

Kay sees me and stops. She then leans in close to the locksmith. All I hear is, 'I'll pay after-hours, whatever' and 'all the windows, doors, everything'. For a while, the man just looks at her. He has that same face that people get when they find out Mum and Dad are dead. 'It's pity,' Kay said to me once. 'That look is pity.'

So the man, with his pity face, nods and says, 'I'll do you a quote.'

He goes inside and Kay turns to us. Her eyes are red and she hugs her elbows.

'Thank you for bringing Jessie home, Mrs Moran,' she says to the old lady from Number 61.

'My pleasure, dear. We had a lovely walk, didn't we, Cornelius?'

The cat meows.

Kay takes my backpack inside and gets me a glass of orange juice for no reason. I sit on the veranda and drink it. More men come, pudgy men who are smiley and hairy like the other locksmith, only younger. They go through the house like it's theirs. The old lady from Number 61 tells me not to worry, that Kay is being 'precautious and very wise'. She goes back to her house and brings us cold pasta, which she makes us eat, and puts a tub of fancy ice-cream in the freezer 'for later'.

When the locksmiths finish, it's very late. Except for the old gate lock, they really do change everything. Kays pays them from the credit card she's only used once before and they leave. Then Mrs Moran and Cornelius leave. The house is quiet.

Kay goes into every room and turns all the lights on. She turns the TV on. She checks all the new locks. Then she goes into the kitchen and takes the ice-cream out of the freezer, the fancy one and our regular one.

'We'll let it soften,' she says.

'What happened?'

She won't look at me. 'Do you want Caramel Honey Macadamia or Mint Choc-Chip?'

'What happened?'

She opens the lid on the fancy ice-cream and tests it with a spoon. 'A guy broke in. I scared him away. He didn't take anything.'

'How did he have a key?'

She looks at me now. 'What? He didn't.'

'The locksmith said.'

Kay looks at me like the office lady did. 'He's wrong. I left the backdoor unlocked.'

'Why'd you change all the locks then?'

'The locks were old and needed to be replaced. Now the house is much safer and I'll never forget to lock the door again, promise. You can remind me every time we leave and you can help me check.'

I want to scream YOU'RE A LIAR LIAR LIAR but I don't. Kay looks sad and tired. Her eyes are droopy. So I ask, 'You okay?'

Kay scrunches up her forehead like she might cry. 'I'm okay. This ice-cream isn't very soft though.'

She microwaves both tubs and gives me the bowl she usually uses for soup. She squirts so much Ice Magic on top that it doesn't fully set and then gives me my favourite teaspoon (the one with the cat on it). She takes me to the TV and gives me the remote.

'I'm going to the loo,' she says. But she goes to her room and closes the door.

She's in there for ages. When I finish my ice-cream, I go to her door. She's crying inside, soft, like she's sobbing into her pillow. The last time I heard her cry like this was at the hospital, where she howled and pulled her hair and said sorry a lot. Then

Grandma came and a man in a suit came with papers, and so many people came with papers, and she was always on the phone. She went quiet then, and stayed that way.

I wonder if I should go in there and give her a hug. But I hate people touching me when I'm sad, so I go back to the TV and count how many times the lady on *Lateline* says 'Prime Minister' as she interviews a man in a grey suit (thirteen in a bossy voice like she thinks he's a liar, four in a calm voice, two with a smile).

When I wake up, the TV's still on and it's raining outside. The rain is so loud I can't hear the TV. Kay's still not here. I peek down the hallway. Her bedroom door is open.

I walk down the hall and find her in the study at the front of the house. The study has a whole wall of bookshelves, with books going from the floor to the ceiling, and a fireplace with old photographs of Grandma, Dad and other people I don't know. There's also a desk and a chair, and a pretty couch that's small enough to fit right under the window. But Kay's not sitting on the chair or couch. She's on the floor in the corner of the room. She stares into the other corner. I look too. There's nothing there. Just bookshelves.

Her eyes flutter as I come into the room.

'Hey,' she says quietly.

I sit down next to her. Thunder rumbles in the distance.

'Would you like some ice-cream?' I ask Kay.

'I'm okay.'

She still looks at the corner.

'What are you looking at?'

'The books,' she says. 'Aren't they pretty?'

The books are not pretty. They're covered in dust. The carpet is nice though, red with dark swirls. It lifts up in the corner where Kay is looking.

I point it out. 'Do we need to fix the carpet?'

Kay looks down and frowns. She scrambles over and lifts the carpet like she's peeling off a sticker. It comes away easily. It's not fraying. Part of it's been cut.

'It wasn't like that before,' I say.

Kay doesn't seem to hear. She tugs as hard as she can. I grab the corner of the carpet and help. Then I see it.

A trap door.

It's a square in the floor, no larger than two rulers across, with flat metal hinges along one side and a keyhole on the other. I look into the keyhole. Darkness.

'Open it!'

Kay sticks her pinkie in the keyhole. She feels around the trap door's edges.

The keyhole looks familiar. Large and old. Like the gate key.

I'm still wearing my school pants. I take the key out of my pocket.

'That unlocks the gate, silly,' Kays says.

'Can we try it?' I ask.

Kay smiles. 'Sure.'

I put the key into the lock – it fits! – and turn it. Something clicks and when I try to pull the key out, the door swings open.

A book.

Just a single book inside a small box in the ground. A dusty black thing without any words or pictures on the cover. I pick the book up. It's small but heavy.

I look at Kay. She smiles and says, 'Go on.'

I open the book *very carefully* but its spine creaks. I stop.

'It's alright,' Kay says, and I open the book again. The first page is blank. The paper is thick, a very dull dirty white. On the second page, written in pretty black lettering, is the book's title:

*The History of Mischief.*

Mischief. Like the key.

A small symbol is drawn below it: two curves, like a smile and a frown, joined by a straight line and a little circle, an odd eye, above the smile. I can't help but touch it. I'm very careful and only touch with my fingertips. Kay turns the page. Just a few words:

*For Pan and The Blackwood.*

'Who's that?' I ask.

'I don't know,' Kay says. 'Turn the page.'

I turn the page. It's a contents page with a long list of names and dates.

Kay points to one of the entries. '316 BC,' she mutters.

'What's BC mean?' I ask.

'Before Christ,' Kay says. 'Two thousand three hundred years ago.'

'This book is over two thousand years old!'

'No, it can't be,' she says, touching the paper.

'Look at all the cracks,' I say, pointing at the spine.

'Yes, but it's too well preserved,' Kay says. 'And look, it says "Transcription Note". It's a copy, not an original.'

'Can we read it?'

Kay turns the page and starts to read out loud.


*Transcription Note*

The History of Mischief *is no ordinary history. It records the secret millennia-old practice of mischief and its practitioners, who, when practising their art, assume the title of A. Mischief.*

*The original* History *was a book of signatures that, upon being touched, granted the practitioner unpredictable magical abilities along with the memories of previous mischiefs. Each entry told*

*of their greatest acts and, as such, the dates listed*
*mark the period of their tenure as a mischief.*
*The History survived thousands of years, but*
*then began to degrade in the nineteenth century.*
*Only some of the histories remained intact. Those*
*that survived were recorded by myself and Chloe*
*McKenna.*

*The histories here take first person form, as they*
*were observed through the memories and emotions*
*held in the original book. More details of the*
*transcription itself feature in my story, at the end*
*of the History. Chloe believed the original History,*
*with its decaying memories, would restore itself.*
*Until that time, this record shall be its history.*

*Henry Byron*
*a.k.a. A. Mischief the Two-Hundred and First*
*5 August 1966*

Kay says, 'That's the year Dad was born.'
And we turn the page.

# A. Mischief the First

*Athens, Greece 316 BC – 236 BC*

Our first day in Athens was fading. The sun was dripping below the horizon, casting a pinky-orange hue across the darkening sky. The bustle of early evening on the agora: food stalls, restaurants, shops. The noise, the blending of human voices, animal cries and slave chains, was life going by. It was the end of the day and, for a moment at least, I was free.

I meandered with a weary, lazy gait towards the Eridanos River. I'd abandoned my shoes as soon as I was given the night off. It was a rare thing, a time where the only one I served was myself. I couldn't remember life outside slavery. I was born into it, or, in my fantasies, perhaps I was the son of a defeated monarch. I was the only slave I knew without a name. I was just 'the boy'. I was a man really, around eighteen or so, but the title hadn't shifted. I smiled to myself, enjoying the feeling of sand between my toes, the scratch of it, the way it stuck to my feet. I felt like the boy of my namesake.

The river came into view. It was not as busy as I expected. There were a few women filling their jugs with water, but no one else. It didn't take long to realise why. An elderly man was resting against the marble steps, completely naked and scratching himself for all the world to see. He held a cup in one hand.

The man's frame was ravaged by hunger, the joints in his

limbs and hips jutting out as though his bones wished to burst from his flesh. His skin was a sunburnt brown, as tanned as it was wrinkled, and he had knotted white hairs on his head, his chin and the scrotum he so publicly scratched. He looked up and considered me. Then he turned his cloudy eyes to the sky.

I returned to the river, equally indifferent, and took those final steps. As marble and sand gave way to moist earth, I dropped to my knees. I cupped my hands, scooped up the water and drank, slurping deeply.

'HA!'

A great exclamation, then – smash! I inhaled a gulp in surprise and coughed, water spluttering from my nose and mouth. The old man stood, his arms outstretched. His ceramic cup lay in pieces by his feet. He fixed his eyes, now wide and blazing, on me. He shouted in a tone that was gleeful and surprised.

'A child has beaten me!'

He laughed, a throaty cackle punctuated with the odd high-pitched gasp. He gripped his belly. He looked *utterly* mad. He gestured at his broken cup and muttered something about human folly and having everything we needed already. Then he pointed at me. He grinned and his eyes sparkled. They were a clear shiny blue, the cloudy white all but gone.

'There is a dog in you, pup!' the old man roared. He hit me hard on the back – too hard for a man his age – and then cupped his hands and drank too, giggling between each gulp. After a long drink, he pulled himself up and walked back towards the agora.

*Dog.* I suddenly realised I was looking at the man my master wanted to meet. I followed him. Eventually his giggly form came to a large wooden barrel, overturned and nestled into a corner of marble between the agora and the Eridanos. There was no doubt: this was the rogue Cynic philosopher, Diogenes of Sinope.

By the time I made it back to camp, the sun was set. So many lanterns were lit among the tents, I could see them before I left Athens' gates. The lights hovered in the dark, like menacing spectres waiting on the edge of the city. I knew Athens wanted us gone, this army camped outside their walls. But no one defied my master. No one defied Alexander the Great.

And yet, as I approached my master's tent, I heard raised voices.

'We cannot advance into Persia without assistance from Athens.'

'It is intolerable that I should have to beg for a few ships!'

'Yes, but Athens knows we cannot sack them as we did Thebes.'

Eventually, his generals shuffled out, looking grim.

I took a deep breath and entered.

Alexander was alone, sunk down in his chair as he gazed absently over the maps in front of him. He looked tired and mildly annoyed. It was an expression I knew well. My first memory was of Alexander, then no more than six years old himself. He had tested his blade skills by stabbing a knife between my outstretched infant fingers. He cut me twice but I didn't cry. He liked that. I was a plaything that lasted longer than the others. I guessed at my age in proximity to his. He was twenty-one.

'Didn't I give you the night off?' he mused.

He didn't look at me.

'Yes, but I found Diogenes, Master, and thought it best to notify you immediately.'

'Immediately?'

'Forgive me, Master, you were engaged with more important matters.'

'So you waited?'

'Yes, Master.'

'Good boy,' he replied, a small glance my way. 'Did you seek an audience with the philosopher on my behalf?'

I dropped my head. 'No, he was … somewhat confronting.'

Alexander smirked. 'No matter. Tomorrow. You will find him tomorrow.'

He said it like a threat. I mumbled yes as he turned back to his maps. He held out his empty cup. I rushed to fill it with wine.

*Find him.*

I woke early and slipped back into Athens. But Diogenes was not in his barrel, nor was he at the river. I searched through the bustling city streets for hours, trying not to look at the graffiti that marked every building. Many of the drawings mocked Alexander. The first one I saw depicted him as a dwarf with a giant sword, cutting the head off his father Philip II. His other tiny hand was outstretched to catch the crown of the fallen king. Rumours about King Philip's death followed wherever Alexander went. If he caught any such whisper, he cut the tongue out of the person who spoke it. Yet, they still rumbled on like faraway thunder, a common theme in the gossip of Athens.

Then, I saw him: Diogenes, fully-clothed this time, lumbering down the middle of the road, swinging a lantern with theatrical flair. The lantern was lit, despite it being midday. He swung it at passers-by, narrowing his eyes to study them. He then scowled, disappointed.

I followed as he trawled up and down the agora. People frowned back at him, others laughed, many smiled.

'It's daytime, dog! Is the sun not enough for you?' one man yelled. Laughter rippled through the crowd.

Then he turned and fixed that craggy, fierce scowl on me. He held the lantern up to my face and leaned in so close our noses almost touched. He grimaced, as if the sight of me offended him. He spun back around and went on his way. I paused, then trotted up alongside him.

'What are you doing?' I asked.

'Looking,' he barked.

'What are you looking for?'

'An honest man.'

'I can show you one.'

He stopped. His bright, suspicious eyes turned on me. 'Oh yes?'

'Alexander the Great, King of Macedonia. He desires an audience with you.'

Diogenes laughed and continued walking. 'Any man who calls himself "the Great" is as honest as I am young.'

A tiny seam of mischief opened inside me, and I grinned. 'My master is visiting the great philosopher Plato at his academy. I believe there is a lecture today. Perhaps you'll find an honest man there.'

He smiled wickedly. 'Perhaps you are right, pup.'

As we approached the amphitheatre, I spotted Alexander, surrounded by his generals and various Athenian noblemen. He looked uninterested in Plato's lecture. His entourage watched nervously. A bored tyrant was no good for anyone.

Diogenes walked to the front seats. He stopped right beside Alexander. He didn't acknowledge him, nor anyone else, and turned his back on the king. A small gasp echoed around the chamber. Diogenes ignored it, watching Plato with exaggerated mock interest, nodding despite the philosopher's sudden silence. Plato glared back with open contempt.

'Sit. Down,' Plato instructed.

I whispered who he was to Alexander.

'Oh! Make space for the philosopher,' Alexander said to his

men, shooing them so Diogenes could sit on his left. 'Sir, won't you join us?'

Diogenes ignored him. Plato commanded him to sit again, and then added, 'Friends, I may have said that man is a featherless biped, but perhaps we have found the exception. A man as dog.'

Diogenes grinned. 'A featherless biped? I will fetch you a fine man.'

He left. Just left.

The entire audience, including Alexander and Plato, looked confused.

'Go after him,' Alexander commanded.

So again, I followed. Diogenes marched through the streets with purpose.

'My master would like to speak to you,' I said.

'I'm coming back,' he snapped. 'No need to follow.'

'What are you doing?'

'Getting Plato his man.'

'A featherless biped?'

'A featherless biped.'

'What's a featherless biped?'

'A two-legged creature with no feathers.'

'Oh, that's quite clever. Man is quite unique in that regard –'

Diogenes grunted his disagreement.

He stopped at a chicken stall, where dead creatures hung in varying degrees of featherlessness. Live chickens squawked in a cage, stuffed in so tightly that their wings bulged out in tufts.

'One of the plucked ones!' Diogenes commanded.

The man behind the stall smiled at him. 'I don't mind giving you scraps but a whole chicken, Diogenes, that is too much.'

'Send your boy to me. I will counsel him and his friends. The importance of listening to parents.'

'The last time I sent my boy to you, I found him barking outside your barrel.'

'A fine lesson in humility.'

The merchant, though still smiling, shook his head. 'No, Diogenes. I can give you a head or a foot.'

Diogenes turned to me. 'Do you have money from your master?'

'No,' I said.

He sighed. 'No matter.'

'What do you need it for?'

'To make a point.'

*To make a point.* For some reason, this enchanted me. A feeling of playfulness prickled my skin. I spotted the cage full of chickens. There was a pin in the cage's door, keeping it bolted shut.

My eyes fluttered between that pin and the crowd. No one seemed to notice me. I grinned and something surged inside me. The pin magically flew from the latch and the door burst open. I gasped, astonished. The chickens spewed out, squawking and flapping as they flooded the streets. The merchant yelled for his son as he tried to grab the chickens nearest the cage. I snatched one of the plucked birds from his chopping block and fled alongside the escaping chickens. I ran through a cloud of feathers with a featherless biped in my hands.

Diogenes didn't thank me but he grinned, took a feather from my hair and wiggled it in front of my nose. A gaggle of the escaped chickens followed us as we walked back to Plato's Academy. Diogenes didn't seem to find this strange.

By the time we reached the amphitheatre, Plato's lecture had finished. The audience was clustered in groups, debating or gossiping. When Diogenes arrived, a hush descended. The philosopher held up the chicken and proclaimed loudly, 'This is Plato's man!'

Some men stifled a laugh, others scowled. Suddenly, the live chickens burst forth, flapping and squawking as if this use of their dead kin offended them so. Diogenes laughed, a delighted throaty roar.

I saw something I'd only seen a handful of times in my entire life: Alexander smiled.

In the following days, Alexander sought out Diogenes on multiple occasions. We witnessed him lift his leg and urinate on men who labelled him dog. We visited as he snoozed in his barrel, his fake snoring getting louder the more we tried to speak to him. Once, when Diogenes lay in the sun, Alexander stood over him and said, 'I can bestow upon you anything you desire, Diogenes. Tell me. Is there anything I can give you?'

The philosopher squinted at the figure towering over him and then knocked him with his foot. 'Yes, you can get out of my sun!'

Alexander stepped aside, moving his shadow off Diogenes. The philosopher promptly went back to ignoring him.

Alexander was never fazed by Diogenes' blatant rudeness. If anything, it amused him.

'He adds some spice to the tedium of this city,' he commented once.

And tedium dogged Alexander everywhere. He spent most of his time with Athenian noblemen who were openly gracious but quietly despised him. For me though, Athens was the very antithesis of tedium. It was alive, wicked, mysterious and layered. The graffiti about Alexander seemed to multiply, and yet so few people were shocked by the blasphemy that filled their surrounds. No one noticed things that in other cities would stand out. *I* didn't stand out. It was odd not to be seen, as I'd often garnered attention due to the colour of my skin. In Athens, there was too much happening to be noticed as strange.

As I wandered through the agora, I noticed lanterns hanging above stalls, in windows. I smirked, and suddenly they flickered to life. My eyes widened. I walked past another and blinked. A tiny flame sparked out of nothing.

I stopped. I looked for every lantern, candle and torch I could see. I willed them to life. They all burst into existence. With a small wave, but never touching a single one, they went out. I looked around to see if anyone noticed. I heard one woman exclaim from inside a restaurant, but nothing else.

A man shoved me and told me to get out of the way. I willed his hair to ignite like the lanterns. No such luck.

Being an anonymous face in the crowd had many advantages to exploring my newfound abilities. I experimented with moving things with my mind, knocking objects off stalls and opening cages or crates. I learned that I couldn't be seen to overtly do these things. I witnessed a man beating a child. I yelled at him to stop and thrust my palms towards him, willing him back. Nothing happened. He turned on me. I learnt something new though. As I lay on the ground from his first blow, he came to hit me a second time. I watched him pull his fist back fast and then he just stopped, or seemed to stop. His fist came towards me so slowly it was like he was moving through rock. His features, his words, even his hair, slowed as well, and passers-by were reduced to a snail's pace. A bird lagged in the sky above, its wings beating the air like one might wade through water. It was as though time itself had lost momentum.

I marvelled at the world's sudden sluggishness until I realised that the fist was still moving towards me, albeit slowly, and that I was the only one not affected. I rolled out of the way, got to my feet, and walked off. Time returned to normal. The man's fist hit the ground. He jerked around.

I ran. He took chase. Again time slowed. I sprinted as others crawled. Looking back, I still don't know if I could slow time, or if I could just run very fast when I needed.

I rounded a corner and climbed onto the roof of a house. By the time the man lumbered around, I was lying on my belly, enjoying the view. Time returned to normal. He stopped suddenly, looking for where I'd gone. With a mere thought and a flick of the wrist, I knocked over a barrel. It banged into the man's legs, and he toppled backwards.

I don't know where it came from, or why, but I sank happily into this new … mischief. I say mischief because it seemed, well, mischievous. A feeling of impishness shivered through me when I worked this magic. I could be playful, but couldn't cause direct or significant harm. The magic itself seemed to choose when and how I could use it. It also didn't want itself spoken about. If I tried to tell anyone about it, my throat dried up, only squeaks escaping my mouth.

Yet, once, as I was running through frozen time, I swear I saw Diogenes' eyes track my movement. He smiled and then turned away, as if catching me running at such an impossible speed was a mere passing amusement. It was so fleeting, I'm still not sure if I saw it.

I served as Alexander's messenger, taking sealed notes between him and various Athenian senators. My speed was noted by both parties. Alexander became so suspicious I started taking breaks between errands, racing to retrieve a message, then sitting with Diogenes or dangling my feet in the river, before racing back to my master. I played with the wind, blowing out lanterns and swirling sand into shapes between my hands.

As negotiations intensified, Alexander was no longer bothered by my speed. In fact, he demanded it. I didn't know what the sealed notes contained, but I heard talk of ships, soldiers and Persia. The Athenians, I imagined, would be happy to see Alexander turn his ire towards another foe. But I suspected Alexander asked too much.

Occasionally, when no one else was around, he would engage me in conversation. It always felt like a trap.

'What do you see when you ferry notes from one end of the city to the next?'

Such an innocent-seeming question asked with such malice. He didn't look at me as he spoke, his eyes glaring, unblinking, off into space.

'I see many people, Master. Athens is a busy city.'

'Do you see graffiti?'

I held my breath. We'd all been so careful, scouting ahead to ensure his path never crossed any of the offending artworks. Behind Alexander's back, the crude drawings were painted over, only for them to appear in new locations overnight.

'No, Master. I run very fast when I'm delivering messages. I don't see much.'

Alexander sneered at my evasive response.

'Take me to the dog philosopher.'

We left camp and made our way to Diogenes' barrel. That day, the philosopher sat cross-legged, sifting through a pile of bones. He examined them closely, squinting as he compared them.

Alexander stood over him.

'I won't look up to you, boy,' Diogenes said absently, focusing on his bones.

I assumed he was speaking to me. But Alexander knew it was directed at him and obliged, sitting on the ground in front of Diogenes. He mirrored the philosopher by crossing his legs, like a child seeking the wisdom of an ancient sage.

'Do you know why I like you?'

Diogenes finally faced Alexander. 'I don't care why you like me.'

Alexander smiled. 'Exactly. You don't care. You don't care about anything.'

Diogenes narrowed his eyes. 'I don't care, do I?'

'Of course, you don't,' Alexander scoffed. 'You show no reverence to the powerful, you dismiss any wealth or comfort, you parade your body around without shame. People come from all over Greece to seek your counsel, and you bark at them.'

'Some dogs bite their enemies. I suspect you are like that,' Diogenes quipped. 'But I bite my friends as a parent hits a child who plays with fire. Dogs do not bark for no reason.'

Alexander leaned forward. 'What kind of bite would a dog like you give a man like me?'

Diogenes tilted his head towards the pile of bones and picked up a large, distinctive rib. 'I was looking for the bones of your father,' he said. 'But I couldn't tell them apart from the bones of a slave.'

Alexander's face suddenly darkened. 'History remembers kings,' he sneered, 'not slaves.'

Diogenes smiled and shrugged. 'But what does the king have when history is all that remains of him?' He held a second rib, identical to the first, up to Alexander, but he glanced at me. 'Probably as much as the slave.'

Alexander stood and stamped on Diogenes' pile of bones.

Alexander didn't say a word on the way back to camp. Another note was waiting for him when we returned. He tore it up without reading it. He stewed in silence for hours, brewing over Diogenes' words. This direct challenge to the status of kings, and the reminder of the rumours about his father's death, touched a nerve.

'The dog philosopher should be put to death.'

The first thing he said in hours.

'The Athenians are quite fond of him, Your Majesty,' one of his generals said tentatively.

Alexander ranted long into the night. He drank and played with the candles on his desk, running his fingers through the flames just long enough to scorch his skin. He never flinched. I begged for the flames to erupt, to envelope him in fire. But all I felt was sand, swirling between my toes and up my legs, as if the earth was teasing me for the inability of my powers to extend towards this tyrant.

The sand dancing at my feet started to form more shapes, resplendent in the knowledge that no one paid attention to me. Tiny hands climbed up my toes, and laughing heads, no bigger than my palm, bloomed upon my feet. As I ducked to avoid a knife that Alexander threw, the face of his father, King Philip, took shape by my ankle. It winked and a hand held out a tiny sand rib. Then every grain of sand dropped to the ground.

I smiled. I stood up and filled Alexander's cup.

Alexander went to bed drunk. I waited until the rest of the camp was snoring too, all the while feeling the sand between my toes again, just as I had on my first day in Athens.

There was more sand in the camp, and I beckoned it to follow me. Little whirlwinds tickled my feet as I summoned the extinguished candles from around the tent. We slid like snakes – the sand, the candles and I – as we came upon Alexander. For a moment, I stood over him, watching him sleep. It would have been so easy to plunge a knife into his belly. I was struck, for the first time in my life, with power. He was so vulnerable. It would be easy.

But whoever or whatever gave me the power to command

wind and give birth to fire had something else in mind. All the malice in my heart melted into play. I cast the sand into the air and ducked behind Alexander's bed.

'Alexander!'

It was a whisper, but the mischief amplified my voice. Alexander's eyes flew open, and I lit every candle that floated above his bed. I felt him jolt from where I hid, but before he had a chance to sit up, I beckoned the sand to rush down upon him. He gasped and gripped the sides of the bed as it swirled around him. The swirls started to take shape: feet, legs, torso and arms, then finally a head. It was Philip II.

'Father?' Alexander gasped.

Time, wind and space; the world was at my command in that tent. I felt connected to every grain of sand. The ever-swirling form above Alexander came in closer, its nose almost touching his. I projected my voice again, letting it boom in on Alexander from all sides, as if it was Philip speaking.

'I am your blood,' the ghostly figure spat. 'I gave you the eyes that would look upon the world and seek to own it. And you gave me *this*! Ash and sand.'

'Everything I've done has been in your name!' Alexander blurted out.

'Liar!' I shouted. I made the candles spark. 'Everything you did was in the name of Alexander. You couldn't wait for my time to come before taking my empire, before spilling the very blood I gave you.'

'I swear, Father, I had nothing to do with –'

The ghostly figure spat sand in Alexander's face. In my mind, I saw its eyes grow wider, never blinking. The sand obeyed.

'I. Know. Everything,' I rasped. 'And I will haunt you, boy. I will haunt you every night until you leave these shores. You will have to flee far across Persia to escape my wrath. Greece was to be my empire. Every soul you take in this land will become a soldier of death in mine.'

Sand from Philip's head spiralled off, forming hundreds of little faces, all bearing down on Alexander.

'*And we will haunt you.*'

I clicked my fingers. The sand ghosts melted into nothing. Sand rushed over Alexander. The candles winked out and dropped to the ground. In the pitch-black tent, I heard him thrashing about, trying to brush the sand off his body.

I slipped away. Time slowed. I left camp before Alexander had a chance to call his guards.

The next day, Alexander left Athens. The whole camp was packed up before midday, the gossipers said. He was going to Persia with five, twenty, thirty ships, others claimed. Hiding between market stalls, I listened to Athens speculate all day. By nightfall, merchants assured others that yes, it really was true, he'd gone just before dusk.

'Come to the port,' one said. 'You can see the ships on the horizon.'

I didn't need to go to the port. I'd felt him leave Athens. The air changed, as if the city breathed a sigh of relief. But I didn't move, didn't dare think that perhaps, truly, I was free. It seemed odd that I hadn't been looked for or, at least, not in earnest. Maybe Alexander was so afraid he didn't care if a slave or two slipped away. What did it matter? He was gone. They were gone. I was in Athens.

*Free.* I repeated the word a thousand times that night. What did it mean to be free? Wouldn't the world know what I was, even without a master calling me as such?

A whole new day dawned without Alexander before I accepted it.

I was free.

Mischief sparked in me again.

I jumped up, surprising a woman unpacking her wares for the day. I shouted an apology as I took off, running towards the Eridanos River. The sun was making its steady climb into the sky. As I approached, I could see the light reflecting off Diogenes' barrel. It was a beacon to fools like me. I grinned as I saw the philosopher's withered form leaning against it. He glared out at the sun, his eyes lazily narrowed but unblinking. He had such a knowing smile on his face. I wanted nothing more than to know what caused it.

I opened my mouth to speak but then closed it. Something wasn't right. He was too still.

'Diogenes?'

He didn't blink.

I held my hand towards his mouth to feel for breath. Nothing.

I slumped beside him. Fat tears dropped down my cheeks as I sat with the dead philosopher, looking ever up at the sun.

Another man, middle-aged and scruffy, joined me soon after. For a moment, he just sat there, casually, as if he was enjoying the dead man's company.

'He held his breath,' the man said. 'He just held his breath.'

'Why?' I asked, my voice barely a whisper.

The man never answered. A woman came next, filthy and wearing the same rough cloth as Diogenes. We all sat there in silence. As I stared, I noticed a single piece of crumpled papyrus in the philosopher's hand. I carefully tugged it from his rigid fingers, watching my two companions nervously. They didn't seem to mind. I unfurled it and saw Diogenes' scribbles surrounding a strange symbol. It was like a smile, with a single dot for an eye. Suddenly, the odd little eye winked, and the words around it faded, the ink slipping from the page. The symbol disappeared too. In its place, a single word appeared in the philosopher's scrawl. I didn't know how to read, so I had no idea what it said, and I was too afraid to ask Diogenes' students and have it taken off me.

Years later, when I finally learnt to read, I discovered what it said:

*Pup*.

# *Jessie*

I'm at school before anyone else. This isn't new because Kay often has work early and doesn't trust me to walk to school on my own. But today, I'm here for a different reason.

I want to learn more about the boy, Diogenes and Alexander the Great. Last night, I asked Kay about them but she kept saying 'I don't know' and put me to bed. I wanted to read the next history but she said 'maybe tomorrow' and that was that. I couldn't sleep. I got out of bed on my own in the morning and woke up Kay for once. I said it was important: 'I need to go to the library.'

I haven't been to the library before school. I know it's open before school, after school and at lunch, Tuesday to Thursday, because the librarian Mrs Harper tells us all the time.

It's 8:15 when I arrive. The door's wide open and there's someone's backpack outside. Bags aren't allowed in the library because a boy took his inside and his drink bottle leaked cordial everywhere. Mrs Harper was very annoyed. There's still a big blue stain on the carpet. I leave my bag by the door and peek inside.

'Come in, dear.' Mrs Harper is putting books away in the non-fiction section. 'Can I help you?'

'I want to learn about someone,' I say.

'Okay!' Mrs Harper sings, abandoning her trolley and swishing over to her computer. She always wears swishy pants and coats. It looks like the wind is rushing around her whenever she moves. 'Who do you want to learn about?'

'Diogenes.'

'Oh, Diogenes. Who's he?'

'Ah … he was a … he lived a long time ago in Athens. He liked to annoy people like Alexander the Great.'

She laughs. 'Sounds like a philosopher.' She clicks away at her keyboard. 'He didn't like Alexander the Great, huh?'

'No.'

Mrs Harper keeps searching, hitting the Esc button after every few clicks, and finally makes an 'oh!' sound and jumps out of her chair. Her clothes bob like a jellyfish. She goes to the shelves and gets me a book. 'Might be something in here.'

*Horrible Histories: Groovy Greeks.* The book has a wooden horse on the cover with lots of soldiers. One soldier says, 'NOW THAT'S WHAT I CALL HORSE POWER'.

I go to the mat area with all the cushions. That annoying boy is here, lying spread out on his belly on the giant giraffe cushion. He's reading a tattered copy of *Guinness World Records 2010.*

'Good morning, Jessie!' he says.

'Hi,' I say. I turn around and go to the desks on the other side of the library. He follows, pulls up a chair next to me. I hold the book up to my face.

'Horrible. Histories. Groovy. Greeks,' he says slowly. 'That's on TV.'

I just *hmm* at him and hold the book up even higher.

'Did you see the episode about the Roman emperor who made people eat rocks for dinner? His name was Elagabalus and he lived from 203 AD to 222 AD, which means he died when he was nineteen, which is very young but not that young back then.'

'I'm reading,' I tell him.

He says 'okay!' and plonks the *Guinness World Records* book on the desk. He flicks through it and makes 'woh!' noises.

Before I find anything about Diogenes, Mrs Harper says, 'Kids, the bell's about to go. Could you put the books back or come and borrow them?'

The boy slams his book shut. 'Sure thing, Mrs Harper!'

He runs over to the shelves where the record books live.

'No running in the library, Theodore!'

'Sorry!' he says, and then walks dramatically out of the library, swinging his arms.

I borrow the book and leave, only to find him waiting for me.

'Let's walk to class together. I bet the doors are open now.' He jumps on the spot. 'Race you!'

He takes off. I walk after him, flipping through *Groovy Greeks* until I get to class.

I wake. Mrs Armstrong is saying, 'Up you get, kiddo!'

I'm under a tree near the top oval. It's no longer recess. Everything's still. I must've fallen asleep.

I blink a few times.

'Rough night?'

I shrug.

Mrs Armstrong takes me to the office and they call Kay. I try to read *Groovy Greeks* but I fall asleep again while I'm waiting.

Kay is annoyed but doesn't say so. As we walk home, she says things like 'how could you not have slept at *all* last night?', 'did you have a nice morning?' and 'walk faster please!' She has a day off so she didn't have to leave work. I don't know why she's so grumpy. When we get home, I see why. There's a man in a van waiting outside. The van has flowery writing on it that says ALCHEMY WROUGHT IRON – FOR ELEGANCE AND

SECURITY. CALL US FOR AN OBLIGATION-FREE QUOTE TODAY.

'Sorry,' Kay says to the man.

'No worries, gave me a chance to look at this gate. To be honest, it would be a real shame to tamper with something like this. Beautiful metalwork.'

'Jessie, go inside,' Kay says.

I go inside but listen by the door. The man talks about putting metal bars on all the windows and doors. Kay says she wants a new lock on the gate too but the man tries to convince her not to because it will change the gate somehow. But then I feel tired so I go to bed.

'Okay, you've had a nap. Get up.'

Kay opens the curtains.

'Come on, if you sleep any more you won't sleep tonight.'

I wish I had mischief. As Kay turns away, I flick my hand at the curtains. They don't move.

I read *Groovy Greeks* while Kay calls people and stomps around the house. I wonder who else could be a mischief. Maybe a mischief lived in this house. Maybe one of the men who went to war and got buried in the park was a mischief.

When Kay finally gets off the phone, I ask if we can go to the park. She says no but I bounce around and tell her I could stay up *all night* so she says *'fine!'* we can go to the park to 'let off steam'. She checks every lock. As we go out the front door, she says, 'just wait' and then checks everything again.

At the park, I step out the graves again and say in my head:

BOWRA F.D.A. – *Maybe A. Mischief* – *I'm sorry.*

BAILEY B.H. – *Maybe A. Mischief* – *I'm sorry.*

BAILEY J.L. – *Maybe A. Mischief* – *I'm sorry.*

Kay stops me when I get up to RICHARDS E.W. because it starts to rain. As we walk home, I ask her, 'Did you know

Alexander the Great died when he was thirty-two?'

'No.'

'He got a cold. He drank too much.'

'Did you read that in the library book?'

'Yeah. It doesn't have anything about Diogenes in it yet.'

'Whoever wrote the story probably made up Diogenes.'

I stop.

'No, they didn't,' I say. 'It's a history, not a story.'

'Well, that kind of thing can't happen. You know, magic powers and all that,' she says. She tugs on my arm. 'Come on.' She says it softly, like I'm being silly but she's trying to be kind.

'You don't know that!'

I cry. I don't mean to. I'm not sad, I'm angry. I wipe my cheeks on my jumper but they keep coming. Kay huddles in close.

'I'm sorry, I guess I can't know for sure.'

'The book was hidden for a reason,' I tell her. 'It's secret.'

'I guess that's true.'

'Why would someone hide a fake story?'

'I don't know.'

'They wouldn't.'

'You're right, I'm sorry.'

I nod. We start walking again. Kay strokes my hair, just like Mum used to do when I was upset, only now I've just got short bristles poking up around my scar. And Kay's gentle fingers are not Mum's.

I try to be nice. I try to sound sad, not angry, as I ask, 'Can we read some more tonight please?'

'Okay,' Kay says. 'As long as you go to bed early and actually sleep.'

I nod and try not to smile too much.

# A. Mischief the Second

*Alexandria, Egypt 236 BC – 205 BC*

We set out from the warehouse for the last time that day. Dusk. The sun looked ready to drop into the ocean and fizzle out, but the world still glimmered from the light that shone off the waves. There were five of us, a small company given the ship we were to inspect, but the merchants were not considered hostile. We wore only thick leather, no armour today, though our swords were heavy at our hips and we had daggers strapped to shins and chests in positions chosen more for visibility than practicality.

The ship itself was a sight to behold. Ships were as common as books in Alexandria, yet I'd never seen one of this shape, with pointed corners and glorious red sails that fluttered like silk. I'd been told the ship came from the East, but ships from the East didn't look like this, at least not the ones I'd seen. We were greeted by a man and a woman, both dressed in thick, embroidered clothes. Behind them, seamen went about their business. I recited the speech I'd already given five times that day.

'Please allow me to welcome you to the city of Alexandria. I am Aristophanes, a humble servant of our king Ptolemy III. On behalf of our great monarch, I pray that your visit is as fruitful and joyous as our fair city itself.'

'Thank you, Aristophanes. It is humbling to finally visit the glorious Alexandria,' the man said, his accent foreign but his Greek perfect. 'We're here for trade, yet we already feel richer for having come to your shores.'

'We are pleased to have your trade, my lord,' I said. 'As this is your first time in Alexandria, you may not be familiar with our many laws and customs. One in particular must be adhered to before you leave this ship. I hope you'll permit me –'

'We know we are required to forfeit every manuscript to the Library of Alexandria,' the man said. 'We commend your wise king for his policy. If every empire collected books like him, perhaps we'd have a much more enlightened world.'

I wasn't sure how to respond. We were normally met with refusal, outrage, sorrow, shock and disheartened resignation. Though copies were often made for our visitors, the taking of their original books did something to them. Those who were lucky enough to be provided with a rushed replica were rarely appeased. Never had we been congratulated for the king's policy of searching every ship that came into port and confiscating all their books.

'I'm pleased to hear that, my lord,' I managed.

'We've already taken the liberty of collecting the books in our possession.'

A seaman came forth, carrying a small chest. He opened it to reveal a collection of scrolls, about ten or so.

I gestured for my men to retrieve them.

'Thank you,' I said. 'I hope you won't mind if we inspect your ship for other manuscripts. It's merely procedure.'

The woman's smile faltered but the man bowed, smiling warmly. 'Of course.'

Three of us set out, descending below deck. We split up as we went through the many barrels and bags of grain. I prodded the bags, keen to check them quickly and be on my way.

It was then that I felt something hard in a bag almost my height. It didn't feel like a scroll, but something about it felt foreign, perhaps dangerous. Together with the men, one of whom had found a scroll in the merchant's quarters, I dragged the bag up to the deck. I deposited it at my hosts' feet. The man gestured to the scroll, ignoring the bag.

'Forgive me, that is an inventory of our stock. You're welcome to inspect it, but I hope you'll let us keep it,' he said.

'My lord, may I ask what's in this bag?'

The man still wouldn't look at it. 'Rice.'

'There appears to be something hidden inside.'

'Not at all. Rice forms into clumps if the moisture gets in. It can feel quite hard.'

I bent down and felt through the rough fabric of the bag. It had a definite shape, with sharper corners, and no amount of squeezing or prodding broke it up. I drew my dagger. The woman cried out as if I'd cut her. The man placed his hand on mine.

'Please, sir, you can feel, it is not a scroll.'

'Scrolls are often stored in intriguing ways. We just have to check. You will, of course, be compensated.'

I cut the bag open and rice spilled over the deck. Inside I found a strange object. It was like a box, rectangular in shape, but covered in dark leather. As I opened it, leaves of papyrus fanned out. It looked as if many scrolls had been cut up, the pieces then piled on top of each other. They were attached to the leather, stitched in on one side so the leaves could be turned. I flipped through it, gazing upon the unfamiliar writings. The papyrus itself felt unusual, tougher; perhaps it wasn't papyrus at all.

Whatever it was, this cut-up scroll enclosed in leather, it most certainly was a book.

'I'm sorry, this will need to be confiscated –'

The man reached out. I stepped back. Behind me, my men placed their hands on the hilts of their swords.

'Please, sir. We'll pay handsomely if you look the other way.'

'I'm sorry –'

The woman launched herself at me. She scratched wildly, grasping for the book even as her own seamen pulled her off me. She cried in a language I'd never heard, and then collapsed into wordless wails.

'It's nothing of any import to you,' the man pleaded. 'Just a small thing of a small people. Nothing of any worth to Alexandria.'

'The law on this matter is very clear. I assure you, if the librarians decide it's of no value, it'll be returned to you.'

This was a lie, of course. The woman knew. She screamed at the man, bitter, accusatory. He looked at the book in my hands. That same look of resignation I'd seen countless times came upon his face.

'Please ask your scribes if they'd be good enough to make a copy for themselves and return the original to us.'

'I will,' I said, another lie. I knew such a novelty would never be returned.

As we left the ship, the woman cried out in Greek. 'Your library will burn!'

We took the confiscated scrolls to the warehouse overlooking the port. The clerks were busy, labelling each item with the customary 'from the ships' and loosely sorting them in preparation for their trip up to the library.

'What's that?' the clerk asked, pointing to the leather-encased book under my arm.

'I'm not sure,' I said. 'I better take it to Old Pup straight away.'

The clerk nodded, his eyes still lingering on it.

The other men departed for home while I made my way to the Royal Quarter. The library sat within the great Mouseion, dedicated to the Muses. Its entrance was open to the air, with gardens and elegant colonnades so scholars could debate among nature and the cool sea breeze. I rushed past its beauty, through the cavernous open doors, into the covered section of the library.

My footsteps echoed as I fast-walked through the high-ceilinged halls and their wide ornamental columns. I passed the reading rooms and dining halls, and came upon the shelves, piled from floor to ceiling with scrolls. My destination was the belly of the library, the stacks, where the acquisitions department would be winding down for the day. When I arrived only Cleon was there, making notations on a brightly coloured scroll.

'Old Pup gone already?' I asked.

'First floor,' Cleon replied, not looking up from his work.

To the staircase. In my haste, I didn't notice the young slave carrying a pile of scrolls so large he could barely see over them. He bumped into me and our books went flying. Scrolls unfurled across the marble floor, my leather-wrapped book disappearing among them. The boy apologised in clumsy Greek as he stumbled about, picking them up. I snatched my precious find from him. His master, a scholar with a gnarled walking stick, descended upon him as I rushed up the stairs. A cry reverberated through the library's great silence.

I searched the labyrinth of the first-floor shelves, but couldn't find Old Pup. He'd entrusted me with many responsibilities that weren't afforded to other confiscators. It'd been a day much like this, two years previous, when I discovered a merchant was hiding great works of literature by stitching them onto the end of stock reports, assuming no one would check their entire contents. I still remember Old Pup's wrinkled face smiling at me as he said, 'You have a good eye, my son. You may bypass the clerks whenever you see fit.' He was someone I genuinely liked.

As I surveyed the alcoves in the walls, I noticed the slave again, wavering slightly as he stood by his master, who sat in one of the niches. I felt a pang of guilt. His cheek was split open and his left eye swollen.

The lamp in the scholar's alcove went out. He grumbled and had the boy move his books to the niche beside it. Once he was settled, that lamp, too, went out. Oddly, the lamp in his previous alcove was lit again. Both of us stared at this, then looked around. I saw Old Pup, sitting on the opposite side of the floor, going through a scroll. He was absorbed in his work and couldn't have had time to relight the other lamp. The scholar then glared at me. I shuffled away, pretending to look for something among shelves of … astronomy, it seemed.

As the scholar moved again, I caught a glimpse of Old Pup. His eyes were lifted, though he still leaned into the scroll. His hand made the tiniest movement, as if plucking something from the air. The lamp by the scholar went out. He then opened his fingers suddenly. The second lamp lit again. A smug grin flashed across Old Pup's face, and then disappeared, eyes returning to the scroll. The scholar glanced up in frustration.

I wasn't sure what I'd seen or if I'd even seen it. All I'd really witnessed was flickering flames under the watch of an old librarian who happened to delight in his patron's annoyance.

The scholar sent his slave to Old Pup, who requested a candle for his master's alcove. Old Pup was pleased to oblige. After the boy gave his master the candle, he was sent to the shelves on some errand. The flame by the scholar was steady. I was about to approach Old Pup when suddenly, despite the absence of any breeze, it went cleanly out. The scholar fiddled with the candle impatiently. Just as he brought it close to his face, Old Pup clicked his fingers and the wick caught in a great flash that singed the scholar's eyebrows.

I returned to the shelves, Old Pup to his scroll. A few moments later, the scholar left, barking instructions at his slave. Old Pup winked at the boy. Then he turned to me.

It was only then, I think, that he noticed me. He frowned as if I was the one who'd done something strange. I felt suddenly afraid. His questioning eyes suggested he was in fact very responsible for the bizarre happenings with the lamps, and that perhaps I shouldn't have seen them.

Old Pup stood. I turned to go.

'Just a moment,' he said.

I ducked between some shelves near the stairs. Suddenly, the scrolls slid off the shelves and slotted together like bricks. Invisible, nimble hands erected a wall, blocking my way. I turned to retreat, but another wall of scrolls awaited me, the last few volumes stacked well above my reach.

Silence. Then, the clacking of wood on marble as Old Pup made his way towards me and my prison of books. I realised then that there was no one else on the floor; in fact, I couldn't hear any other sound.

'I'm sorry to restrain you but it's quite remarkable that I can, to be honest, and I must speak with you,' Old Pup's voice came from beyond the wall of scrolls.

I pushed on them, leaning with all my weight, then tried to climb the empty shelves. Both the shelves and the books shifted around my efforts.

'I'm not going to hurt you,' Old Pup said. 'If anything, I wish to embrace you!'

There was joy in his voice. Elation.

One of the book walls parted. Old Pup hobbled towards me. I thought of running, of shoving him aside, but his smile disarmed me, that same smile that was given so readily whenever I brought him an oddity from the ships.

Old Pup held out his hand. A scroll fluttered down to him, levitating above his palm. As he tilted his head and observed me, the scroll unravelled and danced like a ribbon caught in the breeze. As he returned his head to centre, the scroll wound itself back up and, with a delicate gesture, fluttered softly back to the shelves.

Yet it was Old Pup who seemed amazed. He said, 'You see this!' with awe.

'My wife!' I shouted.

It surprised us both. Old Pup frowned.

'She'll be waiting for me,' I managed, much quieter this time.

The wall of books came up behind Old Pup. He dropped his cane and grasped my arms. 'I've waited for years! I just thought this was it! But now I have you! You've seen it!'

'I don't know what I've seen.'

'But you saw it!'

'I can *not* have seen it?' I suggested nervously.

'No, it's wonderful! We must talk! Let me buy you dinner. I can tell you of the mischief – I *can* tell you, I can say it!' He lost himself for a moment, delirious. 'Will you come? I'll take you to the finest establishment I can afford.'

'I must get home,' I said. 'Please.'

My final word was a cowardly beg. Old Pup frowned sadly at me and slowly nodded. He let go of me and gestured at his walking stick. It flew to him, slotting neatly into his hand. All his exuberance was gone.

Yet, we were still walled in by the prison of books.

'Will you come tomorrow?'

'Yes, yes, I will,' I said a little too quickly.

'I can do no harm,' he said. 'I'm an old man with strange tricks. That's all.'

I nodded. 'I will.'

The scrolls at my back parted and slotted gently back onto the shelves. I backed away, knocked my elbow and then scurried off. Once I left the library, I ran home. Only when I sat down to dinner did I realise I still had the unique book from the ships. Its novelty was suddenly lost on me.

I couldn't sleep that night, and happily got up when the baby cried. As I rocked my son to sleep, I went over the stacks of my mind. I liked to think of my mind as a library, with memories curled up like scrolls and grouped together on shelves. I went over everything I could find on Old Pup.

When I was first employed as a confiscator, gossip about the library and its inhabitants were regular topics of conversation. Confiscators rarely left the port, going only between the ships and the warehouses that stored their loot, so we often mused on the goings on of the institution we all served but did not visit. Occasionally, we were required to help transfer scrolls from the warehouses to the library. Men who were given such a task came back with stories of the cloistered bookworms in their chicken coop of the Muses.

Old Pup was in charge of acquisitions. He once came to speak to us about the importance of our work. From that point on, every man who delivered scrolls to Old Pup and his team came back with rumours. He had no real name. Some said he went under the title of 'the boy' for decades. When he came to the library, he took the name Old Pup but no one could say when that was.

Wilder stories circulated beyond the oddity of his name. His life spanned a century. He'd travelled the world, going even further than Alexander the Great, then settled in Alexandria for a beautiful but barren woman. Others insisted he'd never left Alexandria, born within its walls and never venturing out. One rumour claimed he'd once been a slave.

In my dealings with him, he was kind. Whenever I brought him scrolls, he expressed gratitude even if he had six of the same on his desk. After he gave me the right to bypass the clerks, I didn't gossip about him. Now I wished I'd made more of an effort to listen to the stories.

Old Pup was waiting at my door the next day.

'You've got the morning off,' he said, taking my arm to steady himself. 'Come, let's have breakfast. I'm sure you've eaten but a morning without work is a day for two breakfasts!'

He led me away from the port, away from the house I shared with my family, away from the library. I gazed at his frail, hunched frame, leaning against me and his walking stick, and chided myself for the fear of yesterday. Whatever I'd seen, surely it wasn't dangerous.

Then again, what kind of sorcery could extinguish and ignite flames? What wicked magic could move objects without touching them?

The fear set in again as we entered the Jewish Quarter.

'Here,' Old Pup said, motioning down a narrow lane. 'The place looks shabby but the food is excellent.'

I paused. I still felt nervous. Old Pup smiled as he waited for me to walk him down the alley. Then something came over me, something that lodged itself between the fear and the self-assurances that he was just a harmless old man: curiosity. I smiled back.

The café was unkempt but no more so than the restaurants near the port. Old Pup and I were not scholars; though we worked for the library, we didn't receive a tax-free stipend or lodgings within the Royal Quarter. We existed on the fringes, often near the port warehouses. As we were served surprisingly delicate wine, Old Pup took a small piece of papyrus from inside a chest pocket in his robe. He lay it on the table in front of me, smoothing it out delicately. It was crinkled, with a small tear in the top right-hand corner, and blank save for a single word: *Pup*.

'This is a memory,' he said.

The word on the page suddenly bled, the ink dispersing across the papyrus, and then reformed back. I glanced up. Old

Pup looked even more surprised than me.

'It hasn't done that in a long time,' he said.

I stared back down at the papyrus. Then, tentatively, I touched it.

Suddenly, I was somewhere else. A busy agora. Walking towards a river. Athens. I drank water and choked as an old naked man laughed. I served wine to Alexander the Great. I played with fire and ran with chickens. I defied time, slowing it. I turned sand into a dead king to threaten a living one. I took the papyrus from the stiff hands of a dead philosopher.

I snatched my hand away. The world shifted back to the restaurant in Alexandria.

Old Pup frowned. 'Are you alright?'

I looked at my fingers and then the papyrus. 'I saw ... I saw where you got this.'

'What did you see?' Old Pup asked urgently.

'The river, Diogenes ... I played a trick on Alexander the Great,' I mumbled. Finally, I looked up at him. 'Was I ... was that you?'

Old Pup smiled. Tears filled his eyes as he nodded.

I was shocked. 'How ... why did you ... show me this?'

'It's never done that before,' he said. 'What else did you see?'

'Plato's Academy. Graffiti.'

'No, after all that.'

'I – you found the paper and the ink shifted.'

'After that.'

'That was the last thing I saw.'

'Oh. Really?'

'Should I have seen more?' I asked, nervous that I'd upset this strange sorcerer.

'I don't know. I just ... I've done a lot since then.'

We went silent as a serving woman delivered warm bread to our table. Old Pup indicated that I should take some, but he did so absently, waving his hand limply. He took a piece himself, but his eyes never left the papyrus.

'I didn't expect it to do that,' he said. 'But I'm surprised it only showed you one … event.'

He put the bread down without taking a bite. He finally looked at me.

'You know what I am now, or at least, what I came from. This mischief, magic, whatever you wish to call it, has been with me since those memories you just saw. The papyrus –' he picked it up and tried to rip it '– it doesn't tear, burn or stain.'

He dipped it in his wine and lifted it out dry. 'I don't know what these abilities are for, but I've done such wondrous mischief. When I was younger, I'd leave small slips of paper; 'A. Mischief' I called myself. I calmed storms when I crossed the seas, slowed time to steal scrolls from kings. But I couldn't do anything when someone was looking at me.'

He then placed the papyrus back down in front of me. 'Until now. You've seen me.'

'Yes,' I said.

'Not even my wife knew. I lost my voice when I tried to speak of it. I wrote letters but the ink always shifted into something else. She died some time ago now. It never allowed me to tell her.'

I felt uneasy. What did he mean by 'allowed'?

'I thought about this yesterday,' he said. 'Perhaps you are to be the next mischief.'

'But … this seems wicked. I don't want this.'

Old Pup took my hand, his eyes full of sympathy. 'Maybe you're just to record it before I die so the scholars will have something new to ponder. I don't know. But you mustn't worry.'

I nodded. He let go of my hand and finally, we ate. The serving woman came with two bowls of stew. She winked as she gave me the one with more chunks of meat. Old Pup smirked as she left. He clicked his fingers and our bowls magically switched places.

When we finished our meal, we walked slowly through the streets, Old Pup showing me a few of the things he could do. We found that when he slowed time, it slowed for me too. Even as he hobbled along, we overtook passers-by, all of whom failed to notice us. He encouraged me to try to snub out candles in shop windows, but my attempt to stare down the humble flames only garnered confused frowns from the shops' patrons. Old Pup waited until their backs were turned, waved his hand, and the whole street went dark.

Suddenly, I remembered the odd book I found the day before. We would pass by my home, so I insisted we drop by to get it. When we arrived, Adoni, my wife, was flustered by the impromptu visit. She ran fingers through her uncombed hair as she held our son.

'Don't worry, dear, you're a vision,' Old Pup said.

She smiled. 'Thank you, sir. Please sit. I'll bring some wine.'

He sat as I retrieved the book. When he saw it, he took it eagerly, almost snatching it. He held it up to examine what bound it together.

'It's a book, isn't it?' I asked.

'Oh yes,' he said.

'You've seen one before?'

Old Pup didn't respond, lost in his inspection. Adoni served wine but he didn't notice. I tried to penetrate his thoughts.

'So, this cut-up scroll –'

'Codex,' he said. 'The future of the book.' He used his mischief to hover it above his hands. The pages fanned out elegantly. 'Look at it. I tried telling Eratosthenes but had no example to show him.'

'Have you seen many codexes?'

He smiled warmly. 'Codices,' he corrected. 'And no. Only heard about them. Long ago.'

I waited for an explanation. Instead he pointed through the single window behind me. The sun was almost in the middle of the sky. My shift would start soon.

We set out towards the library. Old Pup grasped the codex under his arm. When we arrived, he fished a piece of papyrus from his pocket and placed it into my hands. For a moment, I thought he'd given me the old page he'd taken from Diogenes. I looked down to find an address.

'I live nearby. I'm old now, so the king moved me closer to the library. You may come any time you wish, especially if you ever notice anything unusual.'

We both knew what he meant. I nodded and wondered what mischief he performed to get himself so close to the scholars' official lodgings.

'Do visit me though, even if nothing changes. At least, you can record my story. I'd be very grateful,' he paused, bowing his head in some small embarrassment, 'even for a little company. Bring the family.'

'I will,' I assured him.

He grasped my arm again. 'But be careful.'

I nodded.

'Those letters I wrote to my wife. The last time I did it, the ink shifted into the most horrible note. She cried for days. I couldn't tell her I didn't write it.'

'You speak of it like it's a living thing.'

'It is. It's not always you wielding the mischief. Sometimes it wields you. And sometimes, it will punish you.'

I nodded, trying not to show how terrified I was. I waited for him to enter the library and then ran out of the Mouseion, my eyes on the sky. I would be late. Yet, if I think back on it, I made it to the port so quickly it was as if time had stopped.

Six ships, all with hidden manuscripts. I'd never seen so many actively hiding their literary cargo. Yet, after the fifth ship, I began to wonder if maybe this wasn't so unusual. Perhaps it was me who'd changed, suddenly able to know where things were hidden as if a beacon marked them on every ship. As I parroted the same request for books, my mind was elsewhere; a captain's mattress, a bag of wheat, the stitching of a lady's skirt. Otus, a fellow confiscator and friend, laughed as I insisted the woman forfeit the scrolls in her gown or have her clothes removed.

'You've found more scrolls this afternoon than I have all week,' he said. 'In fact, you've found more than *you've* found all week!'

By home time, the thrill of finding so many books drained away. I felt sick. My eyes went in and out of focus. Otus steadied me, holding my shoulders as he walked me away from the port.

'Just a bit of seasickness,' he said. 'Bound to happen when you jump from ship to land all day.'

No, that wasn't it. Something was wrong. The beacon that showed me all those hidden books now called to me from the library. It came with pain, dizzying pain. Otus had to carry me to my door. When she saw me, Adoni took me to bed and stroked my hair. Just like Old Pup, delicately stroking the pages of the codex.

The next morning, I knew I had to see Old Pup. I left home before sunrise. If I had the correct address, his flat was right next to the scholars' marble lodgings opposite the library. I knocked but no one answered.

The sun was lighting up the streets as I made my way to the library. It seemed strange that he'd leave for work before dawn, especially when he lived so close, but the acquisitions team famously spent more time at the library than the scholars themselves. I met Cleon on the way. Old Pup's wry second-in-command looked weary.

'Little early to be coming from the ships,' he said.

'I forgot to give something to Old Pup,' I lied.

Cleon sighed. 'Come on then.'

We made our way through the gardens. As we came towards the main doors, I felt sick again. There was someone lying on the ground. Their robes were spread out, stained red. That violent colour pooled beside them. The blood slowly spread, fresh.

Old Pup. His eyes open wide and unblinking. He stared up at the windows on the highest floor, as if he was still glaring at the place from where he had fallen. Or been pushed. His mouth was open. He looked surprised.

'For goodness' sake, call the guards!' Cleon shouted.

I stumbled, my sight blurred. Cleon barked something about watching the body as he ran, shouting, towards the gates. My sight returned to normal and a sense of urgency gripped me. I went to Old Pup's side and lifted the robe at his chest. The hidden pocket was empty.

I took off. I ran all the way to acquisitions. The codex was missing. I ran to the top floors, to where Old Pup's dead eyes stared with fear and accusation. Scrolls were scattered on the ground. But still, no codex.

I returned to a garden full of people. Guards surrounded the body. Shouts, gasps and questions drowned out the subtle sound of the sea in the distance. Cleon touched my arm. I looked down at him and noticed I had blood on my hands. I shivered. His robes were stained too.

'Come,' he said. 'There's nothing we can do.'

In an unprecedented move, the king closed the library. Work at the port was to continue, but the library itself was closed. Never had its doors been shut, its scholars sent scurrying back to their dormitories. Guards from the palace came to the library on the king's command, and Cleon and I were questioned for so long that the blood on our robes stiffened. Finally, we were given leave to clean ourselves in the kitchens, with fresh clothes given to us and our own sullied ones taken. We were then pushed out the gates as officials from the palace came in. We stood there in silence, our backs to the hushed voices and barked commands that filled the gardens.

Cleon sighed.

'Walk me home.'

He took my arm just as Old Pup had the day before. As we walked to the edge of the Royal Quarter, whispers snaked out of alleyways and windows. News of Old Pup's death filtered through the capital.

'Did you know him well?' Cleon asked me.

'Only a little.'

He glanced up at the windows above and scowled. 'Whispers do him no justice.'

As we came to Cleon's house, the stern librarian softened. 'Go home and rest. Sleep if you can.'

I nodded and waited for him to go inside. Then I turned towards the library. I had to know if the codex, and the papyrus Old Pup held so close to his heart, were safe.

I stood some distance from the library, watching the guards stalk the perimeter. I looked for my moment to run. At last, the guards nearby turned their backs. I ran on tiptoe along the buildings. Time slowed. As I slipped behind the apartments' walls, the guards had only taken three steps.

I found Old Pup's flat. I pushed my weight against the door but it didn't budge. If doors prevented me from searching ships in the port, I picked the lock or broke the door down. The lock on this door was incredibly intricate. I took my dagger and went to insert it into the lock when the thing clicked three times of its own accord. The door opened.

Light streamed in from two large windows. It was so very still but signs of life – a dirty glass, bedsheets unmade – were everywhere. A mosaic of a beautiful woman stood pride of place in the middle of an overburdened desk. But the codex and Old Pup's papyrus were nowhere to be found.

The port called to me then. I remembered the woman on the ship with the red sails.

*Your library will burn.*

I ran out of the apartments and raced down to the port. The codex was calling me. I could feel it, throbbing like a beating heart.

But the ship had already left. Its red sails were specks in the distance.

'Didn't think you were coming in today,' Otus' voice came from behind me.

I pointed to the red sails. They were so small, I could've scooped them off the horizon with my little finger. Otus stared at me. 'What?'

My left ear burned. I turned to the docked ships. They were bobbing about as the sea swelled beneath them. The clouds overhead were turning black and the winds whipped at the folded sails and lengths of rope. My inner beacon sounded, a silent pinging. I took a few steps to the left. The pinging became louder. I didn't know what it was – there was no sound that fell or grew with each step I took – but it felt like a bell dinging inside my skull.

The pinging became a painful chime as I came across a small vessel. I jumped aboard.

'Aristophanes, ah, that's the ship they've been working on for the princess.'

I could feel the beacon below in the unfinished sleeping

quarters. I drew my sword.

Otus followed. 'What's going on?'

I descended below deck. There was an odd smell, musty and smoky, like crumbling charcoal. It was strong, with foul notes of rotten eggs. I threw open the door. There, the woman from the boat with red sails sat, holding the codex close to her chest. A loose page peeked out of the book: Old Pup's papyrus. She wore a beaded necklace with a wooden bulb pendant, which hung over the book. Black soot marred her fingers, jewellery and clothes.

Her eyes narrowed. She stood, raising herself proudly, and walked towards me. I flicked my sword at her, keeping her back.

'The book,' I said, holding out my other hand.

'I won't forfeit this treasure to you. Not again,' she said. 'If I must forsake it, let me give it to someone of a more respected position.'

I thought of Old Pup. 'You killed the man of a more respected position.'

'Yes, and I'll kill you too.' Her eyes flickered over my shoulder. 'And him.'

I glanced behind and saw Otus. He pushed past me, unafraid, and grabbed the woman by the arm. He shoved her forward. 'Come on then,' he barked.

She glanced back. Our eyes met. She ran her blackened fingers upon the codex.

We took her to the library to face the palace officials. I'd begged the port manager to keep her in the port, to have the officials and guards come down, but the messengers from the library insisted we bring her to them. They wanted to question her at the scene of the crime, to have her show them how she was able to penetrate the city's famous library and kill one of its most beloved employees.

Palace guards escorted us. Though we had six armed men, I felt nervous. The musty smell that emanated from her made me nauseous. She didn't seem worried; in fact, she was defiant. Her eyes were fixed on the library that loomed ahead. No one took the book from her.

We were led through the gates. Thunder rumbled back near the port. As we entered the library itself, past the giant windows in the great hall, it was difficult not to notice how the sun was almost completely hidden by the growing black clouds. Guards were lighting the night lamps in and around the library.

We were taken to acquisitions. Palace guards stood in attendance as an unarmed man wearing fine white and purple robes shifted through the items on Old Pup's desk. I knew him instantly as the Ophthalmos, the King's Eyes. Like Old Pup, no one knew his real name. When he turned and saw us, it was as if he recognised us all. Even her.

'Dear girl,' he said. 'Such a big fuss you've made.' He gestured at the codex. 'You have no use for that anymore.'

The woman gripped the codex tighter. 'That is not for you to decide.'

'Oh, but it is,' he said, smiling. He was so at ease he played with the lamp on Old Pup's desk, dancing his fingers through the flame. I shivered as I remembered Alexander doing the same thing in Old Pup's memories. 'Everything about you is for me to decide.'

She fingered the wooden pendant that hung around her neck. 'I can give you more than a book.'

The Ophthalmos raised his eyebrows, mocking her.

'A prophecy and a weapon,' she said.

His fingers flickered through the flame, bored. 'Oh yes?'

'Your library will burn,' she said.

I stepped back, feeling dizzy. The beacon sounded again, a burning sensation in the back of my head. A guard whispered something to me. Otus too. But all I heard was the exchange in the middle of the room, and the subtle swish of the flame as the Ophthalmos ran his fingers across it.

'And the weapon?' he asked.

She yanked the pendant from her necklace, snapping the cord. Beads chattered around her feet. She pulled a plug from it and a plume of black soot escaped. She tossed the orb at him, the black powder arching in the air. The Ophthalmos caught it above the flame. I stepped back, out of the room. It boomed like thunder. Fire, sound and fury threw us all into darkness.

I woke. First, all I registered was a long buzzing sound, like a mosquito burrowed into my ear. Then I felt the heat. Smoke billowed out of acquisitions. The scrolls and shelves around me were on fire. I tried to pull myself up but my hands slipped. They were wet with blood, my arms blistered and red. I tried again. As I struggled to my feet, a dull sound from far away pierced the ringing in my ears. It was screaming.

I stumbled to the office. I couldn't go beyond the doorframe, where the door had been blown clean off. Fire engulfed everything. Guards near the door were screaming. The desks and bodies at the centre were completely consumed, the fire so hot and bright you couldn't see if the shapes inside were moving or simply fuelling the flames.

Another beacon went off in my head. The kitchens nearby. I ran towards them as burning scrolls fluttered down on me. I burst through the doors. The library was the only place I knew of with pipes delivering water directly to its kitchens. With a flick of my wrists, I used mischief to snap every faucet. Water gushed forth. I directed it out, through the halls and down to the office. But it evaporated into air. The fire spread through the shelves. The air shook with heat.

I burst into tears. Like a child. The flames bore down on

me. My only hope was to run out of the kitchens and escape through the gardens. The fire jumped from shelf to shelf, eating book after book. I felt exhausted and so incredibly sad. I wished it would all stop, that the ground would split open and a flood would come rushing out.

I smiled then, thinking of the pipes that snaked under shelves and desks before coming to the kitchens. The mischief, that tingling in my chest, sparked. I thought of Old Pup, throwing sand into the wind to create ghosts, and clenched my fists. I felt the pipes snap as if they were my bones. The marble split open and water gushed from the floors and walls, spurting out. I ran back towards acquisitions.

Three burst pipes flooded the office with water. It was still blistering hot, the heated marble melting my shoes, but I stayed. The fire was under control. I heard voices somewhere. People were coming. Guards and water. Thunder rumbled over us now and though my ears were still ringing too loudly for me to hear it, I knew it had started to rain.

I should have gone then but I didn't. Something compelled me forward, past the smouldering furniture, books and bodies. It was a little voice, another beacon calling *just here, just here …*

Among the wreckage, I found it. Untouched. The codex lay on the ground in a pile of ash. I bent down and touched it. It was cool, completely unscathed. I opened the book and found Old Pup's treasured papyrus. It suddenly fused into the book, becoming one of its first pages. A gust of smoke washed over us, turning each leaf. The magic trapped in Old Pup's papyrus ran through the rest of the codex in a ripple of red flame. As it did, the ink on the rest of the pages bled out, leaving them blank. Then they flipped back the other way and settled on the page just after Old Pup's. I touched it, leaving fingerprints of blood. The blood sank into the paper and reformed as a single word in black ink: *Aristophanes*.

Whatever mischief Old Pup had held in that page, whatever magic he had passed onto me, laid claim to the codex. This, I knew, would be its home. Its history.

I took it and left. Past shouting guards, men with buckets of water. They moved slowly, as if time worked differently for them. They didn't even glance at me as I limped out into the rain.

I didn't turn back until I got home. There, I saw the plume of black smoke from the library billowing up and meeting its ominous cousin in the clouds above. Then I went inside. I didn't hear Adoni's words as she embraced me. I stumbled to bed and hid the codex. The mosquito buzzed in my ear. I went to sleep.

I slept for days. My hearing returned only partially, with the buzzing an ever-constant accompaniment to the sounds of my life. Someone came from the library to tell Adoni I was dead, only to find me sleeping in my bed. The guards came then. I told them the Ophthalmos had dismissed me when he had the woman responsible for Old Pup's murder. I didn't see what happened. That was all.

For each person who came, every time my wife or children spoke, the codex under the bed whispered to me. At first, I wondered why it hadn't done this before, but then I came to realise that it was the mischief, not the book, that spoke to me. The codex was just a vessel the mischief had taken. The magic in Old Pup's papyrus wanted something permanent, something special, to call home. And there was nothing more special than this new breed of book. Old Pup's memories were now recorded in this tome. I remembered the ink forming my name. What great act of mine would it record, what would it trap within its pages? Perhaps finding the codex. Perhaps saving the library from fire. Maybe it would record something decades from now, some little but mischievous thing done by an old man, or maybe something tomorrow, something innocent and simple.

A week after the fire, I left before Adoni or the children woke. I raced through the dark, jumping over walls, sneaking into gardens. I slowed time enough so that an hour stretched for days. I crept by guards at the palace. I tiptoed past families sleeping together. I flittered through the gardens of the library, still smoking from the great fire. I took every flower I could find, every bud waiting for spring. I filled our house with blooms as the whole of Alexandria, as my dear sweet wife, lay sleeping.

As the dawn crept through our window, I willed every shrivelled bud to unfurl, every petal to sigh open. A hundred gardens filled our tiny house. Adoni opened her eyes and gasped. I smiled sheepishly, suddenly embarrassed as I too realised how much I'd stolen.

Then she laughed. She waded through the floral rainbow and took my face in her hands. She said, 'My mischievous boy.'

# *Jessie*

I'm excited. It's Saturday and we're going to visit Grandma. Maybe she can tell us more about Old Pup and Aristophanes and *The History of Mischief*. I think Grandma was A. Mischief. She must be. It must be why Dad didn't sell the house when Grandma went to the nursing home. He knew somehow and wanted to find the *History*.

Kay says we can read two histories *in a row* if I let us go to Grandma's in the car. I can't read any histories if I'm dead so I say no.

She says, 'That's disappointing.'

I say, 'That's fine.'

We have to take two trains, a bus and walk seventeen minutes to get to Grandma's nursing home. It takes between one and one and a half hours. Kay doesn't bring the *History* even though it would be a perfect time to read. She listens to comedy on her iPod and doesn't laugh. I'm not allowed to listen because it's 'for grown-ups'. She gives me an old Winnie the Pooh book to read instead.

We get off at our stop. Kay tells me not to bother Grandma about the *History* because she's old and tired.

'Grandma isn't tired,' I tell her. 'She's just old.'

'Just leave it to me, okay?'

The nursing home is nice. It's like a hospital in a big home, with beds and nurses but comfy chairs and TVs too. There are flowers everywhere.

'Hello girls, how are you?' one of the nurses says as we arrive. She has a long name I can't remember, so she lets me call her Lulu. Lulu is the prettiest lady I've ever seen. She has hundreds of long braids in her hair and she always smiles. She's the only nurse who doesn't seem frightened of us since Mum and Dad died.

'Kay, can I have a word?' she says. She stands close to Kay, leaning in, and talks softly about 'erratic behaviour', 'nothing to be too worried about', 'still upset about your dad'. Both she and Kay turn away from me.

There's a weird guy staring at us from down the hall. I look at him, he looks at me and then he jumps into a room. I stand there for a little while. Kay and Lulu keep talking. The weird guy peeks out. He sees me again and his head shoots right back inside.

'Umm …'

Lulu strokes my arm. 'Oh, honey, we're talking too long. Why don't you go down to the kitchen? We have chocolate cake in the fridge. Grab a piece for you and Grandma.'

I walk down the hall and stop outside the room where the weird guy's hiding. It's a storeroom full of boxes. He tries to hide in the corner. He wears white like a nurse but I've never seen him before. He looks Kay's age and has very blond hair. He clutches needles wrapped in plastic.

'Who are you?' I ask.

'Ahhhhhhhhh …' He seems to say *ahhhh* forever. 'Daniel.'

His name tag says David.

'No, it's not, it's David. Your name tag says so.'

He glances down at his shirt and then looks straight back at me. 'Yes, it does.'

'Why are you being weird?'

'Ah, I'm a prac student.'

'What's a prac student?'

'I'm learning to be a nurse. I'm practising here,' he says. 'Is your sister around?'

'How do you know my sister?'

'Your Grandma talks about you two all the time. She's got lots of photos. You're Jessie, right?'

'Yeah.'

'Right, and so … where's your sister? Kay, yeah?'

'Why do you care?'

'Well, I … I like your sister!' He shouts it, like he's just come to some big realisation.

'You don't know her.'

'No, but she's very pretty. Pretty girls are scary.'

'Kay's not very pretty.'

'I think she is.'

'She's not *very* pretty.'

Kay calls to me. David jiggles on the spot like a scared dog and then turns around, opens a cupboard and shoves his face in there.

'Please don't tell her about me,' he says. He sounds so frightened, I feel sad for him.

'Jessie, what are you doing?' Kay says as she spots me in the doorway of the storeroom. David goes through the cupboard like he's looking for something. 'Leave the nurse alone, come on.'

I follow her but don't tell her about David. I'm sure she'd be happy someone thought she was 'very pretty' though.


Grandma is reading when we arrive. She puts her book down, hugs us both and brings down her biscuit tin. I like her room very much. It has a bed, a table, a bookshelf, a TV and three comfy chairs. There are blankets everywhere, on each chair, even hanging from the coat hook on the back of the door. There used to be lots of photos but she put them away when Mum and Dad died. I wonder how the weird prac student knew what we looked like.

The first thing Grandma says is, 'Have a biscuit, dear.'

I take a Tim Tam and she gently touches my face like I'm the most special girl in the world. I love Grandma. She's very short, but she sits and walks tall. When she moves, she seems to float, like everything is easy, like she's not old.

Kay and Grandma talk about nothing things. Grandma asks a thousand questions. *How is work? How is school? How is Guildford? Isn't it pretty? How are the trains? Aren't they fast? What are you reading?* And on and on. I eat six Tim Tams (four normal ones, two double coat) and no one notices.

'Grandma, we found something interesting in your old house,' Kay says.

I start listening again.

'Isn't it lovely? Have you been down to the bakery? Didn't I tell you they have the best jam donuts? What is your favourite thing about Guildford so far?'

'Well, I like the house mainly. Jessie likes the park.'

'I like the big gravestone,' I say.

'She means the war memorial,' Kay says to Grandma.

'No, I mean the big gravestone.'

'Anyway, we found a book in the study. It was in a secret compartment in the floor,' Kay says. Then she brings the *History* out of her backpack. I can't believe she made me read Winnie the Pooh on the train. She hands it to Grandma, who looks surprised.

'What's this?'

'It's *The History of Mischief*!' I say. 'Are you A. Mischief, Grandma? We haven't read it all yet, Kay won't let me. Are you in there?'

'Jessie, calm down,' Kay says.

Grandma hands the book back. She doesn't really look at it.

'I've never heard of it,' she says. 'It must've been left there by the people before us.'

'Really?' I ask.

'Sorry, dear.'

I put my hand in my pocket and then remember Kay has taken all the keys. 'It's on the gate key, Grandma, *Property of A. Mischief*. Don't you remember?'

'Not really.'

But Grandma never forgets anything. I wonder if this is what Lulu meant by 'erratic behaviour'. Grandma changes the subject and Kay seems fine with it. They talk about pointless things for another half-hour. I eat ALL the Tim Tams (one normal, four double coat, two chewy caramel). I feel angry but no one notices.

Kay won't let us read the *History* on the way home. She tries to talk to me on the train but I ignore her. It is raining but the train is on tracks, so we can't go anywhere even if the wind blows really hard. And there are walls between the tracks and the road. Even if a car slips it won't hit us.

It's still raining by the time we get to Guildford.

'If you stop sulking and keep dry, we can read the next history before bed,' Kay says.

'Okay,' I say. 'I'm sorry.'

Kay opens up her umbrella and puts her backpack on her chest. She hugs it with one arm and holds the umbrella with the other. We both get a bit wet but the backpack stays dry.

'Thank you for taking me to Grandma's,' I say when we get home. I smile so Kay won't think I'm sulking.

## A. Mischief the Forty-Ninth

### Northern Wei, China 423 AD – 445 AD

The day the mischief came my daughter left for war.

She handed me a leather-bound collection of papers and smiled casually, like she was simply handing me a cup of tea.

'Don't worry, Mother.'

Then she rode off.

I never thought she'd go. Not even when she came home dressed as a soldier, her long hair cut clean off. Even when she galloped away, I thought she'd loop around the bend, disappear for a moment, and come back.

Mulan should have been a boy. She started moving when she was just a small bump in my belly. Friends declared that the great Hua Hu had a son who was already practising the martial arts that earned him such respect as a younger man. When she arrived, Hu laughed as he was told his son was actually a daughter. He announced she'd be fiercer than the lazy sons of our neighbours. And she was.

I complained when Hu gave Mulan her first sword at age five, but there seemed little I could do. Soon she picked up the bow, and then the lance, and by this point I'd given up. It was easy, in a way, because she also sat with me at the loom. She went hunting in a face made up with powder and rouge. She was my little girl and her father's son. She was nine when

I finally managed to give her a sibling, her sister Munan, and twelve when our first and only son, Yao'er, was born.

She was sixteen when she handed me *The History of Mischief* and left.

The cock crowed. I opened my eyes and counted twelve, twelve days she'd been gone. I wanted nothing more than to stay in bed. But Hu was waiting.

I got up, dressed, and went to the kitchen. I prepared a simple meal, some rice and soybeans with a little pork, and went to Hu's room.

I opened the door slowly and said, 'Good morning, my darling.'

I didn't wait for his response. I came in, placed the bowl on the small table beside his bed and went to the windows. I opened a small wedge in them, letting the morning light and cool air seep in.

I helped him sit up. Some days, he wouldn't need help. Some days he would. Some days his hands shook and he couldn't hold his chopsticks. That day, he hung his head as I propped him up against a pile of cushions. His hands trembled.

I retrieved the bowl and fed him. He chewed slowly, clenching and cracking the shaking hands in his lap. I smiled at him the whole time, offering encouragement – 'There there, eat up, no rush, enjoy' – as he made his way through the bowl. He didn't look at me, his shame so heavy it left him hunched over, but just as I put the bowl down and wiped his face with a damp towel, he glanced up and our eyes met. In those sad eyes I saw every unspoken apology, every feeling of guilt, his emasculation coupled with his gratitude, and he said so quietly and earnestly, 'thank you'. I stroked his cheek and said as sincerely as I could, 'my pleasure'.

When I took the bowl back to the kitchen, I noticed the

strange gift from my daughter, sitting by a cold teapot. Why had I ignored it for so long? It was thick and heavy, like a block of wood. As I opened it, it cracked, as if the leather was centuries old. I flicked through the pages. They weren't particularly remarkable. Strange squiggles and symbols on each page, all in the same black ink. Some scripts I recognised: Chinese names of men and women. I saw my husband's name and then Mulan's, the last one listed in this strange book of sorts.

I felt the ache of missing and touched Mulan's handwriting.

Flashes of other lives filled my vision. I saw through the eyes of so many different souls, of people with rounded eyes, black skin, and hair the colour of wheat and fire. I lived – and it was living, for I felt their heartbeats, felt their fear and joy. I felt the heat of fire blazing through a library. I laughed as I was thrown off a tower and flew. I questioned a thousand different gods as centuries passed. I wondered every time where the mischief had come from.

Then I saw myself, young, through my husband's eyes. I saw him use this strange magic to orchestrate our meeting, to save my father from a group of robbers who were but shadows he commanded. Then I saw Mulan, five years old. Hu gave her the book on the same day she received her first sword. Through her eyes, I saw her sneaking around me as she and her father trained. Then I saw her great act of mischief, at the age of twelve: stealing a penjing tree from a wealthy lord, a beautiful gift she simply left outside my room, one I always assumed was from her father.

As the memories became mine, not a second passed in my world. I was shocked to find myself back in my kitchen, the day still so young.

My penjing tree had long been neglected. I felt guilty as I approached it under the veranda, knowing now the effort

Mulan had gone to in stealing it. Penjing require maintenance, care. My tree, a trident maple with its roots stretched taut over a large rock, was overgrown and a thick layer of its three-pronged leaves rotted at its base. I touched it lightly and its leaves quivered, as if to wave at me. I spent some time pruning it, listening as the world around me woke: chickens rustling in their coop, doors opening and closing in the house, the squeal of a kettle.

It was strange that the magical book set me back to my mundane routine. I'd done nothing but the bare minimum since Mulan left, only feeding my husband and children. I had no feats of sorcery in me. I was a sphere of a woman who went from one chore to the next, my once milky skin tanned almond from hours in the garden. What great mischief could a woman like me muster?

I remembered a moment early in Hu's sickness, as I went door to door selling eggs. A neighbour's husband asked how I did it, how I managed to do everything now that my husband was an invalid. How did I manage the finances, care for my family, grow the vegetables, clean the gutters, build the chicken coop, keep out thieves? I resented everything in those questions, the fake pity, the way he emphasised the word *invalid*. More than anything, I resented the implication that the task was bigger than me, that all these things were new. I narrowed my eyes and said, 'Women have always done this.'

So, let the *History* record this: the chores of Hua Yingtai. Let it follow me as I clean out the chicken coop. I've quietly done more than every tale in its wicked pages.

Every day, I sat with the trident maple. Long ago, I had fashioned wire over its branches to shape it into a leaning position. Shaping required months and years. As the plant grew and aged, the shapes that had been wired into its hardening bark were fixed in place. With the mischief, I could shape the branches like they were sand. The tree, such an old thing, sang as its aged bark dissolved and twisted into the shape of a dragon. I smiled as I wondered if Yao'er would be able to spot the shape in this one. He checked the tree daily, waiting for new figures to appear.

'Spirits live in our garden! They're trying to trick me!' he claimed. No one took much notice. A boy who saw spirits in plants was just a silly child telling stories. I hoped he'd stop when he got old enough for childish eccentricity to be taken for adult madness, but the delight I felt when I heard his squeals of joy tear through the house made it worth the worry.

'It's a dragon today, Mummy, a dragon!'

And I would say, 'Of course it is,' and that would be that.

I tried to speak to Hu, tried to share the wonder of surprising our sweet boy with such tricks, but the mischief wouldn't let me. This made no sense. Mulan's memories showed Hu talking about the histories with her quite freely. Mischiefs who passed the *History* on, often coaching their successor, didn't lose their abilities either. So why was he bedridden, when once the mischief helped him move so freely? Sometimes I dropped rice when I fed him and looked away, hoping he'd use the mischief to pick it up. When I turned back the rice was still resting on his chin or lap, and he looked at me with sad eyes. The rules of mischief, it seemed, were not fixed. It was as if it couldn't settle on what it was. I concluded that was why the word mischief had been chosen to describe it. It was benign and troublesome, benevolent and cruel, seen and unseen. It was fickle.

Outside was where I felt it most. I carried my shears only for show now, pruning plants just by running my hands over their branches. I drew water out of the soil and into the roots of starved crops. Sometimes, I gathered insects without touching them, their little bodies hovering behind me in a swarm, and flung them into my neighbour's yard. I knew it was wrong but that little tickle of mischief took hold sometimes.

I boiled water with the click of my fingers. I could feel when the water reached the optimum temperature for more delicate tea, bringing it to just below boiling and resting it there. I could smell when a cucumber was ripe. I could hear when eggs were waiting for me in the coop. I saw Yao'er pinch Munan behind my back. Mischief wasn't an unlimited form of power; it was an enhancement of one's existing abilities. I spent years doing this. Making mischief out of managing a house.

As time went by, I sank into the magic like one settles into a chair that has, over the years, moulded around you. It was a feeling more than anything. I was bound to the world, to the house and the life within it. My body was tethered to the heartbeats of my children, the germinating seeds outside, and the wind that rustled between the trees that shaded the vegetable garden.

Seven years passed.

Yao'er stopped checking the penjing and Munan, in the spirit of her older sister, gave up any pretence that she was 'watering the garden' when she was firing arrows into a now thoroughly splintered tree behind the chicken coop. We received three letters from Mulan in that time. She signed them with her father's name and said the war was going well, that she was happy and had many new brothers among the ranks. I read them to Hu, leaving out the part in the most recent letter where she warned us that there were bandits looting villages close to the mountains near our home.

I started dreaming of her, or, *with* her. She was older, stronger, her skin rippled with gashes and scars. I sat on her shoulder as she fought, listening to her grunt and pant.

'Behind you,' I warned.

She turned and slashed the man who snuck up on her. I felt her thoughtless panic, fear so primal it left her mind blank, as she battled like she was trying to fight a sea of ants from enveloping her.

'To the left.'

They felt like more than dreams. They didn't come often, but every night when I lay down to bed, I stretched the tendrils of my mischief out into the world and begged them to find her.

Plumes of black smoke billowed out of the forest-rimmed horizon. It was far away, so only the faintest smell reached us, but it rose like a warning. I didn't say anything to Hu, keeping the windows closed so the smell wouldn't disturb him. He fed himself that morning, eating his breakfast angrily as if he knew I was hiding something.

'Fetch Munan and Yao'er,' he said as he handed back the bowl.

I sent the children to him and went about the day's routine, cleaning and watering mindlessly, my thoughts on the fire and the bandits in Mulan's letters. *Please come home*, I begged her silently. As I walked to the chicken coop, my sandals squelched. I was drawing water out of the earth with every step I took.

'It's alright,' I muttered to myself, wishing my worry away from the mischief. 'It's alright.'

'Mother.'

Yao'er's voice was quiet but I jumped. He'd snuck up behind me.

'Father asked us to call the neighbours to meet with him. He didn't want you to know, but I thought maybe you should. Some of them have already arrived,' he whispered.

I nodded and touched him briefly on the cheek before going inside. He followed a few steps behind. When I came in, Munan scowled at him.

There were four men in Hu's room, all from nearby houses. One lent heavily on a walking stick, and sagged as we bowed our greeting to one another. The same scowl from Munan appeared on Hu's face as he looked for Yao'er behind me.

'Sit, boy,' the walking-stick-wielding elder commanded to Yao'er.

'He's eleven,' Hu said. 'My daughter will sit with us. Yao'er, help your mother with the tea.'

Munan bowed deeply, I suspect to hide her smile, and drew up a chair for herself. Yao'er followed me to the kitchen.

The kitchen was some distance from Hu's room. I sent the mischief out, leaving my ear in that room.

'Not even I, confined to this bed, can ignore the whispers,' Hu said. 'Smoke rises from our neighbours in the mountains. The forest is the only thing separating us from the looting that has befallen them.'

'My son calls them leopards,' one man said. 'Their leader is a man known only as Leopard Skin. They say he is twice the size of a normal man, thrice as broad.'

'I don't doubt the veracity of your son's testimony but these aren't hardened warriors burning our villages. They are petty vandals. They can be frightened away.'

'By what? Whoever they are, they've taken advantage of the fact that we are without our strongest heirs. We are towns of elders and children.'

'Perhaps we can bribe them,' one man suggested.

'One cannot bribe men who have the power to take everything,' the elder's voice came, deep and low. 'I sent my youngest to the capital a week ago. Hopefully he can convince the Emperor to release our sons before the bandits arrive. It may be too late, but we can do little else.'

Yao'er's voice, so little and young, came into my ears. 'Mother.'

My attention returned to the kitchen. He stood there, a teapot in his hands.

'The tea is ready. Shall I …?'

I took the teapot from him and smiled. 'No, darling, let me.'

I listened to the voices in Hu's room as I approached.

'They have a pattern,' Hu said. 'They burn the surrounds of a village to frighten people and force them out into the open. They'll burn the forest first.'

I served the tea. The men looked through and around me as if I wasn't there. Only one, the same man who'd questioned how I was managing all those years ago, bowed as I filled his cup.

'Perhaps we should run,' he suggested. He gestured at Munan. 'We cannot have our daughters face the same disgrace as our sisters in the north.'

'Perhaps if your daughters could fight like me they wouldn't have to,' Munan said.

Before any could rebuke her, Hu spoke. 'My daughter is right but there's no time to train them. Perhaps fleeing is our only option.'

As I filled the last cup, Hu motioned for me to leave. I left the pot by his bed and listened from outside.

'I've lived seventy-two years in this village,' the elder said. 'I'm not abandoning it to some roaming phantoms. Flee if you wish, but these gangs roam every road. If we put up enough of a fight, they'll leave and never come back. Gather your grandsons. Better to fight at home than fight on the road.'

The back and forth continued until the tea went cold. There was no resolution. Some said they'd run at any sight of fire in our forest; others said they'd fight with what little men they had. As they left, the elder rather gloomily told them that whether they fled or stayed, they should give daggers to their wives and daughters. The men nodded soberly.

Munan was annoyed by this. As she cleaned up after they'd

left, she seethed. It was unfair, she said, that those were the only options for women: be protected by good men or commit suicide to save oneself from wicked ones. She yelled at Yao'er for the rest of the day.

Hu slept, fatigued from the neighbours' visit. When I brought him his evening meal, he was revived, his eyes alert and hopeful despite the shaking in his hands.

'We only need to frighten them, you know,' he said to me.

'Sorry?'

'The bandits. We only need to frighten them. These are just leopards separated from the pack, not an army. There are too many for us to fight, but we could easily scare them. They're deeply superstitious.'

'How do you know this?'

He shrugged and offered his explanation nonchalantly. 'Magic.'


The next day, seven boys and one girl from the neighbourhood came to the house. Munan, they said, would train them to fight. She'd promised.

I sent all of them away and relegated Munan to the chicken coop.

'Clean it properly,' I ordered. 'I don't want to see a single stray feather.'

I sat by the trident maple and followed her every movement with eyes narrowed like a cat.

'You don't need to watch me, Mother,' she said.

*Don't I?* I knew, the second I went inside she would flee to the neighbours, determined to train her own little army. I'd dreamt I was with Mulan the night before, flying through the trees on a beast of a horse. A group of men were either riding with her or pursuing her. She rode hard, whipping the horse and ignoring the branches that snatched at her face.

One daughter off fighting a war; another preparing for battle on her doorstep. I would not allow it. No. No no no.

Without thinking, I made the branches of my trident maple spin, its three-pronged leaves whirling like swords on a battlefield. It shifted into the shape of a woman, a slender thing much like my daughter, with its branches stretched out like arms. I clicked my fingers and watched it unfurl, the branches twisting back into a more relaxed shape.

I wished the mischief was good for something other than shaping plants and boiling water.

'They'll reach the forest by sunrise tomorrow, Yingtai.'

Hu said this dispassionately as I fed him his morning meal. I dropped the chopsticks.

'What?'

'The bandits,' he said. He tried to pick up the chopsticks in his lap. 'They'll be here by sunrise tomorrow.'

I stared at him, the relaxed way he fumbled with the chopsticks as he spoke of the impending attack.

'You don't know that.'

He abandoned the chopsticks and clenched his trembling hands. 'I do.'

'How?'

He nodded towards the chopsticks. When I did nothing, he tilted his head towards the bowl and then nodded again at the chopsticks in his lap. I picked them up and started to feed him. I felt the world breathe around me, all the life swimming in the soil and the air. My mischief branched out, connecting me to the forest. There was a darkness beyond it, creeping closer.

'What do we do?'

'What you've always done.'

'Me?'

What did that mean?

Hu didn't answer. He lay back, sinking into the cushions that propped him up, and closed his eyes. The slow deepening of his breath told me he was asleep.

*What you've always done.*

I have always just dealt with things, done what needed to be done. That's all.

So what needed to be done now? I felt the darkness on the fringe of the forest sneak closer as I went about my chores. Then the maple sang again. I glanced at it. Its branches sharpened into something sinister like claws.

Something sinister.

I smiled.

That night I lay in bed, listening to the heartbeats of my family slow into slumber. I got up when everyone was asleep. It was cold and my joints ached. I put on a few extra layers and made my way out into the garden. I left my lantern behind. The world was dark but I could feel where everything was.

The world was only quiet at night if you didn't really listen. People were still, birds didn't sing or cluck. But the wind never slept. It rustled through everything, even the dust on the road, and carried the noise of nocturnal creatures. I left our yard and walked through the streets, letting the moon and the mischief guide me.

I hadn't been out to the forest since before Yao'er was born. Mulan and Hu used to hunt there, coming back with rabbits and the occasional boar. It was on our village's doorstep, a mass of life framing our little collection of families and separating us from the mountains.

When Mulan was younger, Hu took us to the tallest tree in the forest. I waited with the horse as he climbed, Mulan's little agile body clinging to his back. I was never game. They disappeared above the leaves, where Hu pointed out the mountains, our village, our home, and the tiny glimmer on the horizon that was the Yellow River. Sometimes, they sang, Hu first, and then Mulan, loudly, willing her voice to bounce off the mountains. But the trees always swallowed their songs. Now, I searched for those melodies, letting my mischief sink into the forest's memories.

I walked for an hour, following the songs the trees had trapped in their trunks. Hu and Mulan's singing got louder in my right ear, so I veered off the main path. I found our tree. It was even taller now, its branches fanning out above the canopy of leaves from other trees. I sighed as I laid my hands on it, wishing I'd once had the courage to chase Hu and Mulan up into its branches. Hu cut a few notches into its trunk long ago. Lichen and insects now made their home in the nooks. I brushed them away before placing my slipper in the first foothold.

The mischief surged around me as I laboured up the tree. I stopped often, clinging onto branches and looking where to go next. When I finally made it to the top, I clung onto the trunk, my back to the forest, too frightened to turn around. There was a curve to the tree here. I imagined Hu and Mulan resting in it.

Finally, I turned. Awed by the sight, I sagged further into the tree. The forest stretched out, a rolling sum of green. Our village was to the east, a collection of roofs and a few tiny lights. The mountains loomed above, so still and massive. I saw how small I was.

Lights twinkled in the north, torches from the approaching leopards. There were more than just a few renegade soldiers; at least thirty trampled the road ahead. As I sank into my mischief, that connection to the earth, I heard their sniggers and proud talk. I rested as comfortably into the tree as I could, listening again for the lingering memory of Hu and Mulan's songs. I thought of the penjing, my dear old maple.

The forest and I became one. I was in the eyes of every owl and insect, in the dirt under the leopards' feet. I crept into the trees and sank deep into their trunks, twisting them into dragons, snarling faces, and slender women with limbs outstretched to the sky. The trees shifted only when they weren't watched. I jumped from branch to branch, behind each man's back, shaping the trees in front and behind them. Whispers started. Then gasps and shrieks. The forest surged. I felt them shiver.

All the movement woke the animals of the forest. The birds chattered; somewhere, a monkey screeched. The wind howled. The leaves that framed the wicked trees quivered. I was everywhere and everywhere was me. I angled the limbs of tree women into claws, blocking the way ahead. The men at the back deserted. The remaining men thrust their torches into the branches. I brought all the water out of the earth, dampening the trunks. Water dripped from the leaves. The wind followed me and blew the torches out. The forest was lit only by moonlight. It wasn't long before they all fled.

I returned to my body and opened my eyes. The forest around me shifted back. The leopards retreated to the west. The next town in their path was three days away. I hoped they were frightened enough to leave them alone.

Then I got down from the tree and went home.

The days that followed were much like the last. Cleaning, cooking, feeding Hu. Rumours circulated, followed by confirmed reports: the bandits had left our region. Some speculated that the Emperor's men had come and scared them away; others believed spirits protected the town. No one asked for my opinion.

I dreamt again of Mulan. The men who galloped after her were friends, men under her command. They found the leopards on the road and dispatched them, capturing their leader and killing the rest. I sat on her shoulder as her gaze turned to the forest, *our* forest, her heart yearning for home. But then she turned and commanded her unit back to the capital. The elder's son, the one who'd been sent to beg the Emperor for help, was the only one to venture into the forest. He was home by the time I woke up.

That morning, as the town celebrated their returned son, I fetched Hu's meal. He was so tired, he struggled to hold his head up. I fed him in silence, save for my regular little encouragements.

'I wish they knew,' he said to me.

'What, my darling?'

'That it was you.'

In that moment, the tendrils of our mischief, his and mine, connected in the earth beneath us.

'The people who matter know.'

# Jessie

It's Sunday. Sunday's a resting day where we do nothing and I'm allowed ice-cream after dinner. But we're not resting. I didn't even get breakfast. We're on the train to Perth. Kay woke me up early and said she had to go to work. I have to come with her because I'm not allowed to stay home alone.

'They've covered for me so much. I couldn't say no. It'll be fun, I promise. There are only two of us who work on Sundays. Well, there are more than two, obviously, but in Stock and Stack, there are only two of us and we're out doing retrievals, so you'll have the whole workroom to yourself. I'll find you a computer or some books, and we can get milkshakes and muffins for breakfast. There's this takeaway place at the station that does the best milkshakes. And there's a bakery. We can get a jam donut.'

Kay rambles the whole trip. I'm tired because we stayed up late reading the *History*. I really like Yingtai. I wish we'd talk about her and not Kay's work. I saw the movie *Mulan* a few years ago. I used to like it but now I don't because they got so many things wrong. Mulan's mum was barely in it.

We get off the train at Perth. Perth is a big station, where all the trains come together. We go up the escalators to the bakery, where Kay buys me a jam donut and a gingerbread man. She waves the gingerbread man in my face and says, 'Look at my big smile, Jessie, let's see your smile!' like I'm three. I don't smile. Then she orders a caramel milkshake and a flat white with an extra shot and two sugars from the place that has lots of ice-cream. I slurp the milkshake as we walk over the bridge towards the art gallery.

Kay works at the State Library. It's a funny, ugly building, a big block of concrete with weird sharp angles that lives behind the art gallery and next to the museum. The side of the building where the main door is looks like the library was even bigger once but then some giant came along, sliced it open and covered it in glass. It's like a big cake with lots of layers that get smaller as they go up, with windows instead of walls. But that's only the front of it. Around the back and sides, it's concrete, like maybe they used up all their windows in the front.

Inside, the library has two caverns that go through its centre. You can stand on the bottom floor and see all the way to the top. There's a set of stairs you can climb, or you can take one of the glass lifts like from *Charlie and the Chocolate Factory*.

Kay takes me to the back of the library, away from the main entrance, and through a secret door. She has an ID card that lets her in. We go through a dark corridor and then get to some lifts that are silver and very wide, like hospital lifts. We go up to the first floor, out into the library, and then to a door behind a desk. Kay taps her ID next to the door and it flashes green. It makes a click. She pushes it open.

We enter a room with long desks and lots of mess. There are trolleys everywhere with old books, newspapers, all sorts of stuff. There are no windows but the light feels too bright. It smells strange in here too.

'I'll set you up on this computer,' Kay says. 'You can go on YouTube and watch Pokémon or whatever you like.'

'Can I read the *History*?'

'I didn't bring it. *Groovy Greeks* is in your backpack.'

The door makes that loud clicking sound. A lady comes in.

She has grey hair so long it goes past her bottom. She sees me and smiles.

'Hello there. You must be Jessie.'

I nod.

'Jessie, this is Lily,' Kay says.

The lady holds out her hand while she juggles a stack of newspapers in her other arm. I shake it but don't really know what to say. Lily has a nose-ring, which I thought only teenagers got. She and Kay talk a bit about 'who's taking what floors'. Kay asks if she can do ground, first and second so she can keep an eye on me. Lily says she's happy to do Battye, which I think is the third floor.

Kay sits me down and puts her hands on my shoulders, which means I'm about to get 'a talk'.

'I need you to stay here, okay? The first-floor stacks are through that door –' she points to an open doorway '– but you're *not* allowed in there. There are things that could fall on you and books that are very old and expensive. I retrieve books that people request, so I'll be in and out all the time. I'll know if you move.'

'Can't I sit with everyone else and look out the windows?'

'No, I want you to stay here.'

So I'm stuck. Kay goes away for seventeen minutes before returning with some green slips. She disappears into the stacks, returns with a small trolley loaded with three red boxes, and then goes out again.

I'm bored. I finished *Groovy Greeks* ages ago. It says nothing about Diogenes. I try googling Diogenes but I can't stop glancing at the doorway to the stacks. If I push my seat back, I can just see a set of stairs going up.

Kay comes back after thirty-one minutes. She glances at me on her way into the stacks. Again, those green slips. She seems to swap them for books or boxes. Then, she comes back after twenty-eight minutes, and then again after twenty-four.

'Reading something cool?' she asks as she walks past, this time holding a long slip with pink, yellow and blue paper. She doesn't wait for a response. When she comes back, she has a small book-shaped box with gold lettering. Then she disappears.

She won't be back for another half-hour. If I have a very quick look, she won't know.

I go to the doorway and peer in. The stairs go up to another floor. Behind them, there are so many bookshelves, I can't see where they end. The bookshelves are so tall, they almost touch the roof. They are metal and stacked right up against each other, with no room between them. What's the use of them if you can't get to the books? How did Kay get those books out?

I've got more than twenty minutes before she comes back.

I tiptoe into the stacks, past the stairs and into the land of giant bookshelves. There's a sign on each one, sometimes with just letters like a secret code. Each bookshelf has a handle, not like a door handle, more like the wind-up handle on my jewellery box, the one that makes the ballerina inside turn. I try to turn one of the handles but it won't budge.

I walk further and find a gap between two bookshelves. I peer inside. There are many books, with a few of Kay's green slips sticking out between them. All the books look old. It must be why it smells in here. Kay once said there's lots of leather books decaying in the stacks, and it smells like off honey. I can see what she means. It's sweet but kinda sickly.

I try the handle on this bookshelf. It's heavy but it moves. The whole bookshelf rolls along tracks on the ground, like a train. I try another and another. They squeal a little and make a little knocking sound when they come together. Then I turn the handles until the shelves are back to where they were before, so Kay won't know I was here.

I've got plenty of time so I walk around the stacks. At one end, I find a secret room. It has a tiny glass window in the door, but it's so dark I can only just see a few bookshelves inside. I touch the glass. It's cold.

Kay told me about these. A rare book room. A fridge for special old books. Could there be something as old as the *History*? I try to go in but the door's locked. I notice the card reader. I think about stealing Kay's ID. She'd be so angry she'd never let me read the *History* again.

I go back to the workroom and check the time. Better not risk it.

When Kay comes back, she smiles at me. I smile back thinking, *you don't know what I did*. She has those long slips again, the ones that are three joined together. They look important. She swaps them for two of the book-shaped boxes.

'I have one more retrieval shift and then we can have lunch, okay?'

'Okay.'

She leaves.

Another half hour to explore the stacks.

I go back to the rolling bookshelves. This time, I step over the little train tracks. The bookshelves are so tall, like walls. I want to see the books at the top. There are steps on wheels all around the stack. I wheel one over, pick it up (it's heavy!), and put it inside the shelves. When I step on it, I can see some of Kay's green slips. They sit in the gaps between books. I pick one up. It's a form: TITLE, AUTHOR, CALL NUMBER. It has scribbles on it, like a doctor's writing. I can't read it.

A little squeal. The bookshelves behind come towards me! The shelves bang into the step and shudder. I scream. Someone grabs me and pulls me out of the shelves. It's Kay.

'What the fuck are you doing? I could've killed you!' she screams, shaking my arm. She digs her fingernails in. She won't let go. 'I tell you to do one thing for your own good. One fucking thing! Why can't you help me? Why do you have to make everything so hard?'

Then Kay cries and hugs me really tight. Her ugly sobs echo around the stacks. It's horrible.

'I'm sorry,' I say.

Kay just bawls. Eventually, she calms down and lets go of me. She wipes her face and takes a big breath.

'Let's have lunch.'

In the café downstairs, I have a cheese and salad sandwich and Kay has another flat white with an extra shot and two sugars. She looks past me as she sips her coffee. Doesn't say a word. Her eyes are glassy like she might cry again. She doesn't buy me a muffin, even though the lady behind the counter says I should try Kay's favourite, which is raspberry and white chocolate. Kay tells the lady I don't deserve it.

After lunch, Kay takes me to the first floor, but this time to the public area. She sits me in front of a librarian called Neil.

'If you move, you are *never* reading the *History* again,' she says, shaking her finger at me.

Neil watches me while Kay retrieves books. I've never met a man librarian before. He is very smiley, but he looks big and tough, like a rugby player. He sits behind a desk that is too small for him. It has a sign that reads REFERENCE DESK. People ask him where to find things and request books from the stacks. He puts the request slips in a magazine holder that Kay fetches every half hour, though she comes more often now to check on me. It's nice to be out of the workroom, but I'm not allowed to sit by the windows. I swing my feet and sigh.

'A computer just became free, if you're bored,' Neil says, pointing to the monitors behind him.

'I'm not allowed to move,' I tell him.

'I'll tell Kay I said it was alright.'

There are six computers behind Neil's desk. I sit next to a teenager who's googling something called Othello. I go to Wikipedia and look up Diogenes again. It says he died in 323 BC. But in the *History*, he dies soon after the boy gets the mischief, which is 316 BC. Weird.

'Can I have some paper?' I ask Neil.

'Of course!'

He gives me a piece of paper and a pen.

I write out the things I remember from the *History*. Using my notes, I find many mistakes online. Wikipedia says Diogenes met Alexander in a place called Corinth, not Athens, and that their stories are 'apocryphal', which means 'works, usually written works, that are of unknown authorship, or of doubtful authenticity, or spurious, or not considered to be within a particular canon'.

When I look up Aristophanes it says he was a comic playwright who lived from 446 to 386 BC. When I google 'Aristophanes Library of Alexandria', I find a Wikipedia page for Aristophanes of Byzantium. It says he was the head librarian after Eratosthenes. I guess he got a promotion. It says he invented things like full stops and commas. But it says nothing about him being a confiscator.

When I look up Hua Yingtai it says, 'This page does not exist'. I find Mulan though. She's from a ballad, which is a kind of poem. It says, 'Hua Mulan is treated more as a legend than a historical person.'

I'm annoyed.

'Wikipedia is wrong,' I tell Neil.

He laughs. 'Yes. You can't trust Wikipedia!'

I'm more annoyed now.

'What are you looking at?' he asks, peering at the screen. 'Hua Mulan? Like the Disney movie?'

'No! Like the real person!'

'I bet we have books about her.'

'Really?'

Neil looks it up on his computer.

'Do you want one?'

I nod. He writes something out on a green slip and puts it in the magazine box. Eleven minutes later, Kay comes to take the slip. She glances at me and looks angry but she gets it. The book is boring, but I learn there are lots of stories about Mulan. One of them is a play. The play lists everyone except Yingtai. She's listed simply as MOTHER, performed by *lao* (old female).

'Can I get more?' I ask Neil.

'We don't have any others on Mulan, unless you want some sheet music from the Disney movie.'

'Can I get books about other things?'

'Sure! What do you want?' Neil asks, really jolly. Neil seems happy about everything. That kinda makes me happy.

He writes up more green slips for books on Alexander the Great, Diogenes the Cynic, the Library of Alexandria, and codices. He even finds a book about libraries on fire. Kay still looks annoyed but she fetches them.

'Most of the books you're looking for aren't at this library,' Neil says. 'They're at libraries all over the state. You can request these from your local public library, did you know?'

I shake my head.

'Inter-library loan. Basically, you can order any book in WA and they'll send it to your local library. What's your library?'

'We have a library at school.'

'Hmmm, no, it needs to be a public library. Where do you live?'

'Guildford.'

'Lovely. Let me look it up. Here,' he says, and swivels his computer screen around to show me. 'It's on James Street. Is your school Guildford Primary or Guildford Grammar?'

'Guildford Primary.'

His fingers fly across the keyboard.

'Hey, it's on Helena Street. That's super close to James Street. You could walk there with Kay.'

'Really?'

'Absolutely! How about I write up a list of books you can request from Guildford Library? Then you can take them home. You can't borrow books from here.'

'Okay!'

Neil types out a list with codes for the librarians at Guildford. I ask for some books on penjing and he does a quick search and some googling.

'Penjing is the Chinese version of bonsai. You know, those little Japanese trees? Penjing came first according to this … oh!' He stops, looks at me, looks at the clock and then back at me. 'Stay here. Man the desk. Tell anyone who comes up that I'm in the loo.'

He runs out from behind the desk and races down the stairs. I sit behind the desk but he's back really quick, like only three minutes. He has a book.

'I saw this in the discard bookshop the other day,' he says. 'It's an old library book. Not penjing but similar. You can have it.'

I take the book. It's about bonsai trees. It has black marks and scratches on the cover, which has gone a little yellow. Inside, there's a barcode that's been stamped over in red with DISCARD BY THE LIBRARY OF WA. It has so many pretty pictures of bonsai trees, some with wire on them. Neil shows me the index at the back of the book. I find a trident maple like Yingtai had.

'Is it really for me?'

'Of course!'

'Was it expensive?'

'Three dollars. Cheap as chips. *Cheaper* than chips!'

'I can pay you back. I get pocket money every fortnight.'

Neil laughs. 'Don't worry about it. You can pay me back in *bonsai facts*!'

I like Neil a lot. I write out bonsai facts from the book on strips of scrap paper and sign them 'FROM A. MISCHIEF' on the back. When Neil goes to the toilet, I hide them under his keyboard, in his notebook, in his jacket pocket and in the hat sitting on the floor. I smile at him when he comes back. Later, when he puts his hat on, I think about the bonsai fact tumbling out when he gets home.

This is my first act of mischief.

## Jessie

Today Kay promised we can go to Guildford Library after school and request all the books Neil typed out for me. We'd have gone Monday, but the men from the iron bars place were over and they took forever.

School goes on and on. I go to the library at lunch and read a Disney Mulan book (which is stupid) and then the bell goes. I can't wait for the day to be over.

Kay is sitting on the brick steps in the courtyard when I come out of class. She smiles and takes her earphones out.

'Okay, off to Guildford Library!' she says. 'Oh, and look what I got.'

She hands me a red library bag made from the same material they use in the green shopping bags you keep forever. It has flowers, people and hearts on it, and says 'LIVE LOVE LEARN with Public Libraries' on one side and 'Proudly supported by public libraries Western Australia' on the other.

'For all the books we're going to get,' Kay says.

It's even bigger than my backpack. I love it.

One of the mums tries to stop Kay as we're leaving.

'Hi, Kay, you're Jessie's sister, right? Do you have a minute?'

'No, sorry,' she says. We keep walking.

We cross the busy road next to school and go down the hill with the petrol station and the little park. Finally, we turn onto Meadow Street, which has lots of pretty houses on it. At the end of the street, tucked behind a theatre, is the library. It faces the train tracks and the park with the big grave. I never even knew it was here.

Inside, it's small, only a few shelves, some couches and a few desks, but it has very tall ceilings. There are pictures on the walls, old maps and old faces, and a pretty stained-glass window above the librarian's desk.

I go right up to the desk. The librarian looks up.

'Hello there.'

'I would like these books please,' I say. I hand her the list. 'Neil from the State Library said you could get them for me.'

The librarian smiles and takes the list. 'Well! He's even written down which ones can be found here. Neil from the State Library is very helpful.'

I nod.

'These are very mature books. Are they for you or ...' she glances at Kay.

'They're for me!'

'It's fine,' Kay says.

'Okay, let me get the three we've got here and then we'll request the others.'

The librarian gets the books as we fill in some forms. I get my own library card.

Then she starts on Neil's list. She types really fast just like Neil and, when I think about it, Mrs Harper. You must have to be a fast typer to be a librarian.

'Okay, Jessie, all of those are on order for you,' she says. 'They'll be coming from other libraries in WA, so you'll have to wait, but you can definitely borrow these three today. Would you like to get anything else? We have a great kids' section just around the corner, see?'

'No thanks,' I say. 'How long will the books take to get here?'

'It depends where they're coming from.'

'Will some get here by tomorrow or the day after or do I have to wait for weeks?'

'Not by tomorrow but I bet one or two will be here by next week.'

'Do I have to come every day to check?'

'No, we'll email you.'

'I don't have email.'

'We'll email your sister. She'll tell you.'

'What if she's grumpy and doesn't tell me?'

The librarian smiles but tries to hide it. 'I guess you better not make her grumpy.'

At home I try to read the three books I got from the library. One of them is about Chinese myths and has the story of Mulan in it. It also has a story about a lady and her lover who turn into butterflies, and the lady's name is Yingtai. The second book is 'sayings and anecdotes' from Diogenes (the cover has a picture of him *naked* and with his lantern). The third one is a thick book about Alexander the Great.

I read the Mulan story while Kay is making dinner. It says Mulan was the youngest daughter, not mentioning Munan, and that she was away for twelve years. The Alexander the Great book is too big to read now, so I flip through the Diogenes book. It lists things he did and said. I don't really understand everything, but I do find conversations between him and Alexander. In one bit, Alexander asks if Diogenes is frightened of him. Diogenes asks if he is good or bad. Alexander says he is good, so Diogenes responds, 'Who's afraid of what is good?'

We have fish fingers and peas for dinner. I eat mine with tartar sauce. Kay has tomato sauce.

'Can we read another history tonight?' I ask.

'No, I'm really tired.'

'Can I read it on my own? I'm not tired.'

'No, you need to sleep,' she says grumpily. Then, nicely, she says, 'Plus, it's fun when we read it together.'

I think it would be fun if I read it on my own but I don't say so.

'You need to finish those library books anyway. We'll read the next history when you finish your research on the first three. Then we can read another and do more research. Won't that be fun?'

*No.*

Kay makes me go to bed early. She tells me off when I put the light on to read so I just lie there and think about mischief. Kay watches TV for a long time and goes to bed late.

After a while, I get up and go to the toilet. Kay doesn't come out to check on me, so I go to the study and look out the window. Mrs Moran from Number 61 is outside with Cornelius again, but she isn't vacuuming. She sits in a chair with Cornelius on her lap. She seems sad. She looks around, from one end of the street to the other. Maybe I could do some mischief to make her feel better. I decide to do something tomorrow.

I bet Mrs Moran likes flowers. She spends a lot of time outside, and she has rosebushes in her front yard. We don't have any flowers in our garden because everything's dead. On the way to school, I look at our neighbours' yards and think of Aristophanes stealing flowers all over Alexandria.

At recess, I walk around the gardens at school. There aren't a lot of flowers because it's winter, but I find a few purple ones and some big spindly red ones. At lunch, I return with scissors and my backpack. We're meant to stay in the undercover area to eat lunch for ten minutes before we can play, but I sneak out when the teachers on duty aren't looking. I fill my bag with flowers, right up to the top.

Someone sees me and tells the teachers. I have to sit on the bench for the rest of lunch and they take my backpack. Then I have to go to the principal's office and get told off. Mrs Fraser returns my backpack but the flowers are all gone. I make mistakes on my worksheets for the rest of the day on purpose.

Kay won't let me take flowers from the neighbours' yards and won't give me money to buy any from the petrol station.

'What do you want them for?'

'Mischief,' I say.

'What kind of mischief?'

'Secret.'

The next day, I try to think of where I can get flowers without getting in trouble. Then I spot a book on the trolley near Mrs Harper's desk. It's about origami and has a paper flower on the cover.

'Can I have that book?' I ask Mrs Harper at lunch.

'Sure,' she says.

In the book, there are steps with pictures to show you how to make all kinds of origami things, like birds, elephants, boxes and flowers. I ask for paper and Mrs Harper gives me some scrap.

My flower is terrible. The steps are too hard. I scrunch it up and get another piece of paper but I ruin that one too. Mrs Harper won't give me a third piece so I get the scrunched-up paper out of the bin and try again.

'I like origami!'

Theodore. I ignore him but he sits down at the desk with me.

'Can I make origami with you? My favourites are cranes. Have you read *Sadako and the Thousand Paper Cranes*? It's so sad. Stephanie taught me how to make them like Sadako and I'm trying to make a thousand too.'

I scrunch up my paper again. It's no use. I can't make it properly when the paper's all crumpled. I look at Theodore.

'Can you ask Mrs Harper for a piece of paper and then give it to me?'

'Sure!'

Theodore goes over to Mrs Harper and says, 'Jessie would like another piece of paper please.'

He's such an idiot.

Mrs Harper looks a little annoyed but she smiles too. 'I'll give *you* a piece of paper. If you want to share it with Jessie, you may.'

'Thank you, Mrs Harper.'

He snatches the paper and sits back down with me.

'Let's share,' he says. 'We need to make the paper square first. That's why your flower didn't work, you didn't make it a square. We can get two squares from this.'

He folds part of the paper into a triangle and then folds the extra bit at the end. He opens it up to a square and carefully tears off the bit on the bottom. He does the same thing to the leftover piece, making another smaller square.

'I'll show you how to make a paper crane,' he says. 'It's easier with bigger pieces of paper so you can have the big square.'

'I want to make a flower.'

'I'll show you how to make a crane first.'

'I don't want to make a crane.'

'Cranes are nice. Here, first you fold it into a triangle like this. Then, you unfold it and fold it into a rectangle, like this. You're not doing it. Follow along with me.'

I sigh but follow along. We fold our squares over and over again, and then unfold them and put them back together in a different way. It turns out a crane is a bird, not a crane that works on buildings. Theodore asks for a pen and we draw smiley faces on our cranes. They're nice actually.

Mrs Harper comes over, slips us more paper and winks.

Theodore shows me how to make the flower and rose in the

book, and then he shows me how to make a lily and a lotus flower. We make flowers and birds all lunch, him chatting on and on while he shows me what to do. He talks about the book with the girl and her paper cranes, and how she got sick from a bomb dropped on her city. He boasts that he and his mum have a secret language, Korean. Even though his dad is half-Korean, he was born here and doesn't speak it well. He talks about his nanny Stephanie, his dog Broom, and other things like how paper's made and what he had for breakfast.

The bell goes. Theodore lets me keep all the origami and helps me carry them to my backpack.

'Let's meet tomorrow. We can make more! Thank you for playing with me!' he says before we go back to class.

I take the origami home and hide them under my bed.

The next day, Theodore brings lots of coloured paper already cut into squares, some with pretty patterns. At lunch, we make lots of birds and flowers. He talks a lot and asks me questions. I don't answer. He doesn't seem to mind. He lets me be quiet.

I start writing 'From A. Mischief' underneath the cranes' wings. You can only see it if you turn them over. When Theodore asks what I'm writing, I say 'None of your business!' He just says 'Okay!' happily. That afternoon, I hear a teacher complain that he's 'undiagnosed' and 'the parents are in denial'. I guess it's an adult way of saying annoying.

At home, I take a cardboard box out of the recycling bin, one with pictures of bananas all over it that Kay got from the market. I put all my origami in it and hide it under my bed.

When it's full, the mischief can begin.

On Friday, Kay gets an email. We go pick up five books from Guildford Library. Two are about penjing, full of beautiful photos. I learn that penjing is different from bonsai because penjing is more about 'landscape' and 'creating a scene'. The other three are about the Library of Alexandria, well, two of them are. One of them is about books and has a section on Alexandria. It has lots of pictures. Some books used to look like fans and some were written on bone. It says that the book (or 'codex') was invented in the first and second century, which is two to three hundred years *after* Aristophanes' history.

I think the real *History of Mischief* was the first book ever made. All other books before then were scrolls. Paper didn't even exist. Paper was invented in China in the second century. Before then, they used papyrus (plants from Egypt), parchment (animal skin) and vellum (calfskin). I'm happy we make paper from trees and not from animals anymore.

I write down all of the things I learn. The dates are often different from the *History*, but historians always get things wrong or argue. Some of them even name the other historians they think are wrong. They argue a lot over Alexander. Some think he was clever, while others think he was cruel and mad.

None of them know about *The History of Mischief*. I know something kept secret from the whole world.

A week later, more books arrive. I write down anything linked to the *History*, even if it's wrong. Kay asks what I've found.

'I'm still researching,' I say.

'Then you'll give me a mischief report, hey?' she asks.

'If you let us read the fourth history.'

'Deal.'

The box of origami birds and flowers is full. There are three hundred and sixty-three: one hundred and two paper cranes, eighty-four lotuses, sixty-eight lilies, sixty-two roses, and forty-seven simple flowers. I have so many coloured and fancy-patterned ones that I throw out the ones Theodore and I first made on scrap paper. Except for the first two paper cranes. I keep them in the back of my cupboard.

Mrs Moran has a veranda around her house. She sits there with Cornelius, even if it's raining. Sometimes Cornelius sticks his head out and licks the rain. He's clever, and hides under one of the hanging baskets for protection. I look for the ones that hang completely under the veranda. They'd make perfect nests for the cranes.

Kay used to leave the keys in a bowl in the kitchen, but since the break-in, she carries them around with her. It's Thursday night. Kay's asleep in front of the TV, the keys next to her on the couch. It's 2 am and the lights at Number 61 are off. I sneak into the living room and take the keys really slowly so they don't jingle. Kay's snoring. I think I'm safe for a while.

I open the front door and run over to Mrs Moran's house with the box of origami. I quickly put the paper cranes and flowers all over her veranda. I put them in her hanging baskets, on her chair, the table where she puts her tea, and next to Cornelius' water bowl. There are so many. It looks so bright and colourful, even under the dull street lamp.

I run back home. I return to the living room, where Kay is still snoring, and leave the keys next to her on the couch. The empty box goes under my bed. I get under the doona where it's nice and cosy.

I smile and smile.

The paper cranes and flowers are still there when we walk to school the next day.

'That's interesting,' Kay says.

I shrug.

I don't need to make any more origami so at lunch I read a book about codices. Theodore still wants to make paper cranes. He sits on the cushions with me and chats until I tell him to be quiet. He then hums. I can't read, so I just make cranes with him, even though I don't need to. He tells me everything he remembers about Greece from a documentary Stephanie let him watch, so I guess I'm still doing mischief research.

Later, Kay takes me to Guildford Library because the last two books have arrived. There's one on Diogenes and the Cynics (which were the grumpy philosophers) and one on the burning of libraries (it has a chapter on Alexandria).

On the way home, we see Mrs Moran sitting on the veranda with Cornelius, who's batting a paper crane with his paw, and a lady I don't know. Mrs Moran has a mug of tea in one hand and a golden crane in the other. I remember writing 'From A. Mischief' on that one. She grins and waves with the crane in her hand.

'Hello girls!'

'Hello Mrs Moran,' Kays says. She then pokes me. 'Say hello!'

'Hello Mrs Moran,' I say. Then, I feel mischievous. 'I like your paper birds.'

'Aren't they marvellous?' she says. 'Oh, girls, this is my daughter Helen.'

Helen looks about Mum's age. When she smiles, she doesn't look like she means it. 'Hello.'

'Helen doesn't like the paper birds,' Mrs Moran says. 'She doesn't even like the flowers. What a party pooper.'

'I didn't say that, I just … you know why.'

'She thinks I did all this myself! Can you believe it?'

'Mother, please,' Helen says.

'Anyway, girls, would you like a cup of tea?'

Kay says 'no thank you' and we go home.

On Saturday, I read the new books (they don't have many new facts) and flick through the old ones while Kay listens to her podcasts, cleans the bathroom and sleeps.

At dinner, I present Kay with my report. I give as much

detail as I can, checking my notes, so she won't have any reason to say I didn't do enough research. She gets us both a bowl of ice-cream as I finish my report.

Finally, I ask, 'So, can we read the next history please?'

Kay looks tired but smiles. 'Sure.'

# A. Mischief the One-Hundred and Twenty-Third

### Wieliczka, Poland 1436–1489

As I placed my foot on the first rung of the worn wooden ladder, stepping back into the abyss, I felt immediate calm. Soft light and shadow danced from below as I went further down into the heart of the earth. I hadn't wanted to leave the mine, but when the doctor discovered I hadn't been aboveground in two years, he prescribed sunlight and a small vacation. I spent my enforced holiday at the nearest inn, blacking out all the windows.

A barrel slowly passed me as it was winched up to the surface on a set of pulleys. The familiar creak of the ropes made me smile.

'Serafin!'

As I stepped off the ladder, the miners below secured the winch and patted me on the back.

'Welcome back!' one of them said cheerfully. He crossed himself. 'We missed you, old man. The boys have had a terrible time with the horses.'

I sighed. This didn't surprise me. 'Did I miss anything?'

'Not unless you count the dragon,' he laughed.

The other miner went suddenly dark, scowling at his friend fiercely.

'What … oh … sorry,' he said to me sheepishly.

I shoved past him and descended deeper, heading for the stables. The mention of a dragon set it off again – that hum, that wicked sound from the *History*. I'd left the book in the stables, hoping it wouldn't be there when I returned. The thing had been with me for almost fifty years. What a fool I'd been to think it would abandon me after so long.

Each level down, the hum grew. It was reminding me: *You are back. But don't forget before.*

I went down a sloped corridor, another set of worn steps, and out into an expansive cavern. Miners, carpenters, engineers, penitents, doctors, cooks and horse-handlers like myself crossed at this large intersection, nodding our greetings as we found the corridor or shaft that would lead us to our work. There were over three hundred of us in this underground kingdom. Truly, there was no place like the Wieliczka Salt Mine. Corridors tunnelled haphazardly down into the earth as miners followed the salt wherever it went. Some areas were so low and narrow, one had to get on hands and knees and crawl. In others, the caverns were taller than buildings, and wooden archways and stairs wound around the walls. I went down a corridor that sagged, like it laboured under the weight of the earth above. The walls bulged like they were riddled with gout.

I then had to take a boat over our biggest brine lake, a body of water as vast as any lake aboveground. Among all the fears of living down here, few were greater than smashing through rock and breaking into a lake. Flooding killed men every year. But as I watched its lightly rippling surface twinkling in the light from the tallow lamps, I couldn't help but admire the lake's beauty. There were worse ways of dying here.

Once past the lake, I descended a staircase that wound down a wide shaft. Then I followed the wooden gutters that snaked around the mine, draining brine from leaking walls and lakes. Pine and fir stakes held up the ceilings, supported the walls, and arched in bridges over brine lakes. Since wood became as hard as rock when exposed to salt it was used in the carts, winches and horse mill that hauled the greatest salt deposits to the surface. Metal corroded too quickly, only finding a place in the pickaxes.

I then noticed something. Three new crosses carved in an overhead beam. Markers of the dead. I touched those few I hadn't seen before. I often wondered if they would carve a cross for a Jewish man like me, or if they'd afford me a marker in Hebrew. At the start and end of every shift, the miners crossed themselves. They crossed themselves for me, when they saw me start work. It annoyed me as a boy. Now I saw it as a sign of affection. I was one of them.

I heard the horse mill creaking as I approached the stables. The stables housed twenty horses that lived and worked belowground with us. Five were driving the biggest mill in the mine, a winch that wound ropes as thick as a man's torso to pull salt blocks to the surface. The horses calmed as they felt my presence. The men who monitored them did not. I saw them stiffen. They knew something was wrong. Whatever this talk of a dragon meant, they knew. They offered only meekly mumbled welcomes.

I ignored them and went to the stables. Most of the horses were gone, no doubt pulling carts to the various shafts that brought the salt up to the surface, or here to the mill. There were three mares resting. A boy, only a little older than me when I started, groomed their manes. He bowed nervously. I snatched the brush from him.

My day passed in the heavy silence of my men creeping around me. Eventually, a familiar voice, its deep timbre wry yet gentle, sounded behind me.

'I could've mined an entire mountain in the time you've spent grooming those horses.'

It was Władysław.

'It hasn't been done properly in a week,' I snapped and continued brushing the horses who'd returned after the main shift of the day.

Władysław watched me for a moment.

'You're upset.'

I said nothing.

'Someone mentioned the dragon, didn't they?'

Ignored him still.

He sighed. 'Come, sit down. I brought dinner.'

'I'm not hungry,' I said, but he took me by the shoulders and sat me down. He placed a small box with bread and stew in my lap. He sat and nudged me. Though a full foot taller than me, he tried to make himself smaller, resting his elbows on his knees and slumping forward. Władysław was an imposing figure, a frontline miner who spent his days digging into virgin rock. He smiled at me gently. Sadly.

I looked away.

'It's nothing, you know,' he said. 'Just Lolek. He's convinced there's a dragon on the lower levels.'

Lolek led the penitents, the men who burned off the deadly methane gas that leached out of the rock and hung above our heads.

'Why?'

'Why else? The poor bastard's mad. His men aren't helping. Ulryk's been roaring like a dragon all week.'

My hand went to my pocket. I felt the little wooden dragon hidden there. A child's toy. My only possession from life before.

Władysław's voice jolted me back.

'Lolek's given Ulryk double shifts as punishment but he still does it.'

I got along with most of the men in the mine, but Władysław and Ulryk were the only ones I considered friends. We had all been in the mine for decades, longer than the rest. We were permanent fixtures, some joked, as old as the rock itself. Even our long beards matched, though Ulryk hadn't been able to grow his back since the accident. Ulryk was another penitent. The long pole he lit and poked into the caverns to burn off methane was his constant companion. His face was partly melted, burnt when methane had built up too much and exploded in his face. Yet he laughed constantly, always playing games. He'd make a better mischief than me. I tried giving the *History* to him once, but he flipped through it only to find blank pages.

'Give it back to me when you've written your great opus,' he said. 'Tales of Serafin, Handler of Horses, Miserable Old Bastard.'

That night, after Władysław left, I went up to my bed in the loft. I banished everyone else to the stables below with the horses. Many of the miners went back to the surface after their shift, but there were a number of us who stayed for months, even years, on end.

I let out a sigh as I settled into bed. Talk of dragons aside, I was home. Not even the *History* beneath my mattress, with its gentle humming, could ruin that.

I sunk into the mine. My mischief took me into the rock. I swam in the brine lakes. Like Yingtai some nine hundred years ago, I knew how to feel the earth, how to be one with it. While she shaped the trees above, I snaked through rock below. That was all I could do. I had no magic in me. And I was fine with that.

I used my mischief to follow Ulryk as he finished his double shift, listening to him hum some happy tune. He extinguished his pole-mounted torch and took a small lamp back up to the middle level to sleep.

I lingered in this new cavern. It was full of a darkness without shape or end. As I drifted off to sleep in the stables, I dreamt of finding dragon eggs, smooth oval things, ready to split open. I dreamt of Feliks.

I don't recall how I found the *History*. I just remember, suddenly, the feelings and experiences of so many people blooming in my mind. My first memories were theirs. I caught my reflection in a window. I was a boy. Black hair, face pale and freckled, with startling green eyes. But I was also a slave who outran time, a woman who shaped forests, a princess who turned limestone to salt. I experienced all those memories as my own. I knew a dozen languages before I could fully speak. I was one hundred and twenty-two souls in a tiny boy who had yet to form his own identity.

I became mute, trapped in the *History*, staring at my reflection for days, trying to understand who or what I was. My parents put me to bed. I wouldn't eat. Then Feliks sat on my bed and put a wooden dragon in my hand. Feliks made me Serafin. Feliks gave me back myself.

'Your name is Serafin. You are three and a half years old. Your favourite food is gingerbread, which Father makes in the bakery downstairs. You like dragons and stories. Maybe you've forgotten them, like you've forgotten yourself. I'll tell you again. You shouldn't be sad, little brother. It'll be nice to hear them as if they're new.'

He motioned down to the wooden dragon. It fit neatly in my palm, like it was made for me. My fingers wrapped around its neck. It had bulging eyes and a long, curved tail. 'This is your favourite toy. Smok Wawelski, the Dragon of Wawel Hill.'

He told me the story of the dragon and the founding of our town. King Krakus was looking for a place to build the seat of his realm. He discovered Wawel Hill, a tall mound where he could see his whole kingdom. Below, the hill was full of caves. Fertile fields surrounded the hill and a crystal-clear river wound through them gracefully. The only problem: a giant egg found in the caves. The king was afraid, but his men convinced him it was nothing to worry about. The egg was heavy and thick. It would never hatch.

A grand castle was built on Wawel Hill, and a village of merchants and farmers sprang up at its base. The city was named Krakow after the wise king. Then one day, a cracking sound came from the caves, loud enough for all to hear. A dragon hatched. It crawled out of the caves, already a giant, and tormented the city. The king promised his daughter's hand in marriage to anyone who could defeat the dragon. Many tried. Many died.

A cobbler had an idea. He knew the dragon couldn't resist a juicy plump sheep. He stuffed the carcass of a sheep with sulphur, fluffed its wool so it looked alive, and left it outside the caves. The dragon devoured it immediately. The sulphur burned the dragon's insides. He flew down to the Vistula River but no amount of water could quench his thirst. His belly swelled and then BANG, he burst! The dragon was no more. The cobbler married King Krakus' daughter. Krakow was at peace once more.

'When we play,' Feliks said, 'you're the cobbler and I'm the dragon. I pretend to explode and you always laugh.'

As Feliks told me the story, I started to understand who I was, separate from the *History* and its memories.

'I like the story,' I said. I heard my voice for the first time. I had so many voices before. This little voice, with its ill-formed words: this was my voice now.

'I know, it's your favourite,' Feliks said. 'I think it's a little sad though.'

'Why?'

'The dragon was just hungry. He didn't have a brother or friend to help him.'

'But he killed people! He was a bad dragon.'

'He was lonely. Maybe that's why he was a bad dragon. I was naughty before you were born. Mother always says so. I was lonely. But we're never lonely, you and me.'

So Serafin was born again in the things Feliks told me. He told me about the king who was eaten by mice, the glass mountain and the tree of golden apples, gingerbread bees, and stories from the Torah, of Abraham and Moses. Even at ten, I felt disjointed at times, unable to discern between my memories and the histories. Feliks locked eyes with me as if he knew.

'Your name is Serafin. You are ten years old. You have eyes as bright and green as dragon scales. You are fun and you love gingerbread. You are my little brother.'

There were whispers when I woke in the morning. As the handlers and I led the horses through the mine, rumours were shared with us too. The penitents had found rocks in the new cavern that were not there before. Four rounded rocks, as large as a man, oval and smooth. *Dragon eggs*, they said, laughing.

Had I dreamt finding those eggs? Or had I maybe … made them?

No, it wasn't possible. I had never been able to wield mischief. Not properly. Since I'd found the *History* so young, I didn't really have any abilities for it to magically enhance. I could be one with the mine, feel the life within the rock, but beyond that, nothing. And ever since Feliks, well … I had never tried.

I needed to see those rocks.

Echoing shouts became louder as I approached one of the main caverns. It was rare for men to shout, as everyone was always listening for the creaks that foretold a collapse. Lolek and Jozef, the mine administrator, were arguing. The penitents assigned to the cavern, including Ulryk, waited behind their commander, looking a little embarrassed.

'They weren't there before! They weren't!' Lolek protested.

'Then you are either going blind or someone put them there because they knew what a gullible fool you are,' replied Jozef.

I came close to Ulryk. He smiled faintly and gave me a tired embrace. His clothing was damp, a precaution for any good penitent. 'Good to see you,' he said.

'What's going on?'

'Lolek's lost it.'

'Were the eggs really not there yesterday?'

'I didn't notice them, but it's a big cavern,' Ulryk said. He stroked the horse at my side. 'We haven't lit it properly because there's still so much gas to burn off. We only see the place in flashes and dull light.'

'Can I ... can I see them?'

Ulryk smiled and raised his eyebrows. 'They're just rocks.'

'I'm curious.'

He shrugged. 'Sure. I'll take you down when we break for lunch. We'll say you're inspecting it for horse mills or tracks or whatever.'

Lolek refused to go back down there, so when lunchtime came, there was no one in the lower cavern. Corridors branched out ahead of it, with men like Władysław chipping away at new deposits, but when we descended deeper, there were no torches, only Ulryk's small handheld lantern. The cavern itself was so vast I couldn't see the ceiling. Only the tips of pointed stalactites, menacing as fangs, poked out of the darkness. Cauliflower salt formations bloomed on the walls. It felt oddly familiar.

We walked through a puddle of brine, ankle deep, and came to a side of the cavern where dripstone columns parted.

'Your dragon eggs, sir.'

There – four massive stones, smooth but oddly not damp like the salt domes we'd passed. They were all separate, complete

rocks, not connected to any of the other deposits. Four. *Feliks.*
*Dorota. Mother. Father.* Dreams from the night before came to
me: running my hands across the rock. That sense of mischief
bubbled up again. They really looked like eggs.

'I've never seen anything like this before, have you?'

'To be honest, no,' Ulryk said. He shivered and crossed
himself.

'Just smooth rocks?'

'Just smooth rocks. Shiny white gold.'

White gold. Salt's other name. With salt blocks that size, you
could buy a whole kingdom.

Dorota. Our little sister. When she got old enough to play Smok
Wawelski with us, she was not content to play the princess
offered as reward for killing the dragon. No, she played the
king. She loved bossing me to 'save the kingdom, good cobbler!'
as she motioned at the bakery as if it was hers.

We loved playing near the Wawel Hill caves, just at the base
of the castle. We weren't supposed to, and the soldiers guarding
the castle always tried to scare us away. One day, we were
chased by an especially aggrieved soldier.

'How many times do I have to tell you brats?' he shouted,
bolting towards us.

We shot away. Dorota and I sprinted down the hill. Feliks
ran into the caves. The soldier went after him, his voice
booming as it echoed off the cave walls.

'Come back, you little monster!'

Another soldier carefully made his way down the hill after
us.

'It's alright,' he called. 'We just want to talk to you.'

The first soldier's voice bellowed from the cave. 'God help
you!'

Though the voice was not as loud, its reverberations coming

from deep inside the cave, it was enough to send us scampering into the streets.

As we arrived home, the most hideous crack sounded within my skull. It was like a dragon egg, giant and deadly and final, splitting open. I fainted.

That night in the mine after the eggs were discovered, all I could think of was that sound. That crack. Something breaking. Yet, for the first time in my life, it didn't feel sinister. It felt … mischievous.

I lay in the loft until all the heartbeats below, horse and man, slowed and their breaths became deep. I crept past my sleeping colleagues and took a lantern down to the lower levels. The threat of methane bothered me – the air seemed thicker – but I consoled myself that the lantern was mostly contained and smaller than the one Ulryk used to show me the eggs. As I went down, I noticed a tiny flickering light coming from deep within one of the corridors. Men working late, perhaps? My destination was much further ahead. They wouldn't notice me.

As I entered the cavern, I felt I was stepping into the mouth of a dragon. My light wasn't strong enough to reveal the stalactites above my head, but I sensed them there. I made my way to the egg-shaped rocks and placed my hand on the largest of the four.

I spread my fingers. The rock cracked. That same sound. I gasped, thinking it really was a dragon egg. As the salt splintered, I realised the fracture was emanating from my palm. I felt a surge of playfulness and pushed it further. The rock split. As the two halves separated and smacked against the ground, the cavern shook. Stalactites above trembled. Some came crashing down. I looked up at the cauliflower formations and, with a grin, bent my fingers into claws and swiped the air. Claw marks scratched the wall.

Then I felt something else. Something up in the nearby corridors. A groaning, like something bending out of shape.

An impending collapse.

I left the cavern. I ran. I'd never been this close before, never felt the corridors around me moan. Then I saw the light again. It pulsated in the middle of the creaking. I focused on the light and heard familiar voices.

'Hold the light closer, I want to refine the detail in the face.'

'It's looking good. Perhaps we can start defining the arms.'

Władysław and Ulryk. Their talk was punctuated by the sound of a pickaxe, but this noise was delicate and quick. Surely they'd noticed the rumbling coming from the walls.

Something snapped. They didn't hear. They weren't moving.

I hurled my voice down the corridor. It echoed into the chamber where their light flickered, bouncing against the buckling walls. I screamed 'RUN!' but it came out distorted, like a roar. The corridors shook. As the earth crumbled, I ran back to the level above.

I caught my breath in the main cavern on the upper level. Plumes of dust and powdered salt billowed out of the corridor that descended below. Rescuers arrived, lanterns swinging. Then Władysław and Ulryk emerged from the cloud, coughing and covered in dust.

'Are you alright?'

'Is anyone else down there?'

'What happened?'

Jozef rushed forward and gave them water. They drank heavily.

'A collapse,' Władysław rasped. 'Corridor 15B.'

'I don't think it's gone into the main corridor,' Ulryk added between coughs.

'What on earth were you doing down there?' Jozef demanded.

Władysław looked guilty.

'A chapel, sir,' he said. 'We were carving a small chapel off Corridor 15B. For men to pray before descending –'

'There's something down there,' Ulryk interrupted, looking frightened. 'Something big. It warned us. Or it wanted us out of there.'

'What?' Lolek's voice came, steeped in fear.

'It was a roar, like a lion,' Ulryk said.

'Or a dragon,' Lolek whispered.

'No, it was a voice, it shouted RUN, didn't you hear?' Władysław said. 'It was familiar.'

'Was someone else down there?' Jozef asked urgently. 'Could someone else be trapped?'

'No,' Władysław said. 'It came from the walls, from the stone, from everywhere. Maybe ...'

'What?' Jozef pushed.

'Maybe,' Władysław said slowly, 'it was a ghost.'

Dragons and ghosts. Nothing else was spoken of for weeks. On inspection of the corridors, it was found that two had collapsed, but the main corridor and the cavern were intact. The findings in the cavern – the egg split open and the claw marks – only fuelled debate about the possibility of a dragon living in the tunnels. Those who believed in the ghost dismissed the dragon theory. If there was a dragon, it would've eaten us all. Dragons didn't warn miners. Ghosts did. They started referring to the ghost as Skarbnik, Treasure Keeper, though most men called it simply 'him' – out of fear or respect, I wasn't sure.

It was wrong, but I couldn't help myself. Each night I slept for an hour or two, then woke suddenly, ready for mischief. I walked silently through the mine, no need for a lantern. I could see in the dark now. It wasn't the same as seeing, exactly, but I knew where everything was, like walking through a house you'd lived in your whole life. I stroked the walls, leaving behind claw-shaped gouges. I carved LISTEN FOR SKARBNIK OR HEAR DEATH into a wooden bridge over a brine lake.

It was as if my mischief had been lying dormant, waiting. I finally understood that playful tingle other mischiefs had known. Some nights I moved things. I shaped ropes into warped hearts and lopsided smiles. I switched boots beside beds so that men who slipped their shoes on in the dark found the left shoe on their right foot.

'Catch the clown who's doing this!' Jozef snapped one day.

But no one believed a man could scratch through rock in a single night. No one believed a man would hang upside down above a brine lake to carve words into a bridge that was petrified by salt. They said they did, but they didn't. Hearsay about the ghost and the dragon followed miners into every cavern and corridor.

Then one night, I ran into someone. We both bounded around a corridor and collided. I was knocked to the ground. When I looked up, Władysław was standing over me.

'Serafin? Is that you? What are you doing here?'

I didn't have an answer. 'What are *you* doing here?'

Władysław glanced at the claw marks in the wall above my head. 'I asked you first.'

'If you must know, I'm trying to find out who's doing this nonsense!' I said, pointing at the marks.

'Since when did you get involved with gossip and mischief?'

'I notice you're holding tools there,' I said as I tried to get up.

He held up his small carving instruments. 'You think *these* can do *that*?'

'You tell me.'

He helped me up. 'I'll show you what I've been doing. Then you can tell me what you've been up to.'

We crossed the main cavern, towards one of the heavily mined corridors. We didn't go far. Just off the cavern was a small room. There, a sculpture of Jesus on the cross, his arms outstretched and head drooping, was carved into a makeshift nave. Then, to the side, a woman was taking shape. Her form, with its billowing dress and crown, was carved crudely. Her face was half-etched, a delicate eye and nose, and that was all.

'Another chapel?'

He nodded. 'With permission this time.'

I looked at the woman. 'Kinga?'

'Yes,' he said. He smiled at her incomplete form, as if he could see her beneath the salt.

Władysław's devotion to Princess Kinga wasn't unique. Miners prayed to her for protection. It was said that as a Hungarian princess promised to a Polish king, she threw her engagement ring into a salt mine in her home country, only for it to magically follow her and turn the earth below Wieliczka from stone to salt. She brought riches to Poland but was more famous for her chastity, even in marriage, and became a nun after her husband died. None of the miners knew she was a mischief before me. I felt a sort of kinship looking at the statue. For a moment, I too could see her under the salt.

'It's beautiful,' I said.

'So why are you roaming the corridors?' Władysław asked, his voice kind and playful.

I didn't completely lie. 'I'm looking for a ghost.'

'Skarbnik? I think he's real, you know.'

'No, I'm looking for the Smok.'

Władysław laughed. 'Why would you want to find a dragon?'

I gave an honest answer. 'I think he's with another ghost I'm looking for.'

Władysław nodded, and grasped me around the shoulders. It was brief, and then he patted me on the back and said nothing else, but I felt so many years of unspoken sorrow gently acknowledged.

Of course, he knew. They all did. Everyone knew of the boy who died in the Wawel caves playing dragons.

It was to be my great act of mischief, saving Feliks. Why else had the book come to me? If the *History* allowed me anything, surely it would have given me the power to do that, even as a child. Yet, back then, after I woke from the hideous crack in my mind, all the mischief gave me was his voice.

*Serafin?*

It came from within my head. A little voice, wounded, frightened.

*Little brother?*

I sank into myself and followed the whisper. I flew out of the bakery like a spirit, followed the rescuers with their torches, past the soldiers looking guilty, into the mouth of the cave. I went further than the voices that called Feliks' name, down jagged shafts and uneven corridors, and finally, down one almighty drop. I didn't see any of this with my eyes. It was like a thread of light in my mind, guiding the way.

*I'm here, little brother. My back. I can't move. Please help me.*

I couldn't respond. I tried but nothing came. Feliks cried.

*It's so dark. Please help me.*

I jumped up and ran out of the bakery. Mother grabbed me.

'I know where he is! Let me go!' I screamed.

I bit her. She slapped me hard.

'You're not going down there too!' she cried.

I fought but it didn't take much for her to barricade me in my room.

*Serafin, I'm here*, Feliks begged. *Just here. Please. Help me.*

I thumped the walls, tore the bedsheets, pulled hay from the mattress, made as much noise as I could. As night fell, I collapsed in a heap of torn cloth and cried, all the while Feliks' voice begging, *little brother, I'm here*, in my head.

The search went on for days. Men even came from the mine to join the rescue effort. Some said they could hear Feliks calling to them, but no one could find him. His voice, light and faraway, bounced from cave to cave.

Feliks still called to me. He slept, nodding off every now and then, but when he was awake, he called out.

*I'm so hungry, little brother.*

By the fourth day, he sounded drowsy. His begging slipped into wistful nostalgia.

*Do you remember the first time you had gingerbread? The smells came through the floorboards and drove you mad. I stole one for you. Your eyes! It was like you'd never tasted anything before. I feel that now. Anything, just a piece of bread, would do.*

The next day, he barely said a thing. Just a few words.

*I'm thirsty.*

When he spoke, something rattled in my brain. When he slept, it was a quiet hum. When Mother brought me food, I threw it at her. I felt so helpless, trapped in my room. But even I couldn't reject the water. I was thirsty from screaming. I felt guilty as I sipped.

*There's a giant smooth rock here. It's oval like an egg.*

*It could be a dragon's egg.*


On the fifth day, I heard nothing but humming. Then, as night fell, Feliks woke suddenly. He was frightened, like he didn't know where he was. He made these tortured rasping sounds.

*I'm here,* I called out to him. *I'm with you.*

I don't know if he heard me, but he calmed down.

*It's alright,* he said. *It's good in a way. I'm here so he won't be lonely anymore. The dragon, I mean. We'll be friends. The Smok and me. I'll be fine.*

He sounded resigned to his fate, almost happy.

*You are Serafin. You are ten years old. You are my little brother.*

Silence. Not even the humming I felt when he slept. I lay there for a long time, straining to hear. As the silence crept throughout my body, like cold seeps into bones, I started to cry.

I was going to do it, I'd been sure of it. I was going to follow Feliks' voice through the cave, raise his body like magic out of the long drop and snap his spine back into place. We would walk out of there together, hand in hand. Because I was Serafin. I was ten years old. And I was his little brother. What other mischief could I do?

The search continued for another week. But there was nothing left to do.

He was already dead.


Decades later in the mine, the *History* hummed like Feliks still living. The sound seemed to grow as the miners dug deeper, adding more corridors from the artery that ran between the main cavern with its many shafts and the new cavern with its dragon eggs. As weeks went by, a new labyrinth appeared. Corridors crossed, some were abandoned, others lengthened. Those that collapsed were repaired. Makeshift rooms were dug into naturally occurring caves, where endless drops and jagged rocks were dispersed between smoothed salt domes and saline puddles.

And the *History*, oh, it hummed.

I went down a few times. We brought a horse to the main corridor between caverns, but the animal wouldn't go further. The air was too thick, I suspected. The penitents' work was crucial. The whooshing sound of gas being burnt off, as well as the pops and bangs of mini-explosions, were heard even up in the main cavern.

I tried to stop the mischief, to ignore that sizzling hum that once told me my brother was still alive. If I couldn't sleep, I sat with Władysław as he worked on the chapel. But sometimes, I went other places with my mischief, places no one went, places where lanterns couldn't be brought for fear of starting a fire. I told myself to stop, but I ventured out involuntarily in my dreams, exploring the maze, both natural and man-made, that sprawled beneath. Searching for him. Some claw marks were found, ambiguous enough that the Smok's detractors argued they were just normal gouges from mining the rock. I didn't remember doing them, but then I did.

In some dreams, I was ten again. Feliks and I ran through the mine. He roared and pretended to explode, and I chased him.

'The Smok has a friend now,' he said to me, touching the cracked rock in the dragon egg cavern.

And he was right. We were both dragons now, naughty boys roaring through the mine as men slept. We poked holes in the brine gutters so water leaked out, broke stalactites from the roof and pretended they were teeth, and blew in Władysław's ears as he carved through the night. I knew Feliks was still dead. He could only exist in my imagination. And yet, our mischief marked the mine.

They died soon after Feliks. All of them. Dorota. Mother. Father. A fire in the bakery, like dragon's breath, ripped through the house while I was out. I saw their bodies pulled from our home while it was still on fire. They were only partially burned, a mercy, I was told. They likely suffocated from the smoke. A kinder death than burning. A kinder death than starving.

Play and mischief were dead to me. I never opened the *History* again. Yet I couldn't help but take it and the toy dragon with me as I found a new home in the mine. Though the

*History* had hummed before, a painful reminder, it had never tempted me to play like this, not until work on the lower caverns began. Though sometimes I thought of Dorota as I conducted my mischief, it was always Feliks, the brother who made me Serafin, who seemed to follow me.

Of course, the thing about a child's mischief is that it becomes quite macabre and sinister when in the realm of adults. Dragons, ghosts, things moving on their own. No one knew this as play between brothers, as a man reaching out to the memory of his dead sibling. Lolek certainly didn't. It took just a few more scratches in the walls for him to throw his pole at Jozef's feet and leave for good.

Within days, we had a new penitent. Jakub, his name was, and he was only twelve. Ulryk was annoyed. He was charged with training the dim boy.

'Idiot, how many times do I have to tell you? Go back and wet your clothes. Do your hair and shoes too, and hurry back,' Ulryk snapped at him.

The boy scratched his head. 'I don't like being damp. It's uncomfortable.'

'It's not as uncomfortable as burning alive, let me tell you. It's the only reason my body isn't as ugly as my face. Now go and wet your clothes, or so help me God!'

The boy sulked off.

'I've told Jozef we can't rely on him. He's reckless. He'll get us all killed,' Ulryk complained at one of our late-night gatherings in the chapel. He kept glancing at us to check that we too were outraged, as he worked on a cross that had been recovered from the collapsed chapel.

'He's only been here a week,' Władysław said absently, chipping away at his Kinga statue.

'A week too long!'

'Maybe the Smok will eat him for you,' I said.

Władysław chuckled but Ulryk wasn't amused.

'It's that dragon that lost us our head penitent.'

'The Smok owes you then,' Władysław said. 'Leave the boy near the eggs.'

Ulryk smacked his chisel hard and chipped a shard of salt from the cross.

'Lord Almighty!' Władysław exclaimed.

'Sorry!' Ulryk crossed himself and bowed to the cross. He held his tools out to me. 'My nerves are shot. Can you take over?'

I just looked at him from where I sat. Władysław glared at him too.

'Oh,' Ulryk said. He sat next to me and slapped me on the knee. 'So shot I thought grumpy old Serafin was one of God's children.'

'We are all God's children,' Władysław said tersely.

There was silence for a moment.

'Anyway, pray for me, lads,' Ulryk said. 'I don't care who you pray to, whether it's God, Yahweh or the bloody Smok. I need all the help I can get.'

Władysław promised he would, but I didn't. I hadn't prayed since Feliks died. For all the things that happened next, I wish I had.

The next day there was an explosion.

I felt it before the others. It was a buzzing in my head that steadily grew, distinct from the *History*'s hum. The horses bucked and ran on the horse mill, trying to get away. The rumbling started. In my head, it was like pieces of my brain broke apart and dissolved. Salt showered down on us.

I quickly sank my mischief into the mine and felt corridors collapsing. I heard penitents scream as they fell onto the jagged rock beneath them. I saw fire.

The shaking stopped and men rushed past me holding buckets of brine. The chaos was remarkably quiet. As rescuers descended, they didn't say a word. We all listened for those telltale creaks.

I snapped at my stablehands to retrieve the horses. I ran to the mill and placed my hand on the closest horse, using my mischief to calm her. The boys came from all directions, moving quickly to put the horses back in the stables. I tried to send my calming energy out.

Men streamed between the caverns, water sloshing as they ran. Quickly, I took one of the mares down to the brine lake where men were frantically filling buckets.

As I went back and forth between the lake and the cavern carting water, I listened to the wordless action below. There were pops and whooshes, and the occasional scream.

Something stank. There was too much methane to risk lighting any lanterns. The men below worked only to the light of the fire they were trying to put out.

It took three hours to extinguish the flames. Now the rescuers, empty buckets or heavy stretchers in hand, were in need of rescuing. They traipsed slowly through the tunnels below, completely blind. I sat on the ground, tired from hauling around drums of water, and put my head in my hands. I could see them in my mind, like ants crawling closely together. I reached out my mischief and called to them.

*Straight ahead, then right here, yes, now straight.*

They started going the right way. I kept calling out.

*Left, step over the debris, and straight. Keep going. Over the rocks, raise the stretchers high. Keep going, brothers, keep going.*

There were still two men trapped below, their heartbeats pulsing beyond where the fire and collapse had occurred. One of them was Ulryk's, slow and laboured. The other was Jakub's, frantic like a rabbit. I tried to ignore them while I focused on the thirty or so men lumbering through the dark towards the main cavern.

*There's another collapse to your right. Walk past carefully. There's heavy debris on the ground. Climb over. Abandon the stretchers. Carry the men over.*

A heartbeat in the group fluttered and failed. They still laboured to climb over the fallen rocks with him. I wondered if they knew he was dead.

Light from the main cavern must have touched their eyes. The men who cleared the debris sped up, moving with purpose. They turned around a corner without me telling them and streamed into the main tunnel between the two caverns.

I opened my eyes as they flooded out, all bloodied, burned and covered in soot. Jozef stood by the tunnel's opening, his eyes jumping to each face, taking a mental inventory of the living and the dead. Bodies were brought up, burned, some missing limbs, some alive, some dead.

The doctors rushed forward. I stood off to the side, watching from the shadows.

Władysław was the last to emerge, cradling a man with burns all over his body. He took him straight to a doctor, and then looked around.

'Where's Ulryk?'

They ignored him, attending to the injured or staring blankly through him, as if their brain was trying to catch up to the question. Finally, he stared into the darkness from where he'd come. Tears streaked his soot-blackened face.

'Lead him out, Skarbnik,' he whispered.

Ulryk and Jakub couldn't move. They seemed suspended in the salt below, like their bodies were part of the rock. I tried to call to them, giving directions. This frightened Jakub more. His heart fluttered so madly I feared it might burst. They couldn't follow Skarbnik's commands. Perhaps they'd broken their legs. Perhaps their backs.

Jozef dismissed any talk of a rescue party. There was too much methane to light a lantern and we couldn't search for men in the dark.

But I didn't need a lantern. I could see everything. I knew where they were.

No one noticed as I entered the tunnel that descended into the caverns and corridors below. I was quickly enveloped by darkness. I glanced back and locked eyes with Władysław. I wondered if he saw me. He looked as though he was searching. I winked and smiled, confident he couldn't see a thing, and then made my way down.

There was debris everywhere. Abandoned shoes and pickaxes rested alongside fallen slabs of rock. As I went towards Ulryk, past collapsed corridors and blackened wood supports, the air became heavier.

I entered a cavern with cauliflower formations sprouting from every surface. Smoke had flooded this place, turning the white salt black. The air tasted burnt. Ulryk's strangled breathing, which rasped around the chamber, quickened.

'Who's there?'

I found him. His left foot was twisted. His skin was burnt, a screaming, blistered red with parts that yellowed and shone. He was dusted in fragments of salt, and his right hand was bloodied from having dragged his body along the ground in an attempt to get out. He stared into the darkness, his wide eyes going straight through me.

'It's Serafin,' I said.

I crouched down and touched him lightly on the shoulder. He jumped.

'I can't see you.'

'There's too much methane to light a lantern. We have to go back through the dark.'

'I can't ... how can you see?'

'I have dragon eyes. I see in the dark.'

He paused, clearly afraid. I thought he might even refuse my help. But then he grasped at me with his right hand. 'Okay, Smok, off we go.'

Every step was a battle. Ulryk couldn't put any weight on his left foot, so he hopped on his right, grunting with every movement. His blisters ruptured and oozed. We stopped often. I tried carrying him.

'You're too heavy. Keep hopping,' I said as we cleared another pile of debris.

'I'm a rabbit now, am I?'

'Yes, and best get a move on, or the Smok will catch you.'

I don't know how long it took for us to inch our way up through the collapsed corridors but finally, we saw light.

'Not long now,' I said. We climbed up to the main tunnel. As we emerged from the darkness, men rushed forward to take Ulryk from me. Some of them looked at me with suspicion. I just turned around and went back down the tunnel.

Jakub wasn't far from where I found Ulryk. There were a few tunnels branching out from above the blackened cavern, and one of them was partially caved in. I squeezed through a crack between collapsed support beams and salt blocks. Everything was burnt here.

Jakub shouted out. 'Who's there?'

'A rescuer, Serafin. Ulryk's friend,' I called back.

I rounded a corner and found the boy, burnt and cut all over. His right leg was trapped under a rock.

'Help me, please!'

I hauled the rock off his foot. He let out a strangled cry, and then held his arms out like a child begging for his mother. I tried pulling him to his feet, but he wasn't even able to stand on his good leg. So I just picked him up.

'We need light!' he cried.

I started walking with him in my arms. 'We can't have any lanterns. There's too much gas down here.'

His head darted around frantically. 'But it's black!'

'It's alright,' I said. 'I can see.'

'God, I'm blind!'

'No, you're fine. We'll get to some light in a minute.'

He was still looking around as we came to the collapsed corridor.

'There's a collapse here. There's just a small gap between the rock and the broken supports. It's not big enough for me to carry you through, so you need to hop on your other leg and squeeze through. I'll hold your hand. Just be very careful, the supports have been damaged. Try not to touch anything.'

'I need to see!' he cried as I positioned him beside the gap.

'You don't need to see, I have you.'

He wept as he battled through the gap. As he cleared it, he fell face first on the ground. He let out a feeble cry.

'It's alright,' I reassured him from the other side. 'You've cleared the hardest obstacle. I can carry you the rest of the way.'

'I need to see!' he cried. He felt around on the ground next to him. I began to make my way through the gap, carefully avoiding the beams which looked even more splintered than when I first came through.

'It's alright,' I said to him and myself.

But the boy was terrified. He grabbed at anything he could find. A penitent's pole, a shoe, a pickaxe. Then his hand fell on a tiny metal box sealed shut. He flicked off the lid and felt inside.

'Matches!' he gasped.

'No, Jakub –'

He struck the match. The tiny flame burst as it caught the air.

A sudden, piercing heat seared through my very being as I was swallowed by the explosion.

And yet, my soul ripped free.

Somehow, as I was blown apart and burnt to ash, a part of me soared defiantly out, flying through the tunnel, riding the explosion, bursting into the main cavern and yelling, 'RUN!'

I saw them all – Władysław, Ulryk, Jozef and the rest – and somehow they saw me. I roared with the fire that surged out. I lived as I died in it.

Then, as the smoke ventilated through the shafts in the main cavern, as the men rushed once again to the brine lakes, I began to recede. I couldn't follow them. Like a heavy fog, I sank. The fire raged, but they'd been warned with enough time to escape the worst of it. A darkness crept into me. I drifted back to the ash that was once my body, to the walls and the floors I'd worked, to the salt.

The fire raged for a month. All the while, my soul slept like a hibernating dragon. After the fire was extinguished and the men returned, their voices stirred me from my slumber. I came and went, my consciousness dispersed among the salt, bleeding out occasionally like brine. I witnessed the men carve a cross into the horse mill in my memory. Władysław was annoyed.

'Do you really think that's appropriate?'

They looked at him, dumbstruck.

Over the following nights, I rested in the air around him as he added the tiniest embellishment to Princess Kinga's already ornate dress. צ, followed by the outline of a dragon's head breathing a single flame. It was so small, hidden in the hem of her skirt, that it was barely perceptible.

But I saw it. The Hebrew. The dragon. *Here lies Serafin*. I wondered where Władysław had seen it, who he'd asked. I saw the effort, the searching, that went into this marker. When he finished, and touched it with such kindness and sorrow, I began to fade. The world went out of focus, but I knew I'd be back again, every time there was a fire, an explosion, an avalanche.

I couldn't save Feliks. But I could save them.

I'd always be there.

## Jessie

There's nothing in *the whole of WA* about the Wieliczka Salt Mine. NOTHING. The librarians at Guildford couldn't even find one book. I told Kay to ask Neil to do some searching for me. She said she did but he couldn't find anything. I don't believe her because Neil can find books on anything.

I do some googling and find many pictures of the mine's statues and chapels. They mined salt up until 2007, though 'commercial mining' stopped in 1996, which is ages ago. People can visit and see all the statues. Sometimes they even have concerts and weddings down there. I also find some books online. I write them out in my neatest handwriting and present them to the librarian at Guildford.

'I would like these please.'

The librarian looks at my list.

'These are tourist guides. We don't have things like this.'

'Yes, you do,' I say, and point towards the blue books about countries. The book on Poland had a section about Krakow and the salt mine, but it was very small.

The librarian smiles. 'Those are Lonely Planet guides. What you've got on your list are guides you'd buy at an attraction, like a souvenir.'

'Can I request them?'

'No, dear, you can't request books that aren't in public library stock.'

'What's that mean?'

'We don't have them at any of our libraries.'

'You didn't even check.'

The librarian sighs. 'Okay,' she says. She types for two seconds and then says, 'Sorry, there really is nothing. Remember, we searched for books on the mine a few days ago. I bet you can do some great internet research. Or you can read some books about Poland, oh, like that one you've got in your hand. Well done!'

'Why can't you order these? I found them on the computer!'

Kay comes over and says, 'Keep your voice down.'

'She's not even looking properly!' I yell.

'Don't be so rude,' Kay says. Then she looks up and says, 'I'm so sorry,' to the librarian. That makes me even madder.

'You're a bad librarian! You didn't even try!' I yell at her.

I throw the Poland book and storm out of the library. Kay runs after me and grabs me by the arm.

'Ow!'

'That was unacceptable! You don't treat people like that, especially when they're trying to help you!'

I try to tug my arm free but Kay grips it really tight.

'You're hurting me!'

'Go and apologise now!'

'NO!'

Kay snatches my bag and pulls me back to the library. She dumps all the books I renewed, the ones about codices and Alexander and Mulan, in the returns shoot, and then drags me back home. I scream at her the whole way. I tell her to let go, she's hurting me and I hate her. No one does anything, even the lady walking her dog. She just looks away.

Kay finally lets go of me when we get home. 'Go to your room!'

'You're not the boss of me! You're not Mum!'

'Well, Mum's dead, so go to your fucking room!'

I run to my room and slam the door. I jump on my bed and scream and cry. After a while I feel tired. I just lie in the bed and feel sad.

It's raining. Raining really hard. The TV's blaring. Kay hasn't called me for dinner and it's past midnight.

I'm hungry. I'm embarrassed. I acted like a baby.

I'm sad about the rain too. Kay used to love the rain. She'd get this look in her eyes, wild and excited. Sometimes she stood outside looking at the sky until someone asked her what she was doing. She'd say, 'It's going to rain today.' And it would.

She loved the sound of it most and would open every window so the house was full of noise. She'd close her eyes, smile and just listen. Mum and Dad never minded. We were a family who loved winter. Mum put us in stupid matching jumpers. On the weekends, Dad made hot chocolate with real chocolate and cream, and we'd watch movies up loud so we could hear them over the heaters. We all sat shoulder to shoulder, even if we'd had a grumpy day.

Sometimes I wish the accident had happened in summer. When it rains now, Kay shuts the house up. She turns the TV on or puts her iPod up so loud I can hear it through her earphones. She doesn't let us go out when it rains unless it's school or work, and if it's really bad she calls in sick and lies in her room all day. I don't mind the rain so much. It never sounds like it did on that day. Maybe I should tell her that. Maybe then she wouldn't be so sad.

The TV goes off. Kay goes to the bathroom and then her bedroom. All the lights go out. The rain gets louder. I want to tell her I'm sorry, but I don't.

The next day, Kay wakes me up and says, 'I'm sorry I hurt your arm. I was worried about you running onto the road. I'm still really disappointed with how you behaved. It really hurt when you said you hated me. I shouldn't have said that thing about Mum, but neither should you. It's not fun for me. I don't want to do all the Mum and Dad things, but I have to.'

I want to apologise but I don't say anything. I can't even look at her. Kay sighs.

'I've got a day off today. Some tradies are coming to put bars on the windows and doors. They're going to make our house really safe. And pretty too.'

I don't think I can say sorry now because she's talking about something else.

'Anyway, let's get ready.'

I get up without making a fuss.

'What have you got on at school today?' Kay asks as she gives me a bowl of cornflakes.

I don't answer. I don't know how to say what I want to say. I just eat my breakfast, have a shower and get dressed. Kay walks me to school. When we get to the school gates, I run to the library.

It's Wednesday. Dance again. Mrs Lornazak makes everyone dance to 'Poker Face' by Lady Gaga.

'You do realise what she's talking about when she refers to her "muffin", don't you, Audrey?' Mrs Armstrong says to Mrs Lornazak when she tries to make me join in.

Mrs Lornazak goes red.

'It's interesting what kids learn from pop music these days,' Mrs Armstrong continues. She takes a big sip of her coffee.

Mrs Lornazak changes the song to something else. Everyone complains. Theodore asks if they can dance to it again. He asks eight times before she threatens to send him to the principal (he asks two more times but she doesn't send him).

Theodore sings the chorus all the way back to class, especially the *na-na-na-naaaa!* part. Miss Sparrow *does* send him to the principal's office for disrupting silent reading.

I still feel bad. I wish I'd apologised when Kay said sorry. I get funny with this stuff.

At lunch, Theodore teaches me how to make an origami box, so I make two. Then I make two little cranes and put one in each box. I write the word SORRY on the box lids and FROM A. MISCHIEF on the bottom.

When Kay picks me up, I give her one of the boxes. She smiles as she reads the lid. She doesn't look on the bottom. Adults never look at things properly. Maybe she'll find it later and it'll be a nice surprise.

'It's okay,' she says. Then she opens it. 'This is ... cute. Looks like the paper birds from Mrs Moran's garden.'

I don't say anything.

'Anyway, thank you.'

'That's okay,' I say. I look at the ground. 'I don't hate you.'

She strokes my cat ears beanie. 'I know.'

She says it softly, just like Mum.

'Can we go to the library so I can apologise to the librarian?'

'Really?'

'I made her a box too.'

'Okay, sure.'

We walk to Guildford Library and I go straight to the desk. I hand the librarian the box and say, 'I'm sorry I was rude yesterday.'

The librarian smiles. She also doesn't look at the bottom. 'This is very sweet. Did you make it?'

'Yes. There's a bird inside.'

She opens it. 'How charming! Thank you,' she says, holding it up to her face. Then she looks at me. 'I hope this means we won't have another episode like yesterday.'

'No.'

'No throwing books?'

'No throwing books.'

'Good,' the librarian says. 'By the way, I found something you might like. When you threw that book at me, I noticed you'd put a Post-it note on the page about the Dragon of Wawel Hill.'

'Kay says it's okay to put Post-it notes in books because they don't leave a mark.'

'You're not in trouble!' she says. She ducks under her desk and comes back with the Poland book and another small book with a picture of a dragon on it. 'It just made me think that maybe you were interested in the dragon. And would you believe it, we have a book called *The Dragon of Krakow and other Polish Stories* right here at Guildford. Krakow is the city of Wawel Hill. It's the same story.'

She hands it to me. The dragon on the front is green and there's a castle ablaze in the background.

'I know you read lots of adult books but this one's for kids.'

I don't know what to say. I flip through the book.

'You can borrow it if you like,' the librarian says. Then she goes behind her desk again and brings out a pile of books. 'I also saved those inter-library loans you wanted to renew yesterday.' The librarian looks at Kay. 'If it's okay with you.'

Kay nods. The librarian takes my library card, scans all the books and puts them in my giant red library bag. There are so many it's almost full.

'There you go,' she says. 'The inter-library loans are due back sooner than the two Poland books, so make sure you keep your docket with the due dates.'

I look at the dragon book and then at her and say, 'Thank you.'

'You're very welcome.'

I want to say more. I want to say how I don't deserve this,

how I don't deserve Kay, how I've been grumpy and mean and I'm so sorry. I just feel so angry and sad all the time, but I love the mischief, I love the books and I love the library.

I can't say any of this, but I do smile.

She smiles right back.

## *Jessie*

When we get home, there are black bars on all the doors and windows. They are like prison bars with pretty twists.

'See? Look how strong they are,' Kay says, pulling on the bars. 'They're made specially, just for our house.'

They aren't as nice as the fence with the roses but they look okay. 'How do you open them?'

'You don't. We can still open the flyscreen and the glass window, but you can't open the bars.'

'Why?'

'It keeps us safe. No one will ever break in again.'

'What if there's a fire?'

'We go through the doors.'

'But the doors have bars on them.'

'We can open the doors. We have keys. You can swing them wide open.'

'What if you get trapped in your room and you can't get to the front door or there's a fire in the way?'

'Go to the backdoor.'

'What if the backdoor has fire in front of it too?'

Kay looks annoyed. 'It won't happen, so don't worry about it!'

I take the Dragon of Krakow book to school and read most of it at lunch. In this book, the king offers the shoemaker anything he wants, so he asks for the dead dragon's scales and makes shoes with them! There's a story about gingerbread bees that makes me think of Serafin. Some of the stories are sad because people or animals die and lots of princesses have to marry the heroes, even though no one asks if they want to.

Theodore still bothers me, but after I tell him I want to read, he finds a book about dragons (copycat) and reads next to me.

On Thursday, after school, Kay and I go to the park. I count out the graves again. I imagine the soldiers are like ghost Skarbniks or Smoks. Maybe they are counting along with me.

Afterwards, we go to the bakery. I get a gingerbread man with Smarties for eyes.

Then Theodore and a blonde lady come into the bakery.

'Jessie!' he yells. He puts his arms out for a hug. I don't hug him. He wraps his arms around himself and smiles.

'Hi,' I say.

'Oh, is this Jessie?' the blonde lady asks. She looks about Kay's age. She's got curly hair, long eyelashes and a big smile. She looks like a Disney princess, but in jeans and a woolly jumper.

'Yep!' Theodore says. 'Jessie, this is Stephanie. She bought the nice origami paper for us and got me that documentary on Greece! You remember!'

I nod. I chew on my gingerbread.

'It's so nice to meet you,' Stephanie says. 'Theodore tells me about the things you read. You've taught him so much. You're obviously a very smart young lady. And I love your cat ears beanie.'

'Who's this, Jessie?' Kay asks.

'Boy from school,' I say. I chew my gingerbread some more.

'You must be Kay! You're Jessie's sister, right?' Stephanie says, holding out her hand to Kay. They shake hands. 'I'm Stephanie, Theodore's nanny. I've wanted to meet you for a while but I can never seem to catch you after school. Theodore talks about Jessie every day. I'm so grateful he has such a lovely friend. I love how they spend their lunchtimes in the library. Jessie's very considerate to include Theodore in her reading and origami.'

Kay nods. 'Oh, good.'

'Maybe we can organise a playdate,' Stephanie says. Theodore goes 'yay!' and does that funny bouncing-on-the-toes thing he does all the time.

'Maybe, yeah, but we're really busy,' Kay says. 'Even the weekends are jam-packed, you know. Maybe another time. We really gotta get home.'

'Sure, um ...'

We leave. Stephanie calls out, 'We'll catch up at school,' and Theodore yells, 'BYE JESSIE!'

I think Kay hates meeting new people as much as I do.

'So, you have a friend,' she says as we get closer to home. 'You didn't tell me. That's nice. Should I have organised a playdate?'

'No.'

'Okay. But it's good. What's his name again?'

'Theodore. And we're not friends,' I say. 'He just taught me origami and sometimes we read together because he won't leave me alone. He's annoying.'

'He seems nice though.'

'I guess.'

'It's good you're being nice to him.'

I don't think I'm that nice to him. I finish my gingerbread and don't say anymore.

The next day is a Friday, which means the school library isn't open. Kay drops me off early and I sit in the courtyard so the ladies in the office can watch us. There are only a few other kids around. It's cold.

Theodore's here early too. He does what he always does when the library's closed: listens to his iPod and dances. He has it up so loud, I can hear it. He listens to the same songs over and over again. Today's it's one with English words like 'fight till the end' and 'we ain't playin', no' in between Korean words. There's this part that keeps repeating – 'Ready! Set! *POW POW POW!*' – where he pretends to fire a gun.

He dances up to me and wiggles his shoulders as he raps in Korean. I tell him to 'GO AWAY THEODORE!' He just wiggles somewhere else. During class, he gets told off four times for humming it.

He sings it at recess and lunch, '*POW POW POW!*' at everyone. That part is kinda fun. It gets stuck in my head. I get told off for humming it too. Mrs Armstrong points her fingers like a gun and goes 'PEW PEW PEW!' at Miss Sparrow. Theodore laughs so much I think he might wet himself. Miss Sparrow looks annoyed at Mrs Armstrong but doesn't say anything.

When Kay picks me up, she looks pleased but won't tell me why. She smiles like she knows something I don't.

When we get home, I find a piece of paper on my bed. It says: *A jousting knight shows the way. Pointiest regards, A. Mischief.*

I run to Kay, who's making dinner and listening to one of her podcasts. 'What's this?'

Kay pulls one earphone out. 'What?'

I show her the paper.

'Dunno,' she says. She puts her earphone back in.

I read the paper again and remember all the weird figurines in the garden. I go outside and search among the dead ferns. I find the jousting knight with its peeling paint. It points to a spot on the veranda where a white envelope is sticky-taped to a wooden pole. In the envelope is another piece of paper.

*Try to stay warm. Toastiest regards, A. Mischief.*

Stay warm? How do I stay warm? Maybe with a jumper? I go to my room and search through my clothes drawer. Nothing. Wait! The fireplace! I run to the fireplace and find another piece of paper.

*Needle in a haystack? Find the haystack of paper. Then find the needle. Most cryptic regards, A. Mischief.*

This one's confusing. I can't figure it out. At dinner, I quiz Kay.

'What's a haystack?'

'A pile of hay.'

'Why would a needle be in a pile of hay?'

'It's a saying. Imagine trying to find a needle in a stack of hay. It means something is really hard to do.'

'Oh. Would it be easier to find a needle in a haystack of paper?'

'I think A. Mischief wants you to consider what a haystack of paper would be. You're trying to find another note, right? Where would you hide a piece of paper if you didn't want it to be found?'

I try to think. 'Can't you just tell me?'

'Me? I'm not A. Mischief.'

Kay thinks she's so clever. I try to figure out what a haystack of paper would be. I go through the papers on my desk and my homework books, but don't find anything.

At 11:02 pm, I think THE STUDY! I run in and look at all the books, all that paper, and there it is, a piece of paper stuck to the spine of a book with a needle. This note sends me to the oven (*Gingerbread for Serafin? Must face the dragon's breath. Tasty regards, A. Mischief*), then the back of the TV (*Moving pictures and sounds, sure, but not as good as a moving forest. Regards from the couch, A. Mischief*), and even to the freezer (*Treats are only for the weekend? Frostily yours, A. Mischief*). The last clue says *Go to that night-time place you like best in the morning. Restful regards, A. Mischief.* I go to my bed and look under the pillow, the sheets and then finally under the bed itself. In my banana box, I find a postage bag. Kay's name and our address is crossed out and replaced with:

*JESSIE A.K.A. A. MISCHIEF THE TWO-HUNDRED AND SECOND*

*GUILDFORD, AUSTRALIA*

I rip the postage bag open. It smells like orange soap and salt but inside is a large book, a DVD and a postage slip from KOPALNIA SOLI WIELICZKA/WIELICZKA SALT MINE. The book's so big and heavy. It's the biggest book I've ever had by far. There are pictures of the horses, the mills, the lakes, the mine shafts, the chapels, everything. I run to the loungeroom where Kay's watching TV and hug her.

'Thank you!'

She laughs and says, 'No worries, my little mischief.'

We watch the DVD about the salt mine together. We have to pause it a lot because it's in Polish and I'm not very quick reading the English subtitles. The DVD says the mine is still open and you can visit or stay there for health reasons, because salt air is good for you. It talks about Skarbnik. I feel so proud. I know where Skarbnik came from. No one else does.

Kay tells me to go to bed, which I do. I wait till I hear her door close and then turn my bedside light on and read the book until 4:07 am. I dream of horses, ghosts and deep salt lakes. I wake up at 1 pm on Saturday feeling happy.

On Monday, Kay lets me take my book about the mine to school. I plan to make notes at recess and lunch so I can finish my mischief report and we can read the next history. When I arrive, Theodore's there but he isn't singing or dancing. He sits in the corner near the hall, making paper cranes. He looks sad.

I've never seen Theodore sad, and he looks *really* sad, like he might cry. I try to read my book but can't help looking at him. Kay said it was good that I was nice to him. Maybe I should actually *be* nice to him.

'What you doing?' I ask.

'Making paper cranes,' he says. He sniffles loudly.

'Okay,' I say. I go away for a bit, but then come back and ask, 'What's wrong?'

He shakes his head and tries to make the cranes even faster.

'Can I help?'

He nods. I sit down and we make cranes until the bell goes. At recess, he finds a corner in the undercover area and we make more. He's quiet in class and doesn't even smile when Mrs Armstrong tries to do the 'Ready! Set! *POW POW POW*!' thing again.

At lunch, he asks me, 'What does it feel like?'

'What?'

'When your mum dies?'

'It's horrible. You die,' I say quickly. 'But you don't stay dead. You just become another thing. And it's not a nice thing. It's a sad thing. And it's angry. And lonely.'

'I don't want to be another thing,' he says quietly.

We don't talk about it again. I cry when it's Kay who picks me up and not Mum. I cry all the way home and all afternoon. I won't go out, not even to the park or the bakery, where Kay says we can buy jam donuts and gingerbread cooked by dragons. I think that's why she comes into my room with the *History*, strokes my hair and says, 'Let's read the next one, hey?'

After a while I stop crying, and we do.

# A. Mischief the Two-Hundredth

## Paris, France 1870

For weeks we heard them coming. Gunfire and explosions in the distance.

News finally reached Paris. His armies decimated, Napoleon III abdicated and was exiled to England on Bismarck's command. We were a republic now, declared the morning paper, the Third Republic of France. Monsieur Martin, the kindly butcher downstairs, boasted that it was the Third and Final Republic, for we'd never go back to monarchical rule. He had given us a room for free, charity to our late father, his friend and apprentice, so I didn't tell him that 'final' seemed like a prophecy coming nearer every day. The Prussians scuttled across our country. Versailles was taken. Bismarck settled himself there, setting up long-range artillery and pointing it right at us. Some said he'd surely never fire on our fair city – but the nights were punctuated by weapons firing, louder each time, announcing their approach.

They encircled the city. They laid siege. They cut the telegraph lines. All of them. They blew up a few bridges, and barricaded the rest. Even fishermen got turned away, told to make their way back up the Seine. Nothing could leave. Nothing could come in. Not even a letter. Claude was quite pleased to have been picked as a postal runner to get through the blockade.

'An elite group, only twenty-eight of us, handpicked from the whole service. We go tomorrow, just before dawn!' he boasted to Chloe who, being a sweet girl barely fifteen, was mightily impressed.

'Perhaps there are only twenty-eight of you foolish enough to do it,' I countered.

'If by foolish you mean brave, then I'd agree with you, sister.'

*Sister*. The arrogance. He spoke as if we were already family. I suspect he used this claim of bravery to take my sister's virginity. When she came home early the next morning, I told her I'd burned her copy of *Notre-Dame de Paris* in lieu of firewood.

'You just don't understand love, Lou!'

Of course, I didn't. I was sixteen. I knew nothing.

The Prussians shot Claude. They shot most of them. Bernard, a kind boy who also worked at the postal service, came to our room to deliver the news. Chloe cried and soaked his handkerchief. Not knowing what to do, he pleaded with her.

'Please, he wouldn't want you to cry. Please, I beg you. I … um … I'm delivering some mail to a balloon! A balloon, do you believe it? Oh, please don't cry, let me, um, the balloon! It's magnificent! It's going to fly right out of Paris. I could sneak a letter in for you. No charge. Or maybe you'd like to see it. A balloon! To sail right over the Prussians' heads!'

Claude must've told Bernard about Chloe's fondness for the aeronauts. She cried all the way to Saint-Pierre but we went.

It was an underwhelming sight. The balloon was an ugly, limp black thing. The line was still connected as we arrived, pumping coal gas into the balloon, which was a collection of fabric patches and glue. The ropes that tied the sickly swaying thing to the basket made unnerving creaking sounds. One of the aeronauts noticed Chloe's sniffling. Assuming she feared for the flight, he gave her his handkerchief and offered some reassurance.

'It is a noble piece of wreckage, mademoiselle, never fear.'

As Bernard and the other postal workers hoisted the mailbags, some 125 kilograms of correspondence, into the balloon's basket, the aeronauts looked less confident in their noble wreckage.

Now loaded with mail, the men disconnected the gas line and helped one of the aeronauts into the basket.

'That's Jules Duruof,' Chloe whispered to me.

Monsieur Duruof cried out, 'Lâchez-tout!' He cut away a sack of sand as large as a mailbag and shot up like a champagne cork. The sleepy crowd was suddenly entranced. They cheered the rickety balloon. Chloe stopped sniffling and gasped. The balloon cleared the buildings, some nine storeys high, that surrounded it. People came out of their homes to see what was going on. Soon Paris was gazing skyward.

It didn't entrance me, I confess. Instead, my eyes were turned down to the ballast Monsieur Duruof had cut from his balloon. It had split open, and in the mound of sand that flooded from the bag, out stuck the corner of a book. Why would a book be in a sandbag attached to a balloon? The balloon in the sky, floating out towards the Prussian troops, didn't seem as strange as a book hidden in a bag of sand.

Firewood and coal were expensive. We stole all manner of things to burn. Books were the best, for they offered stories first and warmth for the stove and the hearth second. So I took the book while all of Paris looked upwards. It was full of blank pages. I was disappointed but comforted myself that while it had no stories, it would burn.


The balloon was a success.

Monsieur Duruof sailed over the Prussians. Not a single

bullet grazed the balloon or its cargo. Three balloons went up quickly after that, but this time, the clever fellows took homing pigeons with them. Soon messages were coming back. Pigeons became sacred, a sign of hope. While hunger drove men to eat their dogs and scamper down alleyways for rats, pigeons were spared. The siege lines were broken. The first ever airmail service was established. Monsieur Nadar's 'No 1 Compagnie des Aérostiers' was famous.

As the weeks went by, more balloons were needed. Empty train stations became balloon factories. The balloons fascinated Chloe. She volunteered us to help sew the great swathes of fabric needed to make them. Well, rather, she volunteered herself, and due to our arrangement, that meant she also volunteered me.

You see, we looked almost identical. Same face, same height, same long black hair. Only our eyes and cheeks distinguished us, for her eyes were brown, mine blue, and my cheeks marked with freckles.

When Father died, we were left with nothing. Despite Monsieur Martin not charging us rent, we needed money for food. We offered to help in the butcher, but that was men's work. We tried dressmaking, laundry, all manner of female things. But no one wanted the help of girls. We realised that being boys was more advantageous. We could only afford a single boy's outfit. Our arrangement was simple. We took turns. Few people noticed the eyes. Only one or two felt that something wasn't quite right, but could never figure out what. When we grew, we secured more women's work, but men's work paid better and was a deeper well for stories. By the time the siege started, we'd been a butcher's assistant, a courier, a baker's apprentice, and a zookeeper who fed the more vicious animals at the Jardin des Plantes.

On the night before Chloe's first day at the balloon factory at

Gare d'Orléans, we debated who'd take the first shift.

'You're a better seamstress than me,' she said.

'But you wanted the job.'

'I know, but could you go for the first few days? We must establish ourselves as reliable.'

'We'd make more money catching rats.'

'Yes, and I'm a better rat catcher than you.'

She was. The week before, we'd made five francs over the four days she spent chasing them. Rat pâté was in vogue with the wealthier Parisians. Some butchers paid half a franc for three. We were able to save our books and keep hunger away.

So I relented. I took our warmest dress and the pair of stockings with the fewest holes, and she took the trousers and the big cap that hid her hair. She disappeared into the alleyways, and I into the train station full of balloons.

Gare d'Orléans was a grand building, with the high ceilings you'd expect of a train station. Countless panels of glass directed sunbeams down like spotlights, and a giant ornate clock, framed with golden spears, kept the time with hands that were longer than a man's body. Trains were replaced by two balloons, one almost fully inflated, the other on its way. They were far larger than the first balloon we'd seen, taking up two platforms and almost touching the roof, bloated like a beached whale. They were pretty though, made with striped candy-coloured fabric.

There were at least fifty women working on reams of calico. We were to sew and varnish the fabric in a particular way – it was easy enough – and then a group of men hung the fabric up to dry from the iron beams in the roof. Three layers of varnish were needed, and had to dry for twelve hours between coats. There were three limp balloons drying above the tracks while we worked on sewing three more. Sailors worked beside us, braiding the ropes and halliards needed to attach the balloons to the baskets. There was an urgency to our work, but the atmosphere was jovial. Brave sailors flirted with us before Madame Beaufort, dubbed 'the Balloon Matriarch', smacked them with a ruler and shooed them like pesky birds. She made me and the other new seamstress sit with her.

'You're very good, dear', she told me, as kindly as a grandmother. She gave me a ruler too, and instructed me to hit any boy or man who came near me. The woman was an infinite source of pragmatism, caution and, indeed, rulers.

When I arrived home, I found Chloe curled up in bed, bloodied and beaten. I ran to her side.

'Oh, Lou', she sobbed. As she stretched out an arm to embrace me, I noticed the other was bent at an unnatural angle. Her nose was blocked with clotted blood.

'What happened?'

'A gang of boys attacked me when they saw how many rats I had', she said. 'I'm so sorry, I'd caught at least eleven!'

'I don't care how many you caught. All I care about is you.'

Chloe, her face etched more in guilt than pain, still gestured to the floor, where a single rat lay dead. 'I kept one at least.'

'Oh shush', I said, and started cleaning her wounds. I glanced at the twisted arm. 'It's alright. We'll get it fixed.'

Chloe nodded, but we both knew finding a doctor was impossible. In her eyes, I saw all her fear, of the money we couldn't earn now, of the break that would stay twisted.

'Trust me', I said.

That night, she shivered as the cold seeped into her wounds. I burned two books and a handful of newspapers. It's quite a thing, a burning book. The best thing to do is open it up and sit it in the fire, letting the flames climb the paper. The fire eats away at it, red ripples shrivelling the pages. They curl before crumbling to ash. When the flames consume it, they dance out violently above it. Ashy white fragments spiral off, like the stories are trying to escape. A burning book emits pure yellow-white flames, but its heart is black.

Next morning, I made my way to Gare d'Orléans, ruler in hand and thoughts consumed with the problem of how to get a doctor.

'What's wrong, dear?' Madame Beaufort asked as I sat silently sewing beside her. 'Those ruffians not giving you any trouble, I hope.'

Her eyes followed some of the men, including one with hair as black as mine, who winked at me as he walked by.

'No, madame,' I said. 'My sister's broken her arm. I don't have money for a doctor.'

'A doctor?' the winking sailor said. 'My pa's a doctor.'

'No he's not, you common ship rat, move along!' Madame Beaufort snapped.

'Honestly, he is! I fell out of favour with him when I … well, medicine's not me, but he's a good man. I'm his only son, so Mother –'

'Be gone, you monstrous liar!' Madame Beaufort shouted, smacking his legs with her ruler.

He moved along, but kept his eyes on me. There I saw a promise.

'Men will tell you anything, dear,' Madame Beaufort said.

I nodded, but when the time came for an inflated balloon to be prepared for launch, I left my sewing sisters for the spectacle outside. The winking sailor was holding one of the many ropes that worked as a tether. I slipped in beside him.

'Hello, monsieur.'

He nearly let go of his rope. 'Mademoiselle!'

'My name's Chloe,' I said.

'Alexandre Prince,' he offered. He bowed, inadvertently tugging on the rope and jerking the balloon so violently that the aeronaut who supervised our work, the famous Monsieur Godard, had another sailor retrieve the rope. Together we watched as the balloon was tied down and mail loaded into it. Monsieur Prince was only a decade older than me, I guessed. I noted he didn't have a ring on his finger.

'Monsieur Prince, what a regal name,' I said. 'Sir, I hope you don't mind me asking about your father's services. I'm just a poor orphan and we barely have enough for bread. I wouldn't normally ask but I'm desperate.'

I started to cry then, soft little gasps, a tactic I found worked on most men.

'Oh, don't cry!' he said. 'I promise, I'll speak to him tonight.'

I took the handkerchief he offered and gently touched his arm. 'God bless you, monsieur!'

The next day, Monsieur Prince approached the sewing brood and Madame Beaufort chased him away. I found him later, helping Monsieur Godard hoist a basket, sans balloon, onto the iron girders above. I watched on admiringly, trying to show how very impressed I was with their heaving and harring.

'Can I help you, mademoiselle?' Monsieur Godard asked.

'I wish to speak to Monsieur Prince, sir, but it's a pleasure to admire your fine basket up on the beams. Is it easier to tie it to the balloon this way?'

Monsieur Godard laughed. 'Not quite! This basket shan't see flight. Our facility here is becoming a training college for fledgling balloonists. I'm sorry to say that all our professionals have already gone. Now we need good men, like these lads here.'

Once the men finished, I pulled Monsieur Prince aside. He couldn't meet my eyes.

'My father will offer his services but they've inflated in price. I convinced him to halve his fee, but he still asks one hundred francs to treat your sister.'

I was paid half a franc a day. We had nothing saved. I shed true tears, the hopelessness of my situation overwhelming me. Dear Prince, he was one of those men, like Bernard, who found female tears torturous.

'I can give you ten, and you can pay the rest off slowly. I'll vouch for you.'

'Truly, sir?' I asked.

'I give you my word.'

The word of a sailor was as good as nothing, Madame Beaufort told us. But Alexandre Prince kept his word. His father came two days later, took his son's ten francs and my paltry two (with the promise of more) and set Chloe's arm. From that point on, Alexandre and I were friends. Every day at the balloon factory, he found a way to slip me a coin and a wink, even if it meant getting smacked by Madame Beaufort's formidable ruler.

Weeks stretched into months. The siege held. During the day, I worked on the balloons. At night I huddled with Chloe, who was healing well but slowly. If I found some wood or paper, we slept by the fire. I wanted to hunt for rats at night, but the street lamps were extinguished early and the whole city was dark.

Hunger seeped into Paris. The butchers descended into the zoos where only the lions, tigers, and hippopotamuses escaped our dinner plates. Monsieur Martin sold elephant for forty francs a pound. Too many cows were killed for meat, and milk became so scarce that many babies died. I saw the little coffins most days, women's cries the only sound coming from funeral processions that swayed down boulevards that'd lost all their trees to our fires. It was November by then. Almost all our money went to paying off our debt to the doctor. As I hugged myself on the cold walk to the station, I could feel my ribs.

That day, Alexandre was in such a joyous mood, he skipped over to us despite Madame Beaufort's threats.

'Chloe, your debt is paid!'

'Have you completely lost your manners, boy? Calling a young woman by her first name, you improper beast!' Madame Beaufort objected.

I pushed my way between her and Alexandre. 'What?'

'I'm a balloonist now! I fly out on the twenty-eighth. Just a sliver of my wage covers your entire debt. When I get back, when our Republic is freed, I'll spend the rest on the biggest diamond in all of Paris and fashion it on your finger there!'

Madame Beaufort smacked him with her ruler. As she beat him back, he retreated to his comrades by the ropes.

'Say yes?' he called to me.

I liked Alexandre enough. For an orphaned girl, enough was the best I could hope for. I shouted back, 'Yes!'

The sailors let out a great 'hooray!' making enough noise to bring down Monsieur Godard. Madame Beaufort called our behaviour 'most improper', but the master aeronaut didn't agree, saying Alexandre was a fine catch, a hero of Paris in the making. That day, he trained Alexandre in how to use the balloon's valves and guiding ropes.

Later, I chose food over warmth. I used the few francs I'd saved on bread. Chloe asked how my day had been, and I told her about our debt being wiped clean. She didn't need to know about the marriage proposal. Not yet. We ate our bread and two slices of nondescript cured meat Chloe had begged from Monsieur Martin. There was gunfire going off somewhere. A few explosive booms in the north.

'It's so cold,' Chloe said, coughing.

'It's not so bad,' I said, putting an arm around her as we

huddled under all the coats and blankets we owned.

'My bones ache,' she said.

Our little fire, burning from newspapers and a few sticks I'd foraged, was dwindling. It was only seven or so, at a guess. Yet, it was already so cold.

Under the bed, our books. I went for Mother's volume of Shakespeare. Chloe objected. I came across a stack of magazines, all about balloons.

'Something else, please,' she begged.

Finally, the last one: the book with blank pages I'd found in the ballast. Another mystery from this strange book: it'd survived months without going to the fire. How had I burned my copy of *Arabian Nights* before this?

I opened the book and set it in the fireplace. A few embers sparked up and bit my hand. I gasped. Then I heard something. Whispers. They were hushed, joined together. The wind, perhaps?

I settled back down with Chloe as the flames caught on the book … only … they didn't catch. The flames jumped on the book, but the pages didn't curl and blacken.

'Lou,' Chloe said. 'That book …'

The voices … they were louder now. Whispers in languages I didn't know.

'Can you hear that?'

'Hear what?' Chloe said absently, not moving her eyes from the book.

The flames grew, enveloping the book, but the pages didn't burn. The black heart of burning books was absent, no red ripples, no pages shrivelled into ash. Just pure yellow-white flames.

'The book doesn't burn.'

Chloe's voice was tiny in the cacophony of whispers that filled my head. They seemed to be vying for attention, all

speaking at once. I caught something in French. *Espièglerie.*
Then the same word in English. *Mischief.*

The flames leapt from the book. With a great whooshing
sound, they disappeared as if sucked up the chimney. The
voices fled. The red embers from the remaining newspapers lit
enough of the fireplace for us to see: the book was untouched.
Unburnt.

The embers went out, one by one. We shivered in the dark
until our eyes adjusted to the paltry sliver of light the moon
offered. It was enough for us to see the whiteness of those
blank pages in the black ashy fireplace, those pages that had
whispered instead of burned.

The next day, I took the book out of the fireplace. Ash from the
newspapers didn't even stick to it. I tried to light it on fire again,
using one of our precious matches and holding the tiny flame
directly to its pages. The match burned down to my fingers.
A few whispers came and went. Sounds beautiful and soft,
abrasive and violent. I flipped through it to check if it was really
blank. I dropped water on the pages, and it rolled right off. It
felt like paper. It didn't seem to be made of anything special. I
tried to tear out a page. It wouldn't rip.

I left our room with it before Chloe woke up. I was worried
it might be dangerous. Alexandre was already up in his training
basket when I arrived at Gare d'Orléans. He waved and then
blew me a kiss. I waved back and got to work, the book resting
beside me as I sewed a sturdy strip of red calico to one of blue.

No one seemed to notice it. Twice, the ladies beside me
knocked it off the table, but never offered any apology or
acknowledged what they'd done. When Monsieur Godard
inspected our work, he rested one hand on it. He didn't register
when the book moved and his hand slipped. By home time, I
was convinced the book didn't want to be seen. Not by them,

and not by me. So often it was knocked to the ground. I swear, it wished to escape.

'Lou,' Chloe said that night, as we cuddled in lieu of fire. 'You said you heard voices.'

'Yes,' I said. 'From the book.'

'What did they say?'

'I don't know. There were too many.'

I couldn't confide in her that the single word I could discern was *mischief*.

That night, I dreamed I was in a round room with a magnificent dome. Bookshelves climbed towards the sky. I sat on a desk in the middle, surveying it all. Everything was on fire, yet nothing burned. A young man sat next to me, only a few years older than me.

'I don't know yet,' he said to me in English.

'What don't you know, sir?'

'This,' he said. He touched the book, which rested between us. 'I'm not the next one. Neither are you. But I'm the one you'll find.'

I didn't understand. He smiled at my confusion.

'We're thieves, dear. Always hiding in plain sight, disguised as something else. Just like the book.'

I shivered in the room on fire. Not even in our dreams were we safe from the cold of a besieged Paris in late November. All I said to him then was, 'Isn't it cold?'

Alexandre was being interviewed by three journalists when I arrived at the station the next day. He stood tall, chest puffed out, wearing a colourful waistcoat that rivalled our balloons for its gaudiness.

Later, when Madame Beaufort excused herself for the ladies' room, Alexandre found the courage to approach the sewing station.

'Chloe, will you come to the launch?'

'Of course,' I said.

'It'll be 11:30 this evening. Best to travel at night, they tell me. I'll escort you from your home, of course, and have Papa walk you back. It'll be perfectly safe.'

'No need, I'll make my own way there.'

Yet, at 10:30, he came to our room. He gave Chloe (who we called Louise) a loaf of bread and promised I'd return home safely. I couldn't find where I'd put the book. I didn't want to leave it with Chloe, frightened that it might whisper its wicked words to her. But there was an urgency in the air and my search was cut short. An escort of soldiers hurried Alexandre and I out into the night. We saw the balloon from a mile away, even in the dark, it's colourful bulk already fully inflated. This balloon they called *Le Jacquard*.

Alexandre was a gentleman, and only went so far as to kiss my hand and blush. He was helped into the balloon and mailbags were piled at his feet. He took a cage of pigeons and shouted his promise to send word back when he'd completed his mission. Carefully, they cut the ballast. Slowly, Alexandre and *Le Jacquard* rose.

'Oh, Chloe! I hope you don't mind, I took your book,' Alexandre suddenly shouted down to me. 'Sometimes the journey can be short, sometimes long. Best to take something to read, just in case.'

From the basket, he waved my book, the wicked, whispering, unburnt book. I mouthed *no*, but he'd already cut more ballast. The sandbags dropped around us, as the balloon and my fiancé stole away my book. Somehow, I knew this was what the book wanted. *Disguised*. That's what the Englishman said in my dreams.

I promised the book, whatever it was, *I'll hunt you down*.

# Jessie

The history ends. It just … ends. No big act of mischief. Nothing.

'Oh, cliffhanger!' Kay says, trying to make it sound exciting.

'No, that's not how it works,' I say. 'It can't end like that.'

'Well, there it is,' Kay says, showing me the first page of the next history. It's in Ethiopia, nine years later.

I don't understand. Was Lou even a mischief? Why did she hear the book talk but didn't get its memories? I have so many questions but I don't ask them. I sit for a moment.

Annoyed. I feel annoyed.

It's late but Kay makes dinner. We have microwave pasta that takes six minutes and thirty seconds (stirring halfway through) to cook. I poke at my pasta, still grumpy. It tastes like butter and fake cheese.

'Hey,' Kay says. She nudges me.

I ignore her.

'I liked this history, didn't you?'

'It's not a real history,' I say.

'Well, it's in the book. Maybe Lou and Chloe will be in the next history. Maybe they're in Ethiopia.'

*Chloe.*

Wait.

'Give me the *History*!'

Kay shakes her head. 'Not till you do your mischief report.'

'I just want to see the Transcription Note. It mentioned a Chloe, remember?'

'Did it?' Kay asks. She gets the *History* and flips to the note at the beginning. 'Oh, so it did. Here: "Those that survived were recorded by myself and Chloe McKenna." Hmmm ... McKenna's not a very French name. Maybe it's a different Chloe.'

'Maybe it's not!'

Kay smiles, all mischievous-like. 'Guess you're going to have to wait to find out.'

She closes the *History*. I don't need to ask to know *that's that*.

I think about the *History* until it's time for bed and the lights are out. It's school tomorrow. Theodore will be there. I remember what he said. I miss Mum and Dad so much. I imagine I'm in a train station full of balloons. I climb aboard one of them, cut the ropes, and fly away. I hover over Paris, gaze down at the buildings and the river, until I fall asleep.

Over the next few days, I research and make cranes with Theodore (but we don't talk about things). I've decided to just pretend he never said anything. I have more important things to figure out. There's something about Lou's history, something bad. It breaks the rules. So I'm going to figure out what went wrong.

I request books about the Paris siege and find a book at Guildford that's about the history of ballooning. It's got a pretty cover, with many colourful balloons, but inside there's lots of tiny words. I hate when the words are so small. It takes forever to read just one page.

'Oh, a nice big hardcover!' the librarian says as I go to borrow the book.

I nod.

'You always borrow the most interesting things,' she says,

handing it to me. 'You must be learning so much.'

I nod again. That night, I try my best to read it properly and not just look at the pictures. I read a chapter about the balloonists in France and find a menu from the Paris siege. They ate anything they could find, just like the *History* said. Goldfish, elephant soup, roast camel, baked cat!

'Can we have baked cat for dinner?' I ask Kay cheekily.

'Sure,' she says. 'Go and ask Mrs Moran if we can have Cornelius. I'll turn the oven on.'

I scowl at her. 'Cornelius is too clever to bake.'

'Then fish fingers it is.'

Cornelius is at school the next day. When the bell goes, I come out to find him waiting in the school courtyard with Mrs Moran. Lots of kids rush at him, saying how cute he is in his pink harness. But when they try to pat him, he bats their hand with his paw, just once, like he's warning them to back off.

'Better not, kiddly-winks,' Mrs Moran says. 'Cornelius is a gentleman but the next bop might be with claws.'

Mrs Moran spots me. She waves me over.

Suddenly, something grips my heart.

Where's Kay?

Why isn't Kay here?

My eyes burn instantly with tears.

'Come here, dear.'

I don't move.

'Your sister's car just broke down,' Mrs Moran says gently. She smiles, walks over and puts her arm around me. 'Everything's alright.'

*Broke down.* 'What happened?'

'Thing's just old, isn't it? Not sure if she's getting it towed or if she can get someone to fix it on the spot. But she might be a while.'

I feel happy then. Good. Her car is stupid. I hope it can never be repaired.

'Come now, we'll have fun,' she says.

Cornelius bumps my leg.

'Say hello, dear,' Mrs Moran says.

'Hello Cornelius,' I say.

He looks away, like he knows what I said yesterday.

'I'm sorry, Cornelius. I would never let the Parisians bake you.'

'What a moving sentiment,' Mrs Moran says, and we start to walk home.

When we get to Mrs Moran's house, her daughter Helen is there. She's dressed smart in a suit but she looks a bit crazy, with messy hair and smudged mascara. She looks like maybe she was crying.

'Where have you been, Mother?' she demands. Then she spots me. 'What is this?'

'Bessie here is just staying with us for a bit. Sister got waylaid,' Mrs Moran replies.

'Jessie, Mrs Moran,' I say.

'Oh yes, of course. Jessie. Silly me.'

Helen glares at Mrs Moran. 'I need to go, Mother. I'm meeting Paul in an hour.'

'Off you pop then!'

Helen glances at me. 'This isn't a good idea, Mother.'

'It's a brilliant idea. Let's have breakfast, Jessie! When unexpected friends visit we have unexpected food, isn't that right, Cornelius?'

Cornelius meows. Mrs Moran takes my backpack and puts it down by a table with a bowl of keys. Then she takes my hand.

Helen lets out an angry sigh. Mrs Moran takes me to the kitchen.

'Do you like scrambled eggs, dear? I make wonderful

scrambled eggs, don't I, Cornelius?'

Helen follows us. 'No, Mother. No stove.'

Mrs Moran rolls her eyes like a teenager.

'If you insist on this breakfast nonsense, just have some cereal!'

Helen gets Weet-Bix, but Mrs Moran goes into the cupboard and brings out Coco Pops. She shakes the box at me and grins.

'Coco Pops and eggs?'

Helen sighs and speeds away, shouting, '*No stove!*' When she comes back again she's got her keys and a bag full of files. She tells Mrs Moran off like she's a child. She then hands me a card.

'My number, just in case. Please don't let my mother use the stove or oven,' she says, right in front of Mrs Moran. I just nod. She leaves in a rush, slamming the front door.

Mrs Moran turns the stove on as soon as Helen's car is gone.

I like Mrs Moran.

'You can still have Coco Pops if you want, dear, but I'm having eggs.'

'Can I have both like you said before?' I ask.

'Together or separately?'

'Separately, please.'

Mrs Moran nods. 'Unoriginal, perhaps, but sensible.'

We sit at a table made from shiny wood and eat our Coco Pops and scrambled eggs. Cornelius sits on a chair at the head of the table with his own plate of eggs and tuna. His head just pokes up above the table. Mrs Moran pushes the plate close so he can still eat. He turns to look at us whenever we speak.

'Just keeping it warm,' Mrs Moran says.

I don't understand.

'Cornelius. He's keeping my husband's chair warm for him,' Mrs Moran explains.

'Oh,' I say. I've never seen an old man at Number 61 before. 'Where is he?'

'Away, dear. You know men, away for work. Taking care of his family, my George. He'll be back soon. You'll love him, he's a character, isn't he, Cornelius?'

Cornelius meows his agreement.

After our afternoon-breakfast, Mrs Moran says, 'Just need to do a spot of cleaning. Then we can have fun.'

She puts on an old movie, then cleans the house around me, getting out her vacuum cleaner again. I don't know why. Everything's perfect. She dusts and mops and polishes things until they squeak.

'Mrs Moran, I think you polished that already,' I say when I see her polishing a table for the third time.

'Best to make sure, dear,' she says. 'That's what Aunty June always said. Men don't like to come home to a dirty house.'

'Your house is super clean,' I say. 'I bet Mr Moran would love it.'

'Oh, George doesn't mind a messy house. It's just … best to clean up. Aunty June always said.'

I wonder how old Mrs Moran is and if her aunty is still alive.

'Can we go to the park?' I ask.

'Oh, yes, good idea! Let me finish up. Are you bored, dear? Just give me a few minutes. I don't have any good movies, I know. I prefer to read.'

'Me too.'

'Oh, how marvellous! I thought kids only watched TV these days. There's a study down the hall, next to the toilet. Lots of books in there. George bought me Sherlock Holmes for my birthday last month. Maybe you can read that.'

I don't know who Sherlock Holmes is, or what kinds of books he writes, but I nod and go down the hall. To my surprise, the study is FULL of the origami I left on her veranda. Paper cranes and flowers lie on top of bookshelves, books, and a little desk. She's even blu-tacked cranes to the wooden desk chair, with their wings poking up so you can see the 'From A. Mischief' on them. I wonder if she kept them all. I count them to check.

Three hundred and sixty three.

She still has every one.

I look through the shelves, trying to find books on people in the *History*. Then I spot a book with a green spine and gold letters that reads, ARTHUR CONAN DOYLE: COMPLETE ILLUSTRATED SHERLOCK HOLMES. It even has gold edges. I sit at the desk and flick through it. There are pictures of men with moustaches, pipes and top hats.

A card falls out of the book. It must have been Mrs Moran's bookmark. I try to keep her place while picking up the card. It has writing on it.

*Page 774. He says life is full of whimsical happenings. My sweet lady is surely one of them, though perhaps he doesn't mean it as fondly as I.*

*Yours whimsically,*

*A. Mischief*

*2009*

A. Mischief.

2009.

I read it over and over again. I can't believe it. The Transcription Note in the *History* was from 1966. That's forty-three years *before* this note. What does it mean? What are whimsical happenings? Is the sweet lady Mrs Moran? Is Mr Moran A. Mischief?

I turn to page 774 in the Sherlock Holmes book. It has really small words in two columns. It's difficult to read but I find the spot where he talks about whimsical happenings. I still don't understand.

Didn't Mrs Moran say that her husband gave this to her for her birthday *last month*?

Wait.

Maybe the real *History* is here. The one that makes you A. Mischief. The one Lou was hunting.

I flip through the book again to see if there are any other notes.

Nothing.

Mrs Moran's vacuum cleaner is going again. Maybe she'll be a while.

I search the bookshelf, looking for anything that might be the *History*. I pull out fat leather books that smell like the State Library. They all have words; no signatures or magic or anything interesting. If I find a book with blank pages, it might be the *History* hiding its magic.

I search the desk next. I open the drawers and find a notebook full of scribbles. I spot A. Mischief again! I flip back and try to find it. I don't know what this notebook is. There are people's names with entries.

*Helen Louise Moran. Born 21 July 1978. Only living child. She was a bossy thing. Loved Enid Blyton, especially* The Wishing Chair.

It goes on. Towards the end of the page, it says: *She used to love mischief. She's angry and tired of us now. Her divorce hurt her deeply. Don't perform mischief on her. Don't tease her. Be kind. When you're kind, she becomes soft. She needs love. Remember that.*

Mischief again. I wonder if there's something about Mr Moran here. I find an entry towards the start.

*George Frank Moran. Born 2 February 1949. Husband. Married 4 March 1972. Father to daughter Helen and son Anthony (stillborn). Softness and light, kindness and patience. Make him smile and you'll remember everything.*

The vacuum goes off in the other room.

'Finished, dear! You ready?'

I need to read more. Maybe I can take it. I look around for my bag. Maybe she won't know. But I don't have my bag.

Footsteps down the hall. I shove the notebook back in the desk.

Mrs Moran comes into the study. 'Sorry for the wait. Did you find Sherlock Holmes?'

I try not to look guilty. 'Yes, Mrs Moran. It's very good.'

'Isn't it?' she says. 'Come, dear. Let's go for a walk.'

Mrs Moran puts Cornelius back in his pink harness. She gives me the lead but Cornelius flops on the ground and won't move. I drag him through the dirt and he still won't get up. Mrs Moran takes over and he springs up. He walks proudly like he beat me.

We go to the park and I count out the graves. I try to count properly and say I'm sorry, but I can't stop thinking about the card and the notebook, and that maybe the real *History* is somewhere in Mrs Moran's house. I wonder if Mr Moran was confused when he saw A. Mischief on the origami I left on the veranda. Maybe he thinks there's another mischief out there.

I really hope he comes home soon.

When we finish our walk, Mrs Moran makes me play Scrabble. I don't want to play. I want to read the notebook and hunt the *History*.

'I'm bored, Mrs Moran. Can I read?'

'You are reading, dear, look!'

She lays out the word NOTORIOUS with all her Scrabble tiles and some of mine.

'I want to read a book, Mrs Moran. Can I read Sherlock Holmes again?'

The doorbell rings.

Kay.

Not yet!

'Sorry, I had a flat battery. It took the RAC a while to come out,' Kay says as she comes in the door.

I want to scream. I try to think of a way to get back to the study and take the notebook. I ask Mrs Moran if I can borrow Sherlock Holmes, but when I try to go to the study with my bag, she insists on getting it herself. She takes out the card from A. Mischief and hands the book to me. She smiles.

I've been tricked, I'm sure of it. Mrs Moran knows I'm looking for the *History*.

## Jessie

Mrs Moran is onto me. I watch her as she vacuums her driveway at night. Sometimes she glances back. Sometimes she sits in her chair with Cornelius like she's guarding her house. I try to think of a way to get back in and look for the *History*, but I can't think of anything clever.

'How would you break into a house?' I ask Theodore as we make paper cranes at lunch.

He *hmmms*, really thinking about it.

'I would make friends with a thief,' he says.

'I don't know any thieves.'

*Hmmm* again.

'Then I'd try to trick my way in. Maybe take the person some treats and then get their keys!'

The next day, I return Sherlock Holmes and give Mrs Moran a jam donut from the bakery as a 'thank you'. She just takes it and asks if I want to have a tea on the veranda, not inviting me inside. I glance at the table near the door with its bowl of keys.

She beat me again.

I ask Kay if we can keep visiting, but Kay tells me to stop bothering her.

'Why do you keep asking about Mrs Moran?'

'I want to play with Cornelius,' I lie.

Should I tell Kay what I found? Maybe then she'd believe the *History* is real.

In the meantime, I keep doing my research. The books on the Paris siege arrive and I find all the balloonists from the *History*, including Lou's fiancé Alexandre Prince. Turns out, he was the first balloonist to disappear during the siege. They think he travelled too far in the wrong direction. His mailbags were found out near a lighthouse at Lizard Point, which is at the very bottom of England. He must have thrown out the bags when he realised how far away he was, and then shot up into the clouds over the ocean.

I bet it was the *History*. It didn't want to be found, so it somehow got on the balloon and escaped. Then the balloon vanished. I imagine the *History* flying up in the clouds and then falling into the ocean. Maybe a fisherman will be the next mischief.

I have to finish quickly so I can give Kay my mischief report and we can find out.

We've been lazy with visiting Grandma so Kay decides we should go on Saturday.

'Are you sure we can't take the car?' Kay tries again.

'Are you sure we can't put iron bars over the car like we did on the windows?' I reply.

So we take the two trains, the bus and the seventeen-minute walk, and then we're there. It took one hour and twenty-eight minutes in total, which is twenty-six minutes longer than last time (we missed the train and the bus). Lulu isn't there so another lady signs us in. I see that weird guy David come out of a room and then run back in when he spots us. Kay doesn't notice.

We arrive at lunchtime and sit with the old people and their families. I didn't realise the nurses would feed us too. We have roast lamb, potatoes and gravy. Then we sing happy birthday to a lady in a wheelchair and she blows out a nine and a two candle on a slab of cake. Grandma makes sure I get a big piece before we go back to her room. It's vanilla sponge with custard inside and cream on top, which Grandma knows is my favourite.

Grandma and Kay talk while I eat cake. Kay says something about me becoming a 'library goer'.

'Oh, how wonderful,' Grandma says. 'When I was your age, I'd do anything for a good book. What are you reading?'

'I'm researching *The History of Mischief*,' I say. 'I've read books about Alexander the Great and Diogenes, and the Alexandrian Library, which was in Egypt. I've read about Mulan, the real one, and the Polish dragon and salt mines. Kay even bought me a special book and a DVD. I've just been researching the Paris siege and the balloons. Did you know they ate animals from the zoo because they were so hungry? They ate elephant and antelope and …'

I stop because Grandma isn't smiling. I think I was rambling.

'I'm happy you're reading,' she says. But she doesn't sound happy.

'Darling girl, could you refill my water jug please?' she then says, pointing to the jug on her table. 'It has dust in it. And maybe some clean cups? Thank you.'

The jug doesn't look like it has dust in it, but I take it anyway. Adults do this all the time. They give you a chore to make you go away so they can talk about you. I wait by the door and listen.

'These stories don't sound appropriate for a nine-year-old,' Grandma says.

'They've been sad but they're fun too. Jessie loves the magic in them,' Kay says.

'Why is she doing "research"?'

Kay chuckles. 'She thinks it's real. Whenever she finds something that doesn't match up, like a date or something, she's convinced the *History* is true and all the other books are wrong.'

'Why is this funny to you?' Grandma sounds angry.

Kay's voice softens. 'I don't mean – it's not funny, but it's sweet. And, I think she needs this.' Kay then says really quietly, '*I* need this. It's the only thing that makes her behave.'

'Bribery isn't a good parenting strategy.'

'I'm not a parent, Grandma. I'm doing my best.'

Grandma sighs. 'I know,' she says, her voice all soft again.

'It's the only thing she'll talk to me about. It can't hurt, can it? It's like Santa or fairies. She'll figure it out one day. I want her to keep talking to me. I want her to be happy about something.'

'I understand,' Grandma says. 'You're doing such a good job. I know it's been the hardest on you.'

'It's been hard on everyone.'

'Maybe, just read the stories before you read them with her. To check. They sound violent.'

'Okay, Grandma.'

'Just a thought.'

'Yep, no, it's a good idea.'

They start talking about something boring like the nursing staff, so I go and fill the water jug up in the kitchen.

I feel angry. I know Santa and fairies aren't real, but this is different. The *History* is real, I just know. And why don't they want me to read things that are sad or violent anyway? Nothing is more sad or violent than what happened to Mum and Dad. And me. And no one could protect me from that.


I've got to meet Mr Moran. If I can't find the real *History*, I've got to meet a real mischief. I get my chance when we arrive home from visiting Grandma. Mrs Moran's daughter Helen is out the front, going to her car. I rush over and say hello.

'Yes?' she snaps at me.

I decide to ask, even if she's grumpy. 'Is Mr Moran home yet?'

'What?'

'Mr Moran, is he home yet?'

'My father's dead. He died seven years ago.'

'Oh … but Mrs Moran said –'

'Mother forgets. She's not well.'

I don't know what to say. I just go home. I wonder if I should've said sorry. More than anything though, I wonder where the real *History*'s gone now. Maybe Mrs Moran is a mischief but she doesn't remember.

I flip through my notes and books for the rest of the afternoon. I feel sad. Everyone's dead. Mum. Dad. Mr Moran. Alexandre Prince.

I find Kay in her room. She's already in bed, watching TV on her laptop. I cry a little.

'Come here,' she says. I bundle in beside her.

She hugs me. She kisses me on the top of my head, where there's enough hair now that it almost hides the scar. Then we watch a show from Britain where people bake cakes in a big tent. I fall asleep.

The next day, I give Kay my mischief report. I don't tell her about Mr Moran and the A. Mischief note from 2009.

She asks if I want to read the next history. 'We can stay in bed all day and read, if you want.'

I say, 'yes', of course.

# A. Mischief the One-Hundred and Ninety-Eighth

*Addis Ababa, Ethiopia 1879–1890*

*Alemayehu is dead.*

I woke to this, the wordless words of God, a voice so all-encompassing and other-worldly that it was felt more than heard. I listened for Him, waiting for more. Then some sinister realisation sank in, that Alemayehu truly was dead, that I lay there moments after he'd slipped from the world. I wondered if anyone had been with him. A priest. A friend. Anyone.

*Alemayehu is dead.*

The only person I told was Taytu. She didn't flinch, didn't blink. She didn't question how I knew that our prince, taken to London over a decade ago, had passed away. But behind those intelligent eyes, I saw her mind working.

'Thank you, Bezawit.'

That was all she said.

That day, I found *The History of Mischief* on the end of my bed.

God never spoke to me again.

I came to Taytu when I was around four or five. God spoke to me often even then. I gained a reputation for predicting the future, dispensing little sermons and tugging on the priests' robes to tell them what I'd heard. My father, a soldier who fought at the Battle of Maqdala, laughed at this, enchanted.

But his friends watched me with narrowed eyes. Rumours, suspicion and fear followed me.

Somehow, those whispers reached Taytu and she sent for me.

Even then I could tell she was a leader. Her eyes watched carefully, studying every detail. She was beautiful and plump, her skin shone, her braids were tight, and her white dress was embroidered with elaborate red crosses. But those eyes. I couldn't look away.

She gestured for me to come to her. I did so without fear. She took my hands in her long, gentle fingers.

'My child,' she said. 'I hear you speak to our Lord.'

'No,' I said, very sure of myself. 'He speaks to me.'

She smiled. 'And what does He tell you?'

I answered simply. 'Everything.'

Taytu considered me, as if she was searching for something. 'Do you know what I've heard about you?'

'Father says I'm a gift of God.'

'Yes, but some men think otherwise.'

I felt suddenly embarrassed. If this magnificent woman believed what those men were saying, perhaps it was true. 'I'm sorry,' I said.

She smiled and sat back, as if her assessment was over. Then she leaned forward and tapped me playfully on the nose.

'But what do men know?'

I moved into her palace at Entoto, which would soon become the city she named Addis Ababa, New Flower. My father was given a position in her army. She referred to me as her niece and sent away anyone who spoke against me. She told me to be still and listen to God, and that whenever He told me something, if He allowed it, I could tell her.

In her palace, the voice became clearer. Once, she asked what God sounded like. I couldn't tell her, for it wasn't a sound as we know it. The words came to me, voiceless yet loud, neither male nor female, and equal measures strong and gentle. The voice emanated from everywhere and yet it felt as though its origin was a singular place. I had been with Taytu for four years when Alemayehu died.

It wasn't until I came to Taytu that I learnt about the Battle of Maqdala and Alemayehu's place within it. Emperor Tewodros, Alemayehu's father, united the country and started major industrial initiatives. To advance his work, he called on Britain, as a fellow Christian nation, to send him skilled men and equipment. The British ignored his letters and their missionaries were found with documents that insulted him as a barbaric black dictator. In response, Tewodros took them prisoner. The British attacked his mountain stronghold of Maqdala. Instead of surrender, Tewodros shot himself.

After Tewodros' death, the British looted Maqdala, taking so many of our treasures that fifteen elephants and two-hundred mules were needed to carry the bounty back to Britain. Alemayehu, only seven years old, was taken too. What the British couldn't take, they burned. For days, burning manuscripts fluttered down the mountain.

Maqdala seared itself into those around me. Europe was a place of danger and power. Taytu was cautious to assume benevolence on behalf of those who burned and stole our precious books and relics. When she married Menelik of Shewa, this became even more obvious. Though he was not yet Emperor of Ethiopia, many foreigners came to visit. She gazed quietly at them with those intelligent eyes. Her silence felt like a prelude to something significant. She was like a lioness, completely still save for her eyes, which followed every movement.

When God spoke to me, I spoke to her. I wanted to be worthy of her. I wanted to be worthy of God, who blessed me with every revelation. So when He stopped talking to me, I lost my worth. I stayed in my room for weeks on end, fasting, praying and begging for God to speak to me and take this wicked book away, this book that now spoke to me instead of Him.

Taytu asked me many times, 'Has our Lord blessed you with His word, my child?'

Ever the same answer: 'No, my lady. No.'

Then one day, as I was making my way to the dining hall, I heard the unmistakable hushed chatter of foreign visitors. They were Italian, a diplomat and his translator. I stood there transfixed, understanding every word.

Spotting me staring, they stopped. The diplomat was startled, but the translator said to him, 'Don't worry, she doesn't understand. None of them do.'

'Capisco perfettamente,' I responded. *I understand perfectly.*

If I was Taytu, I wouldn't have given myself away. I would've eavesdropped on the secrets they shared when they thought no one was listening. It just rolled out of my mouth, like an instinct.

The Italians were wary of me from that moment. Taytu noticed this and brought me to her meetings with them. I started to correct the translator's Amharic. I then translated the Amharic into Italian, much to his annoyance. I was called on when the British arrived, and then the French. Soon I was translating for the Ottomans and the Germans. I could even read their various scripts.

If it was in the *History*, I knew it. In gaining the mischiefs' memories, I gained their languages too. I spoke with the ease of a native speaker. One's own language never feels foreign. It is the language we start to speak before we form memories. It is the script we use to think, to dream, to feel. These new languages – Italian, English, French, Arabic, and endless others – felt the same. Then I realised I could speak any language, not just those hidden in the *History*. It was easy.

Taytu never questioned it. She stopped asking if God spoke to me. Sometimes she looked at me like Diogenes looked at the boy, with that knowing smile. Those looks were something I could never translate.

A decade passed like this. Despite my prominent role, I had a way of blending in, averting the gaze of others. It was I who heard that Emperor Yohannes was dead. I'm ashamed to admit it was satisfying that my words could unleash the chaos that ensued as Menelik scrambled for the throne. That mischievous feeling, that tickle in the chest that all mischiefs felt, made me praise God for His gift of the *History*. I ignored any niggling thoughts that perhaps, this was a gift from another, more sinister deity.

It happened late in 1889, a decade after Alemayehu's death. Menelik became Emperor, and Taytu our Queen. The day after her coronation, I was summoned. It was so early the birds outside were still sleeping. I was eighteen and had been with Taytu for most of my life. I wondered which guest was so important that Taytu would receive them this early.

When I arrived, there were already three men, all Ethiopian, in her chambers. There was a priest, a strange man dressed in a mix of Ethiopian and foreign garments, and Balcha Safo, a young but respected soldier I'd seen at court many times. I never liked being around him. I went straight to Taytu's side.

'Bezawit, I'm here to address you too,' Taytu said, gesturing for me to stand with this group of men. I went to the priest, kissed the cross he offered in blessing, and stood close to him.

'I've called you here for an important mission,' Taytu said. 'The sacking of Maqdala is a great stain on our glorious history. So many of our holy books live as objects to be gawked at by those who cannot read them. Most intolerable of all, our prince's bones lie in their soil. This is unacceptable.'

Balcha nodded his agreement.

'I am sending you to England to see the British Queen.
Requests for the treasures of Maqdala have so far been ignored.
Though I require you to ask the Queen to return what her
soldiers stole, I accepted long ago that the British do not let go
of their loot so easily. But we must have Alemayehu back.'

Again, Balcha nodded.

'Bezawit is our nation's greatest translator and a skilled
negotiator. If anyone can convince the British Queen to give
us Alemayehu's remains, it is her. She is to take the lead on this
mission.'

I froze. In a thousand languages, my mind screamed out:
*What?*

Taytu continued, giving each man an instruction.

'Aba Kassie, dear Father, I pray you'll go and offer spiritual
counsel to our envoy and bless Alemayehu in the proper
fashion.'

She gestured to the man in a mix of foreign and local clothes.
'Lema, you have been to London. You'll go as a guide to the
places and customs of these people.'

Finally, she turned to Balcha. 'Soldier, you must protect our
envoy.'

'It would be a great honour, my Queen,' Balcha said, bowing.

'Do not forget, gentlemen, you take your orders from Bezawit.'

I glanced at them. They glanced at me.

It was Balcha who asked what we were all thinking.

'What should we do if the British Queen won't return
Alemayehu's remains?'

Taytu didn't pause. 'Take them.'

We left to the sound of birds singing their wake-up songs.
Horses were already saddled and mules loaded. Taytu gave me a

bundle of special clothes and jewellery to wear when I met the British Queen, but I didn't have time to look at them. I was only given a few moments to gather my things. At the last second, I took the *History*.

We travelled for weeks across the mountains and plains of our country, heading for the port at Massawa. Initially, I was nervous about leaving Taytu. It was music – and language – that helped me. Aba Kassie, the priest, was a giant of a man but he was warm and full of good cheer. He wore the typical white robes and turban of a priest, and the brass cross never left his hand, even as he rode his horse. Always singing hymns, he helped me feel more comfortable. Once he realised I could speak our holy language of Ge'ez fluently, he encouraged me to sing too.

Lema, on the other hand, had none of Aba Kassie's cheerfulness. He looked at everything as a potential threat, watching Balcha in particular with his shoulders up like a frightened cat. He was an engineer who'd worked with Emperor Tewodros. He'd been sent all over Europe to learn how the foreigners made their weapons. He was forever sketching in a notebook, marvelling at many of the buildings we passed, pointing out how they stood or commenting on the use of materials. He was an odd mix of curious and nervous. I felt both fondness and pity for him.

Balcha was the hardest to warm to. He was an intensely fierce, yet oddly pretty, man. He was beautiful in a way men were not meant to be beautiful. His voice, though forceful and strong, was quite high-pitched, almost like a boy. There were rumours he'd been castrated very young at a battle in Gurageland. If it was true, it didn't make him any less formidable. His layers of leather and fur made him look bigger, more imposing, as did the muskets, swords and spears strapped to him and his horse. Strangers whispered as they passed us on the road, their eyes lingering on him.

I was frightened of him until one day, when Lema lost his patience with my clumsy cooking, Balcha defended me.

'She's an emissary of our Queen and a woman who speaks to God. You are blessed to eat the bread she burns!' he barked.

He then took a big bite of the blackened bread and, through a wince, smiled and nodded at me. Lema followed suit.

After a few weeks, I felt at home in this new family of mine. Lema's observations and Aba Kassie's songs filled my days with safe, familiar music. As we travelled further north, there seemed to be more foreigners, almost all of them Italian. Balcha rode close beside me, always probing, 'And what is that one saying? What are they whispering about? Why is that one bothering that priest?'

'He is complaining about his wife. They are talking about our food. He is trying to figure out the word for God.'

He seemed frustrated by my answers. 'What do they say when we're not listening, little sister?'

When we reached the port at Massawa, there was already a boat waiting for us. I felt a happy shiver as I stepped aboard. The ship was simple but beautiful, with large white sails. The captain promised us a new steam-powered vessel when we reached the Suez Canal in Egypt, but I was thrilled with what we had, running my hand over the polished balustrade as I strode across the deck. The memories of various mischiefs, of sailors, pirates and gondoliers, floated up to my mind. The movement of the ship, as it lolled gently up and down, was familiar. In my head, I spoke all the languages of the seafaring mischiefs.

With the anchor aweigh, the ship sailed out of the port, away from Ethiopia and onto the Red Sea. I sat at the edge of the bow, my legs dangling off the side. I leaned into the wind and shivered every time the boat dipped into the ocean and my face was sprayed with salt water.

Soon the sounds of men being sick overboard filled my ears. My dear companions all lost the contents of their stomachs to the ocean. Bless Aba Kassie. He still held his cross as he leaned over the side of the boat.

As the days went on, the men gained their sea legs a little more. Balcha was the only one who didn't improve. He descended below deck and wouldn't leave. He was given a bucket to be sick in, which I emptied overboard twice a day. After a week, it only had a pool of bile and water sloshing about in it. He hadn't eaten since we left port.

Then one day, I found him in the darkest corner of the vessel. His bucket sat faithfully by his head. He hugged his knees up into his body, and groaned sadly with every movement.

In that moment, I wondered how many men this pitiful soldier had killed.

'Do you ever think …'

He trailed off.

'What?' I asked.

'The water. Against the hull. Will it break?'

'Never.'

'It presses against us. I can feel it. I can hear the wood cracking,' he whispered, his voice shaking. 'Can't you hear it?'

'No, I hear the boat slicing through the water. The water doesn't press against us, we press against *it*. If you come up on the deck, you'll see us cutting right through it. We'll go tomorrow,' I said. 'You'll see the boat slice open the belly of the ocean. I promise.'

He groaned. Yet, the next day, he was waiting for me, his back against his corner of the ship, his eyes red and full of tears. I offered my hand. He paused before taking it.

We slowly made our way up.

Once we got to the deck, he grabbed at everything he could. He could only stay up for a moment before he was on his hands and knees.

'Shall we go back down?' I asked.

'No,' he grunted.

He battled on, crawling after me as I led him to the bow of the ship. He grasped onto the balustrade that stood between us and the ocean below. Gradually, he pulled himself up so he could see. I caught a glimpse of his fierceness in that slow but determined gesture. His back straightened as he looked out. There was land in the distance, cut in half with the tiny sparkling blue strait that was the Suez Canal.

'Slicing open the belly of the ocean,' he murmured.

'Slicing open the belly of the ocean,' I said back to him.

At Suez, we found a steamboat heading for Europe, as the captain promised. Once we cleared the canal, we were out on the Mediterranean Sea for our longest journey yet. We stopped at many ports along the way. I enjoyed every time we docked, as I got a chance to speak the many languages I knew. Finally, we docked in France, informed that it was much quicker to go over land than to venture out to the North Atlantic Ocean and snake by the coast of Spain and Portugal.

As we stepped onto European soil, it was amazing how familiar everything was to me. The memories of mischiefs past had me yearning for detours. I daydreamed of swinging from the bells of Notre Dame, where a clever hunchbacked mischief had hidden the *History*. I could almost feel the sensation of moulding molten glass with my bare hands in a Venice gripped by plague. I wanted to flee east to visit the salt mines and fly further still to the Yellow River that flowed through forests twisted into wicked faces.

There was something else too, in Paris. A feeling. It

reminded me of a page in the *History*, close to the end, with a name smudged out and no memories. Something unsettling, almost taboo, radiated from it. It was a sensation unique to that page. I always forgot it, like the *History* didn't want me to know it was there, unless something reminded me. That feeling came again as we entered a train station in Paris. I was relieved when we got on a train heading out of the city.

Eventually, having cut through France by rail, we reached the coast again. We boarded yet another ship, this time bound for Britain. I felt apprehensive leaving Europe, with Africa and Asia at my back, for so many memories lived in those lands. No mischief had ever come from or to England, though many had felt its reach. I tried to focus on the sea. It struck me how the diversities of lands and people were not echoed in the oceans. It was comforting to think that the waters around England were much like those along the coast of Ethiopia. It didn't take long for this to change. The island nation loomed ahead as we faced the mouth of the River Thames. The familiar ocean receded into a grey sludge, a colour I'd never seen in any body of water.

For the first time on the trip, I felt sick.

Now I remembered why we were here, who we were here to visit, and who we were here to take home. I vomited, throwing up into the sickly waters of Britain's famous river.

Balcha, who sat with me on the deck, handed me his flask of fresh water.

'Slice open the belly of the ocean, little sister.'

As we came closer to London, the river darkened. The smell was a veil of rot and damp that hung over everything. There were more than just boats floating beside us in the water. On land, the sides of the river swelled grotesquely with human life. I'd never seen so many buildings packed together, so much smoke hanging in the air, or so many people bustling about.

The buildings became somewhat prettier as we came into the heart of the city. The great dome of a cathedral pierced the skyline. In the distance, we saw a building shimmering with gold beside a clock tower at least four times as tall as the obelisks at Axum. We all stood on the bow of the ship, staring up at this giant thing, too in awe to be sick.

'Isn't it glorious?' Lema muttered.

'Shame the rest of the place is so filthy,' Balcha said, as an indistinguishable dead animal bumped against the side of our boat. Lema retreated to his notebook, now blackened to the margins with scribbles. There were children on the muddy riverbank, snatching at things as they went past. I stared at the clock to avoid the unpleasant sights around me. It was only 3:45 pm, yet the sun was already setting, casting its dying lights upon the golden building and the fetid water of the Thames.

Our boat veered towards a small platform beside the clock tower. There was a group of men waiting for us, dressed formally or in military garb. They were all white with one notable exception: a young man as dark as me, dressed in a suit. His eyes sparkled with recognition and fear.

Of course, they assumed Balcha was the head of our mission, and rattled off their official welcome to him. They didn't stop when he gestured at me. He turned to the dark man and spoke to him in Amharic, but the man looked away nervously and muttered some apology to his superiors that he didn't remember any of his homeland's language. Balcha knew no English, and only had a few Italian words under his belt, so he pointed at me and snapped '*Signora!*' Lema added awkwardly, 'He means you speak with the lady.' I stepped in front of them and smiled.

'Gentlemen, thank you for your welcome. My apologies for the confusion. I am Bezawit, representative of the King of Kings

Menelik II and Queen Taytu of Ethiopia. We have come to seek an audience with your most gracious Queen Victoria and pray you will receive us with the British hospitality so famed even in my country.'

An elderly gentleman, a Lord Oliver, was the only one who didn't act openly surprised by my ability to speak English. He bowed solemnly.

'My deepest apologies for the confusion, dear lady. Our Majesty has been in correspondence with Queen Taytu and is most eager to meet such esteemed representatives from the great Christian empire of Abyssinia,' he said.

Balcha bristled next to me. Abyssinia was not a name we had ever used for our country, but foreigners insisted on it. I too felt a little irritated, that he would use it when I had clearly stated our country as 'Ethiopia' just a moment ago. But Lord Oliver continued.

'Queen Victoria was tremendously fond of Prince Alemayehu and welcomes you to visit her, and the boy's resting place, at Windsor.' He then gestured for the Ethiopian man, who came forward awkwardly. 'This is Dr John Napier. He is one of your kind but has been trained here and in the colonies of India. I must apologise, I was wrongly informed that he knew your language.'

In that moment, a glance was exchanged between the two men. It was one of rebuke. The doctor dutifully lowered his eyes.

'It is most comforting to see one of my own countrymen,' I said. 'But there is no need for a translator.'

'Such an accomplished young woman,' Lord Oliver stated. 'The sun is setting and I hope you can forgive my haste. We have carriages waiting to take you to Windsor. You will receive an audience with the Queen tomorrow.'

We were bundled into a spacious carriage with this Dr

Napier. Balcha, ever suspicious, insisted on travelling up front with the driver.

As we went on our way, Dr Napier offered a few mumbled words to us. 'Hello, welcome, it's such a pleasure to meet you.'

Aba Kassie offered Napier his cross for a blessing, but he just stared and then bowed curtly to it. The priest withdrew his cross and said a prayer for him anyway.

'Where is he from?' Aba Kassie asked me.

'Dr Napier, sir, what a pleasure to see an Ethiopian in these faraway lands. Pray, where do you hail from and how did you come to live here?'

'Ah, I don't know, I left Abyssinia very young. I travelled on the same boat as Alemayehu, I've been told. I was orphaned at Maqdala and a good British family took pity on me and saw that I was educated.'

I forced a smile, trying to swallow my annoyance that this man too felt the need to give Ethiopia a foreign name. 'You're a doctor, sir?'

'Yes, it is quite fortuitous that you should come now. I finished my studies in Edinburgh recently and was visiting London to see an old university friend.'

'How fortuitous indeed,' I said. 'You know nothing of Amharic, sir?'

'No, my apologies. I don't know why Lord Oliver assumed I did. I remember nothing of Abyssinia, I'm afraid. The only evidence I was there is my skin. I hope I may still be of service.'

I went to translate but Aba Kassie was frowning, staring at Napier as if he was a long-lost acquaintance he was trying to place. He recognised the words 'Alemayehu' and 'Maqdala' and placed a hand on Napier's arm.

'I know you,' Aba Kassie muttered.

'The priest says he knows you, sir,' I explained.

'A little thing ... he wept over the Emperor's body with

Alemayehu. He had a father, a good man. He survived. Why was he not given to his father? Why is he here?'

Best, perhaps, not to translate that.

'He thinks he remembers a little boy from Maqdala just like you, but who can tell? I'm sure there were many boys at Maqdala when it was sacked. If it was indeed you he remembers, he says you were a very sweet child.'

The doctor nodded and offered a weak smile to the priest and then to me. As was the British way, I smiled meekly back.

It was dark by the time we reached Windsor. The castle at night was a monstrous shadow, its turrets and walls so high they blacked out sections of the starry sky. We could only see glimpses as our carriage approached, but the place seemed so enormous I felt we were visiting an entirely new land, a place distinct from Britain itself.

Our belongings were searched, weapons confiscated. Balcha did not resist the loss of his arms, though he glowered at the strange guards in tall hats. The English guards kept their distance. As we moved into the castle's compound, Balcha grinned at me. It was the smile of a soldier who still had at least one of his weapons.

Even as we were greeted and shown to our guest chambers, Lema spun around, face tilted upwards. He scribbled furiously without even looking at his notebook.

'Good Lord. Would you look at that? Did you see the Round Tower? I must speak to their engineers. How does it stay up? Perhaps the architects will meet with me. Did you see that ironwork? Good Lord!'

Every time he said 'good Lord' he crossed himself with his pencil.

Though none could understand him, Balcha kept asking when we would meet the Queen, thoroughly dissatisfied with my response that we would see her tomorrow. He interrogated Napier, he badgered the maids. I'm sure he asked purely to unnerve those who could only understand the harsh tone in his foreign words.

'You're frightening them,' I said.

'They're frightening me.'

At dinner, we were shown to a dining room with paintings on the ceilings and tapestries on the walls.

Balcha poked at the food in front of him.

'What are we eating?' I asked.

'Pork,' Dr Napier explained.

I pushed my plate away and quickly translated. Everyone recoiled.

'Savages,' Balcha spat. He looked at Napier as if he'd betrayed us.

There was a sudden creak, a door opening, and two men entered. One, tall with sand-coloured hair, was gloomy. He looked as though he'd once been handsome, but his beauty was marked by vicious scars and a dreary demeanour. The other, a man with messy black curls, smiled as if we were beloved relatives. He held his arms out as if he meant to embrace us. For the first time since we arrived, Dr Napier smiled.

'William!' he said. He stood and shook the man's hand.

'John!' he exclaimed. He turned Napier's handshake into an embrace. 'Good to see you, finally!'

'Sorry, let me introduce you,' Napier said. 'Friends, this is Dr William Barrie and ah, forgive me, we haven't met.'

The gloomy man made no attempt to introduce himself.

'This is my brother Archibald,' Dr Barrie said. Still, the man didn't offer any greeting. Dr Barrie continued. 'We're both so happy to meet you. John here is a dear friend, such a clever man at university. Showed everyone, didn't you, John?'

'What are you doing here?' Napier asked.

'Archie works at the British Museum. The Castle requested a Maqdala manuscript as a gift for your guests. When he told me who they were, I hoped you might be in attendance.'

'A gift?' I interjected.

'Yes,' Dr Barrie said. 'I dare not say any more, lest I ruin the Queen's surprise.'

'Won't you please join us at least,' Napier begged.

Finally, Archibald spoke. 'Oh, no, we couldn't.'

'We'd love to! Since the demands of royalty have kept you from visiting me, I must seize this opportunity. Besides, we couldn't refuse such pleasant company, could we, Archie?' Dr Barrie said, physically prodding his brother to elicit a response.

'Yes, brother,' he sighed. I was surprised to find his accent, a thoroughly English tone, didn't match his brother's Scottish one. This was explained almost as soon as the men took their seats. Dr Barrie joked that his brother had spent too much time in London and had lost his accent. Archibald dryly commented, 'Perhaps it is the other way around, brother,' and Dr Barrie laughed as if it was an old joke we all shared.

As we dined, the pork removed, Dr Barrie spoke enthusiastically to everyone, thanking me every time I translated a sentence. He apologised for Archibald, playfully saying that his brother was the 'gloomy sort'. He asked questions about Aba Kassie's cross and invited Lema to a personal tour of the dome at St Paul's Cathedral. He complimented Balcha on his furs and joked that perhaps it was a fashion Londoners could get behind with their terrible climate. At the end of the night, he handed Dr Napier a card.

'I'm living with my brother – this is the address. It's just by the museum. Small, but always open to visitors,' he said. Archibald sighed and glared at his brother, annoyed. 'Come and stay anytime you are in London.'

Napier looked at the address scrawled on the card. 'I will, thank you.'

Then, with the happy doctor and his brother gone, our bellies full, we retired to our rooms. Balcha insisted on guarding my door.

Finally, I was alone, lying on a bed lined with silk sheets, listening to the castle breathe. Though it was so still in the upper levels, I felt movement below, of servants scurrying about, cleaning, cooking, putting things in order. Men in tall furry hats and red coats stood outside doors and gates, guarding their occupants much like Balcha guarded me. From my window, I couldn't see the chapel where Alemayehu was buried, but I channelled former mischiefs who were much more attuned to the earth. I searched for him, digging in the ground with my mind.

I found his bones, remains heavy with loneliness. The feeling made me gasp. For the dead to have weight, a sorrow that lingered even after life had ended – it frightened me. I didn't know if it was real or not, but I reached out to our prince and whispered a promise.

'We are here to take you home.'

The Queen made us wait. We dressed in our finery, were brought to a sitting room and told to wait. The only one not bothered by this was Lema, who quizzed the footmen on this or that triviality to do with the castle. Before breakfast, he somehow managed to find a groundskeeper and an architect. Someone had even given him a few books on the castle's history. I think the people liked him, his friendliness and awe.

I sat at the window and, with my mischief, knocked the furry hats off the guards who stood at various posts around the castle. Most of them didn't flinch, leaving their hat on the ground. Two, clearly tortured, stood in anguish until they dared snatch them up. In both instances, the men were rebuked by their superiors. I felt a little sorry for them. Still, the mischief bubbled over in times of boredom. Perhaps if the Queen didn't make us wait, I'd leave her guards alone.

Finally, we were instructed to come, and began our journey down a long hallway. The walls were lined with paintings of monarchs long dead, their unsmiling eyes following us until we came to another sitting room. Though small, it seemed more like a piece of art than a room for living. Gold was the overwhelming feature. I tried not to follow it up the walls as we approached an unassuming woman dressed in black.

Queen Victoria stood to receive us. This old woman, this ever-mournful widow with her weary smile, was queen of the world's largest empire.

Formal welcomes were exchanged. The Queen insisted I sit with her. I waited for her to sit and chose a couch across from her. I sat alone, my men standing behind me. The Queen sat with the quiet dignity of a woman whose life had been made up of these kinds of meetings, lords and soldiers of her own country at her back. I saw in Victoria the same thing as Taytu: those eyes. Those sharp watchful eyes.

I was struck by the strangeness of it. In a world where men existed with singular authority in every realm, how was it that these two women sat on the thrones of their respective empires? Men surrounded them, served them. How was it that God made these women rulers, yet men thought themselves just in excluding women from everything outside the home? I thought of all the women who surrounded Jesus, who were with Him when He died and when He rose, who held their faith when all the men had left. What wicked sorcery had men worked to sideline us so? I felt the authority I'd been granted by my Queen, and for a moment believed I could do anything.

'Lady Bezawit, I hope you will forgive the informality of

this session. From our correspondence, I feel like an old friend to Queen Taytu, and would like to receive you in the manner befitting friends.'

I bowed as I sat. 'We are honoured, Your Majesty. Our Queen humbly asks that you accept these gifts as a token of our gratitude for your kind reception.'

Lema came forward with a small crate.

'Coffee, a gold cross made by our finest artisans in the holy town of Lalibela, and a Bible in our ancient holy language of Ge'ez,' I explained.

'What generous gifts. You must tell your Queen how very grateful I am for her kindness,' Queen Victoria said. 'I hope you will accept this small gift in return.'

A man behind her extended a book to me. It was a large beautiful tome in Amharic, a catalogue of the Library of Maqdala. For a moment, I thought it was a list of everything that would be returned to us, that all the books in this catalogue would be coming home. I smiled, relieved I hadn't needed to ask. But then nothing else came.

I turned to the Queen. She waited for a thank you, but I was speechless. Did she realise what she was giving me, this inventory of the treasures her soldiers had stolen from us? Or did her people just think that, due to its size, it must be something precious?

'Thank you,' I muttered. 'Ah … it's so good of you to return a lost treasure from Maqdala. Our Queen will be most humbled.'

'It's my pleasure. I must say, it's a delight to meet the countrymen of my dear Alemayehu. I met with him a few times, did you know? The sweetest of boys, such a sensitive, thoughtful child,' the Queen said. 'I still mourn his passing. He was far too young.'

I nodded and took the opportunity to move on to our difficult request.

'Your fondness for Prince Alemayehu touched our Queen's heart. She sent me here because she so admires your kindness and mercy. She requests that I humbly ask that the Maqdala treasures be returned to our country, along with the remains of Alemayehu, so he may finally find peace in his homeland.'

Queen Victoria smiled. It was tender, genuine. Then she said, still smiling, 'It is with a heaviness in my heart that I must deny your Queen's most reasonable request, but so many of the relics she has asked for we cannot find. The others are precious things we fear will not survive if they are not archived and cared for properly. We hope she will find comfort in the fact that the relics will survive forever under our care, so that generations of Abyssinians and indeed the people of the world may enjoy the fine culture and history of your people.'

I stared at her. The sweetness of her tone, the way she expressed a desire that our treasures survive, couldn't mask the truth of what she was saying: you cannot be trusted with your own history. But she went on.

'And dear Alemayehu. I imagine your Queen would not want to disturb his remains, especially in such a holy place as St George's Chapel. He has been buried with many kings and queens of my country, a place befitting such a noble prince. I encourage you to visit him. Our Dean,' she gestured to a balding man behind her, 'would like to give you a tour of our Chapel. I am confident you will see it is the best place for him.'

Her smile was kind but her eyes gave away the inflexibility of her position. I smiled back; no point arguing. We gave our thank yous, our goodbyes, and quietly followed the Dean to the Chapel.

'What did she say?' Balcha asked as we walked.

'She said no,' Lema answered.

Aba Kassie frowned. 'Why?'

I didn't know what to say. There were no words in any language I knew to explain it.

St George's Chapel was a building of grandeur and detail. The windows were tapestries made in glass and the floor was tiled in black and white squares. Its pillars rose up like ancient trees, spreading like branches at the high ceilings.

The Dean showed us a brass plate that commemorated Alemayehu. It listed his name, his birth and death, and a small quote: 'I was a stranger and ye took me in.' It was as beautiful as anything in the Chapel, but seemed very small against the statues and tombs surrounding it. I could understand it. This foreign prince, dead at eighteen, was not British royalty and couldn't feature so prominently. I could see it as a kindness, a great honour, the way they commemorated a foreigner in one of their most treasured places of worship. But I couldn't help but wonder if this was how Alemayehu felt, so small and isolated in a world so alien to his own, a world in which he would never truly belong.

The Dean took us outside, to a patch of land with no markings, and informed us that this was where Alemayehu was buried. I didn't tell him that, in fact, he was standing on top of Alemayehu, not in front of him. I was already planning how to take his bones home.

Lema said, 'Please don't do this.' Napier said, 'You can't do this.' I quietly admired the difference between the two.

'Aside from the obvious logistical impossibility, it would cause a diplomatic incident!' Napier insisted.

'How is this refusal by the British, this stealing of our treasures and our prince, not a diplomatic incident?' I asked. 'Why do we continually have to beg and scrape and be polite?'

Napier shook his head. 'Consider what happened when Emperor Theodore –'

'His name was Tewodros,' I corrected.

'Whatever you call him, think of what she did when he locked up her countrymen. She sent an entire army!'

'She didn't send them to free her countrymen. She sent them to rob us and stop Tewodros' progress. It wasn't in Britain's interest to have an African country with independence and power so close to its colonies.'

'Her motive is irrelevant. Think of what she did. What will she do when you dig up her ancestors' graveyard?'

'She won't spend millions of pounds getting back the bones of our prince.'

Napier exclaimed 'HA!' so loudly Aba Kassie jumped. 'She won't have to! If you get caught even attempting this, you'll never leave this castle!'

'Am I to take it you won't assist us?'

Wordless sounds escaped him, gasps and stutters, as if my request was so incredible he momentarily lost the ability to speak. 'No!' he finally got out.

'Very well. I trust you won't tell our hosts.'

'I have to!'

'She won't do it. No need to tell,' Lema interjected in his broken English, clapping the doctor on the shoulder. 'She is joking.'

'I am not,' I said bluntly.

'She is,' Lema insisted. 'A silly lady. The priest talks sense.'

Lema turned to Aba Kassie and begged him to intervene. The priest responded in Amharic, 'Alemayehu needs to come home.'

Lema, his hands still on Napier's shoulders, smiled. 'The priest says no. Don't worry. The priest talks sense. No need to tell.'

Napier shrugged Lema off him, glancing from Aba Kassie

to me, uncertain. 'Please don't do this, Lady Bezawit. You don't know what these people are capable of, you haven't seen … you haven't seen the way they treat people like you.'

'People like *us*, you mean,' I said.

'No, I mean people like *you*,' he stressed. 'People like me are a different matter. This will not be tolerated.'

One last time, he said, 'you can't do this', and left.

Lema fell at Aba Kassie's feet and begged him to see reason, to think of the danger, to think of the consequences. The priest touched his head gently and said, 'You don't need to participate if it so grieves you. But I'd sooner face the wrath of this queen than live knowing I left our prince here. Wouldn't you?'

Lema hung his head.

'I'm sorry,' he said. 'I can't be a part of this.'

He then tore page upon page from his notebook, ripping them in a violent jerking motion. He chose them methodically, flicking through the notebook and tearing the desired leaves out. Then he got his pencil and circled various sections. Finally, he stuffed the torn papers, around twenty of them, into my hands, and left.

I opened up the crumpled sheets. The first thing I saw was a map of the castle.

Lema disappeared. No one saw him leave the castle, but he was gone. I sat alone, studying his notes, and ignored the call for dinner. There were multiple maps of the castle, some that offered a bird's-eye view, others that sliced open the roofs and detailed the rooms inside. There was another that sketched out basements and tunnels that threaded under and out of the castle. Here, he'd circled a spot in the Horseshoe Cloister outside St George's Chapel. There was a tunnel that went under the Curfew Tower and out towards the town of Windsor. He labelled it *SALLY PORT – CHAPEL – NOT CONFIRMED BY*

*ARCHITECT*. There were many tunnels splitting off from the Tower, all with question marks and a source:

*George – Groundskeeper*
*Big Mary – Cook*
*Little Mary – Maid*

How had he managed to find all this, to convince so many people to share the secrets of the castle with him? On all of the maps, there were little Gs marked out along the walls, gates and entrances, which I guessed were guard stations, with times to indicate a changing of shifts. His other notes were a garbled mess of Amharic and English, with words running into each other, things crossed out or smudged. I discerned one thing at least: there was a way out of the castle. There was no way to make it to the Chapel without crossing a guard station but, once we had Alemayehu, there was a way out that avoided the gates.

I briefed Aba Kassie and Balcha on the plan, with one important caveat: *don't look at me*. They never questioned why. They trusted me enough to follow blindly. We'd made it here after so many months and finally, we'd do what we came to do. We prayed together, muttering the familiar words in unison, our hushed tones a gentle music.

We packed our bags, leaving behind any bulky items. While most of Balcha's weapons were confiscated, no one had been game enough to search beneath his fur-covered back, where he'd strapped a blade. His furs acted as a kind of shield, and he used them again, concealing the weapon. I wore all the gold jewellery Taytu gave me, determined it wouldn't be lost. The *History*, I wrapped in our clothes.

We left our quarters just before midnight. I led the way. Aba Kassie and Balcha kept their eyes off me, even as they followed on my heels. This was enough for the mischief. I sank into it and turned every eye away from us. We walked past sleepy guards, whose slow blinks lasted just long enough for us to walk by them unseen. I thought of the boy, who ran so fast it was as if time slowed.

We made it to the Chapel and came to the spot where Alemayehu was buried. There was a shovel waiting for us, leaning up against the wall with a small note. It was in Amharic, in Lema's messy handwriting: *From Kindly Old Anti-Monarchist Scottish Gentleman, Name Difficult to Discern – Gardener. Do not take. This is his favourite.*

Lema, it seemed, was more of a mischief than me.

'Is it safe?' Balcha asked, the shovel already in his hands.

Lights flicked inside the Chapel, delicate candlelight playing against the stained-glass windows. I probed with my mischief. There was a deacon inside, but he had fallen asleep.

I nodded.

Balcha drove the spade into the earth, splitting the grass. Aba Kassie whispered a prayer, his eyes closed, his hands held out with his palms facing the heavens.

'I'm going to look for the sally port,' I whispered to Balcha. He nodded and continued digging.

I ran to the Horseshoe Cloister on my toes, aware of the many windows that bore down on me, and tried to find the tunnel's entrance. The curved building was made of red brick and black timbers. There was an archway that Lema had circled, and there I found a door. It was locked, so I turned the mechanism with my mischief, and went inside. I came to a long hallway with many doors, all closed. I stood for a moment, quickly going over Lema's notes in my head. *Trap door.* I sank into the ground beneath me and felt something coming from the first door on my right. I turned the knob.

Then, I felt something. Someone waking. The deacon in the Chapel stirred.

I ran back.

Balcha was now deep in the ground. He struck the lid of the coffin with his spade.

'Hurry,' I urged.

Standing with two feet in the earth around the coffin, Balcha tried to prise the lid open. Aba Kassie's prayer came faster, words joining into one.

The deacon was coming.

'Balcha!' I begged.

He drove the spade deep into the coffin. The wood splintered. He hit it again and again, shattering the decaying wood.

'What on earth are you doing?'

We glanced up as we heard those English words. It was the deacon. He looked horrified.

'Away with you! This is God's work!' Aba Kassie snapped in Amharic, his angry tone uncharacteristically threatening.

'Guards!' the deacon called out, running away.

Balcha had smashed away half the lid. We could see down to the skull and skeletoned arms of our prince, dressed so nicely in worm-eaten English garb. Voices and lights emanated from all around us. The whole castle, it felt, was closing in.

I screamed, my voice adding to the chaos. '*Balcha!*'

'Forgive me, my prince,' Balcha said. He crossed himself and then grabbed at the bones. There was a sinister snap. Aba Kassie cried out as if in pain. We all crossed ourselves. Balcha begged Alemayehu's forgiveness for being so harsh, his apology bubbling out in a constant stream. He passed the prince's bones up to me. I bundled them into the bag laden with our clothes and the *History*. His skull, his spine, his arms and legs. The bones crunched and snapped. Tears poured down Aba Kassie's face. For the first time in our journey, I questioned whether we were doing the right thing.

Guards ran towards us, their muskets drawn, as I placed the

last of Alemayehu's bones in the bag. Aba Kassie took Balcha's hand and helped him up.

A shot fired. The bullet soared into the Chapel, showering stone shards over us. Balcha turned to face our pursuers.

'No!' I yelled and grabbed his hand.

We sprinted to the Horseshoe Cloister. Gunfire sounded as I flung open the door on the right where I thought the trap door would be. It was a storage cupboard of sorts.

'It should be here,' I said.

Balcha slammed the door shut and leaned hard against it, fighting against the shouting guards who pushed on the other side. It was somewhere here. I could feel it. I flung crosses and crosiers aside, as if a secret door might hide behind them.

*There.*

The slight outline of a trap door poked out from underneath a large baptismal font.

Aba Kassie and I pushed against it, inching it over to reveal the door. I wrenched it open.

Another shot was fired. Shouts and the sound of wood splintering followed us as we scrambled down slippery stairs. In the dark, I stumbled off the last step and hit the hard, dusty ground of the tunnel below. Balcha, the last to descend, pulled the trap door closed, plunging us into darkness. Aba Kassie lit the small lantern we'd hidden in one of our bags. It barely lit two metres ahead of us. We ran anyway, sprinting blindly into the tunnel.

Light suddenly flooded down from above. At least three English guards came down after us. Footsteps echoed from all directions. It dawned on me that maybe all of Lema's speculative tunnels existed, and we were being surrounded on all sides.

The guards on our heels got close enough for one of them to slash Balcha with the blade on his musket. He cried out and turned, swinging his fist and knocking the guard out. For a split second, we stared at each other in the flickering light. Then that little tickle of mischief told me to blow out the lanterns. So I did.

It went dark, yet I could see everything. The guards, terrified, raised their guns. A hard click sounded as their muskets were cocked.

The tunnel lit up with the sparking of gunfire. In the light, I imagine the men saw a flash of fur and nothing else. Balcha moved too fast for me to fully see, like a lion striking. Bullets rushed by his ears as he slashed the throats of the men. The tunnel went dark and silent again.

I'd never seen a man be killed before, nor had I seen one kill. It was a hideous thing, the speed of it. The singular noise it made, the wet opening of those men's throats. The final sound that marked their fall.

An instinct, the mischief perhaps, told me to light our lantern again. The light shone on Balcha, wiping his blade clean. He crossed himself. Aba Kassie muttered a quick prayer.

Footsteps thumped above and around us. We ran. I led the way, following an invisible beacon, something calling to me.

Finally! A set of stairs. We scrambled up like rats, no thought for where it might lead. Balcha reached the top first and pushed hard on the trap door above. It wouldn't budge. I tried to push with my mischief, tried to search for a hinge or lock to move, but those footsteps pounded in my head.

The door swung open suddenly. A rush of bright light and the nervous face of Lema bore down on us.

'Quickly,' he said.

We surged up into a stable. Lema closed the trap door as soon as we were out and tried to conceal it with hay.

'Quickly,' he said again. We rushed out into the dark streets of Windsor, to a large beaten-up carriage. Dr Napier was at the reins, a look of dismay on his face. He glanced at Lema as if this was not their arrangement or, if it was, he was having second thoughts. I caught his eye and smiled, a silent begging in my eyes. We squeezed in and were off.

Napier's eyes didn't leave the road. I tried to thank him, but he shook his head and muttered, 'God help us.' He took us out of Windsor but back towards London. Was there no other way out of this country than through its heart?

'You should have told us,' Balcha said to Lema warmly. 'I thought you a deserter. But you were there from the very beginning.'

'It was still the wrong thing to do,' Lema said quietly. 'But I wouldn't desert you.'

Balcha's mood soured instantly. 'Alemayehu is free.'

'Is he?' Lema said, accusatory, as if he too had heard the bones snap.

We finally came to a stop outside a set of tall, skinny houses that faced the British Museum. Napier ordered us to stay in the carriage and went to knock on one of the doors. He then ran back and bundled us out, herding us towards the light that flooded from an open door. I spotted the smiling face of Dr William Barrie, beckoning us in.

'Quick quick, there you go, come now.'

Dr Barrie was dressed in a nightgown, but he greeted us like a gentleman, insisting we go through to the lounge where he would have tea served.

'We don't have time, we need to get them out of London,' Napier said.

Dr Barrie clasped Napier's arms and smiled. 'It's alright, John. I'll go out in a minute and organise a ship. We'll get them on their way before sunrise, don't you worry. Let me just put some tea on and get dressed. You can't go anywhere yet. Might as well have some tea.'

Napier nodded. He screwed up his face as if to force back tears. 'Thank you.'

'Not at all,' Dr Barrie said, smiling warmly. He took off down the hall and came back minutes later, fully dressed and with a pot of tea. He brought out five different tea cups, two jugs of milk and a sugar bowl made of glass.

'Sorry for the …' He gestured at the strange assortment of tea wares. 'Archie,' he offered, as if it explained everything. 'I'm off to find a boat. Best be as quiet as you can. Archie doesn't know you're here.'

He picked a coat off the floor, retrieved a scarf and hat from a desk, and went out. It was then that I noticed why Dr Barrie offered the 'Archie' defence. The room was a mess, with papers, books, clothes and strange scientific equipment strewn across the floor. Balcha had to move a taxidermy turtle off his chair.

'What did you tell Dr Barrie?' I asked Napier.

'Not much,' he said. He glanced around the room, refusing to look at me. 'A lie.'

'Would he help us if he knew?'

'I don't know.'

'How do we know he isn't going to the authorities?'

'We don't.'

I paused. 'Doctor, if he calls the authorities, we won't be able to escape.'

Napier looked at his hands. 'You won't be able to escape without him.'

'Can you not procure a boat for us?'

Finally, his eyes met mine. 'Look at me. What do you think?'

Silence. We waited, letting our tea go cold. Dr Barrie returned soon after.

'I've got a boat for you,' he said. 'Small thing, bit old, but it will take you to France.'

He then gave me a small purse. 'Give the fellow three coins at the end of the journey. Not before, and not a single coin more. Don't let him tell you I promised more.'

'What is this?'

A harsh voice cut through the air. Archibald Barrie stood in the doorway between us and our escape.

'Brother!' Dr Barrie said cheerfully. 'John and his countrymen are just saying goodbye on their way home. A quick stop, so generous to spare the time, but they must –'

'What is that?' he asked, pointing to the bag that held Alemayehu's bones.

'It's a bag,' Dr Barrie said. 'You embarrass yourself, brother.'

Archibald's eyes narrowed. He studied Aba Kassie, who held the bag close. 'What's in it?'

'What an impertinent question,' Dr Barrie rebuked. He turned to us. 'My apologies, my brother forgets his manners when he's curious.'

'They've stolen something, haven't they?'

I resisted the urge to insist we couldn't steal something that was already ours. Dr Barrie continued to admonish his brother.

'What a silly thing to say. Truly, you embarrass us both.'

Archibald considered us. He took note of Balcha, who simmered with the energy of an armed man.

Then his eyes settled on Napier.

'It would be quite an ungrateful thing to do. Treasonous even.'

'It is disgraceful that you'd make such an accusation of our guests,' Dr Barrie retorted.

Again, Archibald spoke to all of us, but his eyes remained on Napier. 'We suspected you might try something. Your kind often do. Do you know what we do to traitors, Dr Napier?'

The doctor shrunk. We all looked at him. He tried hard to ignore our begging stares, holding Archibald's gaze. Though his voice wavered, he answered, 'Yes, Mr Barrie.'

I watched the way Archibald eyed Napier, as if he was trying to communicate all the consequences the doctor would face for this. It reminded me of the way Lord Oliver had glanced at him when he realised Napier couldn't translate for us. It would be easy enough for us to escape – Archibald wasn't armed – but it was clear that even if we did, Napier never would. Archibald would make sure of that. I needed to do something to silence him.

I took the bag containing Alemayehu's bones and approached him. 'I have something better than any treasure your empire has ever stolen.'

Archibald smirked. 'Oh yes?'

'I'll give it to you if you let us pass.'

'You could offer me the Kohinoor diamond, and I would still say no.'

'Let me show you,' I said. I opened the bag and reached inside. My fingers brushed against Alemayehu's skull as I picked up the *History* and handed it to him. He took it and sighed, annoyed. As he opened the book, I saw the pages, once scrawled with the names of every mischief, were blank. I felt sick.

'This is nothing,' he said.

Then, on an empty page, my name started to appear, as if the page itself was bleeding out in black ink. Archibald touched it. The flashes of so many lives danced across his eyes.

We left. No one asked what I'd given him. It was as if they hadn't seen.

We made it to the boat. Before we cast off, Aba Kassie begged Napier to join us. I translated, and the doctor, aghast at the very thought, shook his head. As we floated away, I waved. Dr Barrie waved back and smiled, but Napier stared at me, his lips pursed together, as if he had so many things left unsaid. For a moment, I thought I saw regret.

We sailed down the Thames in the dark, our way illuminated only by the captain's dusty lantern and the few lights that danced from the swollen shores. By sunrise, we were already out of London.

Balcha was confident, even before we made it to France. 'We looted Windsor, little sister,' he joked.

I don't know what happened to the *History*. As we made our way to France, trekked back across Europe, and found a boat on its way to the Suez Canal, I could still speak all the languages of the world. Only one strange thing happened. A woman shouted to me as we boarded a train leaving Paris. She had long black hair, and eyes as blue as Serafin's were green.

'Madame!' she called.

I stopped, with one foot on the train, and turned to face her.

'Where is it?' she asked.

I was confused. It was unlikely that she'd mistaken me for someone else. 'Pardon, madame?'

'The book.'

The book? The *History*? Who was this woman? I tried to speak, but my voice was swallowed up. Lema seemed to understand though. He called back to her, one word:

'England.'

We hurried aboard, but from the windows, I watched this woman, and she watched me.

Months later, as I sat with poor Balcha, staring out at the sea that still made him so sick, we spotted a strip of land that was the coast of Ethiopia. My heart swelled with joy. The voice came to me again after so long. I didn't know if it was for me, or for Alemayehu. But the voice was so all-encompassing it could've been for all the lost souls in the world. It spoke from the depths of the universe. It came from everything.

*Welcome home.*

# *Jessie*

'That's Lou!'

I shouted. I didn't mean to.

'The lady at the end, with black hair. I bet it was Lou. Or Chloe.'

'I bet you're right,' Kay says. 'Did you like this history better?'

I nod. I loved it. I loved Bezawit and Balcha and even Lema. I loved slicing up the ocean and stealing the bones. But ...

'Is the next mischief going to be the grumpy Englishman?'

'I guess so,' Kay says.

'I don't like him.'

She smiles. 'But his brother was okay. Maybe he'll be in the next history. Maybe Lou and Chloe too.'

'Can we read it now?'

'No.'

Worth a try.

'Do you think Queen Victoria went after Bezawit?'

'Don't know. You can find out when you do your mischief report!' She tries to be cheery.

'Can I use your laptop?'

Kay pauses. She has a video open. Her baking show. But then she smiles at me.

'Sure.'

I open another browser, careful not to close her video. I go straight to the State Library catalogue. Time to find some books.

Over the next few days, I research and make cranes with Theodore. I request a kids' book about Alemayehu called *The Prince Who Walked With Lions*. I imagine him walking around London with a pet lion on a lead, like Mrs Moran and Cornelius, only bigger and golden. This makes me laugh but later I feel annoyed because there are no other books about him. I request every travel book about Ethiopia I can find on the library catalogue. Kay says I should look into Queen Victoria and Windsor Castle, but there are too many books about her and she's boring, so I just ask for books about the castle.

I do a google search and find photos of Alemayehu. He looks sad in every photo. I also find pictures of Balcha. He's not as pretty as Bezawit makes out. He became a Dejazmach (a General) after the Battle of Adwa, where Ethiopia beat Italy in a big battle. Even though the Ethiopians won, the Italians came back and killed Balcha in 1936. It says he came out of retirement to fight. He killed one of them before they killed him. He was seventy-three.

I find articles from 2007 and 2015 that say the Ethiopian Government asked for Alemayehu's bones to be 'repatriated', which Wikipedia says means 'returning an asset, an item of symbolic value or a person – voluntarily or forcibly – to its owner or their place of origin or citizenship'. Britain said no. I wonder if Taytu buried the bones in secret. Should I write to the Ethiopian Government and tell them they *do* have the bones, they just need to look?

I tell Theodore about Ethiopia when we're in the library at lunchtime making cranes. He saw a documentary about Africa and learnt that in Ethiopia, they have churches carved out of mountains. I tell him about the prince's bones and the requests to have them returned. Theodore says it's sad Britain won't give them back. We don't talk for the rest of lunch.

It takes THREE WEEKS for the Alemayehu book to arrive, but I don't complain because I don't want to get in trouble at the library again. We go to the park on the way home and I tell the soldiers about Alemayehu and Bezawit. Who stole their bones back from the enemy when they were killed? Maybe a lady like Bezawit went around Germany and Gallipoli and all those other places, gathering up the bones of Guildford's dead men. As I count around the gravestone, I scoop up pretend bones and empty them into the ground.

'What are you playing?' Kay asks.

'Secret.'

'Can I play?'

I shake my head and continue.

The next day at school, I take my Alemayehu book. It's so early the teachers are only just arriving with their coffees and papers. Miss Sparrow walks past and says hello.

'You're here early, Jessie,' she says.

I say, 'My sister has to start work early so she can pick me up', but all I'm thinking about is what Miss Sparrow is holding. It looks like a hunk of salt, except it's an orangey-pinky colour. It's bigger than her hand. 'What's that?'

'This is a salt lamp.'

'But it's not white.'

Miss Sparrow smiles like adults do when kids say something that to them is stupid. 'Salt comes in all kinds of colours. The colour depends on what minerals are in the salt.'

'Do you eat it?'

Again, that smile. 'You can eat the pink salt, but this is not for eating. You put this on a wooden pedestal and it lights up. Some people think it purifies the air and makes it healthier. It's a lot more expensive than table salt.'

It reminds me of the salt mine and how you could stay there to get well if you had asthma and things like that.

'Is it from Poland?'

'No, it's from the Himalayas.'

I look at it for a moment, not sure what else to ask. 'It's nice.'

'I think so too. I just had breakfast with a friend and she gave it to me for my birthday.'

'Happy birthday, Miss Sparrow,' I say, even though I don't mean it.

'Thank you, Jessie!'

I think about the salt lamp all day. Even though it's not from Poland, I imagine Serafin's friends carving statues out of it. I ask Miss Sparrow if I can see it again and she says, 'Oh, I must have left it in the staff room.'

'Can I get it for you if I finish my maths early?'

'No, Jessie.'

I finish my maths worksheet quickly, except the last problem, and scribble on my paper until recess.

At recess, I run around being Bezawit, pretending I'm on a mission to get the salt lamp. Theodore won't play because he's making cranes. He's less sad, but he still makes them. He says if he makes a thousand, his mum will get better, like in that book he likes about the Japanese girl.

I think the salt would be better. I imagine having Aristophanes' powers for finding hidden things. I find the salt lamp and use it to help Theodore's mum.

After recess, I ask Miss Sparrow if I can see the salt lamp. She says if I keep bothering her, I'll have to sit on the bench at lunchtime. I don't ask again.

'Haven't you made a thousand yet?' I ask Theodore at lunch.

'Broom got into the box where I was keeping them and chewed most of them up,' he says.

It takes me a while, but then I remember Broom is his dog. 'Oh.'

'I have six hundred and two to make.'

'There's a salt mine in Poland and the air there makes you better. Salt makes the air healthy.'

He looks up from his origami paper. 'Really?'

'Yeah, I read about it. Maybe you should get a salt lamp like Miss Sparrow.'

'What's a salt lamp?'

'It's a chunk of salt that … I think it lights up.'

'Can I use normal salt?'

'No, it's special. It's on a wooden pedestal and it's really big.'

'How much does it cost?'

'I dunno,' I say. 'Miss Sparrow said they're expensive.'

'Oh,' Theodore says. He slumps down and goes back to his paper cranes. I feel sorry that Broom ate his cranes so I make them with him.

After lunch, we have to go down to the oval for the sports carnival. It was on in the morning too, but now it's our class's turn with the rest of the Year 4–6s. I don't know why we're having a carnival now, when it's still raining. You shouldn't have to do sports in winter. Mr Curtis, the PE teacher, says footy is the best sport in the world and you play that in winter, so we've got no excuse. He doesn't let me get out of things like Mrs Lornazak.

Theodore trips over and hurts his foot. Mrs Armstrong takes him up to the first-aid room in tears. I wonder if I can fall over and make myself cry.

There's a lot of waiting. My mind wanders to the salt lamp. Why does Miss Sparrow need it? She's healthy. Theodore's mum needs it more.

'I need to go to the toilet,' I tell one of the teachers on duty (*not* Mr Curtis). He gives me permission to go.

I walk up to the courtyard and go to the toilet. It's very quiet. Most of the classrooms nearby are empty. I glance towards the office. The staff room is on the second floor, up a flight of stairs near the principal's office and the first-aid room.

I walk over. Slowly. I glance through the glass door with a PLEASE USE THE OTHER DOOR sign on it. I can just see Theodore lying on the bed in the first aid room, his face turned away, an ice pack on his foot. The principal's door is closed. I test the door, pushing it open a bit. Mrs Fraser is talking on the phone in her office.

No one's looking.

It would be easy.

Not like sneaking around Windsor Castle.

I slip inside. Theodore doesn't move. I stop at the staircase and look at the hard black steps.

I go for it. I run up the stairs on tiptoe, quickly and quietly, and make it to the staff room. I spot the salt lamp on top of the dishwasher, along with Miss Sparrow's lunch bag. I reach out and pick it up. It's really heavy. Then I grab the wooden pedestal.

The phone rings downstairs. I jump. The lady at the other end of the office answers in her singsong voice. The principal won't be on the phone forever. It's now or never.

I run back down. As I come to the foot of the stairs, I see Theodore, sitting up. I look at him, he looks at me. He sees the salt lamp. He shakes his head at me.

'For your mum,' I whisper.

He looks unsure, but then he shakes his head again. 'Don't, Jessie.'

I ignore him and run out the door. I sprint to the hall where all our backpacks hang outside class. I find Theodore's bag and put the salt lamp inside. I shove my jumper down to hide it and zip up the bag. I feel dizzy and a bit sick but I did it.

'Jessie!'

I drop the bag.

It's just Theodore.

'It's okay, I hid it in your bag!' I tell him. 'You can take it to your mum. Miss Sparrow won't even notice before home time.'

Theodore picks up his bag and tries to unzip it. 'We have to put it back!'

I grab the bag. 'No!'

We tug on the bag. It rips open. Everything bursts out. The salt lamp lands on the floor with a crack.

'We're gonna get in trouble!' he cries.

'Theodore?'

It's Mrs Fraser. We freeze.

'Why did you leave the first-aid room?' she asks. We both take a few steps back. 'Jessie, aren't you supposed to be down at the …'

Mrs Fraser stops talking as she notices the bag and the salt lamp on the floor.

'Isn't that Miss Sparrow's?'

Theodore starts crying.

Mrs Fraser takes us to her office and asks lots of questions about who did what and why. Theodore cries but doesn't dob on me. I feel sad for him, but I'm scared and stay quiet. Mrs Fraser knows it was me. She tells Theodore he'll be in trouble if he doesn't tell her what happened, even if he didn't do anything. It's not dobbing when it's about something serious like stealing. We'll both be in even more trouble if we don't explain ourselves. Theodore keeps crying. He snots all over his jumper.

They call Kay and Theodore's dad, Mr Park. Kay arrives first. She's so angry she won't talk to me. Then Mr Park arrives. He is a tall skinny man. Even though he has a young face, he's bald. He smells like some of the people at Grandma's nursing home, like musty cigarettes. He wipes away the tears on Theodore's cheeks.

'Nothing's worth crying this much, little man,' he says nicely.

Mrs Fraser talks to Kay and Mr Park first and then brings us in. Now Kay looks *really* mad and Mr Park looks … well, bored? He fiddles with a bright red lighter.

'Now, Jessie. Theodore. I'm going to give you one last chance to explain yourselves,' Mrs Fraser says.

I say nothing. Theodore sniffles.

'Just spit it out!' Kay says and prods me.

'It's no big deal, we just want to understand,' Mr Park adds. He smiles at Theodore and gives him a tissue. He smiles at me too, a real smile, and his eyes wrinkle all soft and kind around the edges. It makes me miss Dad.

Mrs Fraser sighs. 'This is a very serious matter. One or both of you went into the staff room without permission, took Miss Sparrow's lamp and then hid it in Theodore's bag. It was broken in the process. Since you won't talk to me, I don't know if it was an accident or if you meant to do it.'

'Well, of course it was an accident,' Mr Park says.

Mrs Fraser ignores him. 'Normally, we'd just give you a warning, but given you have been so uncooperative, I've decided to suspend you both for the rest of the week. Stealing is not tolerated at this school. When you return on Monday, I expect you both to apologise to Miss Sparrow.'

Theodore wails.

'It's alright, little man,' Mr Park says.

'Mr Park, I hope you see this is a big –'

'I will discuss this with my son, Mrs Fraser, don't worry,' he says. He puts his arm around Theodore and they both leave.

Kay doesn't put her arm around me. She doesn't tell me it's alright. She apologises to Mrs Fraser and then grabs my bag and pushes me out of the office. As we leave school, all I get is an angry, 'You're going to explain everything when we get home.'

Mr Park and Theodore are outside the school gates. When

Mr Park sees us leaving, he takes Theodore's hand and catches up to us.

'You're going our way,' he says to Kay.

'I'm so sorry about this,' Kay says.

'No need to apologise,' Mr Park says. He takes out a cigarette. 'D'you mind?' He lights it before Kay can respond. 'The suspension is just to the end of the week.' He turns to Theodore. 'A few days off, then you go back and say sorry to Miss Sparrow. We'll make her a nice card and we'll buy her a new salt thingy, whatever it is.'

Kay nods. 'Of course. Just tell me how much –'

'Don't worry about it,' he says. Smoke billows out of his smile like a friendly dragon.

'No, really,' Kay says.

'Please, it's nothing. Maybe come over with Jessie sometime. She's a star. Theodore loves her, don't you, little man?'

Theodore sniffles but nods.

We walk in silence for a bit, crossing the road. I watch Mr Park smoking. Whenever he breathes out, he points his head away from us and blows the smoke in the other direction. He smiles like he's sorry and waves his hand about to get rid of the smell. His hands shake a little.

'You know, my family … we're going through a tough time,' Mr Park says. 'Jessie's helped Theodore so much.'

Kay just nods.

'It's really nice to meet you, Jessie, even under these circumstances,' he says to me with his head turned, smoke blowing the other way. He turns back and smiles. 'I don't know what happened today, but Theodore's told me enough about you for me to know there couldn't have been any meanness to it.'

What did Theodore tell his parents? I'm not like that.

I stop walking. 'I stole the salt lamp and put it in Theodore's bag.'

'Why would you do that?' Kay yells. 'Theodore's in trouble because of you!'

Mr Park asks gently, 'Why did you do that?'

'Salt's good for sick people,' I say.

'What does that mean?' Kay demands.

But Mr Park knows. 'Thank you, Jessie,' he says, so warm and full, like I've really done something worthy of being thanked.

Kay frowns but doesn't say anything else. We keep walking. When we get to our street, Kay says to Mr Park, 'Well, this is us, um, thanks for being so understanding.'

'We're just two streets up!' Mr Park says. 'Listen, here's my card. If you've got work and can't get a babysitter, let me know. I work, but our nanny Stephanie is a star.'

Kay takes the card slowly, like she doesn't know if she really wants it. 'Okay. Thanks.'

As we walk home, I watch Mr Park and Theodore for as long as I can. He keeps one arm around Theodore, except when he's puffing out his cigarette smoke and shooing it away.

At home, Kay takes my Alemayehu book.

'Go to your room,' she barks.

She phones a lot of people. I listen to her talking through my bedroom door. Then she hooks her iPod up to the speakers in the kitchen and plays old episodes of Hamish and Andy as she makes dinner. It rains a little. She turns it up super loud. I can hear every word, every laugh. The laughs are never her own.

The speakers go off.

'Dinner!' she calls.

We eat pasta she actually cooked, not the microwave stuff.

Finally, she asks, 'What did you mean about the salt?'

I shrug.

'I want to know why you did this. I'm really annoyed, Jessie. You've messed everyone around!'

I poke my pasta. 'Theodore's mum is sick. The salt mine DVD and lots of websites say it can help make people better.'

'Is that why you stole it?'

'Yes.'

'Why didn't you tell Mrs Fraser?'

'I dunno.'

Silence. Then Kay says, 'You know it's wrong to steal things, no matter what.'

I want to yell NO IT'S NOT. What about Bezawit and Alemayehu? What about people who are hungry and no one helps them? But I just say, 'Yes.'

'You'll apologise to Miss Sparrow.'

'Okay.'

'You know, those salt lamps are just pseudoscience bullshit. It's not real medicine. The best thing you can do to help Theodore's mum is be nice to Theodore.'

I think YOU'RE WRONG but I still don't say it. I finish, push my bowl towards Kay and mumble, 'Thank you.'

Kay puts the bowls in the sink. 'What's wrong with Theodore's mum?'

'Dunno.'

Kay sighs. 'Okay, so, I can't get out of work, I've had too much time off. I called Mr Park earlier and he said you can stay at Theodore's house.'

'Okay,' I say. Not like I have a choice.

'Go brush your teeth and off to bed.'

'Okay.'

I do what Kay says. She seems annoyed, but by the time I'm in my jammies, she comes to my room and hugs me really tight.

'I love you,' she says.

She returns my Alemayehu book. I read it until 10:57 pm. I'm close to the end. Alemayehu has just caught a cold after lying next to a cage of lions. His father had lions and he missed them, so when a carnival came to the town, he snuck out and slept with them all night.

The cold seeps in around me. I wonder if Alemayehu felt like he was in a cage, being stuck in England away from his people. Our house feels like a cage now, with the bars on every door and window. I imagine lions peering in, feeling sad for me, wondering if I want to be free.

Alemayehu is going to die in the book soon. I don't want to read that. I go to bed instead and listen to the rain. Kay still has the TV on.

# Jessie

In the morning, Kay drops me at Theodore's house. It's old, but like rich people old, where everything is well taken care of.

Theodore's room is huge. He has posters of Korean pop bands all over the walls and lots of books, some of them in Korean. He shows me the weird letters. He can't read them even though he can speak Korean, but his mum promises she'll teach him when she gets better. He also has a mini-tent in his room shaped like a castle, full of cushions and fairy lights. It's too small for the two of us so he lets me sit in it. He sits outside and we pat his dog Broom, this fat floppy golden retriever who pants a lot so it looks like he's laughing. He's what the dog in *Up* would look like in real life.

'Breakfast's ready!' Stephanie calls.

We run with Broom to the kitchen. Being suspended is great! Stephanie gives us pancakes with strawberries, chocolate sauce and whipped cream. We do an hour of homework and make a card to say sorry to Miss Sparrow. After that, we watch documentaries about tigers and make paper cranes. Broom wants to be with us but he can't be trusted around paper, so he sits outside the living room and whimpers.

'Why didn't you tell on me?' I ask Theodore.

'I didn't want you to get in trouble,' he says.

'But I got you in trouble.'

'You didn't mean to!' he says cheerfully, like he never even cried about it. 'Anyway, we'll make it right! Dad says we'll buy two salt lamps, one for Mum and one for Miss Sparrow. He says only medicine can make Mum better but she might like it because it's pretty. I think they're pretty too. Do you want one?'

Theodore's smile is back. There are photos of Theodore's mum everywhere. She smiles just like him, with her whole face. I wonder where she is but don't ask. We make forty-three paper cranes.

I've decided Theodore is my friend. I don't mind if he's a bit annoying. He doesn't mind that I'm grumpy or don't like the same things he likes. When I go home that night, I promise I'm going to be a proper friend from now on. I'll try not to get angry at him when he sings in my face or tries to make me dance.

I thank Kay for letting me stay at 'my friend's house' and feel warm inside.

The next day, we do our homework after a breakfast of scrambled eggs with sausages and hash browns like you get at hotels. Afterwards, we listen to music and make cranes. Broom howls so we let him in but we yell at him when he tries to pinch one. Theodore teaches me the Korean word for no – *AH-NEE!* – and we yell it at Broom every time he gets close. Stephanie cleans the house and pops her head in every now and then to 'check on Broom' but I know she's checking on us. Theodore talks about albinos, which are animals and people that are completely white, and the time Broom got beaten up by a small dog because he's a bit of a wimp. I want to tell Theodore he's a good friend but I don't. We make sixty-two paper cranes. On Friday, we make fifty-one. Waffles for breakfast.

The weekend comes and I listen to a radio show online about Alemayehu. It features a presenter, a British-Ethiopian poet, and the author of my Alemayehu book. I feel angry listening to it, with all this talk that tries to justify everything the British did. They make Queen Victoria out like she's this nice old lady. The poet sticks up for Alemayehu though, saying how they didn't care for him properly. I google him and find his poem about the Battle of Adwa on YouTube. I listen to it and feel happy again.

'You've done so much research for this one,' Kay says over my shoulder as the video ends. 'Once you finish your Alemayehu book, we can move onto the next history.'

I nod, but I just can't. Not yet.

Monday. First day back at school since being suspended. I hum the POW POW POW! song as I wait for Theodore. He doesn't come at all, not even late after the bell rings. I say sorry to Miss Sparrow on my own.

'I understand you wanted to do something nice for your friend,' Miss Sparrow says. 'But stealing is never the right thing to do, okay?'

I'm sick of adults saying this. But I reply: 'I know. I'm sorry.'

At recess I make paper cranes so Theodore can have extra ones when he comes tomorrow.

But Theodore still doesn't come to school on Tuesday. I spend recess and lunch on my own, making paper cranes and reading. I ask Mrs Harper if I can go on the computers because there's so much more about Alemayehu online. She says no (she always says no). It rains on Wednesday and the library's full of noisy people who think it's okay to yell and run like they do outside. Mrs Harper's useless at making them shut up. I make paper cranes for Theodore and hope he comes on Thursday.

When the bell rings to go home, Kay isn't there. Well, I think she isn't there. Then I see her by the gates talking to Stephanie, who's crying and wiping her nose on her jumper. Kay nods, frowns and touches her arm. Stephanie then hugs Kay and leaves. Something feels bad. Where's Theodore?

Kay says nothing but when we get home, she sits me down. I don't want to have this talk. I don't want to know what's happened.

'You know how Theodore's been away?'

I nod.

'His mum died on Monday.'

*No.*

'Stephanie says it was unexpected. She'd been sick for a long time but they thought she was getting better.'

*No.*

'We'll go to the funeral on Saturday. It'll help Theodore if you're there.'

*No, it won't.*

'I don't wanna go,' I say.

'Neither do I,' she says. 'But we will go.'

'We can't make it better.'

'I know. But we still need to go.'

I look down. I try not to cry. Then I go to my room and get all the paper cranes I made for Theodore. I throw them in the bin, all of them. I push them down and cover them in paper towels so I can't see them.

'Go away!' I yell at them.

'We can burn them,' Kay says.

'Really?' I think of how angry she was when I lit my wig on fire.

'If it'll make you feel better.'

I nod. Kay finds a ceramic pot outside. She pulls out the dead plant, digs out some of the soil and together we put the cranes inside. The soil is damp. It takes eleven matches to light them. They all burn to nothing.

We have leftover pasta for dinner that tastes like oil and feels like glue. I take my Alemayehu book to my room. I still can't read it. I curl up in bed and cry.

Kay comes to me with the *History*. For once, I say no, pulling the covers up over my face. She touches my back gently through the doona. I scream at her to go away.

# Jessie

We wake up late on Saturday. Kay begs me to come in the car so we can get to the funeral on time. I refuse. She grumbles all the way to the bus stop. When we get to the funeral home, she pulls me along to get me to walk faster. We slip into the chapel and sit at the back. The coffin is surrounded by flowers and photos of Theodore's mum. Her smile, Theodore's smile, shines out of all of them.

Theodore's at the front next to his dad. Stephanie's there too, with her arm around Theodore. He's crying, I can hear him. Whimpery cries, like a sad dog.

Mr Park is called up to deliver a speech. For a while, he just stands there, staring at the coffin. Someone comes up and touches him on the arm. He blinks a few times, takes a bit of paper from his jacket, and then stares at it. Tears run down his face.

He reads in Korean. He speaks awkwardly, not fast and easy like Theodore when he sings his songs. His voice gets eaten up by his tears and soon, his words are replaced by these big ugly sounds. I've never heard a man cry like this. It comes from his gut. It makes Theodore cry more. I start crying too. Mr Park drops his paper and says, 'I'm sorry, I can't do this in Korean.' He rambles in English about how he met his wife, how she was kind and funny and beautiful, and such a good mother.

'She never stopped smiling, not with the diagnosis, not

through all the chemo or the surgery or all the dashed promises of remission,' he says. 'She was always cheerful, even when she didn't want to be. She did everything to spare us. Everything.'

I cry and cry and cry. I don't even realise Kay's holding me till after the service and some happy song in Korean comes blasting through the speakers.

When Theodore sees me, he hugs me. His tears make my shirt wet. I cry too and hug him. Even though I hate hugs, in this moment, it's okay.

People go to Theodore and his dad and say how very sorry they are. We go up too. Kay is so careful. She holds Mr Park's hands and says, 'I don't know what you're feeling, but I remember how I felt. Please know … just tell us … if you need anything.'

Mr Park nods but looks down. 'Thank you.'

How many people cry at funerals because they miss the person who died? I think more people cry because they feel sad for the people who are grieving. They cry because they remember people they've lost, or they imagine what it'll be like when someone they love dies.

I cry for Theodore. I cry for Mr Park. I cry for me and Kay.

Later, at home, I scream at Kay. 'WE'RE TOO YOUNG FOR OUR PARENTS TO DIE!'

She says, 'Yes,' with tears in her eyes, 'but I don't think anyone gets old enough for it not to hurt.'

People cry at funerals because they know this is the end we all face; not death, but grief. Like the people in Grandma's nursing home. Old and lonely, everyone they know dead or dying. I remember the kids at my old school who cried when the accident happened. I now realise they didn't cry because they felt sad about Mum and Dad dying. They felt sad for me. They felt sad because they knew their parents would die one day too.

At dinner that night, Kay teaches me the word 'empathy'. I wonder if what we feel is really empathy or self-pity at what's to come. She asks if I want to read the *History*, but I say no, I'm not ready for Alemayehu to die. She frowns at that but says nothing.

Mrs Moran's at it again. One am. Vacuuming her driveway. It's strange to see something so familiar after a day like this. Things just … go on. I feel angry at her, for still vacuuming her driveway when Theodore's mum is dead. She looks like she's singing something to herself, and she's smiling. I wonder if she had a funeral for her husband. I wonder if she went and she just doesn't remember.

'This is what you do late at night, huh?'

Kay's found me. I don't care. I don't even look at her.

She sits down on the little couch with me. Together, we look out at Mrs Moran.

'Poor Mrs Moran. I think she's a little crazy.'

'She looks happy,' I say.

Kay pauses for a moment. 'You're right. She does.'

Then she puts her arm around me. I shrug it off.

'I have something here,' she says.

I glance down. I expect to see the *History* but it's my Alemayehu book.

'You need to finish this so you can give me your mischief report.'

I turn back to Mrs Moran. She's turned the vacuum off and is checking her work. I can just hear her singing something about sunshine.

'I don't want to finish it.'

'Because Alemayehu's going to die?'

I nod.

'Then we change the ending,' she says.

Kay opens up the book and takes out my bookmark. She starts to read from the part where Alemayehu finds the lions. This time though, he doesn't lie by the cages. He doesn't get a cold.

He lets them out.

'Arise, good lions!' Kay pretends to read. 'Off to Windsor! Tonight you shall feast on royalty!'

I want to tell her she's dumb. Alemayehu would never say that. But I don't. And, I don't mean to, but I smile a little.

Kay closes the book. Finished.

'Want to give me your report now?' she says.

I remember then what Kay said to Grandma, how she uses the *History* to make me behave and feel less sad. So I give her my report. I tell her about Taytu and Balcha. I tell her about the articles that say Alemayehu's bones were never returned.

'I think the British are ashamed to admit that Bezawit rescued them,' I tell her. 'That's why they keep saying no.'

Kay smiles sadly. I know she doesn't believe in the *History*. She thinks those articles are right, that Alemayehu's bones really are still there. I glance out at Mrs Moran and think of her husband and the A. Mischief card. Should I tell Kay? Maybe then she'd believe.

But then Kay says, 'I bet you're right. Taytu must have buried them in secret knowing Queen Victoria would never want to admit it. If they don't admit the bones were taken, they can't retaliate, can they?'

I smile. I think of that word again. *Empathy*. Kay always thinking of me. I think of Theodore. I hope, deep down, I can do this for him.

'Time for the grumpy Englishman?' she asks.

I nod. As Mrs Moran goes inside, we go to Kay's bed and curl up. She opens the *History*. I can't help but notice how little we have left.

# A. Mischief the One-Hundred and Ninety-Ninth

## London, England 1890–1895

I ran as I'd never run before. My thief was quick, darting around cabs with the energy of a much younger man. The ground was slippery and a light but icy rain fell around us. I knew how to run in the wet. I'd spent my youth being the thief myself. Unfortunately, this man was just as skilled.

My thief darted onto Haymarket. I followed. He'd kept to quieter streets, ducking between terraces, houses and shops to switch between laneways, but now the streets were getting busier. I saw it before him; Pall Mall ahead. Any quest forward would bring him closer to the Palace and a bevy of law enforcement. Trafalgar and St James Square awaited him on either side.

He stopped, then darted alongside a theatre. I gained ground. The road in the alleyway was uneven. We splashed in the puddles collected in its potholes. I saw my chance, felt that mischievous spark. I froze the muddy slush beneath my thief's feet. He slid and stumbled. I caught up, grabbing him by the collar, and threw him against the wall. My thief gasped as the wind was knocked out of him. He dropped what he'd stolen from me: the *History*.

The book splayed open and its pages landed in the half-frozen slush on the ground. I scooped it up quickly, more to save it from this fiend than any concern for the pages. The

*History* had survived bookworms, fire, and decades at the bottom of the ocean. A bit of ice and mud was nothing. But for another soul to touch it. I remembered my first encounter with the enigmatic book and prayed it hadn't spilled its secrets.

I observed my thief further. His hair was black and covered by a cap that bulged despite it being comically oversized, suggesting he had quite a head of hair. He was slim; his clothes stooped him. His face looked young with its smattering of freckles, but dark hollows under his eyes spoke of many years on this earth.

I took a step closer. A pair of bright blue eyes glared at me with a fierceness not seen in men thrice his size. Something wasn't quite right.

Finally, I saw it. 'Ah.'

I pulled a small penknife from my coat pocket. Those furious blue eyes went wide. I advanced on him, then, a sudden flick! – the blade cut through his shirt. The binding underneath split open, revealing the shape and cleavage of a woman's bosom.

She seemed neither ashamed nor threatened by this sudden reveal. She just smiled.

'You have bested me, sir,' she said. Her accent was French, her tone exaggerated in the way women deliver their most insincere flattery. 'Bravo.'

'Bravo indeed,' I said as I fished into the left pocket of her trousers in a rather ungentlemanly fashion and retrieved my pocket-watch.

'I would like the book, sir.'

I was shocked by her brazen request. 'You'll be lucky if I don't drag you to the authorities.'

'Very well. You may keep the book for now,' she said, and made to leave.

I caught her arm.

'What's your interest in the book?'

She tried to shake free. I held on.

'Exit, pursued by a bear,' she joked, eyeing my ill-kempt hair and the scars that ravaged my face.

'What's your interest in the book?' I repeated.

'I like to read,' she said. 'And I am *very* clever.'

*I am very clever*. I was reminded of an incident in the Reading Room, just a few weeks before. I'd found some obscure tome on botany thought lost in the 1700s. When asked how I'd found it, I responded with the exact same retort. I began to feel sick. Had those eyes that now bore into mine looked upon me before?

I felt it then – icy damp under my arm, right where I held the *History*. Was the book wet? How could that be?

She yanked free of my grip and ran off.

I hugged the *History* all the way home, too afraid to open it. I was apprehensive about my thief's time with the *History*. I reached out to the door that led to my humble home and focused on the raindrops by the brass knocker. I imagined the twin molecules of hydrogen circling that single one of oxygen, then slowed them. The raindrops froze from the knocker out. I could still wield mischief. As I went inside, I flicked the air. The ice evaporated. Tiny wisps of steam danced across the polished wood.

I bolted every lock. I searched the rooms. No one. I checked the windows, bolted them too. I'd been cautious long before the *History*, with good reason, and praised myself for adding the extra security all those years ago.

I went to my bedroom and locked the door. Only then, settled at my desk, did I open the *History*. It was wet. Pages sticking together. I carefully opened it to the section that had touched the road. A name was bleeding out of recognition, not in the way the *History* did when it hid itself, but like ink naturally dispersing from the touch of water.

When I first got the *History*, I'd thrown it into the fireplace. I'd poured a whole bottle of wine on its open pages. I'd left it in a fish bowl for a week. It always remained unscathed. Now this.

I tried to read the distorted name. I looked at the pages before it, trying to remember. Only three pages were affected. The water was being kept at bay, as if the *History* amassed a barrier between the sodden pages and the rest of the book. I remembered Bezawit. I still held her memories. I went back, to the man before her. An ocean. Flashes of war. Cannon fire. But those images dissolved, forgotten.

I lit the fire and sat by it, holding the pages out to dry. I tried to remember. Who came before? Me. Bezawit. Then who? I felt a sharp pain in my head, as if the memories were leaching away through burst blood vessels. Something horrible had happened. This book had survived thousands of years and countless attempts at destruction. I begged the paper to dry, the ink to reform. My nose bled. I wiped it absently on my shirt.

I sat in front of the fire until I ran out of wood. At least a day came and went. The pages dried in ripples like normal paper. Distorted, stiff, discoloured. Once I gathered the courage to finally close the *History*, the dried pages crunched. I took it to bed and cried, as no man should ever cry. Perhaps you'd concede that a man who worked and lived in the British Museum was a man unduly obsessed with the conservation of rare human relics, and as such, allowances could be made for such hysterics. As I drifted off to sleep, I knew that if the *History* was to record my feats, it would record the truth. I was afraid that this great gift was no longer mine.

'Archie?'

How many times could I instruct Will to leave me alone? I wouldn't say it again.

'It's been three days.'

It had been four. I resisted the urge to correct him.

'Your absence has been noted at the museum. Mr Blythe visited this morning.'

Percy. The Superintendent of the Reading Room. How very boring.

Softer then, Will spoke. 'Please, speak to me. Let me know you're alright.'

I was not alright. Whatever was happening to the *History* was happening to me. I spent the days and nights in a fog, as a pain migrated through my head like a parasite feasting its way through my grey matter. My self-confinement had been filled with monstrous nightmares and wicked daydreams. Every time I slept, I met my thief again, this time in the Reading Room. The whole room was on fire, its Pantheonesque dome enveloped. Yet, nothing really burned. We sat together on the Superintendent's desk, the flames licking at our bodies, untouched.

'Isn't it cold?' was all she said to me.

On the third day locked away, I had tried a humble experiment. I added a drop of water to an as yet untouched page, testing if it would repel the liquid as normal. To my horror, the page sucked the water in. Once it dried, the spot was crinkled, minor water damage, but the name and memories that lived in the page survived. Still, I didn't experiment again.

In all the *History*'s memories, nothing could explain what was happening. I hypothesised that perhaps the *History* was reacting against my thief, but the *History* had been stolen, abandoned, given away and lost countless times before. I couldn't account for what caused this. Unless … there was something ominous in the book. A page at the back, stained with a name smudged out. I always forgot it was there unless something prompted me to look, a feeling normally, something unsettling. The foreboding that lived in that page hung in the air now. Was something leaching out? I couldn't escape the thought that it was something I'd done.

Will banged on the door. 'Archie! I will break down this door if you don't speak to me!'

I relented. 'I'm fine. Working.'

'You've never locked me out before.'

I didn't respond.

'Has ... something happened?'

I hated the way he said *something*. I cursed him for the bitter memories he invoked.

'Very well,' Will said. 'I'm going to show a visitor around the museum. I thought you'd be good enough to assist, but never mind. I'm bringing a screwdriver when I return. If you're not out by then, the door's coming off.'

It was no idle threat.

I spent the rest of the day reasoning with myself. *She's a thief. Nothing more. Perhaps this is my great act of mischief. Repairing and saving the* History. *Years in the dark continent has left its mark. That's why the book came to England.*

Yes, yes. That made sense.

I disposed of the indignity in my makeshift chamber pot, washed, and dressed in the clothes that were least offensive to my nose. I took the *History* with me as I did, even to the bathroom where I sat it on a chair within arm's reach. I took appropriate precautions. I wrapped the *History* first in cloth and then in a binding of leather I fashioned from ripping the pages out of a notebook in Will's room. I then placed the book in my briefcase, a hardy thing made of solid dark leather, fastened with two brass clasps that featured a locking mechanism. It'd been a gift from Will long ago when I was devoid of the many scars that scored my face and body. My initials, both actual and mischievous, were monogrammed on its side: A.M. I hadn't always been

Archibald Barrie. I smiled at it as I bathed, remembering Will's disappointment when I got the job at the museum and expressed how I intended to use the briefcase in my new appointment: 'All the better to steal books with, my dear.'

Happy memories brought me back to my old self. I concluded that the *History*'s damage had wrought some damage on me. A day of suffering for each lost entry, and a little extra for the waterdrop experiment, perhaps. No matter. I wouldn't allow a headache, some nightmares and a few blood noses to entomb me in my own home again. There was no better protector for the *History* than I, a guardian (and occasional pilferer) of the British Museum's printed books, the finest collection since Alexandria. The sinister smudged page at the back of the book was forgotten again.

Let my thief do her worst.

Will arrived back late. The sight of him made me laugh. His nose and cheeks were burnt pink from the cold. He wore so many layers his arms stuck out from his sides. He looked like a ruddy penguin.

I told him as such. He smiled at me, good-natured fellow that he was.

'At least I'm not a grumpy old bear,' he said, tugging on my beard.

'I'll shave tomorrow, before work,' I promised.

'It's Saturday tomorrow, you daft old thing.'

'The shave can wait then.'

'It cannot. We have a dinner engagement tomorrow.'

I cursed Will's inability to say no to dinner invitations.

'*You* have an engagement. *I* have work to do.' I motioned at my briefcase as if to supply the evidence.

Will snatched my briefcase. He darted out of my reach as I tried to grab it back.

'That's not funny, Will.'

He wiggled it at me childishly. 'I'll confiscate this till after our dinner. You understand.'

I tried to grab him and he dashed out of the room. I pursued, furious at being taunted with the same trickery that had haunted me for days.

'Will!' I snapped, half-bark, half-growl.

He laughed as he ran. 'Exit, pursued by a bear!'

Her words from his mouth. Suddenly I saw not Will, but my thief. I shoved the air, and my mischief pushed him in the back. He hit a doorframe face-first and dropped the briefcase. I snatched it.

His nose bled. It bled more than should be possible for such a small appendage. I told him as much as he fussed in front of the mirror. He told me I was lucky it didn't break and that I was a right old pain in the arse.

I said sorry.

He said I was bloody well coming to dinner.

I said yes, very well then.

I mused on how like children we still were together.

It was insufferably cold when we stepped out for our dinner engagement. Puddles were fringed with ice. We got a cab heading to the Tower. Will was obsessed with the new Tower Bridge and said he wanted to go for a walk along the river before dining with our hosts.

'It's too cold for a stroll, for goodness' sake!' I objected.

'I have a surprise. It's worth the cold, I promise.'

I hate surprises. I turned every puddle and slick of water to ice, the slippery roads making our cabbie and his horse nervous and, as a result, rather slow. But Will wouldn't be deterred.

'We have plenty of time,' he assured me. 'Dinner's at seven. I only said six because I know what you're like.'

We disembarked at London Bridge and began our intolerable

walk along the Thames, the Tower Bridge looming ahead of us. The bridge, completed the year prior, was gargantuan, its two towers dominating the river. The turrets of the towers were so tall, the fog hanging over the city blocked them from view. A walkway was suspended between them and rope-like steel suspensions draped down on either side. The bridge was one-part suspension, one-part bascule, and indeed it was the bascules that were the most remarkable, though unassuming, parts. They could swing up in a matter of minutes due to some ingenious hydraulic engines, allowing all manner of river traffic to pass under them. The bridge was many things: gaudy and elegant, excessively decorative and eminently functional. A symbol of the best and worst of Britain.

I was so distracted by the majesty of the bridge, I failed to notice the river itself. Will touched my arm and gestured to the water below. Here and there, chunks of ice floated down the rapids. Ice sloshed at the river's edge, broken up and jostling on the surface. This was the surprise, it seemed.

What a miserable anticlimax.

'I miss Scotland when it's this cold,' Will said.

'I miss our residence when it's this cold.'

He ignored me.

'The Thames froze solid up in Oxford. Don't you miss when the lochs froze and we'd spend all day skating?' he said as we trundled towards the bridge. 'Grandpa took me to a fair on the ice when I was little. Carriages were driven over the loch and they even roasted a lamb right there on the ice. It tasted different somehow. I wish you could've tried it.'

The cold condensed our breath into water vapour, smoke-like wisps spilling from our lips as we spoke. I let it come streaming out in an annoyed sigh.

'I fear I'm losing my accent,' Will said quietly.

'You are. It would make things a great deal easier if you lost it completely,' I responded.

He sighed. 'I just thought it was a magical sight, these little icebergs floating down the Thames. This way. Our hosts live off a lane near Fenchurch.'

Fenchurch was a decent walk in this weather. I stifled my annoyance at this unnecessary detour, all for the sake of a few bits of ice bobbing under Tower Bridge.

'Who's the patient this time?'

'Not a patient, a new friend. Mr McKenna and his niece. She fell into the Thames and I happened to be on hand to fish her out. She's visiting London at the moment. I showed her the museum the other day when you were sulking.'

'Why are you the one to play host?'

'I'm being polite, Archie.'

'She has an uncle to show her the sights.'

'Yes, but he's busy and she's rather lovely, to be honest. I enjoy her company.'

Rather lovely? 'I thought you'd given up wife hunting.'

Will put his head down, embarrassed. 'She doesn't look it but she's made a few comments about being as mature as myself. Her disinclination towards marriage seems clear.'

Thirty-five was hardly 'mature' in a man such as Will but for a lady seeking marriage, it certainly was. I was grateful the good lady was aware of this.

We stopped outside a terrace house, slim, two storeys and with stone pillars above its station.

'You are not to steal any books,' Will warned as he lifted the doorknocker and glanced at my briefcase.

'Wouldn't dream of it.'

Will banged the knocker. We were welcomed by a maid who showed us through to the parlour. Will introduced me to our elderly host and his niece but all I could do was stare. It was her. My thief.

I hugged my briefcase. '*You*!'

Confused stares, the lot of them. She glanced at her uncle, frightened, and then back at me. Will muttered an apology and said something equal parts threatening and pleading to me.

'This is my thief! This is her!'

'What thief? What are you talking about?' Will demanded. 'Mr McKenna, I'm so sorry, my brother's not in his right mind.'

Will clasped my arm. I shook him free. '*She*,' I stabbed an accusatory finger at her, 'robbed me! I apprehended her but she damaged a most invaluable thing.'

My thief looked terrified. 'Sir, you must've mistaken me for someone else.'

Scottish accent this time. What a master of disguise my thief was. She was dressed far more demurely, yes, but it was her. Her freckles were gone, no doubt disguised under some tricksy woman's paint, and her eyes were brown ... why had I thought them blue?

'What did you do to the *History*?' I demanded.

'Sir, this is outrageous!' Mr McKenna exclaimed. Was the old man in on it? I didn't care. My fury stayed on my thief. She burst into tears.

A woman's tears can ruin anything. Once they were released, a series of events was set in motion. Will begged her forgiveness, begged our host's forgiveness, delivered a blistering tirade on me, and then bowed and offered a thousand meek apologies as he manhandled me out the door. The dinner, needless to say, did not go ahead. No explanation would suffice for Will. We made it back to the residences separately, Will so angry he chose to walk home and risk losing his toes to frostbite than share a cab with me. Very well. I only heard the slamming of doors when he returned home a few hours later.

I met her in my dreams again that night.

'Isn't it cold?' yet again.

Will didn't entreat me to come to church, as was his tradition every Sunday morning (as was my refusal). He stayed out the entire day. I couldn't help thinking he was with her. No doubt she was graciously accepting apologies, saying how very sorry she felt for the poor unhinged brother of her new friend, and all manner of female flattery and thief cunning.

A day of reflection made me realise how stupid I'd been, showing my hand. It's difficult to know thine enemy when one cannot get close enough to study them. My thief now had Will's ear and no doubt his protection. But I had something she didn't: his heart. When he came home, I caught him in the hallway.

'Trust me, Will. It was her.'

Will sighed, conflicted. 'I trust that you were robbed. I trust you think it was her. But it couldn't have been. The same day you accuse her of stealing from you, I was with her. I told you she fell in the Thames. She was horribly shaken from the event. I was afraid hypothermia would set in. I cared for her the whole day.'

That shook my confidence a little. 'What time did she fall in the Thames?'

'For goodness' sake, Archie! Around midmorning, I suppose.'

Hmm. The robbery occurred in the afternoon. She could not be my thief. Perhaps the Scottish accent was genuine. The woman who had robbed me was French. Yet, something about her still felt uncertain, dangerous even. I felt like a foolhardy boy, making his way across the thinning ice of a frozen pond. I played it safe, retreated.

'Forgive me,' I offered.

'Forgiveness can only be sought from the good lady you've dishonoured.'

'I shall seek it.'

Will was suspicious, but smiled and offered a terse 'good' as a warning.

Monday morning. Briefcase in hand. Hair brushed, somewhat.

I made my way to the Reading Room, my workplace at the centre of the British Museum. There was no finer treasure in the museum than the Reading Room's dome. No drawing, photograph, or literary account could capture its vastness. It eclipsed the desks, the patrons and the books we all coveted. The dome itself was blue, with ribs of white and gold. Tall windows encircled the base, taller than the bookshelves beneath them, and flooded the room with light. The very top of the dome was a brilliant circular window, a rooftop of glass. Below it was the Superintendent's desk, raised so Percy could glower at our readers.

My normal role was assistant to Richard, the Keeper of the Books. Richard often sent me on missions into the stacks or across Britain and Europe to retrieve things. It was Richard, unwell at the time, who insisted I take the Abyssinian manuscript to Windsor, thereby putting me on my path towards the *History*.

For now though, I was an attendant, a fetcher of books, under Percy's dictatorship. I was on loan, like a fine exhibit, for six months. Richard had tasked me with reducing waiting times for patrons' book requests. I was to train the attendants, as my colleagues were uninventive, unable to consider where a book might've been housed if shelved even a few spaces down from its intended position.

Tedious colleagues aside, I enjoyed my new employment. The Reading Room stacks were a fine place to call home. Several storeys encircled the dome. Affectionately known as the Iron Library, the floors of the stacks were made of perforated iron so the sun from the glass ceiling could filter down even to the lowest level.

As the day passed, the dome darkened. The hum of the newly-installed electric glow lamps sizzled a little louder. The Reading Room was one of the first public buildings to experiment with electrical lighting, but a small explosion the year before meant that no risks were taken with the stacks. Once the sun had set, they were thrown into complete darkness. I tasked an attendant with lighting the enclosed oil lanterns and helping me find a few requests. A Russian fellow wanted something on land taxes. I shadowed Jeffery, our youngest but brightest attendant, as he tried to implement my methods. Took him fifteen minutes. I sighed and told him he was still the smartest of a dull bunch.

'Mr Barrie,' Percy greeted me as Jeffery and I returned with the Russian fellow's books.

'Percy,' I responded.

'Could you find this immediately?' he said, handing me a request slip. 'The patron's been here since morning. No need to show us how you do it.'

I resisted the urge to tell Percy to 'say please', took the request and a lantern, and off into the stacks I went.

The author of the requested book was a G. Davis. No doubt a thousand books had been written by such a common name. Indeed, the stacks were full of them. I couldn't find the request at first, but then I took a few books out of the overburdened shelves. Yes, a common mistake. Two small books, eclipsed by larger volumes, had been squashed to the back, hidden from view. One of them was that desired by the patron. The other? I couldn't help a little look. I smiled when I saw the title page.

FROSTIANA :
or
A History of
THE RIVER THAMES,
In a Frozen State;
with an account of
THE LATE SEVERE FROST;
AND THE WONDERFUL EFFECTS
of
Frost, Snow, Ice, and Cold,
in England,
and in different parts of the world;
interspersed
WITH VARIOUS AMUSING ANECDOTES.

To which is added,
THE ART OF SKATING.

Charming! The book claimed to be 'printed and published on the Ice on the River Thames, February 5, 1814, by G. Davis'.

I thought of Will: his childhood fair upon ice, our years skating across every manner of pond, loch or river that froze in our old home. How we laughed back then.

So, yes, I took the book. Unlocked my briefcase, slid it inside against the *History*. I took our patron his request, some small tome that was not 'interspersed' with the promised 'various amusing anecdotes' of the one I stole.

She was there when I got back, sitting by the fireplace of a lounge Will had cleaned as best he could. I promised him a reconciliation. I supposed he was intent on having it. She stood at my arrival. We eyed each other cautiously.

'Archie, this is Miss Chloe McKenna,' Will said.

My thief came forward and offered me her hand. I dutifully kissed it, bowed as a gentleman does, and smiled through gritted teeth.

'Miss McKenna, I must apologise for my rudeness of a few nights ago. I was not myself.'

'Not at all,' she offered. Still Scottish. 'Will tells me of your terrible ordeal with the thief. I'm aghast that one of my sex would participate in the petty crimes of boys.'

Clever words. A small voice reminded me that Will had rescued the lady from the Thames and cared for her during the time of my theft, that this polite but careful creature couldn't be my thief. But my thief she was, I was certain.

We sat. A tray of tea rested on a table whose surface I hadn't seen in years. *Where did Will put my papers? God help him if he lost any on account of her.*

'I hope Mr McKenna can also be so forgiving,' I said.

'Of course. My uncle appreciates it was a misunderstanding.'

I nodded. I found women difficult to engage in conversation. *What should I say now?* Luckily, she continued.

'We're both so grateful to Will. I'd be frozen at the bottom of the Thames if it weren't for him. Has he told you the full story of his bravery?'

'No, he hasn't. My brother is a humble man.' *Dear God, please don't bore me with a tedious tale of heroics.*

She told her story of falling into the Thames and Will jumping in after her. Will. *She keeps saying his name.* That was all I could think. Not Dr Barrie, not even William, but Will.

Only I called him Will.

'My brother, the hero,' I said, realising I hadn't spoken in some time.

She went on, complimenting Will, complimenting London. Asking questions of me, enquiring into my work, on and on and on.

'Mr Barrie, you hold your briefcase with such care. It must contain something precious.'

My expression soured. She noticed.

'Forgive me for prying. I only assumed it was some fine book, given your work. I'm a keen reader.'

*Of course you are.*

'There's always some kind of wonder in Archie's briefcase,' Will said. 'What do you have in there today?'

I thought of our Russian patron. 'Some manuscripts on land taxes. Nothing to bore our guest with.'

'Maybe next time then,' she offered sweetly.

'Next time,' I said, smiling back at her.

The night went on much like this, tedious politeness after tedious politeness. Thankfully, she didn't stay for dinner. Will insisted on taking her home. As she left, she took my hands in hers and said how very happy she was that we were now friends. I could have sworn I saw a flash of blue go across her brown eyes as she glanced once more at my briefcase.

Will returned late. We sat together in my room, on the floor by the fireplace where it was most warm. I gave him *Frostiana* and he flipped through it with a happy smile.

'Listen to this: "Swings, bookstalls, dancing in a barge, suttling-booths, playing at skittles, and almost every appendage of a Fair on land was now transferred to the Thames." Can you imagine?' he said. He laughed and showed me a passage. 'Some fellow wrote a letter to the thaw! Look! "Now as you love mischief, treat the multitude with a few cracks by a sudden visit." What cheek!'

I smiled at the mention of mischief.

'Wouldn't it be marvellous to see the Thames frozen over? I'd do anything to be back there when this book was printed.'

I admired Will, his heart still so young. 'I would freeze all the rivers and oceans if it would please you.'

Will laughed. 'With what divinity would you freeze the oceans?'

I shrugged and grinned back, taking *Frostiana* from him. 'Some sort of devilish mischief.'

The next day, I resolved to find a proper hiding place for the *History*. My thief could freely come into our home now, had figured out where I kept the *History*, and had wormed her way into Will's affections. I set about finding the one place better guarded than my briefcase, a place not even a clever thief could gain access to. The Reading Room stacks.

I woke early and went to the stacks, to the packed shelf where I'd found *Frostiana*. I slid the *History* behind the row of books, behind many volumes of Davises. I felt sure she couldn't get it there.

The next few days were fairly mundane. Just the cold, some students and more Russian exiles. But then, after returning home late one day, Will greeted me at the door with an angry urgency.

'Where've you been?' he snapped.

'Good evening to you too,' I said.

'Your boss has been here.'

I frowned. 'Richard? He's out of town.'

'No, Mr Blythe.'

'Percy? Oh. How tedious for you.'

Will paced. He tugged at his waistcoat, pulled at his sleeves. I suddenly felt uneasy.

'What's wrong?'

'We have been so … *foolish*!'

I grabbed Will by the arms to stop him moving. 'What?'

'He came here asking all these questions.'

'Like what?'

'He kept talking about birth records, about not finding you anywhere. He even checked up on your degree from Edinburgh. He looked into me, found me sure enough, but said he couldn't find an Archibald Barrie anywhere. Even mentioned the initials on your briefcase and your bloody accent.'

'You told him the M on my briefcase is my middle name, Magnus. He can look up Magnus Barrie and find your grandfather.'

'Of course, I told him.'

'Well, you told him about Father's –'

'Of course!'

'And the records?'

'I told him every stupid lie we ever invented!' Will said, jerking his arms free. 'He didn't believe a word of it.'

I shrugged. 'It's of no conscience. He can't do anything. Richard won't have an ill word spoken about me.'

'People listen to these kinds of ill words.'

'We have the degrees, we have the birth certificates. They've never failed us before.'

Will shook his head and mumbled to himself, 'I've made so many allowances.'

'What do you fear? That this will happen to you?' I demanded, motioning at the marks on my face. 'You've made no allowances. None!'

'I can never go home because of you!'

'Me? You can go back to Auld Reekie whenever you wish! It is I who can never go back. Every moment I've lived has been in jeopardy. You think a little snoop like Percy has the power of gangs and wolves?'

'Every man with ill-intent can summon a gang and rally wolves. That is how *this*' –Will gestured at my face – 'happened.'

I was tired and didn't want to indulge fears that ruled my life decades ago. 'We've faced worse,' I offered, and left Will to his frittering. Percy was not a threat I perceived as legitimate. I had all the means to rebuff him.

I was fired the next day. Percy offered no explanation.

'Richard will be hearing about this,' I warned him, loudly. My voice bounced around the dome.

'I look forward to it,' Percy responded coldly. He held out his hand. 'Your keys, Mr Barrie.'

I slapped them hard into his open palm.

'And my keys,' Percy added dryly.

'*Your* keys? I don't have your keys, you fiend.'

'Who stole them then?'

My anger dissolved instantly. Percy's keys had been stolen. It had to be her.

I wasn't allowed back in the stacks. Percy wouldn't even let me approach the desk. The *History* was still hidden with the Davises. And now she had keys to the Reading Room. The stacks.

Will insisted I make no fuss, but fuss I made. We had a week to pack and move our things, but weren't allowed to stay another day in the residences, an absurdity for which there was no precedence.

Mr McKenna somehow heard that we were staying at a local inn. That, apparently, would not do. We were to stay with the McKennas, two guestrooms awaited us.

I spent the cab ride there trying to figure out how she'd done it.

It snowed for days. Heavy sheets of brittle ice piled on the roads, killed off the homeless huddled in doorways, and stopped all telegrams through to Richard. Then the snow stopped and a frost set in. No mail, no travel, no going outside if you wanted to keep your fingers. Our hosts were friendly enough, and their house warm, but the combination of their cheerful conversation and my sudden unemployment plunged me into a gloom so severe I used the fairer sex's oft-employed excuse of a headache to justify confining myself to my room.

My thief spent her time reading or with Will. Their witless jokes and tinkles of laughter were too much to stomach. She read a lot. I even spotted her sitting opposite Will in the lounge, reading silently together. Why did her uncle allow her to be alone with a man who was but a stranger two weeks ago? Did Glaswegians have some perverse sense of morality those of Edinburgh and London were not privy to? The man seemed a civilised gent, why would he allow this? He was unapologetically Scottish though, and if he trusted Will to be alone with his unmarried niece, that was the way it was to be. He reserved all his suspicion for me.

'Where's your accent gone, man?' he asked at one of the few dinners I deigned attend.

'Time in London, sir,' I offered, supressing the sigh of being asked the question a thousand times by a thousand equally as boring gentlemen.

'Your brother managed to keep his.'

'My father thought his eldest son would inherit the family profession of medicine, not his youngest, so it was I who followed him down to London when he was visiting patients. The commonwealth of this nation is not so commonly shared. The wealthiest patients are in England.'

Mr McKenna approved of the dig at England and said no more. The man was clearly a dullard. At first, I'd thought he'd been the one to orchestrate all this, using a woman to try and steal the *History* without consequence, but time spent in his company made me rule out that possibility. Instead, I tried to figure out how she'd done it, how a French woman had convinced a dotty old Scotsman that she was his niece. I asked how she came to live with her uncle.

'Very sad,' Mr McKenna said. 'My drunkard of a brother died with naught a penny to his name. I hadn't seen the poor girl for twenty years when she showed up on my doorstep.'

'Twenty years, sir!' Will responded. 'She must have been a sweet wee girl when you last saw her.'

'Aye,' Mr McKenna replied, nodding soberly.

'How did you recognise her then?' I asked, perhaps a little too pointedly. Will scowled at me.

'Oh, you always know family, don't you?' Mr McKenna said, smiling at her. My thief smiled back. Then she glanced at Will. Smiled at him too.

It would, perhaps, be fairly obvious what happened next. You may think me rather simple not to have seen it. A day after the snow ceased, and the frost plunged the city further down the thermometer, Will came to me.

'Miss McKenna getting a bit boring?'

'She's good company actually,' Will said. 'You would know that if you spent some time with her. Shame about your headaches.'

'Shame indeed.'

We sat for a moment, listening to the fireplace crackle.

'I'm sorry we haven't spoken much,' he finally said. 'I was angry.'

'I understand,' I said. 'So was I.'

'You were right. It was always you who made allowances, you who sacrificed. I never meant ... I never knew how to make up for what happened. I just wanted a peaceful life, for us to be safe.'

'I know,' I said.

'I always wanted to find a way. I wanted so many things for us.'

'I know.'

'I hope you understand, everything I do is for us,' he said.

His words came out slowly, like he was stumbling through them.

'We're fine. Stop this now,' I said as kindly as I could. Perhaps I hoped to stop what I felt was coming.

'There's a simple way to guarantee a peaceful life, and that is marriage. A good family. Respected. Not wealthy but well-to-do enough,' he said. 'I sought Mr McKenna's blessing for his niece's hand in marriage yesterday. He happily gave us his blessing. She said yes.'

I said nothing. He reached out meekly for my hand. I pulled it away.

'We'll still be us, Archie.'

'If you marry her, there is no us.'

'Don't be unkind. There'll always be us.'

I looked at my hands. The cuts and gouges. The ugly red scars.

'You'll always be my brother,' he offered.

'I'm sick of being your brother,' I said.

I left the house, frost be damned. I didn't want to be there in the warmth, among the champagne toasts. I'd lost my job, my mischief and my Will.

I walked past birds fallen out of the sky, frozen by the winter. Some were frosted hard to windowsills. I picked one up, a sparrow, and held it to my chest. I warmed it in the same manner I'd commanded ice to evaporate the day my thief came into my life. The little creature softened, twitched. I felt warmth fill its cotton-thread-like veins. I heard its heart beating, fluttering like a butterfly's wings. Its body twitched with more ferocity. Now awake, it desired to be free.

I couldn't let it go. It would freeze again without me. The sparrow tried to flap its wings. I clamped them down and held it closer to my chest. I wondered if the bird heard my heart beating, if its ears would burst at the drum-like cacophony of a heart that was no doubt bigger than its whole body.

I found myself by the Thames, that star of *Frostiana*. Its current was surely the only thing still moving with ease in London. I thought of the printing press that fashioned the book I swapped for the *History*. Maybe the press had nestled in the spot where the Tower Bridge now stood. Perhaps it faced St Paul's, as men around it walked on water. I thought of Will.

The little sparrow chirped. It looked up at me, frantic. What was better? Freedom and a certain death by freezing, or captivity and warmth? I thought of crushing it, killing it quickly. Perhaps a small cruelty was the kindnest thing. It chirped again, begging mercy perhaps.

I let the sparrow go. Held my hands out to the sky, that grandiose dome, the Pantheon of the world, and it flew away. I bent down, pulled my hand free of its glove, and let my fingers hover just above the Thames. I felt the chill coming off the river.

I sank into myself, sent my mind into the water. I saw the billions upon billions of atoms beneath my hand, remembering pictures of water molecules from stolen books, the way the hydrogen atoms bonded, locking the liquid state into that of a solid. How funny that the first book Will ever caught me stealing was the one I remembered now, a little thing on the states of matter.

The memory triggered the mischief. The water below my fingertips froze. The river pushed up against the patch of ice, but I willed it deeper. I could see right down to the atoms. I danced along each bubble of oxygen, snap-froze those hydrogen bonds in place. It crackled as the ice hardened. I stretched my fingers apart and watched the ice spread.

I had a sizeable platform now, and took the step of a man more mischievous than wise. The ice was solid, at least twelve inches. I threw off my other glove. Holding out both hands,

I froze the ice deeper, extending it into the Thames. I walked forward, watching the river turn solid before me. The ice was dark but smooth. The tides yielded, did not dent or push against the surface. I became cocky, walking faster, and then broke into a run, my feet outpacing the ice. As my shoe hit the water, I froze it. I jumped and ran over the river, freezing it before my feet came down.

The ice hit the south bank. I turned like a skater, letting my shoes act as blades. I sent the ice outward, touching the Tower Bridge, extending past London Bridge. I poured my memories into the water, froze it solid as if to keep my past alive. I laughed.

There was no water to be seen. The ice extended far beyond my eyes. I stood in the middle of the frozen Thames, where once men had drowned. I looked towards the Tower, to the arches of London Bridge and the dome of St Paul's. The power of the mischief still poured out of me. Newspapers would later report that glass shattered in all the houses around the river, as water on dining tables and wine in cellars expanded.

I shivered. It was cold. Very cold actually.

A horrible realisation dawned on me.

I, too, was made of water.

The cold slithered through my veins, like some nasty eel, entering through my hands and feet and gripping my heart. I looked up as the water in my eyes froze them open and saw, if my mind wasn't playing tricks on me, the speck that was my sparrow. As my last breath froze, the water vapour turning to ice crystals in my throat, I felt such joy that its tenacious flight should be the last thing I saw. Let there be celebrations upon the stage of my death. Will would have his frost fair after all.

But I didn't die. I just danced on the edge, tilted over for a second like my sparrow, before being pulled back.

The first thing I saw was her, my thief. I fluttered my

eyes and then wiped them, for they were full of tears. I was incredibly warm, and contained somehow. Ah, a bed. Tucked in so tight she might as well have chained me down. I was back in the McKennas' house. My thief sat on a chair, facing me. I tried to get up but she pushed me down.

'Rest,' she said.

I was in no state to object. My limbs were numb.

'How did I get here?'

She wanted to say something, but couldn't. She opened her mouth and no words came out. She frowned and tried to speak again. Just a squeak. She looked confused. I'd seen this before on the face of a hundred or so mischiefs, trying to communicate their secret. I tried to speak back, to tell her of the magic I'd wrought upon the Thames. Nothing came.

Yet, she managed one thing: 'I saw.'

*You couldn't have*, I wanted to say. Only mischiefs could see mischief being done. Either she was my successor, or the laws of mischief had changed. I thought of the ruined pages and lost memories.

I pulled my hand out from under the covers. I couldn't feel my fingers, but they were all there, none blackened with frost as they no doubt should be. I looked at them for a moment, marvelling that they all seemed to work. I locked eyes with her and clicked my fingers. I saw her brown eyes flash blue just as the bedside lantern, the fireplace and the few candles winked out. I clicked my fingers again. The flames ignited. Her eyes never left mine. She saw what I did. Her eyes were now completely blue, no camouflage to them. She blinked a few times, and they turned back to brown. Was this her mischief? We both considered each other in silence, trying to figure the other out.

She smiled. 'You are *very* clever.'

Then she got up, went to the door and called out, 'Will, Archie's awake!'

I heard the heavy footsteps of a man running up stairs. Will came into the room in a flurry, embraced me, and then rested on his knees beside my bed. His head hung limply, touching the blankets by my chest. I saw the exhaustion of time spent coaxing me back to the world of the living.

'You're a right old idiot,' he said into the blankets.

I put my hand on his head. Touched his hair but couldn't feel it. 'Yes.'

'You only have your life and all your fingers thanks to a good-natured boatman and my medical expertise.'

'Yes.'

He went quiet. I stroked his hair again, willing some feeling back into my fingers.

'Is there a frost fair?' I asked.

Will sighed. His body shrunk. My thief touched him on the shoulder.

'You can't have a stage like that and not erect a fine performance upon it,' she answered. She glowed with the kind of smile women employ to beg reconciliation.

'I would love to be a spectator,' I said, playing along.

'If you can walk before Madam Tabitha Thaw comes to London, maybe,' Will said.

I smiled at the reference to *Frostiana*.

Then, 'Don't do that again.'

'I won't.'

'You're the last of my family. I need you.'

A churlish part of me wanted to say, 'You are to make another family soon. What need will you have of me then?' But I held my tongue. Instead, I hung to the warmth of being worried about. I spent the afternoon wiggling my toes.

'Come on, you monstrous fiends!' I shouted, willing feeling back into them.

I promised all ten of them they could walk again on the ice if they'd just tell the rest of my limbs to move too.

My toes were kind to me, and so was my thief. I walked again with relative ease but Will didn't think it wise to go out. Miss McKenna pleaded with him, saying how unkind it would be to deny a well man a once-in-a-lifetime event.

The dark glass I poured into the river was almost clear now, sparkling sky blues and grand buildings reflected on its surface. Entire avenues were erected on the ice, running from one riverbank to the other, with booths and tents offering all manner of things, from liquor and bread to books and toys. Their brightly coloured flags waved lazily at fairgoers alongside a glut of Union Jacks and signs in screaming capitalisation. The variety of smells were only outnumbered by the people, at least two thousand on the ice itself.

Skaters twirled on the fringes of the fair, racing each other from one bridge to the other. There were women dancing, fiddlers playing, the tinkling of a piano, the hypnotic *shuk shuk* of ice skates, and the constant crackling of fire, of beasts being roasted and chestnuts popping. Even a balloon was set on the ice, its body slowly inflating as its hawkers promised a fine show when the lady balloonist would sail it clean over the Tower. She would only come out when the balloon was ready and her extravagant top hat was filled with coins.

Will bought us lamb that was roasted on the ice. He smiled and said to me, 'I told you. Doesn't it taste different?' I didn't have the heart to tell him it tasted like regular overcooked mutton. My thief dutifully agreed with her fiancé and told him how very wondrous it was. Lapland Lamb. I wondered if she'd been reading *Frostiana*.

At least five printing presses were available. Will waited in line to have Miss McKenna's name printed on a sheet attesting to the fact that she had stood upon the Thames in its frozen state.

A ripple of 'she's here!' went through the crowd. 'She' was evidently a royal she. A carriage with the black form of Queen Victoria was drawn from one riverbank to the other. Fairgoers flocked the procession, waving flags, shouting 'God Save The Queen', and vacating Will's queue so he got his souvenir a little quicker.

The day grew dark, but life still danced upon the ice. Fireworks were set off near the balloon, which was still struggling to rise. The colours in the sky were reflected in the ice, a most magical sight. Grumbles about the forfeiting of coins for the lady balloonist and her non-existent tricks dissipated. The music stopped. Only the shrill squeal of fireworks filled the air, followed by the bang of bright lights and the soft awed rumble of *wooooooooh!*.

Once the show was over, a mass exodus began across the ice. Some tents were packed down. Arguments about the extent to which the ice was thinning by the Tower rumbled through the vendors. We returned to Fenchurch and I went to bed, complaining of a tingling in my feet. Will and Miss McKenna beguiled Mr McKenna with tales from the fair, their frivolity loud enough for me to hear the hyperbole they added to the day's events.

Again, I dreamed I was in the Reading Room with her. The fire was gone. In its place, the dome was flooded to the roof with water. We sat again on the Superintendent's desk, our hair and clothes floating lazily in the water. She held the *History* in her hands.

'Isn't it cold?'

The ice remained firm for another day. I watched the revelry from the riverbank. The balloonist finally set sail, or attempted to. The wind was too unruly. She kept it attached to its moorings as she hung upside down, teetering on the edge in some ridiculous costume that left nothing to the imagination.

Will wasn't content to watch. He spent the day skating. Miss McKenna was as skilled as he, and the two of them circled each other, gliding at speeds only stupid boys dared venture. I wished the lady would fall and break her neck, but rebuked my wickedness with the threat that the *History* would record my thoughts and present me as quite the monster. To make up for it, I picked up a few sparrows in the bushes. Two were long gone, but the last still fought. I held it against me. It started twitching again. A warmth filled my heart that could only be obtained from a good whisky or true happiness.

'Archie!'

I let the sparrow go, looked up and saw the impeccably adorned paunch that was my old boss.

'Richard,' I said, and offered my smile and hand in greeting. The big man spurned my hand and embraced me.

'Good fellow, I've been looking for you all morning. A Mr McSomething waved me towards the river. Could barely understand the poor chap. Glaswegian, your host?'

'Yes,' I said. I wanted to say so much more. How to approach my sacking and the accusations from Percy?

'Quite the spectacle!' Richard remarked. 'Not quite the spectacle that was caused at the museum, but spectacle nonetheless.'

Ah. Ever skilful at bringing the discussion to where it needed to be was our Keeper of the Books.

'Monstrous business, most disgraceful. I sacked Percy as soon as I got back. Never heard of such a thing.'

I tried to stop the relief from showing on my face.

'I understand you've been horribly treated, but I hope you'll come back. You can have Percy's old job if you fancy it, or you can be rid of them and come back to hunting rare books for me. I do miss you, old boy, you're a bloodhound with books.'

I was at a loss for words. Richard chuckled.

'Speak, man!'

'Thank you, Richard. I'd be happy to return as your assistant.'

'Good!' he said and shook my hand in both of his. Then, into my palm he slapped the keys to my residence, my old office, and, hallelujah, the keys to the stacks that housed the *History*. 'Leave the Reading Room to the bookworms, ey! I might send you back there to train the new Superintendent, if that's agreeable.'

'Of course.'

'Good man.'

'Richard,' I broached slowly. 'May I return today?'

Richard laughed, a throaty roar that shook his considerable girth. 'That's why I want you back! Always working! Listen, go back to the residences, get settled in. Come back next week. Few days off for having to suffer this indignity. Full pay.'

I smiled. 'Thank you.'

'Good man,' Richard nodded. I bid him farewell and he seemed to be going, but then he turned back around, his jovial mood slipping into something more … careful. He tried to maintain the casual nature of our chat as he ventured into more serious territory.

'One thing before I go,' he said. 'I don't care if the rumours are true. As long as you display some discretion, my only concern is your ability to do your job. Plenty of folk more wicked than the likes of Archibald Barrie have contributed a great many things to our museum and indeed our empire. I only care what you have to contribute, you understand.'

'Percy's accusations are false, I have proof –'

'I'm sure you do, but I don't care for it,' Richard said pointedly. He glanced again at the fair. 'I hear your brother is to be married.'

'Yes.'

'That is very fortunate.'

'Ah, yes.'

'Shame you haven't been so lucky.'

'Shame indeed.'

He then turned back to me and smiled. 'Discretion, man.' Clap on the shoulder. I could only nod. 'Good chap.'

He left. I sat for a moment, listening to the fair. Then I took off. Retrieved my briefcase and, ahoy, museum-bound! I didn't bother to tell Will. He was too busy circling his future bride. I wished she'd fall and break a leg at least. Rebuked myself again. Perhaps there were far more wicked men than the likes of me, but wicked I could still be.

I searched the stacks for five hours. Pulled every Davis, Davies, Davison off the shelves. Checked the reader requests, found nothing to indicate that the attendants had been anywhere near the *History*. Jeffery asked if he could help find whatever I was looking for. Told him to bugger right off.

It was gone. I knew it was gone. But I kept searching, all day. Noticed numerous books mis-shelved. Didn't bother putting them back in order.

Jeffery came again hours later. Found me checking behind the books on the lower levels, huddled in the dark with a dwindling lantern.

'Closing time, Mr Barrie, sir,' he offered. Swear I heard a squeak in his voice.

I got off the ground, and glared at the youth as I smoothed my waistcoat. 'The stacks are in quite a state.'

'I'm sorry, sir.'

'Have we had any break-ins while I was away?'

'What? No, sir! I'd tell you right away!'

'Could Percy have taken anything before he left?'

'No, sir, didn't have a chance! And I would've told you, sir, I swear!'

I glowered at him. 'Best be going home now then.'

Jeffery nodded like a parrot. 'Yes, Mr Barrie, sir.'

I went back to the McKennas', determined to figure out how my thief had done it. I didn't even get a chance to go in the door. A figure slid out from the side of the house. The big cap was no disguise. I'd seen it before. My thief. She had the *History*. She saw me and ran.

I took chase, following her weaving form through the streets just as I'd done at the beginning of our tale. It was dark; even the street lamps seemed muted. Her cap flew off and her hair unravelled, like a long black streamer flying behind her. Again, I worked my mischief, made the water on the ground freeze. As she ran over those icy puddles, they shifted back to water. She countered my mischief with her own.

My thief opened the *History* as she ran. Then, she ripped out an entire page. The violence of it made us both tumble. A sharp pain shot down my spine. Memories of some fine empire in the Americas leached out of my mind. She recovered quickly and was back up and running. I scrambled up and chased after her. She ripped out another page; I stumbled but kept running. Tasted blood in my mouth, swallowed a wave of nausea. Flashes of something: a woman whose face was ornately tattooed, winking at me as she slipped from my mind. I pushed on despite the burning in my head.

My thief made her way to the Thames. The ice near the Tower Bridge was thinning considerably now. Most booths were packed away, their hawkers moved on. I was struck by a loud creak, like the sound of a door opening on rusty hinges, only magnified. It conjured many memories from the *History* – the creaking of a ship's hull on a violent ocean, the deep timbre of a whale humming. The ice was groaning. A thaw was coming.

She ripped out another entry. The whale slipped away. I felt the memory go.

'Please, stop,' I begged her.

She was already on the ice. I made my way down, trying to push through the blur that the pain brought to my eyes. The Thames was melting; though still solid, puddles made grooves in the ice. There were few people still out. I stumbled a little against some wavering drunk fellow. He shoved me and I fell hard against the ice. I dragged my aching head up and saw her, running for the still-tethered balloon. One of the balloon's minders, drinking nearby, ran towards her.

I tried so hard to get to my feet, but I stumbled like a newborn foal. She reached the balloon, artfully pulled on one of its moorings, and brought it close enough for her to clamber aboard. The ice groaned again, an ungodly sound. Those left on the ice fled, even the balloon's minders. A kindly old man pulled me up and helped me ashore.

She cut one of the moorings. The others yanked free as the ice cracked. The balloon shot up and she floated free. I stumbled along the Thames as her balloon limped upwards. It was heading straight for the Tower Bridge but it wasn't rising fast enough to get over it. It looked set to ram into the walkway between the two towers.

'You won't clear it!' I cried out.

She ignored me. She was battling with the balloon, fiddling with its various contraptions. She threw off as many sandbags as she could. Each one hit the ice below, the last two shattering the thin ice by the bridge before being swallowed by the river.

I was close enough to see the look on her face as she realised the balloon was too low to clear it. The balloon's ropes rammed against the walkway, throwing the basket against the south bank tower. She screamed as it hit the stone hard, shattering half the basket to pieces. As the basket swung around, showering its broken shards on the bridge below, she grabbed onto the balloon's ropes that were now ensnared in the walkway. She tried to scramble up.

By the time I got to the Tower's entrance, she was clinging onto the walkway itself. Remarkably, she still had the *History*. If she fell, it fell too. That would be the end of it, millennia of mischief gone, swamped in the Thames.

One of the bridge's hydraulic engine workers was already making his way up the Tower. I shoved him aside and ran up the inner stairwell. I reached the top quickly. The walkway was completely enclosed. She was caught on its edge, unable to get inside. I smashed one of the windows and climbed halfway out. She crouched there on a sliver of an edge, curled up amongst the ropes and the torn remains of her stolen balloon. As our eyes met, the basket snapped completely off and tumbled down, dashing against the ice below. She stood slowly as I gestured towards her. I offered my hand.

'Please,' I begged.

Tears ran down her face. 'What is it?'

I didn't know what she could possibly mean.

'The book,' she cried. 'Its pages are blank. It didn't burn ... I saw it, all those years ago. It wouldn't burn. But now ... it bleeds memories.'

'That's the book's histories. It works by some magic to record our deeds.'

'What deeds? What is it?'

She was frantic. She kept glancing between me and the ice below.

'It's a magical book, a special thing that gives you marvellous powers,' I said, my voice pleading.

She shook her head. No, no, no, she muttered. The workers on the bridge were at my heels. I yelled at them to back off and then ventured out further onto the ledge.

'It's not working how it should,' I tried to tell her.

'I've been hunting it all this time. Why won't it reveal itself to me?'

'It will in time, I promise.'

'All I see is suffering. Ghosts on fire, tormented forests, the shattered bones of stolen boys. I see you, young, being set on by dogs.'

'That was before the *History*. Something's wrong. It's not showing you the triumphs. I froze the Thames. Did it show you? Or thawing sparrows, bringing them back to life. Think of the majesty in that.'

She nodded, convinced a little perhaps. 'I saw the sparrow. I did the same ... when you froze on the ice.'

'You did, you saved me,' I said. 'Thank you.'

'But there's madness in it.'

'Yes,' I agreed. 'But magic too.'

She wavered. 'Is magic enough?'

'Oh, yes,' I said, and stretched my hand out to her.

She glanced down at the ice. I could see the horrible thoughts that swirled in her mind.

'Please, don't,' I begged. 'We can repair it, you and I. I don't know how you came to hunt it. No one outside those who've owned the book were privy to any of it. It must've wanted you to find it. If you fall, if it falls, we'll lose it. The mischief and its record will be destroyed. I beg you, take my hand.'

Her words were a whisper. They barely carried over the wind. 'Maybe that's why it came to me.'

She looked back at me. I saw how very weary she was.

'Maybe,' she said, 'my great act of mischief is in its destruction.'

She let go. Held the *History* and fell. Our eyes locked and I saw it. The *History* revealed itself. Visions flashed over those blue eyes. She lived one hundred and ninety-nine lives in two seconds, saw what she had been hunting, the magic I promised.

In that moment, she was A. Mischief the Two-Hundredth.

Then she hit the ice hard, shattering it. The river swallowed her. A hundred sparks burst in my mind. My muscles seized in the grips of a fit. I tried to hold onto the memories, but they slipped away. I couldn't for the life of me tell you what they were.

I woke surrounded by the grubby faces of the bridge's engine workers. One man was kneeling beside me.

'You right, fella,' he said softly.

Something was in my mouth. I spat it out. A man's leather glove? The man beside me offered, 'My wife fits like you. Saving your teeth, sir.'

They helped me down, realising I could barely walk. There were no cabs about, so the gent who'd seen to it that I not gnash my teeth offered to walk me home. He gave kind assurances – 'you're doing alright, getting better now, feet comin' back' – as we made our way towards Fenchurch. He was an older man, shorter than me, but he battled on. When I slipped in a puddle and went down, he pulled me back up and said, 'Horrible blight, isn't it? You poor fella.' I was reminded of Yingtai's encouragements when she fed Hu in the forty-ninth history.

The ice of the Thames groaned at our backs. I thought of Balcha, retching along with the creaking of the ship's bow … I realised then that I remembered. Just a few of them. But they were there. I smiled. The workman said, 'Good lad, take strength.'

How to tell Will that his fiancée was dead?

I didn't need to. She was there when I returned. She even helped me to bed. I was surely going mad. Perhaps the whole thing had been a delusion: the *History*, its magic, my thief, everything. Perhaps my entire life had been a fiction. I'd written my own story to escape in, a good book to banish the memories of being chased, my family home burnt down, my parents screaming inside, as the hounds hunted me and tore my flesh and youth from me.

Seeing my terror, she touched my face lightly. 'I'm not her, Mr Barrie.'

A memory. Something new. Her. The forbidden page with the name smudged out. It was her, just a girl, and her sister. Lou and Chloe, caught in the siege of Paris. Balloons and a book that wouldn't burn. She broke the rules. So the book broke her.

I settled into bed. Will sat by my side. The workman's tale of my violent fit left him horrified. He stroked my hair until I fell asleep, said a thousand times he was sorry.

At night, I dreamed of my thief. Again, in the Reading Room. It was still flooded. Books floated around us. Sparrows darted through the water, chasing one another. She smiled at me and said, 'Isn't it cold?' I agreed that it was. I said I was sorry this was how she died.

*Postscript – Chloe McKenna, 1956*

When Lou died, the whispers from the book called me.

I hired a few boatmen and followed the sounds downstream until I found her. She was still holding the waterlogged book when we pulled her broken body out of the Thames. I thought of burying her with it. It seemed right that it would follow her to the grave. But at the last moment, I took it.

The *History* followed me all the way to the colonies, to the most isolated city in Australia. I kept it on the shelf, never really thinking about it. It was torn, wrinkled from water damage, and the leather binding was crumbling. Then, as a woman unmercifully old, a young man came along, noticed it sitting there on the shelf, and said he could hear music.

## Jessie

After Archie's history, there's supposed to be another. The contents page and Transcription Note said there was one more, from Henry, the transcriber himself.

*But it's not here.*

Someone ripped it out of the book.

'Whoever ripped it out didn't do it very cleanly,' Kay says, showing me the strips of torn paper attached at the bottom of the book.

I grab the *History* and flip through them. There's still something here.

I run to my room, grab some paper and a pen, and run back. I can just make out a few words. I start to write them out.

# A. Mischief the Two-Hundred and First

### Perth, Australia 1956–1966

but it sang to me
melody was in

prohibited by
was allowed whi

not mix with
how they raised m

love libraries but
so I have to go wi

quadroon. I
might as well be

should be sad
piano and violin

music came from
walked past the hous

dreamt of that same

hummed it, tried to pla

Weeks and we
old and clever and

'You know, I
out of tune and

library was menac
won't let me so I

I was supposed
every time I visit

tried to help
never mentioned th

just died. Like
she was old but sh

magic. I could
the keys played

as if possessed
surrounded by books

wrote themselv
time signatures mea

each history had
violin string snap

Pan once said I

broke into the con

orchestra. It was
the cellos and the

conductor of some
a mischief never

realised I would
nowhere to call

talent doesn't get
worry, it's okay.'

## Jessie

I don't know how to feel. The *History*'s over. Most of it
destroyed, and the last one ripped out. I thought there would be
at least one more left. Now it's just … over.

So where is the real one? The one that fell in the Thames. The
one Chloe fished out.

On the way to school on Monday, we walk past Mrs Moran
on her veranda, drinking tea with Cornelius. She waves and
calls out, 'Morning, dears!'

I want to scream at her, WHY DON'T YOU REMEMBER?

Or maybe she does. The vacuuming at night. The dead
husband. Maybe it's all a ruse.

Theodore's away for another week. Word about his mum gets
around school and some kids cry. I don't feel angry at them
as I did before. I try to distract myself. I search for books on
the British Museum and the frost fairs, but don't find much.
Wikipedia says the Thames hasn't frozen since 1814. Something
to do with London Bridge. But Archie freezes the Thames in
1895, so Wikipedia is wrong again. You can't trust everything
you read on the internet, that's what Mrs Harper says.

I look into Lou and Chloe again too, wondering how they
hunted down the *History* after it escaped the Paris siege. I feel
silly that I didn't notice that Lou's history was A. Mischief the
Two-Hundredth, while Bezawit and Archie were A. Mischief

the One-Hundred and Ninety-Eighth and One-Hundred and Ninety-Ninth. I wonder what other things I've missed.

When Theodore returns, he comes in with a late pass after the bell goes. He gives it to Miss Sparrow and sits down at his desk. Everyone looks at him. He starts crying straight away. Mrs Armstrong takes him outside for a walk.

At recess, kids ask if he wants to play with them. Kids who teased him weeks ago come up and say, 'Hey, Theodore, wanna play footy?', 'Hey, Theodore, I like your bag', 'Hey, Theodore, do you want my lamington? It's really nice.' Theodore eats the soggy lamington and cries. There are kids who seem frightened of him too. They don't say or do anything.

I don't know how to make Theodore stop crying. After lunch, when he cries again, this popular Year 6 boy holds his hand and walks with him around the oval.

All I say to him is, 'You okay?'

He shakes his head.

'You wanna come over later? Broom and Stephanie can come.'

He shakes his head. He goes home early.

The next day, Theodore comes late again, and the day after that. When he starts coming early again, like he used to, he sits down next to me. He doesn't have his iPod. He doesn't dance or sing.

One day, out of the blue, he says to me, 'I'm a different thing now.'

I remember what I said when he asked what it feels like when your mum dies, about becoming another thing, a sad, angry, lonely thing.

'I know,' I say. 'But I still like you.'

He smiles. I feel warm. This is what Archie must've felt when the sparrows came back to life. I need to remind Theodore that even if he's a different thing, he's still Theodore.

I plan my mischief. I ask Kay to help. When I tell her the idea, she says it sounds great.

'You and me, we're doing mischief together!' she says.

'No, just me. But I need you to take me to the shops.'

'Okay. But I'm still helping.'

'Yep.'

'I'm A. Mischief too.'

She's trying to annoy me on purpose.

'You're only A. Mischief like Archie, keeping the book for yourself!' I say.

She shrugs. 'I'm fine with that.'

We buy a cheap set of earphones that has a long cord. I watch YouTube all weekend in preparation.

On Monday, Theodore comes late, so I can't do my mischief. On Tuesday, he's early, and there's no one else around. He sits in the corner of the courtyard, next to the green door that's always locked. I go over and smile at him. He smiles weakly back for a second, then looks away.

'Stand up,' I tell him. I try to say it nicely.

He stands. I take out Kay's iPod and put one earphone bud in my ear and one in his. I turn the iPod on. Theodore looks confused. It's playing his favourite song, the POW POW POW one.

I bob along. I hate dancing but I try to do Theodore's moves. I take his hands and swing his arms about. It's only when I start singing the Korean rap part that he smiles. He tries not to, I can tell. But he can't stifle his smirk at how wrong I'm getting it all.

'Sing the Korean bits!' I try.

Limply he sings.

I sing the English echo back to him, 'We ain't playin', no!'

His smile gets bigger. He sings the Korean part a little louder.

I sing my part loud and stupid and over the top. 'We ain't playin', *no!*'

He smiles a proper Theodore grin now. We do the 'Ready! Set! *POW POW POW*!' move together. When we get to a part that means 'Friends, put your hands up!', I swing his arms up and he laughs. More kids arrive and a teacher walks past. No one says anything.

Then we get to the part where someone sings in English, 'We can never die!'

Theodore stops smiling. His eyes fill with tears. I try to sing the Korean bits really badly to make him laugh, but the 'never die' part repeats. He bursts into tears and pulls the earphones out.

I feel terrible. 'I'm sorry.'

He just cries.

When Kay picks me up, I return her iPod and tell her I'm a terrible mischief. But the next day, Theodore comes early and sits with me on the bench outside the office. He smiles and shows me his iPod. We listen together. He wiggles his shoulders a bit. I sing with him. He stops it before the 'never die' bit. The next day, we finish the whole song.

In the mornings, sometimes, Mrs Lornazak puts on music in the undercover area before school starts. Usually the Year 6s practise their graduation dances. I give her Theodore's iPod and ask her to put on our song instead of her (stupid) music.

'Sure,' she says. 'But you have to start participating in dance classes. As of next Wednesday, no more sitting on the bench.'

I stare at her, annoyed. She smiles. I look back at Theodore. I agree.

Theodore and I dance around the undercover area to the song. Some little kids from pre-primary join us.

He's still sad. I don't know if the mischief really helped. But he's talking more now. He tells me about the new space documentary Stephanie bought him and asks if I know the life cycle of the butterfly. He says how sad he is that his grandparents have gone home because he has no one else to speak to in Korean ('Dad's almost as bad as you'). He asks me what I do when Kay cries.

I feel guilty. 'Nothing. She cries in her room.'

'Dad cries in his room too. When I went in to hug him yesterday, he pretended everything was okay.'

I don't know what to tell him but we keep having little chats. Theodore still cries a lot, and I miss Mum and Dad every time. I think this is how it's going to be for a while. But that's okay.

## *Jessie*

Kay's been called into work on Sunday again. I have to go too
because she doesn't want to bother Mr Park or Mrs Moran.

'Oh, please, Mrs Moran won't mind!' I say.

I want to search for the *History*.

'I'm sure she wouldn't but I bet her grumpy daughter would,'
Kay says. 'So you're stuck with me!'

I sigh. We get on the train and head into Perth.

Neil's on the first-floor desk again. Kay still doesn't trust
me in the stacks so I sit with him behind the reference desk.
Whenever people come up, they glance at me. One lady says
I'm a pretty little thing. I take off my cat ears beanie to show her
my scar.

I have theories about the last history, the one ripped from
the book. I googled the word 'quadroon'. It's a '*noun* – dated,
offensive' which means 'a person who is one-quarter black by
descent'. I'm guessing the transcriber Henry is one-quarter
black, or maybe someone he knows is. Somehow, Henry got
the *History* to reveal the surviving stories after it was mostly
destroyed. The Transcription Note at the beginning makes me
think he and Chloe worked together. But in the words from
the ripped bits of paper, there are mentions of pianos, violins
and orchestras. Maybe his mischief had something to do with
music. Maybe translating the *History* involved songs.

But where is the *History*, the real one?

'Concentrating awfully hard there,' Neil says to me.

'Just thinking,' I say.

'Looks like some frowny thinking.'

A woman approaches the desk, holding multicoloured request slips. Neil asks for her 'researcher's card' and takes the slips.

'Thank you, Dr Horne, these requests will be delivered to the Reading Room,' Neil says. 'Our retrieval team should have your items in the next half-hour.'

'Thank you,' she says.

She makes her way up the stairs. Kay will collect the slips at 9:30 am, nineteen minutes from now.

'Why are there three slips?' I ask, peeking at the request.

'They're for rare items. One slip goes in the shelf, where the item is normally kept, the other is left with the item, and the final one is given to the staff up on Battye so they can find the item for the researcher.'

'Battye's the third floor, yeah?'

'Yep. WA collection. We have a room up there where researchers can look at old and special things.'

'Like what?'

'Well,' Neil says. 'This researcher has requested two bibles published in 1794 and 1843.'

'Kay gets these, too?'

'Yep, that's one of the jobs of the Stock and Stack team. They fetch everything.'

*Just like Archie.*

I think about the *History*. 'Do you have really old books here?'

'Absolutely!' he says. 'We have surveys from the first fleet, we have maps, newspapers, books made entirely of vellum – that's calfskin, you know!'

I scowl at him. 'I know what vellum is.'

He laughs. 'Of course you do!'

I'm annoyed he finds me so funny. 'Where are the old books?'

'Mainly in the rare book rooms.'

I remember the dark locked room from when I snuck into the stacks. It needed an ID card to get in. I glance at the ID around Neil's neck.

'Are there many rare book rooms?'

'On every floor!'

*The History of Mischief* could be in one of those rooms. The *History* always liked librarians, and didn't the ripped-out history mention a library?

A man comes to the desk and asks for help with the microfiche, which are mini film reels that show newspapers instead of movies. Neil gets up, points at me and says, 'Stay put, missy!'

I watch Neil for a while. It looks like the microfiche machine isn't working. He has his back to me. I glance at his computer.

I hop over to his chair and go to the library catalogue. I don't know what to search so I just type in 'mischief'. Roald Dahl, some adult novels, and some kids' books with hamsters. I type, 'the history of mischief'. A book about student pranks comes up. I'm not surprised. The *History* would hide better than that.

Neil returns. I hop off his chair. He raises his eyebrow but says nothing.

I look at the time. Twelve minutes till Kay comes.

'Neil?'

'Yep?'

'That researcher will have to wait for ages.'

Neil glances at the clock. 'Kay will be here in ten minutes.'

'We should help her.'

He smiles, glancing at his computer. 'So, what's *The History of Mischief* then?'

I left my search open.

'None of your business!'

He shrugs but smiles. 'Okay.'

He goes back to his work. Closes my search. Checks his email. Nine minutes till Kay comes.

'Sorry,' I say.

He shrugs, as if it was nothing. 'Is it old?'

'What?'

'*The History of Mischief.*'

I think for a moment. I don't want anyone else to find it. 'It's a secret.'

Neil nods. 'Okay.'

Lunchtime comes. Kay buys us cheese and salad sandwiches from the café. I ask if she can look in the rare book rooms for the real *History*.

'No,' she says.

'Please?'

'No, it's impossible. There's no listing on the catalogue and you can't search every book in the stacks. It would take years, even if you just went through the rare book rooms.'

'You looked it up then?'

'Shut up and eat your sandwich.'

Neil's on the Battye desk after lunch. A grumpy librarian complained that I was behind the desk and it was 'unprofessional', so he can't look after me anymore.

'Can I trust you to be in the workroom and NOT go into the stacks?' Kay asks.

'If you buy me a muffin.'

She gives me $4.50 and I buy a raspberry and white chocolate muffin. She's retrieving items on Battye too, she says, but she'll check on me at random intervals.

I count to thirty. *Twenty-eight, twenty-nine, thirty.*

I leave the workroom. Kay only said I wasn't allowed in the stacks.

I take the stairs up to Battye, practising all the excuses in my head if she catches me. I go up to the desk and find Neil. He smiles at me.

'You're going to get me in trouble,' he says.

'Will you help me find *The History of Mischief*?'

He grins. 'Sure.'

Neil's clever. He tells me you can't go into the rare book rooms without a reason. The ID reader logs who you are and when you went in there. Then you have to write down what you were getting and at what time in a diary, so the bosses can check if you're doing the right thing. So he waits. He tells the other librarian on Battye that he has a tummy ache and has to go to the toilet a lot. He checks all the floors, gets any rare book requests. Then he gets me.

The first rare book room we investigate is the one I saw when I snuck into the stacks last time. It's very cold. He turns the light on and writes down the request details in the diary. He gets the requested book and rips off the yellow part of the slip, leaving it on the shelf where the book lived.

Most of the books are in green boxes. On the spine of the box, it says the title and the year, all in gold letters. Neil says they are archival boxes.

I gaze at the shelves. It isn't what I imagined. Even with the light on, it's still dark. The books are hidden away in their special boxes, neatly filed in order on the shelves. I thought it would be more, well, like the libraries in the movies with leather books and spider webs.

'The *History* would probably be hiding in a box that had a different name,' I tell him.

'Hmm, well, we can't check every box. Have a quick look and see if anything jumps out at you. If it's really a history of mischief, I bet it would leave clues.'

I look on the shelves. I think of the symbol on the *History*'s title page. Nothing.

'This is mainly science and a bit of history,' he says. 'I've got another request for a bible. That'll be in another room. There are much older books in there. Shall we check?'

The second rare book room is on the other side of the first floor.

'It's a mess,' Neil says as he taps his ID on the card reader. 'Things are being rearranged at the moment.'

This is more like I imagined. The smell of leather and off honey is strong here. The books are not in boxes. They're just sitting on the shelves, some in piles. Neil finds the requested book, leaves the yellow slip and notes down what he's taking in the diary.

'One day,' Neil says, 'the requests will be digitised.'

He sounds sad about it. Then he shows me the requested book. It's in a foreign language, but the letters look English.

'Latin,' he explains.

I look around, searching for the symbol of the *History*. I pick up many books, open them carefully. I look for ones that are water-damaged. When I open them, I find pictures of angels and swirly letters. Neil shows me one where the words are in black and red ink but there are beautiful coloured flowers and fancy borders. The letters at the start of paragraphs are painted in gold.

But still, no *History*. Neil returns me to the workroom and takes the requests up to the third floor. Kay drops by six minutes later.

'You doing okay?'

I nod. I pick at the muffin as I wait for Neil.

He comes twelve minutes later with more multicoloured slips. 'Private archives! We need to enter via Battye. It'll be hard to sneak around Kay, so I asked Lily to get her to help find some scores in the music stack.'

'You didn't tell Lily about the *History*, did you?'

'No, just said the requests were … well, I told her they might make Kay sad, and asked if she could distract her and let me do them.'

'Oh,' I say.

Maybe he said the requests were about death or car accidents. As we walk up to Battye, a librarian walks by and smiles at me. I wonder if everyone knows who I am, if they all know what happened. Maybe that's why Neil's helping me.

Once we get to Battye, Neil leads me to another set of stairs. We go up, towards another stack. Neil uses his ID card. For a moment, I think I see Kay's picture. He puts the ID back in his pocket quickly so I don't get a chance to check.

This stack is different. There are big books covered in paper that looks like marble cake, and cardboard boxes that have 'PRIVATE PROPERTY OF' such and such on them. Neil calls me over to another door, one that has a glass window. I peer inside. It's completely dark.

'Only a few people in the whole library are allowed in this room,' he says. 'You can't request anything in here. We just keep things here to protect them.'

'Like what?'

'Very old things. Things from when white people first came to Australia. Single books that are the only remaining copy on earth.'

The *History* has to be here.

'Can we go in?'

'We can't. My ID won't let me.'

'Can we try?'

'If I do, it'll log that I tried and I'll get in trouble.'

I rest my forehead on the glass. Feel how cold it is. I listen for the whispers Lou heard. All I hear is the air-con humming.

Neil says something about getting the requests. He moves around the archives, tearing yellow slips and leaving them on shelves. He shows me a folder of letters. One of them is for a man who was hung in colonial times. It's decorated with yellow flowers. The paper is so white, like new, but the ink looks old.

'This is cool, hey?'

I shrug. 'We'll never find the *History*, will we?'

Neil closes the folder carefully. 'Maybe it doesn't want to be found.'

I think of Lou and Chloe. 'Maybe.'

'To be honest, I didn't think we'd find it,' Neil says. 'It was worth looking, for sure, but I thought you'd enjoy seeing the secret parts of the library more than anything.'

I look back into the dark nothingness of the rare book room.

'Plus, librarians here are pretty big sticklers. If *The History of Mischief* was here, it'd be on the catalogue. I bet your book is somewhere else, waiting for you.'

'Can I still look?'

'Maybe. Kay's going to get mighty suspicious with me getting her requests though. Let's give these ones to the researchers and go back to the first floor, hey?'

We give the letters to the librarian in the researchers' room. Then Neil takes me back to the workroom. Kay returns and tells me we'll go in the next hour. I try to listen for whispers.

When home time comes, she takes me down to the discard bookshop.

Neil walks past and spots us. He beckons Kay over. Kay tells me to wait in the bookshop. I do, but they're closing. As I come out, I see Neil and Kay swapping IDs. I was right! Neil *did* have her card.

'Thanks for today,' she says to him.

'No worries,' he says. Then he spots me. He looks guilty.

On the train, I tell Kay I'm angry she made Neil play with me like I'm a little kid.

'I did no such thing,' she says. 'I caught him dropping you off at the workroom after he'd taken my requests. He convinced me to let him take you around the stacks looking for the *History*. We swapped IDs so it wouldn't look bad that he was doing my requests.'

I say nothing.

'Did you find anything?'

'No.'

'Maybe you should have researched the last histories.'

We sit in silence for another two stops. I imagine Neil getting busted by Kay. I remember all the pretty old books.

'I didn't say thank you to Neil.'

'That's okay. He knows.'

We arrive at Guildford. We go to Alfred's for dinner and sit by the fire outside, eating burgers and chips. It rains, but it's only a few drops so the fire still burns. We go home smelling of smoke.

# Jessie

The weather's changing. It's spring, Miss Sparrow says.
According to the Noongar people, it's *djilba*, which is when
it's cold but with less rain, and sometimes there are warm
days. Soon it will be *kambarang*, which is when it gets hotter
for longer. Mrs Armstrong taught me that. She says Noongars
have six seasons, while white people only have four. I think the
Noongar seasons make more sense.

Weeks go by. We start getting more warm days than cold. I
ask Mrs Armstrong if it's *kambarang* yet and she says no, it will
be *kambarang* when I have to stop wearing my cat ears beanie.
I'm not looking forward to that. Some days, around lunch, I
have to take my beanie off because it gets hot and itchy. Though
my hair's getting longer, people still stare.

I go over to Theodore's house every Wednesday now.
Stephanie makes us afternoon tea and we watch documentaries.
He still cries a lot. I do too sometimes. Broom tries to lick our
faces when we cry, which is gross but nice.

One day, we're watching a documentary about birds.
Something comes on about cranes.

'They don't look anything like the paper ones,' I say.

Theodore gets teary. 'I never made a thousand.'

'You almost did.'

'Do you think Mum died because I didn't finish making
them?'

'No.'

'But … maybe I could have wished …?'

'Wishes don't work.'

He nods but says, 'Sometimes I think it's my fault.'

'No. Never.'

'I hate them,' he says. I see him looking at a crane sitting on a bookshelf next to a photo of his mum.

'Do you still have them?'

He nods. 'Some.'

I think of Kay.

'We can burn them.'

And we do. There aren't many cranes left, only a few handfuls, but we go around the house and collect them all. We do it in the kitchen sink when Stephanie's hanging out the washing. We use Mr Park's lighter, the bright red one. Theodore shows me how to push down on the little wheel to make the flame come out. It's called a sparkwheel, he says.

When Stephanie comes back inside, she finds us standing on tiptoes over a sink full of fire. She pulls us away, turns the tap on, and floods the paper. All the cranes are destroyed. The sink is ringed with black marks. Stephanie screams at us. When Mr Park comes home, he just blinks at her when she tells him what we did.

Stephanie tells Kay. I get in trouble, but Theodore seems happy, so I'm happy too.

I miss the *History*. Kay lets me keep it now. I look at it every day, especially the bits of paper left over from the final history. I have so many ideas about who Henry was. I'm sure he translated the *History* using music. I try to imagine what each history would sound like.

Kay orders books on frost fairs and the British Museum. She says maybe the secret to the *History*'s whereabouts can be found in researching Archie's history. I just look at the pictures.

One night, when I can't sleep, I go to the study and look out the window. Mrs Moran is sitting on the veranda with Cornelius on the chair beside her. She's already done her vacuuming. Her driveway looks very neat.

I remember the card from her husband signed A. Mischief.

I feel brave.

I sneak out the back door, go around the side of the house and cross the road.

Mrs Moran smiles when she spots me.

'Hello dear,' she says.

'Hello Mrs Moran. Hello Cornelius.'

Cornelius jumps off the chair so I can sit down.

'Bessie, isn't it?'

'Jessie, Mrs Moran.'

'I have a terrible memory, dear. I'll forget everything soon.'

'I'm sorry.'

Cornelius hops up onto her lap. She strokes him but looks out at the street.

'Mrs Moran, do you remember *The History of Mischief*?'

'Is it a book, dear?'

'Yes.'

'Never read it. Is it any good?'

I feel disappointed. Mrs Moran goes on.

'I was a bit of a mischief-maker when I was your age. Used to get up to all kinds of trouble with my sister. You've got a sister, don't you?'

'Yes.'

'She's like a mum, isn't she? Bossy thing. Kate?'

'Kay.'

'Of course. I have a terrible memory, dear. I'll forget everything soon.'

I think again of the card. I don't know how to ask her about it.

'Was your husband a mischief-maker too?'

'Oh, yes,' she says. 'Still is.'

I know her husband's dead. How would it feel, never remembering that Mum and Dad had died? I wonder if it'd be better not to know, just to be waiting all the time.

'He'll be back soon,' she says, looking towards the main road.

I want to ask her everything. About the card. If Mr Moran ever had a book. If he was magic. If he knew anyone called Henry Byron or Chloe McKenna. But I don't.

Instead, I ask, 'Where would Mr Moran hide a book if he wanted to be mischievous?'

She laughs. 'Where else, dear? With other books!'

I go back home and creep into the study. When we first moved to Grandma's old house, I used to look at the books at night. They were so dusty, they made me sneeze. I was frightened about waking Kay, so I never took them off the shelf. Now, I sit in the corner where we lifted the carpet. I start from the first book on the bottom shelf. It's something about a squirrel and has Dad's name inside the front cover. I put it back, pick up the next one. As I go, I check behind the books too, remembering how Archie hid the *History* in the British Museum.

The sun is coming up when I finally find something. There's a section of old science books on the fourth shelf from the floor. Two books must have fallen, as they're hiding behind the others. One is something about chemistry. The other, its spine says:

FROSTIANA G. DAVIS

I open it. Its title page is exactly how it was in the *History*. Its pages are crinkled at the back, like it got wet, but otherwise it's perfect. I find Lapland Lamb, printing presses, the Tabitha Thaw note, and skating. As I flip through it, a photo falls out. It's of three young men standing outside a pub. Two of them are in long black robes with those flat hats. The other is wearing a waistcoat with mismatched buttons. They all grin, holding drinks up to whoever is taking the photo.

'Couldn't sleep, hey?'

Kay's found me.

'Look, it's *Frostiana*! It's been here this whole time,' I say. 'And there's a photo. Maybe it's Archie and Will.'

She takes the photo and turns it over. There's writing on the back.

*Robert, Elliot & George*
*Graduation 1961*

'This must be Grandad,' she says. 'His name was Robert.'

'Really?' I never knew Grandad.

Kay looks at the bookshelf. 'What else is hidden here?'

We go through the books together. Kay forgets the time. I don't tell her when it goes 8:50, and then 9, and then 10. We find books on Greek philosophy and Chinese fairytales. We find a book in French on the *Bibliothèque d'Alexandrie*, and history books on Alexander the Great, the Paris siege, and Ethiopia. Postcards of Krakow and of French balloonists are used as bookmarks in books on World War II. We find *The Collected Works of Shakespeare* full of doodles of bears. Some of the bears have speech bubbles saying things like, *'Back to work, Robert!' 'Careful now!'* and *'Eat your vegetables, laddie!'*.

Kay and I lie on the carpet. She flips through the Shakespeare book, looking for the talking bears.

'Why didn't we think to look here?' she asks.

'Dunno.'

'I guess we didn't think they'd be here, did we? Just … here.'

'We still didn't find the real *History* though.'

Kay finds a drawing of two bears curled up together on the last page of *Romeo and Juliet*. *'I love you,'* one of the bears says.

Kay puts an arm around me. 'Let's go see Grandma this weekend.'

# *Jessie*

It's a sunny Saturday when we make the trip to Grandma's nursing home. We take the *History* in my backpack.

I read *Frostiana* on the train. I like it so much. I like to touch the pages and imagine Archie and Will reading it by the fire.

A man on the train says to me, 'You must be one clever little lady. You don't see kids reading books these days.'

'You mustn't know many kids,' I reply.

Kay tells me off for being rude.

When we get to the nursing home, I feel happy. Lulu's here and she says we match, showing me her watch with cat ears on it. We make our way down to Grandma but then someone comes out of a room and bangs into us. A tray of food goes everywhere.

'Oh, sorry!' Kay says.

I see him before Kay – it's David, the weird prac student. As they both fumble with the tray, David realises who he's run into. He gasps. Kay looks up and frowns. David looks frightened. Kay's face goes from confusion to shock to anger.

'I know you,' she says. Her voice shakes.

David takes a few steps back.

'I know you,' she says again.

'I don't think so,' David says, his voice a squeak.

'You broke into my house.'

David shakes his head.

'You broke into my house!' Kay shouts. People come out of their rooms, including Grandma. Kay points at him. 'You broke into my house!'

'Calm down, dear,' Grandma says, coming up to us.

'Grandma, he broke into our house! Someone call the police!'

David looks around frantically. I grab his arm so he doesn't get away.

'You tried to rob us!' I yell at him.

David pulls his arm free. 'I didn't –'

Lulu's here now. 'What's going on?'

'This is the man who broke into my house!' Kay yells, pointing at David again.

'I asked him to do it,' Grandma says.

Everyone goes silent.

'I gave him the key. I just … can we go into my room please, dears?'

Kay makes David come 'to keep an eye on him'. Lulu follows, like she's keeping an eye on all of us.

'Why would you do that, Grandma?' Kay asks. Her voice shakes like she's trying not to yell or cry.

Grandma sits down in her favourite chair. She sighs. 'When you moved into the house, I was shocked. Your father said he sold it years ago. When I realised he'd lied, all I could think was that he'd found it, and found more, and I couldn't have you find it too.'

'Find what?'

Grandma ignores her. 'I wasn't ready. Not after my boy had just died.'

'Find *what*, Grandma?'

'The *History*.' She deflates as she says it. 'I didn't think you'd be home so early. I didn't think you'd even notice David had been there.'

Kay looks like she might snap. 'Why is this book so important?'

Grandma's eyes are red. Tears flow. 'Because it's the truth.'

*The truth.*

I knew it.

'What do you *mean*?' Kay asks angrily.

Grandma goes to her bookshelf and takes out an old book without any markings. Could it be? The real *History*! Grandma opens it.

I see words. It isn't blank. No signatures. Just a book. No! Where is the *History*?

Then I notice why Grandma picked this book. Inside, like a fat bookmark, is an envelope. She takes it out and hands it to Kay.

'I wrote this to your father last year. I thought I wasn't ... well, I thought I should write it down before I died. He kept asking questions. Elliot said something to him.'

'Who's Elliot? What are you talking about?' Kay yells. 'Grandma, I've been so frightened every time I come home! I put bars on all the windows! I changed all the locks! How could you do that to me? Why couldn't you just tell me, whatever it was?'

'Because I was ashamed,' she says. 'I made a whole life out of lies. I didn't want to be around when they were found.'

Kay cries. I get teary because everyone's crying now. I feel so confused.

'Dear, I'm so sorry.'

'I don't understand any of this.'

'The letter was for your dad. But it'll explain.'

'I'm sick of reading things!' Kay snaps, and throws the letter on the ground. 'I want to know why you sent someone to steal a stupid handwritten book! *You* tell me!'

Grandma nods and then glances at me. 'Jessie, dear, could

you go out? Just for a moment.'

'No, I want to know about the *History*!' I yell. I throw my bag on the floor.

'I'll explain later. Just go out,' Kay says.

Grandma smiles weakly and nods.

'Come on, honey,' Lulu says. 'David, front office, and stay there.'

Stupid adults. I knew they wouldn't let me stay. I dropped my bag on the letter on purpose. I get it when I pick up my bag.

I run to the disabled toilet and lock the door. Lulu asks me to come out but I tell her I need to go to the toilet. She stays outside for a while, talking to me. I keep telling her I'm fine until eventually, I hear her ask a nurse to keep an eye on the door. She tells me she'll be back. She's going to have a chat with David.

The envelope has the word *Harry* on it. The handwriting looks familiar.

## The Letter

Harry, my darling boy,

For years now, you've been asking about the *History*. Long ago, I decided that the truth should die with me. But recently, I've come to realise that would be yet another theft. I feel responsible to tell the truth behind the histories I stole from other people. I feel responsible to you.

So I have written you another history, a *History of The History of Mischief*.

I hope you see that my love for you was the only thing I never lied about.

Please forgive me.

Your Mum,

Elizabeth Stewart

# The History

I was born at a lighthouse in 1950. My father was a lighthouse keeper. He named me Louise, Lou for short. My sister followed two years later. Chloe. Except for the eyes – mine blue, hers brown – and my freckles, we were identical. No one believed we weren't twins.

The closest town, Augusta, was ten kilometres away. In my early years we rarely visited. My town, therefore, consisted of the lighthouse and the three cottages that housed the keepers and their families. Alongside us was a kindly middle-aged couple named Cliff and Molly, and an angry widower and his son. For many years, I thought the son's name was 'boy', for his father only ever addressed him as such. I was ten, and he eleven, when I learnt he was named after his father: Alexander. He acted like the tyrant of his namesake, forever barking orders at his son in an angry mix of English and Greek.

The Leeuwin Township of Light was regulated by the demands of the lighthouse. The keepers worked four-hour shifts – four on, eight off. Meteorological readings were made every three hours, starting at 9 am. Equipment was checked and kerosene poured into jerry cans and lugged up the 176 steps to the lantern above. The metal fittings and the lantern's giant lead crystal lens were polished. Everything was cleaned.

Our nights were marked by the lantern. It filled our homes with a sudden flash of ethereal light every 7.5 seconds, so strong it pierced the curtains. If we couldn't sleep, Chloe and I would sit at the window, our backs to the lighthouse, and watch its spotlight run across the faraway cliffs covered in bush. Roly-poly hills, my father called them. We imagined all the things the light was chasing: kangaroos, possums, the ghosts of shipwrecks past. It was the heartbeat of the lighthouse, pulsing strong.

Here, stories became currency. Books were scarce, the nearest library fifty kilometres away in Margaret River. When there was work to be done, Father promised stories in exchange. He shared stories of his childhood: football, dances, scoping out caves, and hunting quokkas back when the marsupials lived in Augusta's forests.

One day, Molly gave Chloe a book on balloonists. We loved the book so much, Father bought us bubble wands from the general store in town. Together, the three of us stood at the top of the lighthouse, the crystal lens twirling above us, blowing 'balloons' into the wind. Our first attempt was thwarted; the wind just blew the soap back in our faces. The second, we went up on a day so calm that the meeting of the Southern and Indian oceans, which clashed against each other before our lighthouse, could barely be seen.

It was that day that it was first said. Alexander Senior, upon finding us on the balcony, growled, 'What you mischiefs doing up here?'

We laughed and fled down the stairs. We became mischiefs. We did mischief things. We played tricks on visitors by never being seen together, appearing far from where the last one had been, and making them think there was one girl who could just appear out of nowhere. One of them, a fellow from the meteorological department, called Chloe a 'panther' with her black hair and seemingly incredible speed. I shortened it, a nickname shared only between us. We signed secret notes to each other as 'A. Mischief' and 'Pan'.

As we got older, we took our mischief to school. We often rode to town, Alexander Junior in tow but never welcome in our conversations. If we were lucky, whoever wasn't on shift would take us in Cliff's salt-sprayed ute. When winter came, the rains made travelling on the hilly roads dangerous. We stayed at home. Letters were sent from the School Board, informing our parents of the compulsory nature of attendance. Fines were mentioned.

Soon after, Mother sent us to the lighthouse to speak to Father.

'Darlings. You're going to stay. With Aunty June. And Uncle Martin. In town,' he said through laboured breaths. He was winding the crank handle that raised the giant weights through the centre of the tower and set the lens turning.

'Just. During the rains. A few weeks. For school.'

We nodded but knew the truth: Mother's nervous episodes were increasing.

Alexander Junior was to stay. Alexander Senior cared not for fines.

Mother was a cloud that hung over those happy days. People said she had a nervous disposition, which I understood as 'gets headaches and sleeps a lot'.

Our first stay with Aunty June and Uncle Martin, who ran a butcher in Augusta, was justified as 'for school'. This was used the next few times, until eventually the pretence was dropped and 'Mummy needs rest' was given instead. From then on, we only returned home for the holidays. Though we missed our lighthouse life during term, we didn't mind so much. Uncle Martin was endlessly jovial, a giant Frenchman who found every opportunity he could to compliment me on my French name. He took us fishing on the weekends. We'd dangle our legs in the water from the precarious flying fox that hung across the bay and listen to his stories about the war.

Aunty June drove us up to Margaret River to visit the library every fortnight. There, I met Henry. I didn't think much of him. I was eight, he was eight. He had a book I wanted.

'I was looking for that. Could I have it please?'

'Sure!' he said, happily giving it to me. 'My name's Henry!'

I took the book. 'My name's Lou.'

Aunty June called me over and told me off for talking to strangers. I'd never heard the word 'stranger' before, except in books. Strangers in books were unknown and dangerous. I looked at the happy boy and wondered what made him strange.

Next week at school, our teacher came in with an arm around the strange boy.

'Class, we have a new student. This is Henry Byron. Say good morning, class.'

The class droned, 'Good morning, Henry.'

'Henry, why don't you tell the class about yourself?' the teacher said. 'Don't be shy.'

His words came out in a stream. 'My name is Henry! I come from Perth. I live with Mr and Mrs Byron. They have a dairy and they taught me how to milk cows. I love books and music. I learnt how to play the piano at Sister Kate's, which is where I used to live. I used to have a mum and dad but not anymore.'

Sweetly, the teacher said, 'Mr and Mrs Byron are your mum and dad now.'

He nodded, slowly, as if unsure. He took the empty seat at the back.

The kids at school called him names like 'abo' and 'coon'. They were said in the same teasing tone as 'wog,' which was directed at Alexander Junior in the playground. But these words were dropped into the hushed conversations of adults, something I hadn't heard before. Some women spoke loudly, as if they wanted to be heard: 'Bless the Byrons. Very charitably minded.' 'So lucky, the poor mite. Bless him.'

At first, I didn't know why Henry was different. He was cheerful and liked the same things as us. I knew what an Aborigine was, but he was lighter skinned than Alexander Junior and only a little darker than me. I didn't understand what all the fuss was about. Though the gossip about him died down, I'd been quick to learn. In the eyes of the world, I was better than him. And that was a nice feeling, to be better than someone. Especially a boy.

In 1961, everything changed. The summer was uncharacteristically hot, even at the lighthouse. Father didn't send us back up to Augusta when school started, as if he knew what was coming. A few years prior, the Forest Department banned people from backburning on public land, but hadn't kept up with their own schedule. The dried leaves, fallen branches and wasted trees collected in mounds around the living forest.

No one knew how it started. It could've been a cigarette or a bolt of lightning. Whatever it was, something ignited in the dry earth. It caught with the fragrant oil of the eucalyptus, and lit the world on fire.

We stood at the top of the lighthouse, watching the spotlight roam across an entire valley ablaze. Father had one arm around me, one around Chloe. In the bush, fire was part of life. But this was an inferno so bold it crept up on the ocean.

Chloe leaned in close. 'Daddy, will it reach us?'

'No, darling,' he said.

It seemed to span from one side of the coast to the other.

'What if it does?'

'The lighthouse will protect us. Stone doesn't burn.'

The fire tore through a hundred thousand acres and

completely flattened the nearby town of Karridale. Remarkably no one died, though many lost their homes. When we visited Aunty June and Uncle Martin, we found the Byrons and their seven cows. Their farm had been badly damaged.

Father offered to help Mr Byron clear some debris. Chloe stayed while I went with Father and Mr Byron. Henry had walked ahead, Mr Byron said. I could just make him out, sitting by a timber skeleton that had once been a shed. He sat in the ash, his back to us.

'Louise, will you go and see if Henry's alright?' Mr Byron asked. 'Fire's really torn him up.'

I nodded though I didn't want to. I approached him. 'Hey.'

Henry didn't look up. He muttered only 'hey' back. He was playing with the charred chunks of wood. He had charcoal smears up his arms.

Henry was different now. After his arrival, his enthusiasm and cheerfulness faded. He was quiet, he read alone. He had, like me, learnt his place.

He dragged charcoal along his arm, watching it blacken his skin. He rubbed it between his fingers, and then touched his face. He tenderly smeared it over his cheek and stared into the twisted dead forest that stretched out before us.

'What are you doing?' I asked.

He seemed lost somewhere else. His voice was soft when he said, 'Mum used to do this. Every morning.'

'Why?'

A tear ran through the soot on his face. 'So they wouldn't take me.'

As an eleven-year-old, I didn't really know what it meant. I knew he'd said something taboo, one of those things you just don't talk about. I ignored it.

'Sorry about the farm.'

With the fires out, Father could no longer find an excuse to keep us at the lighthouse. Mother was clear. Chloe and I were sent back up to Augusta. The Byrons moved into a friend's house between my uncle's butcher and the hall while their farm was repaired. The hall had a piano, and music soon joined the main street chorus of birds and summer crickets. Henry broke in and just played. I snuck behind the hall and sat by one of the windows. It was the first thing I ever did without Chloe.

I started taking books down to the hall, reading as Henry played. I got braver, sitting under the window closest to the piano, my back against the wall, feeling the clang of the keys vibrate through my chest. As soon as he stopped, I waited to see if he'd play something else. One, two, three, I'd count. On four, I ran back to the butcher.

Then one day, I fell asleep to something gentle. I woke to a creak, saw him climbing out the window. We stared at each other. He jumped down and ran away. He didn't play again for four days. On the fifth, I cornered him at school. I didn't even say hello, I just said, 'You play piano very well.'

He looked afraid. Said nothing.

'Please keep playing. I won't listen if you don't want me to.'

I was lying of course. I would listen, just maybe not from the window. His eyes then dropped to the book in my hand: *The Jungle Book*. They lingered a while. I remembered his eager proclamation on the first day of school: 'I love books and music.'

His eyes jumped back to my face. 'Please don't tell on me.'

It seemed a silly thing to say. Everyone knew it was him. Had no one told him how much they enjoyed his music, how they left their windows open to hear him?

'Promise,' I said.

That afternoon, I heard him playing. I went to the hall, left my book there for him. At school, I caught his eye. He smiled sheepishly. *The Jungle Book* found its way back to me, by a tree behind the butcher, three days later.

We became friends through the secret exchange of books. For five years, we barely spoke to one another. Just books, left on top of a bin near the butcher, on fence posts at the rebuilt farm, snuck into bags at lunchtime. In '64, when the Blackwood River flooded, library books I left for him were taken away by the waters. When they receded, he left a small envelope of money with a note: 'Sorry, from The Blackwood.' I left a book with a message inside: 'All is forgiven, from A. Mischief.' Chloe would've been so upset if she knew: mischief was our secret. I felt a little guilty, but Henry, I knew, wouldn't tell.

Though a small library opened up in Augusta, we both began to frequent the 'big library' in Margaret River once we started high school. I selected things I thought he might like, and he for me. High school was much larger than primary school, bringing together kids from all over the region. Buses roamed the highways. I was in a separate class to Henry, so my only time with him was on the bus, stealing glances between stops.

It was 1965. We were fifteen. Our very occasional conversations were monitored. Aunty June said it would be best if I made friends with someone else.

Then Chloe got sick. She was sent back to the lighthouse to recover and spent weeks in bed. Away from my fellow mischief, I searched for another.

I snuck up on Henry on the bus.

'Have you ever heard the ground whistle?'

He glanced nervously at our classmates. 'No.'

'I can show you.'

'No, thank you,' he said, and returned to the book I'd left in his bag the day before.

But then, as we got off the bus, he let his words drop beside me as he walked past. 'Yes please.'

That afternoon, I told Aunty June I was going to the library. Then I made my way to the Byrons' farm. Henry was waiting by the milking shed. He smiled at me. I smiled back. We set off for Jewel Cave.

Jewel Cave had only been discovered in 1957. Just two years later, it was open to the public. After a long night shift, Father sacrificed his sleep to take Chloe and me into the underground cathedral of sparkling jagged teeth and stone waterfalls. The monstrous black root of a karri tree penetrated deep into the cave in its hunt for water. Another had done so centuries before and then died. Its root rotted and fell away, leaving a hole in the earth for intrepid cave hunters to find. It was this, the 'Wind Hole', that I promised was the ground whistling.

It didn't whistle, not really. But the cave breathed. Together, we stood over the padlocked grate that had been placed over the hole, and felt the cool air of the cave's exhale.

'How long has this been here?' he asked.

'I don't know,' I said. 'They found animal skeletons in the cave that were crusted over with crystals, so it must have been ages.'

He smiled. He held his hand over the grate. I held my hands over too. Our fingers briefly touched. We pulled away. Blushed. Went home.

These little incidents continued. Requests were left in books, notes of acceptance in others. Finally, he got up the courage to show me a cave he'd found in the hills that faced the lighthouse. We rode as far as we could and then walked, high up to a ridge of shallow blackened caves. We could make out the lighthouse and the clash of the two oceans. That day was particularly windy. The oceans hit each other with force, clearly marking the place where they met.

'Like me and you,' he said, pointing out to sea. 'Two oceans, two worlds.'

I smiled. I held his hand. He didn't pull away.

I loved him. He was gentle. He was clever. Our times together were marked by happy silences and tiny shy touches. Sometimes we talked about books or complained about our chores. Occasionally he spoke of 'the time before', when he lived at Sister Kate's in Perth. It was an orphanage, he told me, but I later learnt it was a house where stolen 'quarter-caste' or 'quadroon' children were taken under the guise of assimilating them into white Australia.

'They never told us what we were,' he said one day. 'We thought we were white kids, you know. I never realised what I was. Not till I got here.'

Those conversations always made me awkward. I didn't want to think about it. I told myself how light he was, how he lived with a white family now, in a white world. I never thought how the white world didn't really want him.

Our first embrace was behind the milking shed. Our first kiss was by the bins. Our first time was in the cave. We watched the oceans clash against each other afterwards and promised we'd love each other forever, silly young things that we were.

By the time we turned sixteen, A. Mischief and The Blackwood had codes for everything: every meeting place, every date, every 'I love you'. It seems inconceivable that we were able to hide what we were doing, and indeed it was. The land was vast, but the population small. Still, there was so much we managed to get away with by virtue of messages left in books and two rusty bicycles.

The Byrons bought Henry a second-hand violin for his sixteenth birthday. He took it with him everywhere, even when milking the cows. *Songs are like books,* he said to me once. *They tell stories.*

I turned sixteen during the school holidays. Our lighthouse community came together to celebrate, save for Mother who rested and Alexander Senior who was on shift. Alexander Jnr took a piece of cake to him and had it knocked out of his hand. He was just shy of his eighteenth birthday, and taller than his stout father, yet he shrunk as the man berated him for failing to polish the iron balcony to an acceptable standard. My day was spent listening to a man's shouting compete with the ocean dashing itself against the rocks. I felt sad.

Soon, my sadness slid into terror. I hadn't had a period for two months. I developed a nasty 'stomach bug'.

I stood at the top of the lighthouse stairs, wondering if the fall would hurt me enough to miscarry but not to die. Father caught me staring many times.

'You afraid of heights all of a sudden?' he'd tease.

I smiled but said nothing. The terror consumed me completely. All I thought was how to escape it. One night, I couldn't take it anymore. I needed to see Henry.

I snuck out soon after Father started his night shift. I hopped on my bicycle and made my way towards Augusta, the beam from the lighthouse my only light.

Then the spotlight seemed to be following me. It was the ute. Mother was in the driver's seat.

'Get in,' she said to me. Not 'where are you going?' Not 'why are you out late?' Just 'get in'.

We returned to the lighthouse. Mother sat with me at the kitchen table, a cup of tea in one hand and her head in the other. She looked at me through glazed, angry eyes. Tears were already spilling out of mine.

Finally, she spoke, 'You were going to see a boy.'

I said nothing.

'You girls think I don't know anything,' she said. 'Who were you going to see?'

'No one, Mama.'

She leant into her hand and closed her eyes. 'Do I need to get your father?'

A fresh wave of tears came as I thought of Father finding out. I shook my head.

'Who were you going to see?'

My answer came out in a whisper. 'Henry.'

'The Aboriginal boy?'

I nodded.

'You're a monstrous little girl.'

I put my face in my hands and wept. I don't know how I got the courage to say it.

'Mama, I'm pregnant.'

She said nothing at first. She just stared at me. Then she threw her cup at me. I gasped as the hot tea hit me. The cup smashed. Mother hit me.

'How could you do this?' she screamed.

She hit me again, this feeble angry slap. Then, I can't remember how, I hit back, just to block her. She fell. Everything stopped. It was quiet. Mother was on the floor. She wasn't moving. No one came running. Nothing moved. Only the spotlight, flashing through the windows.

'Mama,' I said.

She just lay there.

I ran out of the cottage. The wind buffeted me about as I made my way to the lighthouse. I ran past it and stumbled down the rocks. The clashing oceans pulsated every time the light passed over them. I stood on the edge, crying as I remembered all the times Henry and I had watched those two oceans colliding from his cave. His tender little comment, 'like you and me', as if he could ignore how violently the waves hit one another. I cried bitterly, letting the howling wind take away the sound of my anguish. I saw my only solution in the waves. I jumped.

Someone grabbed me from behind. We stumbled and went down hard.

'Lou, it's okay.'

A young man's voice.

For a moment, I thought it was Henry. The light passed over us. In a flash, I saw Alexander Junior. I writhed like a rabbit in a trap, trying to escape. He held me tight, muttering over and over again, 'It's okay, it's okay. Whatever's wrong, I can help.'

He dragged me off the rocks, bundled me up and took me to the foot of the lighthouse.

I cried and cried. It felt like hours. He whispered promises, told me he'd hide me, protect me, help me escape whatever was bothering me. He said he hated his father, he was so alone. He was leaving, tomorrow if I wanted. He even had his own car.

He took me to the cottage he shared with his father. Hid me in his room, told me not to make a sound. My whole being was a blur, as if my mind was disconnected from my body. I waited for him to take me back to the cottage where Mother lay motionless on the floor. But he never did.

'I can't stay here,' he said.

Finally, I spoke. 'Neither can I.'

We got in his car. We drove over those roly-poly hills, the light chasing but never catching us. We drove through Augusta, through Karridale, through bush still black with the fire from years ago.

I left everything. I left Henry. I left Chloe. I left my mother, unsure if she ever got up. There was no going back, I told myself. My mother. The pregnancy. It was better to be missing. It was better to be dead.

We drove non-stop, Alexander talking incessantly, like he was making up for lost time. He told me how he'd wanted to do this for years, just run away.

'And now,' he said joyously, 'we're both free.'

I didn't think to ask where we were going.

After hours on the road, tall dark spires erupted from the horizon, muddied by smoke from a bushfire. As we got closer, the skyscrapers came into view. Their blocky-concrete-metalness contrasted with vibrant green hills that I'd later learn was Kings Park. We went over the Narrows Bridge. I stared at the water, hoping we'd fall in.

We bypassed the city centre, veered off to a suburb nearby. Finally, we stopped on a street with five shops. It looked like Augusta's main street, only with thinner roads and buildings in the background instead of bush.

Finally, I asked, 'Where are we?'

'Bookshop!' he said, as if that explained it all.

We approached a two-storey, terrace-style building, with a sign in calligraphy: *Summers' Books – Antique, Rare and Unique Bookseller.* We went through a front door with a sign that read, in similarly elegant font, *NO TIME WASTERS.* A bell tinkled to announce our arrival.

The bookshop was very romantic. Dusty shelves bowed in the middle from the weight of all the books. Countless volumes scattered on the floor. An old man with a shock of white hair sat behind a desk and a glass cabinet displaying what promised to be the store's most precious collection. He looked up, saw us and dropped his book.

'He's dead!' he proclaimed.

'No, Papu, I left,' Alexander said.

'Oh,' the man said, disappointed.

He shuffled over, his back stooped. He grasped Alexander's arms, pulled him down and kissed him on both cheeks. 'You sure you didn't push him off that lighthouse?'

Alexander smiled. 'No, Papu.'

'Bugger,' he said. He looked at me. 'Who's this?'

'A friend.'

He eyed me suspiciously, glancing at my belly as if he knew. Then, he turned his head and shouted, 'Owen, come here!'

'Coming!' A voice came from deep within the bookshop.

'*Now*, you wretched thing!'

'*Coming*!' the voice yelled back. 'I've just found those Dostoevskys you wanted, *Christ*!'

A young man came out, cobwebs in his hair and three giant books in his arms. His look of annoyance vanished when he spotted us.

'Alex!' he exclaimed. The two embraced. Then he turned to me. 'Lizzy, right? Or Chloe?'

Alexander tried to correct him. 'No –'

'Yes,' I said. In that moment, my name changed. 'Lizzy.'

'Heard all about you! You're a reader too, yes?'

I nodded. Tea was put on and chairs relieved of their book piles as we gathered in the back room. Despite calling the old man 'papu', Alexander wasn't his grandson. I never figured out how they knew each other, but gathered it had something to do with his mother. Old Man Summers called Alexander 'pup', 'a little papu' he joked, because who would want to share the name of a father like that.

We were welcomed to the bookshop, told to consider it home. We lived upstairs. I was given a storeroom filled with books, broken bookshelves, and a sagging bed. Alexander slept on the floor in Owen's room.

I was to help in the shop and read only good books. Old Man Summers regularly smacked books out of my hand and replaced them with something that 'wasn't garbage'. Here, I read all the classics. I was given science textbooks and tomes on Greek philosophy. The only good books I wasn't allowed to touch were the ones in the glass cabinet.

New books arrived daily, so the same patrons would come in often to see what fresh rarities had arrived. Owen was particularly skilled at finding books. He also had no qualms about stealing them. He called it 'confiscating' or 'rehoming'. He'd disappear for days. Come back with boxes. Say he'd had a successful meeting with a client. Old Man Summers would nod and say, 'good lad'. Alexander took up this cavalier attitude, assisting Owen with his 'rehoming'.

Me, I just did what I was told. I cleaned up. I made lunch. One of my first jobs was the morning run: to the baker opposite to buy bread, the newsagent on the corner to get the paper, then back home to make a pile of fresh sandwiches and a pot of coffee. I never looked at the paper, frightened as if I knew what was written in those pages. One day, Old Man Summers waved it at me. I saw a glimpse of my face.

'You want to be here, girl?' he asked.

I nodded.

'What's waiting for you back home then? What's worth all this?'

I cried but said nothing. From this, he assumed I'd escaped a monster like Alexander Senior or some other violence. He instructed me to cut my hair and never fetch the newspaper again. Newspapers, after all, were a poor man's literature.

I cut my long black hair, the same hair that earned Chloe her nickname of Pan. As I glared at my reflection, I knew this was it. I was never going back. When I went to fetch bread the next day, the baker didn't recognise me. A. Mischief was dead.

Books grew tiresome. Yet, my love of stories never died. I missed days spent getting tales out of Father, Uncle Martin, or anyone with something interesting to share.

I started to linger in the bakery. It was a charming place, with loaves stacked high in wooden shelves behind a glass counter filled with delicate pastries. Many of the special items were named after people. The most popular bread, a twisted ring-shaped roll studded with poppy seeds, was called Mama and Tata's obwarzanek. There were sweet pastries named Władysław's and Ulryk's rugelach, one filled with jam, and the other with nuts and raisins. An intricately braided chocolate loaf was Dorota's babka. But my favourite was the treacle-coloured biscuits with a dusting of icing sugar in the shape of a dragon's head – the Feliks.

Though the bakery was inviting, the air sweet with the smell of baked bread and burnt sugar, the baker himself was not as welcoming. He was a gruff Polish man with a black beard forever flecked with flour. He was never rude, but his clipped manner didn't invite conversation. Normally, his teenage daughter served the customers, but when it got busy, he had to help front of house. I tried asking once, 'who do all these names belong to?'

'Family,' he answered. He handed me my loaf, my change, and turned his back. He tinkered at the till. I left but resolved to figure out his story.

'You have a nice big family,' I said the next day.

'Had,' he corrected, and gave me my bread.

The next few mornings, he wasn't there. His daughter served me. I learnt her name was Irena. In the afternoons, when everything was quiet, he sat outside the bakery, smoked half a pack of cigarettes, and talked animatedly to her. Smoke billowed out of him as he spoke. Despite the way he wildly gestured, the way her laughter filled the street, it seemed private.

I tried a busier time. He was there again. I spoke as if we were still having the same conversation, 'I don't have a family.'

'I hope you only have friendly ghosts that haunt you,' he said.

Irena glared at me. When I bought bread the next day, she gave me the most squished loaf.

I examined her insult. 'I'm sorry if I upset your dad.'

She stared at me until I left. I gave up, though I still spied on the afternoon storytelling sessions with envy.

Two weeks later, on the way back from the general store, I saw the baker smoking outside. He nodded a greeting.

The bottom fell out of my bag. An entire carton of eggs smashed. I was feeling isolated, lonely. I missed Chloe. I missed Henry. I was sick all the time. So, of course, I burst into tears.

The baker didn't rush to console me. He just said, 'There, there, love,' and took the smashed carton inside. He came back out, the carton refilled.

'You don't need to do that,' I said.

'It's fine,' he said.

I wiped my face. 'I'm sorry. I'm not crying about the eggs.'

He nodded. 'I know.'

These little encounters continued, tiny moments during the daily bread run. He asked, 'Who's looking after you then, love?' I answered, 'Friends, at the bookshop.' Another day, he asked, 'No siblings?' I said, 'Not anymore.' A week later, 'What happened?' I lied, 'Car accident,' then truthfully, 'I messed up.' Two days later, 'Who, love?' I answered: 'Mum, Dad, sister, boyfriend.'

Finally, on a quiet afternoon, he came out from behind the counter. His finger traced along the glass, following the names.

Mama

Tata

'Mum and Dad. Gas chambers.'

Feliks

'Starvation.'

Dorota

'Gas chambers.'

Władysław

Ulryk

'We were separated. I like to think they escaped.'

I couldn't say anything. I felt a terrible fraud. I was a pregnant teenager who ran away. No one had been taken from me.

And what do you say anyway, to something like that? I stared at those names, sad memories baked into something sweet, wanting to say how sorry I was. Instead, I asked, with as much kindness as I could, 'What were they like?'

He looked surprised, then he smiled sadly. He said, 'They were good.'

He never said anything about their deaths again. Never commented on the numbers inked into his left forearm, the ones that peeked out from his rolled-up sleeve on hot days. Instead, he told me about the family bakery in Krakow. He was especially attached to his brother Feliks and cousins Władysław and Ulryk. He spoke at length about the games they played, of times spent slaying imaginary dragons. Once they'd managed to convince his Uncle Jozef, who worked in the salt mines, to take them down for a tour.

Though the war was never spoken of directly, there was always sorrow in his tales. He spoke of 'whispers', of how life had been filled with some murmur of what was to come. There were also so many gaps. He'd forgotten his father's gingerbread recipe and most of his mother's folktales.

'Death kills more than people,' he told me.

It took a week of searching, but I found a book of Polish folktales. I stole it when Old Man Summers was snoozing, though I suspect he knew, as he insisted on ordering me around in Polish for the rest of the week. It was worth it.

When I gave it to the baker, memories came out of those

pages. He flicked through, showing Irena and me stories he remembered. He came across ones he'd never heard, but then halfway through he'd cry out and retell it with different details. We came across the Dragon of Wawel. He ran his fingertips over the faded line drawing of Krakow's dragon.

'My name is from this,' he said. 'Serafin means many things … all names do, I guess. Something to do with angels, I think. But Feliks said it meant 'burning one' in Hebrew. Feliks wanted a dragon, so that's what he called me. I had another name, the one my parents gave me. I forget it now.'

Slowly, his tales of joy and loss were interwoven with kind, soft questions about my own history. The real lying began here. Thinking of Uncle Martin, I made my father a butcher, said my grandparents came from France and that they'd fought in the resistance. Lie upon lie poured out. I too didn't tell of their deaths. A car accident seemed enough. One doesn't talk about death, I learnt, one talks around it. I was Elizabeth, Lizzy to her friends, the pregnant orphan. Lighthouses, mischief, sisters who moved like panthers, and stolen boys who shared books: these stories were written out of my history.

The next well of stories came to me through flowers. Owen was smitten with a young woman at the newsagent. She was willowy, delicate, and always had fresh flowers in her hair. Owen started bringing her blooms, all of which were stolen. He went around with a pair of scissors. Nothing was off limits: clients' gardens, neighbours' window-boxes, the roses in the Nedlands War Memorial.

'You steal flowers like you steal books,' I said one day.

'I don't steal books, I confiscate them,' Owen said.

'Rehome!' Old Man Summers called from his desk.

'Yes,' Owen echoed. 'Rehome.'

Owen roped Alexander into his misadventures. Soon I was

receiving flowers, left in a vase outside the storeroom. The boys never crossed the threshold into my space. Anything in the store could only be retrieved with my permission.

The flowers annoyed me. Not because they were, I suspected, the rejects, but because they were the spoils of mischief. Finally, when I found a colourful bouquet outside my room, I took the whole bunch and threw it at Alexander.

Later that night, his voice came from the other side of my door, soft and careful.

'Lizzy?'

I ignored him.

'I'm not sure what I did, but I'm sorry. I know you're going through a lot.'

I was showing now. Five months, I guessed.

'I'm sorry if I've been unkind.'

I didn't answer, but he stayed there. He sent through little acknowledgements of how I must be feeling. Every allusion to my pregnancy brought tears. I wanted to be that little girl again, the girl who blew bubbles into the wind at the top of the lighthouse. Eventually, I ripped the copyright page out of a water-warped book. Wrote on the blank side. Slid it under the door.

*Can I come with you on the next flower heist?*

A few moments later, he slid it back to me.

*YES!*

It was a week later. Owen planned to flood the entire newsagent with flowers. We left the bookshop around 4 am, visiting nearby houses and parks he'd scoped out on a map. Each of us held a large garbage bag.

We moved quickly through the streets, barely seeing what we were cutting. We judged often by the feel of them. Giant kangaroo paws, fat roses. We all got pricked by thorns.

Our last stop was the house that backed onto the bookshop. By then, dawn was creeping up on us. The place looked like a forest, with many trees and paths made of sliced repurposed tree rounds. Frangipani filled the front yard, overburdened by blooms of white-yellow, pinky-yellow and deep crimson. Our fingers became sticky with the sap the flowers excreted. Owen clipped whole branches. He then pointed towards the gate by the side of the house. We spied more colourful trees in the backyard.

There were two colossal magnolia trees, with pink flowers bigger than our hands. The trees had shed an ankle-deep carpet of petals. Only the garden beds, the area around a chicken coop and a small vegetable garden had been raked clean. Alexander and Owen cut all the blooms they could reach. We went quickly. The chickens chirped their morning welcome as we left.

Finally, we came to the newsagent. Owen showed us his key.

'How'd you get that?'

He just winked and let us in. We made the store a garden. Flowers were filed with magazines, propped up among newspapers and woven into signs. Flowers with sap were left on counters that could be wiped clean. We left one magnolia flower on the welcome mat.

'Won't she get in trouble if her boss sees this?' I asked.

'Boss's away. She's it till next week.'

Later that day, we had two visitors. One was her, Owen's crush. She came in with a frangipani flower behind her ear, invited Owen outside. Alexander and I peeked at them kissing. The second visitor came later, a plump middle-aged Asian woman. By this time, Owen and Alexander had left for the day. I'd done my regular chores, spoken to Serafin, and was now re-shelving a section of rare children's books.

I greeted the woman. She looked at my belly, not me, and

gave it a smile. She made her way to Old Man Summers, who had his feet up on a desk piled with invoices.

'Yes?' he said.

'Your employees came to my house this morning and stole many flowers,' she said. I expected her voice to be soft, like her movements, but it was confident. She had a very refined, almost English accent. 'The bandits left particularly gruesome cuts on my magnolia trees.'

Old Man Summers put his book down. 'You saw them?'

'Yes. There was a dark boy, a fair lad with wavy brown hair, and the pregnant girl sorting books over there.'

'But you didn't apprehend them?'

'I am the wife of a disabled war veteran,' she said. 'I am not going outside at dawn to confront people stealing from my yard.'

'It's not my business what my employees do when they aren't working here,' Old Man Summers said. Bored, he picked up his book again.

The woman plucked it from his hands.

'Sir, let me be clear. You are to send your employees to my house with an apology and some offer of compensation. I would suggest gardening assistance for a time I deem appropriate,' she said. 'It would be most unfortunate if I needed to contact the authorities, especially if they felt the need to examine not only the misbehaviour of what are, essentially, your wards, but also the dubious ways in which you procure your wares.'

Old Man Summers smiled, impressed. 'I'll send the little buggers to you as soon as the boys get back.'

She nodded her thanks.

'You may keep the book, madam.'

She glanced at its spine, then placed it back on his desk. 'Sadly, sir, I don't have time for bad literature.'

Like that, she left. Old Man Summers laughed.

'Touché, madam!' he called after her.

When Alexander and Owen returned, we were sent to this woman's house like naughty children. She sat on her front porch, under a pink frangipani tree that now looked lopsided.

'Good afternoon, children.'

Owen stiffened. 'I'm twenty-one.'

'My. A few decades ago you'd have been on the front or in a foreign grave. Instead, you steal flowers from old women.'

Owen shrunk.

'We'd like to offer our sincere apologies for stealing your flowers,' Alexander said. 'We shouldn't have taken so many.'

'You shouldn't have taken any, boy.'

Alexander nodded quickly. 'You're right. I'm so sorry. We're so sorry.'

I followed, mimicking his rapid, apologetic nods. Owen was next, all of us nodding like parrots.

'You'll make amends by assisting in my garden,' she said. 'You'll come every Tuesday, Thursday and Saturday morning at 7 am for an hour until I deem the damage to be repaired. If you have any problems with this arrangement, I suggest you speak to your employer Mr Summers.'

Gardening with Mrs Li became part of our routine. Alexander was given the job of cleaning out the chicken coop and fetching eggs. When he finished, he joined Owen in raking the magnolia petals and weeding the paths. Mrs Li gave them simple jobs, ones they couldn't mess up, and did her own careful pruning alongside them.

Me, I was to 'supervise the boys'. She insisted I tell them off when they did something wrong. It took me a while, but eventually I learnt what she expected, and had no qualms about telling Alexander not to carry so many eggs at once or pointing out when Owen failed to pull a weed out by its root.

'If your belly wasn't so fat, you'd be doing this,' Owen said.

Mrs Li didn't speak to us beyond giving instructions. We never saw her husband, though once we heard his sad voice, calling 'Mary, darling?' We never went in the house. Not ever.

Old Man Summers, clearly impressed, found a few books in Chinese characters and sent them over with me. Mrs Li handed them straight back.

'I can't read this, dear.'

'Oh, I thought –'

'I was born here, just like you. As were my parents, and my husband's parents, and our grandparents before that. Unless your ancestors came on the first boat, my family was probably here before yours,' she said. 'We lost the language long ago. Better not to learn it.'

Awkwardly, I asked, 'Really?'

'So Mother said.'

I took the books back. A week later, Old Man Summers tracked down a book of fables, poems and plays with stilted English prose and Chinese names. I read it first, and here I found Mulan. When I gave it to Mrs Li, I felt excited, imagining the same response as when I gave Serafin the book of Polish folktales.

She opened it and sighed. 'I've never heard these stories,' she said. 'I wonder how accurate they are. Who translated these? Did this English fellow –' she tapped the name on the front cover '– ever visit the country?'

'I don't know.'

'I have a daughter like this,' she said, stopping at the tale of Mulan.

Her tone didn't suggest that to be a compliment.

'Oh.'

She gave the book back to me. 'Keep it for the bookshop. I'm sure someone interested in the Orient will pay good money for it.'

Though she was always kind, she gave little else. I read books to try and know her, ones on Chinese history and legends, forgetting that they held no reference to her. They were just stories which others like me ascribed to her. I read a few books on World War I and II, not sure when her husband served or how old he was. I tried to ask what happened, how he was, but got nothing. I asked her about her daughter, the one like Mulan, but she only offered, 'She's a sweet girl, busy,' then, 'When's your due date again, dear? You're looking so big.' The direct mention of my pregnancy surprised me. I stopped asking questions.

The truth was, I was getting big.

Talk of adoption began. It was assumed from the outset that I'd be 'giving the baby up'. It was never *my* baby, it was *the* baby. Or *it*, as Old Man Summers said one night, pointing at me with his fork: 'It won't be staying here, of course.' I was never asked what I wanted to do, not by anyone.

I lie, there was one person. Robert, he asked. We met in the bookshop. I was directing Owen and Alexander where to position the fake holly and tinsel outside the shop, trying to do it through silent hand gestures. Old Man Summers had ordered 'No decorations, especially not this bloody early!' so we tried to get them up high while he was napping at his desk. The boys shimmied up the veranda, and were stringing decorations from the eaves.

A young man in a three-piece suit came towards the shop. He stopped to admire our handiwork, when Owen spotted him.

'Where have you been, Doctor?' He called from up on the veranda.

'England,' he said. 'My father was ill.'

His hair was curly and very black; no silver had crept in yet. He was so well dressed he seemed out of the time, out of the weather, which was so hot it felt like you were wading through the air as you walked.

'Hope the old fella's alright.'

The doctor offered a polite smile. 'Bless him. He refuses to die.'

Owen made his way down, then helped Alexander.

'Dr Stewart,' Owen introduced. 'Alexander, Lizzy.'

The doctor shook our hands, insisting, 'Robert, please.'

We answered, 'Nice to meet you, sir.' Though he was only ten or twelve years our senior, he seemed mature, like he'd crossed that line into adulthood we had yet to reach.

'We still have those first editions you requested,' Owen said.

'Oh, marvellous!'

Inside, Old Man Summers was woken by the bell. When he saw the doctor, he snapped, 'Well! Where've you been?'

Robert smiled, clearly familiar with the old man's demeanour. 'England, sir. Visiting family.'

'For that bloody long?'

'Only a month, sir, but before my trip my brother had rather misbehaved so I swore I wouldn't buy him any more books.'

'Your brother behaving now then?'

'No, but I thought it best not to be angry with him for too long.'

'Lucky brother, you have.'

'Quite.'

Old Man Summers opened the glass cabinet and fetched three books. 'You know, there's a holding fee.'

'Of course, sir. Your price?'

'Fifty dollars.'

'Forgive me, I still struggle with this new decimal currency. You quoted me twenty pounds for all three.'

'Yes.'

'The conversion rate is two dollars to the pound, if I'm not mistaken.'

'You are not. Ten dollar holding fee.'

The doctor sighed. 'Of course.'

He handed over a pile of folded notes.

'Give your brother our regards,' Old Man Summers said as he handed over the books.

'I always do.'

I expected that to be the last time we saw him, that this expense was some one-off splurge, but Robert was back a week later.

'How's that brother of yours doing, then?' Owen asked.

Robert darkened. 'Well enough.'

Owen wasn't even sure the brother existed. No one had actually met him. Nothing was known about him, except that he had a fondness for old books and was something of a troublemaker.

One day, I found Robert sorting through some crumbling tomes. He pulled out a copy of *On the Origin of Species*.

'This is stamped State Library Stock,' he said to me.

'One of their discards!' Old Man Summers called out.

Robert smiled, unconvinced, but took the book and paid for it nonetheless. At the counter, he spotted something in the glass cabinet.

'My God, is that …?'

Old Man Summers squinted at the shelf. 'Spit it out, man.'

'*Frostiana*.'

'Oh yes.' Old Man Summers opened the cabinet, lifted out a small book. '1814.'

Robert put his hand out to take the book. Old Man Summers did not oblige.

'One hundred dollars.'

It was clear from his expression that he'd heard perfectly. Yet still, he said, 'Pardon?'

'A hundred dollars is reasonable. Printed on the ice at the

last ever frost fair in London. Just a handful of these left in the world.'

Robert's hand didn't move. Old Man Summers still wouldn't give up the book.

'This is a rather obscure book, Doctor.'

'Yes,' he said. 'It has eluded me.'

Old Man Summers put the book back in the cabinet. 'Perhaps it will elude you again. One hundred and twenty dollars. The price will continue to rise. Best make up your mind quickly.'

Robert's eyes lingered on the book for a moment but then he turned for the door. Despite his annoyance, he rushed to help me as he spotted me carrying a pile of books.

'You shouldn't be doing this in your state,' he said, taking them. He then called behind him. 'Mr Summers, this young lady shouldn't be doing any heavy lifting.'

Old Man Summers just held his book up to his face, ignoring him.

I showed Robert where the books belonged. He started shelving them for me. I wanted to stop him, but was so tired, I just let him. I made an attempt at conversation.

'Your brother likes expensive books then?'

'Yes,' Robert said. He quickly moved onto something else. 'When are you due, miss?'

'Ah, I don't know,' I said. 'Soon I imagine.'

'Your doctor hasn't given you a due date?'

'I haven't seen any doctors.'

He looked alarmed. 'You haven't seen …? No one?'

'No,' I said, a little embarrassed.

He took out his business card, handed it to me. 'I'm an obstetrician. Come to my consulting rooms. Just to check everything is alright.'

'I don't have any money.'

'I can waive payment if you sneak me a good book.'

'I heard that!' Old Man Summers yelled.

I must have looked aghast. Robert smiled and said, 'Don't worry, it was a joke. Come after 5 pm. I'm in the office late, unless there's a delivery.'

I just nodded.

'Perhaps you'd reduce the price of *Frostiana* if I care for your granddaughter, sir,' Robert called back to Old Man Summers.

'Not my granddaughter, not my problem,' Old Man Summers shouted. 'And it's one hundred and forty dollars once you walk out.'

Robert paused, but only for a second. The bell on the door tinkled as he left. I looked at his card for a long time.

I was nervous about seeing him. I was too shy to ask for a lift, so I took the bus and endured the stares. Robert's rooms were nearby. I could've walked if the heat wasn't so punishing. I arrived around 6 pm, and the sun was still blazing. The door to his rooms, which were in a beautiful colonial house, featured the names of three other men, all obstetricians. It was locked. Though I knocked hard, no one responded.

I thought I heard something, so I peered around the side and noticed a window half open, fine white curtains fluttering in the breeze. I heard voices, faint English accents. Surely one was Robert. I only intended to call through the window, to alert them I was here. But the fabric over the window was so sheer, I could see inside.

Robert was sitting at a desk, making notes. Another man was there, taller, older, surly. He paced around, cracking his fingers.

'Would you stop doing that please?' Robert asked tersely.

'Would you finish, please?' the man replied.

Robert ignored him. The man sat in the chair opposite the desk. He lent his elbows on Robert's papers and started cracking his fingers again. They were rough, bulbous in parts, like they'd once been badly broken.

'I'm hungry,' he said.

'Go and eat. I have to finish this.'

The man pulled his chair around to Robert, right beside him. Close. 'Come back to it tomorrow,' he said.

Robert grunted at him, annoyed. The man started running his fingers tenderly through Robert's hair. At that angle, I could see the man had a chunk out of his ear and a small but deep scar along the top of his left jaw.

'Not here,' Robert growled, and elbowed him away.

The man jumped back. He smiled mischievously, then nipped forward, landing a quick kiss on Robert's neck. 'Here?'

Robert batted him away. He went in again, kissed him on the cheek. 'Here?'

'Elliot!'

He kissed him on the nose. 'Here?'

'Elliot, would you fuck off!'

The man pulled a face, unimpressed. 'Give me a kiss and I'll take my book and fuck off then.'

Robert breathed out through his nose, thoroughly annoyed. He relented, giving this man a brief kiss on the lips and then returned to his paperwork. The man smiled, smug but also giddy, happy with even the tiniest affection. He came towards the window, but I was so shocked by the odd intimacy I'd seen, I just stood there.

The man started to say, 'I won't have you cursing like –'
But then he saw me. Our eyes met. Then he ran for the door. I moved as fast as I could. He got to the door quickly, and was outside just as I made my way to the front yard. He was quick. He caught up and grabbed me by the arm.

'Who are you?'

I couldn't answer, I was so frightened.

'What are you doing?' I heard behind him. It was Robert.

Elliot dragged me around to face him.

'Lizzy,' Robert said, his voice suddenly soft. 'You came for an appointment.' Then, harshly, 'Elliot, let her go, for goodness' sake! She's a girl!'

'She saw,' he said.

'What?'

'She was looking in the window.'

Robert changed. He was suddenly cautious, almost afraid.

'The front door was locked,' I said quickly. 'I didn't see anything.'

The two men looked at me and then each other.

Then Robert offered, 'This is my brother Elliot, the awful one I buy books for. He likes to play games. Very silly games. Let the poor girl go, please.'

Elliot released me. Slowly.

'Come this way, Lizzy. I'm terribly sorry.'

I did what I was told. Elliot and Robert didn't exchange any words, but I felt Elliot watching us as we went inside. Robert acted like nothing had happened.

'Are you putting the baby up for adoption?'

'I ... I don't know.'

'Be aware that they'll mark your records as such when you go in. You're young and unmarried. If you want to keep it, you should make that clear.'

I nodded. 'Will you be there?'

'Unlikely. The midwives will take care of you, unless you have complications.'

'Please,' I said.

He smiled reassuringly. 'You mustn't worry. You'll be in good hands.'

'I'll steal *Frostiana* for you.'

He let out a surprised laugh. I smiled, enjoying the way it

burst out of him. 'A tempting offer, but I fear Mr Summers' wrath wouldn't be worth it.'

By the time I left, it was dark. Elliot was waiting, smoking in the dark. He glowered at me, his eyes as wicked as the shrivelling red embers on his cigarette. He said nothing, not even when Robert told him he was taking me home.

The next day, I got up early, bought the bread, made my daily mountain of sandwiches, and went to work. Alexander came down late. That was when I noticed.

Old Man Summers sat in his chair, his head slightly bowed. He sagged like the overburdened shelves behind him. He smiled. His classic napping pose. But his eyes were open. He didn't blink.

I touched Alexander's arm and gestured towards the old man. He said, 'What?' but then frowned. He took a step towards him. Then another. Slowly he made his way over. He knelt down, looked into those yellowed staring eyes. Checked his breath.

'If you're pulling my leg, Papu.'

Checked his pulse.

Owen was called. But no one wept like Alexander.

There was no funeral. Old Man Summers' will was direct: *Scatter my ashes somewhere inconvenient. Remind the world what's coming to them.* A week later, we went to Forrest Place, threw the ashes over a balcony, watched them shower down onto annoyed shoppers. In the following days, Alexander sat on the floor by the old man's chair. Eventually, Owen replaced the chair with another, and started to go through the accounts.

That night, as I was gripped by pain, Alexander noticed how I was sweating and breathing heavily. He brought me a damp cloth and wiped my face.

'Lizzy, after the baby's born we should go. Visit somewhere, or work somewhere different. Maybe Greece or Turkey. Papu said how beautiful it was. All that history.'

'How?' I asked. 'We don't have money.'

'I saved a little.'

'How can we travel with a baby?'

'Well, we won't have the baby, will we?'

I didn't say anything. We sat in that awkward silence. Then, 'I want to go home.'

'We can never go home,' he said.

I nodded.

'I want –' he stopped himself, paused, then took my hand. 'It's okay. We can see every place on earth in the books downstairs.'

I nodded and squeezed his hand back. He took the damp cloth from me, turned it over and placed the cool side back on my forehead.

After an evening of building agony, my waters broke. Alexander was out. Owen took me to the hospital and just left. I begged him to stay, but he seemed even more terrified than me.

I didn't tell them I was unmarried. They just guessed from my age and lack of a wedding ring. The way I was treated confirmed I could never go home. I was left on a cold, narrow bed, nurses, doctors and trolleys rattling past as the pain flared.

I started to scream for Robert early on, begging them to find Dr Stewart, or just to help me, please, do anything. One nurse told me off for all the noise I was making. I was checked periodically, to see how far along I was. Other than that, I was left with that growing crescendo of agony for hours, alone. I kept begging for Robert. He never came.

But you did. Because of course, Harry, the baby was you. As the pain reached its zenith, I was taken to a delivery suite. I was sure I was dying, being torn apart. Then I felt you slide out of me, and a beautiful warm wet relief flooded me. The nurses lifted a sheet so I couldn't see you. I heard you cry, and the relief was washed away with terror. They wouldn't let me see you. They were taking you away.

'Please,' I begged. 'My baby.'

One of them said, 'It's not your baby, dear.'

I screamed in a hysterical voice that was not my own. 'Let me see my baby!'

The nurse that held you, her back to me, stopped.

'It'll do her more harm than good,' one of the others warned.

The nurse turned. 'Let her just see him.'

Then I saw you, this tiny red thing with a big mop of black hair. Black hair like mine. Like Chloe's. In that moment, I knew you were mine, always would be. The nurse gave me one sad smile, and took you away. I screamed and cried and swore. I was given an injection, a sedative of some sort. As the poison leached through my body, something bloomed deep in my heart. You were mine. You, this baby with my hair. You were mine.

When I woke, my breasts were bound. They were swollen, hard as rock, and no milk came. Whenever I heard the babies crying or cooing in the beds of the married women next to me, they throbbed.

I was not alone. There was an unmarried girl next to me in the ward. During the day, a social worker's insidious whispers wafted through from behind the curtain. This man told the girl she needed to sign the consent forms, that a perfect married couple was waiting for her baby, that she couldn't possibly provide what they could. Only a selfish girl kept her baby when she couldn't provide for it.

'If you truly love your baby, you'll let her go to this nice family. You love your baby, don't you?'

Eventually, she echoed his words. She spoke to herself, as if her brain short-circuited so badly that all she could do was mutter, in a constant stream, all the things he said to her. 'It's better, you know. She'll have a better life.'

I screamed for Robert.

The social worker came for me next. He probably didn't guess it from all the fuss I made, but I did feel shame. He was right. I couldn't take care of you like a married couple with a proper house and income. But I kept asking to see you.

'You can see him after you sign the forms.'

But I wouldn't sign the forms. I screamed again for Robert.

Finally, after all my cries, after two attempts to get into the nursery, Robert came.

'Lizzy, I hear you've been asking for me.'

It was meant as a greeting. He smiled warmly, like someone there to take care of me. He looked at my charts, marked with that insidious red triangle, shaped like an A for Adoption, with a big arrow pointing at it for attention. He saw my breasts, squashed under the hospital gown. And he just smiled.

I pulled myself up to get closer to him.

'If you don't give me my baby, I'll tell them what you are.'

His face changed. His smile gone.

'Pardon?'

'I'll tell them!' I screamed, loud enough for anyone on the ward to hear.

He took a step back.

A nurse appeared. 'What's this about?'

'Nothing,' Robert said quickly. Then, he added, 'Get the girl her baby.'

'Doctor –'

'Just do it.'

They brought you to me. They brought their scowls, but they brought you. As soon as I held you, I could see nothing else.

You, with your black black hair.

From that moment on, they could say nothing to me. The kind assurances that adoption was the best thing to do. The cruel accusations that I was a selfish girl. Robert must have said something to the nurses, because they fetched you whenever I asked and eventually brought a cot so you could stay by my side. I listened to the social worker, you in my arms or on my now liberated breast, and smiled. *You can't do anything to me*, I thought. *My baby is the only thing I have.*

I left that hospital with you in my arms. No one was waiting to collect me, so I just walked home. It wasn't such a long walk, and you only cried once. As we came into the bookshop, you and I, we were greeted with disappointment.

'You kept it,' Owen said.

'His name is Harry,' I said, and went upstairs. I lay you down on that little bed of mine in the storeroom. I stroked your fat cheeks as Alexander and Owen argued downstairs.

I went from wonder to terror overnight. No one had explained anything to me, how to breastfeed, how you couldn't regulate your own body temperature, all the thousand terrifying sounds you'd make. I took you to Mrs Li on a daily basis. She sighed with every visit, but took me into her garden and explained what any good mother or midwife should've told me.

Slowly, we got used to one another, you and I. Owen got used to you too. Robert came in once, to ask how I was. He then played with you for half an hour, singing to you, laughing at the way you looked around wide-eyed.

'I always wanted a family,' he told you.

He left that day without buying a book.

Three months, we settled in. Still frightened. Still getting it wrong. No sleep. But we were safe. We had a home.

That all changed when Alexander finally decided to do the

long-overdue chore of taking down the Christmas decorations. He went out early to clean them away before we got up.

They said he fell. From the top floor balcony. A footprint on the balustrade was offered as evidence. I found him when I went to get bread. In the middle of the street, on the asphalt, eyes wide open. They said he broke his back. Burst internal organs. I can still remember how shocked he looked, how surprised he was to have fallen. Owen cried more than when Old Man Summers died. I didn't shed a tear. I felt only fear. My guardian was gone.

It started after the funeral. You would be quiet for days, just the occasional mew, but then you'd unleash hours of relentless screams and crying. If the shop was open, Owen banged on the roof with a broom handle. When customers left, his footsteps pounded up the stairs. He flung open the door to my storeroom without knocking.

'Would you shut that bloody thing up?'

'I'm trying.'

'Try harder!'

Your cries continued to turn patrons away. Owen's girlfriend stopped coming around. And I was useless. I couldn't help in the shop. I couldn't serve people when Owen was away without having you in my arms, cooing or crying.

Eventually, he said to me, with his first attempt at gentility in weeks, 'You need to go home.'

'I can't go home,' I told him.

'If you don't leave, I'll tell them where you are. You're from the lighthouse. I could just send a letter,' he said. 'It's best. Your family might be angry but they could help you. I don't know what to do, I'm sorry. A shop is no place for a baby.'

I thought of the last time I saw my mother.

'I know it's difficult. But it can't be worse than this.'

'Okay,' I said. 'Can you give me a few days?'

He nodded. Smiled as if we were friends again. I hugged him then. Because he was a friend, once. We were playmates, fellow mischiefs. I'd miss him, despite what he was doing to us.

Early next morning, I wrapped you up like Mrs Li had shown me. I took a few sandwiches made from Serafin's bread. I half-filled a backpack, noting how few possessions I had. I left the bookshop, but then came back. Gazed at that forbidden glass cabinet full of treasures. And I took it. *Frostiana*. Put it in my nearly empty backpack.

I was seventeen. I walked to Robert's rooms as the sun was coming up. I sat down outside, right under his window, and waited.

I didn't hear him come in, but he heard you, crying. He poked his head out of his window. He looked alarmed to see us. He disappeared. Then I heard the backdoor slam. In a few moments, he was there, standing beside us.

'Hello Lizzy,' he said.

'Hello,' I said.

He carefully adjusted the way I was holding you. You went quiet. I smiled at him. He didn't smile back.

With one free hand, I took *Frostiana* out of my bag and handed it to him. He took it gingerly, opening it to the title page. He then tried to hand it back, but I was holding you in two arms now. He lay it down on the backpack.

'This is a gift,' I said, motioning to the book.

'It's not yours to give.'

'No. I stole it. Those of us with secrets must do what we can to survive.'

From his face, I could tell he heard my threat.

'I'm homeless,' I said. 'I don't have anywhere to go.'

He didn't know what to say, or what I wanted. He was nervous.

'You need to help me,' I said.

'Okay,' he said, drawing the word out. 'How can I help you?'

'I need somewhere to live. Just for a while.'

'Lizzy,' he said with a sigh. 'I know you love your boy, but there's still time for adoption. You could find a job then. Perhaps I can offer you work in the office here, but most single mothers ... there's nothing for you. Who can look after him when you're working? Who will employ you? If you don't have family, there's nothing you can do. This world won't help you.'

'I'm not asking the world to help me. I'm asking you,' I said. 'Who do you think the world hates more, you or me? What world will help you, Doctor?'

He let out a long sigh. 'Come inside,' he said. 'We'll figure something out.'

That afternoon, we drove into Guildford. When we came over the bridge, onto the main street, we were transported to the past. The romantic shops with their tin signs of peeling calligraphy. The train tracks lined with giant sugar gums. Colonial buildings in various states of majesty or disrepair. The town looked like it'd remained in the 1800s, with cars the only object of modernity to be welcomed. We pulled up outside a beautiful little house.

'I'm moving into general practice,' Robert explained as he took us inside. 'The local surgery was looking for a new doctor, and they liked the idea of having a GP who could offer obstetrics. I'll be moving here in a few weeks. We haven't moved much in, but there's a bed in the master bedroom.'

I walked around in a daze, into tall ceilinged rooms with a hodgepodge of boxes and furniture.

'We don't have a cot, obviously. I will ... I'll get one soon. You can keep it when you leave.'

*When you leave.* I nodded. 'Thank you.'

'Oh, the cupboard's empty. I'll get some food from the local store.'

I stood on the patio and watched him go. Sat with you, admiring the view of the street. An elderly woman was out in her garden. She kept glancing at us.

Robert came back, two bags of food in tow, and then handed me the key. Aware we were being watched, I took his hands suddenly.

'Thank you,' I said and kissed him on the cheek.

He pulled back and nodded. 'It's alright. This is only temporary.'

'Of course,' I said.

The woman, watching from across the road, smiled and waved.

I explored my new home, rudely going through boxes. I found a jewellery box that I later learnt belonged to Robert's late mother. She'd left him many trinkets, including her wedding ring. I put it on.

'Where did you find that?' was Robert's immediate question.

'I was looking for some blankets and found a jewellery box. I just … I wanted to go to the bakery and didn't want anyone to think badly of me.'

And go out I did. I made myself seen with that ring on my finger. Strangers stopped me to comment on my beautiful baby and ask when I'd moved in. 'You're the new doctor's wife?' I smiled and nodded.

Every day, Robert checked on me, though he paid more attention to you, singing and playing games with you. He bought a cot and a pram. Then a few toys. Some clothes. Every time: 'You can keep these when you go.'

A week later, Elliot came in without knocking. I heard his footsteps thumping down the hallway as I was feeding you in the living room. I covered myself as he flung open the door.

'You're leaving soon,' he said.

'I know,' I replied.

'You remember what you are,' he said, coming close. 'No one's going to believe the word of a whore. You remember that, darling.'

He didn't speak to me again, but visited often to unload his books in the study. When it looked as though the house was ready to move in, Robert sat me down. I was prepared to rebuke the eviction notice I knew was coming.

'The neighbours keep asking about my wife,' he said.

It wasn't the sentence I expected.

'How odd,' I said.

'I met with my new colleagues yesterday. One doctor said his wife met mine as she was strolling in the park with my son. Thought she was very witty.'

'They must've been confused by the ring.'

'Hmm,' he muttered. A moment passed. Then, 'What do you want?'

'Somewhere safe,' I said. 'To keep my baby.'

'Is that all?'

'That's all.'

He sighed. 'You've made this difficult for me. I can't be a man who seemingly abandons his wife and child. It would look very bad. I couldn't stay here.'

'I'm sorry,' I offered, though I meant none of it.

He looked down, shy. 'You want safety. To keep your baby. We can, perhaps, you and I … we can come to an arrangement,' he said. 'I don't trust you, but I like you. You're quite formidable. And you're smart. And I like your boy. As long as I live in this town, we can, if you wish, be a family.' Then, quietly but earnestly he said, 'I would like a family.'

I nodded.

'We wouldn't be, it wouldn't be, what it normally is, if you understand me,' he added quickly. 'But I'd look after you. I'd be a good father. Boys need good fathers. And, maybe, you can look after me … and Elliot.'

I nodded again. I smiled.

Robert and Elliot fought. Their arguments shook the house. Neighbours noted their concern to me. I told them Elliot was unstable, an eccentric troubled sort. They developed a mixture of suspicion and pity for him. 'What a good man, your husband,' they'd say, 'caring for his disturbed brother.'

Elliot wouldn't be in the same room as me, would scream through walls at you whenever you cried. Eventually, though, something changed. He grew quiet, brooding but accepting of what we had. Both men, I realised, were tired. They never spoke about their past, about life in England.

Years into the arrangement, we forgot we'd once lived different lives. Robert was the model husband. Always kind. Upon seeing me admiring the roses in the church courtyard, he planted an array of them in the front yard. Though Elliot never came to like me, he came to like you. You were naughty and loud. He enjoyed getting you worked up and creating more trouble for me and Robert.

Every Saturday afternoon in the summer, as soon as you could walk, Robert and Elliot whisked you away to the ocean. I was rarely welcome at these outings, though for your seventh birthday, we all went together. That was the day that opened a door I could never close again.

Elliot kept giving you swigs from his hipflask. It only contained cordial, but fellow beachgoers looked on disapprovingly. You ran around, sugar high. I grabbed you as you were about to do a bellyflop on another child's sandcastle. We'd already been in the sun for an hour, and were all looking pink. Robert let out a long sigh.

'Hot today, isn't it?' he said.

I let you go. You decided to make your own sandcastle to destroy.

'I read it's snowing in London. Back home, some of the lochs have frozen,' Robert continued. 'I bet Harry would love the Christmas fairs, you know, the ice rink and the gingerbread.'

'Harry's fine,' Elliot said. 'He has the whole ocean. Little thing's a fish.'

You decided, as if you agreed, that the sandcastle was boring, and went running off towards the waves. I chased after you and brought you back to our picnic blanket.

As we sat down, I heard Elliot say to Robert, 'I would freeze all the rivers and oceans if it would please you.'

'With what divinity would you freeze the oceans?' Robert asked.

Elliot shrugged. 'Some sort of devilish mischief.'

*Mischief.*

Elliot snatched you from me and tickled you. You roared with laughter. 'But maybe I'll freeze *you* instead!' he said. He chased you across the beach, and then, when you didn't want to be chased anymore, you turned around and roared at him, 'You can't freeze me, I'm a dragon!'

I smiled. That night, mischief crept into your bedtime story. I told you about the Dragon of Wawel and a magical boy who went down the salt mines and became a ghost. The next day, you asked me how the boy got down the mine. I thought of Serafin, the sad baker who lost his family. I gave him a sad end, but one where he could save others, escape the guilt I knew lingered in the real man's heart.

You said, 'How did he become magic?'

I made it up on the spot. 'He found a book.'

'A book?'

'A magical book. A book that held the stories of every other person who had those powers.'

'What was it called?'

'It was called … *The History of Mischief*.'

'There were more like him? More mischiefs?'

*Mischiefs.* Like me and Chloe. 'Yes.'

'Do you have the book, Mum?'

'No, it's hidden somewhere. But I read it once. I can tell you the stories. But you can't tell anyone. It's secret.'

'I promise I won't tell anyone, not even Dad,' you said.

'Not even Uncle Elliot?'

'Not even!'

I tucked you into bed. As I went to turn out the light, you said, 'Who was the first mischief, Mum?'

Who was the first? I thought of Chloe, of course, but pushed her away. I went for Alexander.

'A boy. A boy without a name. I'll tell you about him tomorrow.'

And so, the *History* was born. I took the people, stories and books I loved, and added magic. I tried to share with you the things I cherished in a life that otherwise filled me with shame.

You became obsessed with the book. Where was it? How did I know about it? You knew it wasn't real, but you liked to pretend. Years passed. I invented a few mischiefs off the top of my head, not drawing from anyone in my life. You always found these boring.

'They're not real,' you'd say, as if you knew which mischiefs were based on something true, and those that weren't.

The last few histories – of your father and me – I resisted telling for years. But you kept asking, kept playing. I watched you in the garden, tossing up sand as if you were the boy casting ghosts. I thought you'd grow out of it, but you played with sand ghosts until you were eleven.

Eventually, I gave in. I said I found another history, hidden inside Uncle Elliot's old book *Frostiana*. The story was patchy back then. I only had a few fragments about a man who froze the Thames. Much later, when I felt brave, I added myself, the French girl Louise, who came between the two men and stole the *History*.

Then Robert's father finally died. You were twelve. Arguments sprung up between Robert and Elliot, fights about the funeral, the family, and 'the way things were'.

Robert booked three tickets to London. The arguments stopped. You were thrilled initially. Your first overseas trip, and to the land of Archie and Will. But your excitement was dashed by the resentment that emanated from your uncle. Elliot wouldn't eat with us, wouldn't talk to us.

'Why is Uncle Elliot so angry?' you asked Robert. 'Why isn't he coming with us?'

Robert sighed. 'Uncle Elliot and the family don't get on. You can't talk about him to anyone, alright? Otherwise you'll upset a lot of people.'

You nodded but seemed confused. 'What did he do that was so bad?'

'He just … wasn't very nice.'

You didn't understand, but you didn't question it.

London was everything we expected from the books. Black cabs. Old buildings. We drove by the Thames and exchanged a secret smile.

We stayed with your father's old university friend. On the cab ride there, Robert issued you a warning.

'George's wife is Ethiopian. Her name is Adanech. Please don't call her Mrs Campbell. Ethiopian women don't take their husband's name when they marry. Just stick to Adanech. Please be polite.'

My boy, you were not polite. When this beautiful dark-skinned woman opened the door and exclaimed 'Welcome! Come in!' you just stared at her. I realised then you'd never met anyone who didn't look like you. You were afraid.

But Adanech took us to the Tower Bridge. She took us to the British Museum. You kept pointing at the great dome that was the Reading Room, forgetting your apprehension and begging to go inside.

'Sure, but we might have to be a little mischievous.'

You lit up.

We went to the clerk's desk. She told us to wait back, but we still heard her hushed lie. She spoke in a friendly tone, like she knew the man well.

'Rich, I'm doing some translations for David again, but the old man's lumped me with the wife and kid of the Australian ambassador. Let me give them a quick tour. The Mrs is a librarian and would love to see the Pantheon.'

'Of course,' he said. 'Just tell Percy it's Foreign Office business.'

'Thank you.'

She ushered us along a corridor. It ended so suddenly, in such an expansive space, we gasped. We stood transfixed by the dome and its windows, streaming with light. Adanech asked a clerk to give us the 'Foreign Office tour'. He showed us the stacks with a great many sighs.

Later that night, you declared, 'That's where the *History* must be hiding!'

So I gave Archie the British Museum. For the first time, you saw me stealing from our surroundings to make the histories. You pretended not to notice.

The next day, we met Robert's only sister Edith. The first thing you said to her was, 'You look like Dad!'

And she did, right down to the curly mess of black hair.

'Aye. All us Stewarts look alike,' she said with a sigh. 'Lucky you take after your mama.'

'Uncle Elliot doesn't look the same.'

Silence. At realising you'd mentioned your uncle, you glanced at Robert, your glassy eyes begging forgiveness. Bless Robert. He gave you a small, reassuring smile.

'I don't know who you mean, dear,' Edith said.

Edith was a creature of sighs. Her body swelled with those long releases of breath, and she deflated with every sentence. Her Scottish accent was deep and dreary.

'You know, you could've stayed with me,' she said to Robert. Sigh.

'I didn't want to bother you,' he said.

She looked at me, staring a little too long. 'It's good to meet you finally, Elizabeth. We never thought Robbie would find anyone.' Sigh.

The funeral was the next day. The sermon was dull. Kind words were said unconvincingly in flat tones. At the wake, some distant relative demanded to know where Robert's accent had gone. You asked why no one cried.

We saw little of Robert after that. He spent his days with lawyers, in discussions over the Stewart estate. A week passed before George insisted that he find some time to 'have a day with the lads'. They took you to the ice rink by the Thames (which I heard endless stories about) and, I suspect, the pub (of which I heard nothing). The night before, Adanech promised to counter the boys. After I expressed some interest in visiting Windsor Castle, she promised we'd make a day of it.

Our trip to Windsor took some time. I apologised, saying I didn't realise it was so far away.

'No one does,' she said. 'But it's worth it.'

'Do you have many places like Windsor in Ethiopia?' I asked.

'Oh yes, Gondar is very impressive if you want castles.'

'Do you go home often?'

She smiled sadly. 'No.'

'Do you miss it?'

'Every day.'

We arrived around midday. Adanech insisted we have lunch first, at a sweet cafe that served high tea. She went straight for a scone and piled it with clotted cream, ignoring the finger sandwiches.

I saw it as an opportunity to pry. 'What's Ethiopian food like?'

'Wonderful,' she said. 'But you can't go past an English scone. Have one.'

Adanech, I realised, was very good at avoiding talk about herself. This made me want to pry even more. As one in possession of many secrets, I was curious what other people were hiding.

I reached for a scone. 'They must be good to keep you here,' I joked.

She smiled. 'George is rather lovely too. And my work. But yes, clotted cream makes up for these ghastly winters.'

'Why don't you go back? Would they not accept George?'

Her eyebrows raised a little, a flicker of annoyance. 'Not at all. My family were close friends with Hakim Workneh, the first Ethiopian to be trained as a doctor. Mother thought it wonderful my husband shared the same profession. It was George's family who were less than accepting.'

'Oh.'

'We don't see them anymore.'

'I'm sorry.'

'It's alright. Love's worth it.'

Was it? Was it really? I couldn't help but think of Henry.

'We all make sacrifices,' she continued.

'You'd never go home?'

'I can't. The Emperor was assassinated a few years ago. The country is under military dictatorship.'

'Oh … I'm sorry. Is your family okay?'

'I don't know. My father was an engineer under Haile Selassie. I'm sure he was killed long ago.'

'My God. That's awful.'

'Yes,' she said. 'But don't let that colour how you see us. Ethiopia is a beautiful country. We had Christianity before Europe. We were never colonised. We were never your slaves.'

*Your* slaves. I turned red.

'Sorry, I didn't mean … it's just … people like to make assumptions.'

I nodded. 'I'd love to learn more than the assumptions.'

'Okay,' she said. 'Let me introduce you to Alemayehu.'

Our tour of the castle was leisurely. Adanech opened up, sharing how her father had once been to Windsor long ago. As a child, she spent days going through his notebooks. She vividly remembered the drawings of the castle, maps with sprawling rooms and speculative tunnels. There were funny notations about the people who gave him information or gossip, alongside technical specifications.

As we came towards St George's Chapel, she told me the story of Alemayehu. I saw the plaque that commemorated his death.

'I'm sure one day he'll go home,' I said.

She smiled. 'That's a nice idea.'

'Perhaps … we could steal them.'

'What?'

'His bones.'

She laughed. 'What a marvellous adventure that would be.'

Adanech became my first real friend since leaving the bookshop.

The following week, snow fell suddenly. Flights were cancelled, our trip home pushed back. Robert felt bad about all the time he spent dealing with his father's estate, and spent the rest of the trip with you and George. I was always invited out on these excursions, but by then, I had other plans. I asked Adanech if she could spare some paper. I started to write *The History of Mischief*.

It took months. As I wrote, back at home in Guildford, my own history lingered with me. Chloe sat on one shoulder, Henry on the other. When you went to school, when Robert and Elliot went to work, I wrote. I hid it in a shoebox. Robert suspected something. Dishes were left in the sink, dinner was late. At church, the newsagent asked Robert what we needed all the paper for.

'What was he talking about?'

'I think he mixes up his customers. Sometimes he calls me Rachel,' I lied.

I finished and let it sit, curled up in that shoebox for another month. I was frightened, really, of what I'd written, of what it really meant. I debated removing the Henry story altogether. I kept thinking about him. Every day. Seeing George and Adanech together made me wonder: *what if?*

I bit the bullet. I took it to a bookshop that did repairs and binding. A fortnight later, I received a book bound in leather. All those pages were stitched seamlessly into the spine, like they'd never known life as single sheets. It felt so heavy. I hugged it all the way home.

Two nights later, Robert and Elliot took you to Alfred's for dinner. I feigned a headache, then hid the book under your pillow. You all came back smelling of smoke from the firepit. It only took you ten minutes to find the book and come running into my room. You threw yourself on the bed.

'Thank you, Mum!'

'I told you I'd find it.'

'There are histories in here you've never told me!'

'Really?'

'Can we read them together?'

'Of course.'

It took us weeks to read the whole thing. You said it was scarier and sadder than the stories I'd told you. I felt terrible, but then you said you liked it better, that it felt alive and true and magical. Like the people were real.

Just as the *History* tormented Lou, it started to torment me too. I missed Chloe. I missed Henry. I stared at myself in the mirror every day, noting how I'd changed myself. Cut and curled my hair to match the older ladies at church. Picked out clothes for a woman twice my age. Glasses. More to age me than anything. Would anyone even recognise me back home?

I told myself, maybe I'd just go down and see. Maybe, I'd just find Chloe. No one else would recognise me. I'd just go to see my sister. You and me, we packed our bags. Just a little trip. While Dad was away. We'd be back.

We took the train to East Perth Station, found a bus going to Augusta. I told you the truth, in a way. I said, 'We're going to the place where I found the mischief.'

We made it to a stop just outside Margaret River. You were hungry. We had a twenty-minute stop. We went into a roadhouse with tables festooned with dusty plastic flowers. I forgot my wallet, and told you to order while I went back to the bus to get my bag.

Elliot was there. Waiting. His car parked right beside the

bus. He had a handful of papers that swished in the breeze as he came towards me. He slapped me so hard, he knocked me to the ground. He threw his stack of photocopies and cut-out newspaper articles at me.

'How could you do this?' he shouted. 'After everything Robert's done for you?'

I looked up at him, not daring to get up. 'I just … Harry and I were just taking a trip.'

'Don't lie to me, Louise. I know who you are. I read your stupid book. You even gave your bastard lover the same bloody name. Look at those papers. Go on, look at them!'

I glanced at the scattered newspaper cut-outs. Black-and-white photos of myself stared back at me. Then a few of my sister. My father. Henry.

LOCAL GIRL AND BOY MISSING

SEARCH-AND-RESCUE CALL OFF HUNT
FOR MISSING TEENS

FAMILY'S HEARTBREAK: BRING BACK LOU

BOY, 17, ARRESTED IN MISSING GIRL CASE

'ABO BOY STALKED MY GIRL!'
MOTHER'S CLAIM IN MISSING GIRL CASE

HANGING SUICIDE AT JAIL:
STILL NO ANSWERS FOR THE FAMILY

*Suicide*. I lingered on that. Held the brittle, yellowed paper in my shaking hands.

'Suicide?' Elliot mocked. 'A black boy arrested for killing a sweet little white girl?'

I cried, staring at the pictures of Henry, looking so frightened in handcuffs. Chloe, crying, pleading with the newspaper's readers for any information.

'I know all your secrets,' Elliot spat. 'Your son's a bastard. His father's dead. You tortured your family.'

You saw everything from the roadhouse. You came running.

'Are you going to tell Harry?' Elliot shouted. 'Or are you coming home?'

'Mum?' your little voice dared.

I gathered up the papers in a panic, frightened you should see them. 'We're going home, Harry.'

Elliot grabbed my wrist and yanked me to my feet. He shoved me towards the car. You tumbled as he shoved you too. We both got into the back seat. Elliot slammed the doors. He got in. The tyres screeched as we sped off.

For the whole trip back, we were silent. When we got home, Elliot pulled out every rosebush in the front yard. He left them in a twisted pile in the barren flowerbeds.

'What did we do?' you asked.

What could I tell you?

'Go to your room, love,' I said.

You needed some comfort, but I couldn't give it to you. I spent the next few hours poring over those papers. The newspaper articles told a tale of a missing girl and boy from the lighthouse. At first, they assumed Alexander and I ran away together. Then my mother claimed that Henry had been stalking me, that she'd seen us that night, by the edge of the rocks. 'He pushed my girl in, I just know it!' Our bodies were never found, but we were presumed dead. Henry begged his innocence; no one listened. There was no evidence but my mother's insane ramblings. The paper reported that he hung himself. No reports of foul play. I don't know what would have been worse. For him to end his own life, or for others to end it for him. Either way, I knew who was to blame.

That night, I went to the backyard with the *History*. I lit a fire in an empty ceramic pot. I cried. I threw all the newspaper articles, all the photocopies Elliot had made, into the flames. Sobbed. Tore page after page out of the *History*. I started with Henry's story. Watched the pages with his name burn. I was about to tear out the next history – Archie's history – when a hand came out of the dark and grabbed the book.

'What are you doing?'

Robert.

I wailed. Robert knelt down and embraced me. He stroked my hair and whispered, 'Shhh, shhh, it's okay.'

'I killed him,' I cried.

'It's okay,' he said.

'I killed him.' I muttered it over and over again.

Robert took my face in his hands and made me look at him.

'I love you,' he said. 'I know it's not what you had, but I love you. You gave me a family. I thank God for you every day.'

I pulled my face away from him.

'I'm so sorry we couldn't be brave, you and I,' he said. 'But I'm happy. Aren't we happy? Our boy's grown up with joy and mischief and love.'

I felt numb. I'd been crying for hours. Noticing the fire was going out, I remembered my task. I grabbed the *History* and tried to rip it up again. Robert wrestled it from me.

'Let me burn it,' I begged.

'No.'

I tried to grab it again. Robert backed away.

'Lizzy, this is a testament of your love for our boy.'

'Don't let him know what I did, Robert,' I begged. 'Please. He can't know.'

He shook his head. 'Elliot showed me this weeks ago. He was so angry, but I loved it. You found all the magical, beautiful things in our sorrows, and the sorrows of others. You made the past beautiful.'

'Please, Robert.'

'Elliot said you'd leave us one day. I never thought you would, but I don't begrudge you trying.'

'Please,' I begged again.

'Maybe one day Harry will want to know. Maybe one day he'll figure it out. Maybe that'll be nice. We can make him understand, he was loved. You turned our past into this for him. We sacrificed for him.'

'We sacrificed nothing! That's what I've realised, Robert. We've lived an easy life. We could hide.'

'It wasn't easy. I know you've suffered.'

'I haven't suffered. You and me, we could pretend. He couldn't. Henry never could.'

Robert nodded slowly. 'You're right. I'm sorry. But I can't let you destroy it.'

Robert hid the book somewhere. I wouldn't find out where until decades later. It was easy for him to move on. He wanted his family, consequences be damned. But the guilt over what I'd done haunted me. It created a rift between you and me. You kept asking where the *History* was, why Elliot behaved the way he did. I never spoke about it again. First you were confused, then angry. You never forgave me.

Robert tried so hard to bring back the mischief. Elliot continued to do various threatening things. Pulling out more flowers. When he did, Robert had those metal roses welded to the fence. He even put 'Property of A. Mischief' on the gate key.

'Good luck to Elliot now, hey?' he joked.

I said nothing, never commenting on how beautiful they were. Eventually, Robert asked Elliot to leave. I said nothing again, ignoring this attempt to bring us closer. We grew old like this. He tried to make amends, to make us a real family, to his dying day.

When Robert died, I was alone. You were married, had your own family. Elliot lived a few suburbs away, barely spoke to me. Then, the most unbelievable thing happened. A woman, almost as old as me, moved into the house across the street. She came over one day, introduced me to her oddly well-trained cat, and explained that she was staying with her daughter. She seemed a bit mad, this poor woman. When I asked her to repeat her name, she told me.

'Chloe Moran, at your service.'

*Chloe.* The name made me sad.

'My husband's away. He'll be back soon though. You got a good man, dear?'

'My husband died a few years ago.'

'I'm so sorry to hear that. Loss is a horrible thing, isn't it? Stays with you. My sister Lou was killed when I was just a girl. I miss her every day.'

I stared at her. Could it be?

'I'm so sorry,' I muttered.

The woman looked down at her cat. 'We all are, aren't we, Cornelius?' When she looked back up, I saw my sister's eyes. Deep. Dark. Brown. 'I'll tell you about her sometime. You can tell me about your old man. We'll have tea.'

'That would be nice,' I said.

'Right you are,' she said. She gestured to her cat. 'Come, Cornelius.'

That night, I called you. Said I was tired. The house was too big. A nursing home. Might as well. I gave you the house to sell. I never saw her again. I don't even know if she's still alive.

Soon after I moved into the nursing home, Elliot visited me. As an old man with skin further gouged at with the removal of skin cancers, he exuded this weary energy.

'You know, I saw Harry the other day.'

You'd distanced yourself from Elliot as well, so this was a

strange piece of news. 'Why would you see him?'

'He wants the *History*.'

We hadn't spoken about it in years. 'Why would he want it now?'

'Trying to get a passport to go away with the family. Wanted his birth certificate.'

You'd asked me for it weeks before. I lied. Said I didn't have it.

'He went to the Office of Births and Deaths. Robert's not on there. The father isn't even listed. He wants to know why. He wants the *History*.'

I sighed. 'Why is he asking you?'

'He doesn't trust you, Lizzy.'

'He doesn't trust you either.'

He let out a long sigh. 'Guess he had no one else to ask.'

'Do you know where Robert hid it?'

'He never told me. But he had a floor safe in the study. He got that carpet put in and covered it, remember? Never let me have the key.'

I did. 'Why would he do that?'

Elliot shrugged.

'Well, Harry sold the house. If it's there, it's gone.'

'Good.'

Elliot died a few months later. You came to me with questions, careful, polite and a little begging at first. Then, you became angry.

Guilt is such a powerful thing. It rots you. Disables you. I couldn't tell you.

So why am I writing this? The same reason I wrote the *History*. So I could share my past with you, the people I loved and the people who loved me. I write this only to explain, and to honour them. I don't deserve any pity. As I said to Robert, we *could* do this. We could write new stories for ourselves. We could steal the stories of others, pick from tales of war, and refashion other people's mythologies to hide the violence in our past. We could make the past mere fiction, something that happened to other people.

I try to tell myself nothing is worth the sorrow I caused that little town with its beautiful lighthouse. But if I'm honest, you were. You, my darling boy, were worth everything.

*Jessie*

I finish Grandma's history. I fold it up carefully, then throw it, like a piece of rubbish, by the bin. I feel angry. Grandma lied. She hurt so many people. My grandad, my real one, died because of her. But I'm not angry for that. The *History* isn't real. It's a lie. All of it. I know it was stupid to believe in it, but I did. It was mine, this secret. And she ruined it.

I leave the toilet. The nurse has gone. I go. I walk straight out of the nursing home. No one even sees me. I walk to the bus stop. I wait. I get on the bus, ride it to the train station. I don't really think about it. As the train rocks me back and forth, I'm somewhere else. My friends are gone. All those adventures, running around school with the mischiefs by my side, being a dragon made of magic and fire … I feel like an idiot.

'Next station, Guildford.'

I get off the train. The *History* and *Frostiana* are still in my backpack. It feels heavy as I walk along the main street. I cross the busy roads, make my way to Theodore's house. I creep around the side and peek through his window. He's inside, sitting in a beanbag, singing along to something on his iPad.

I knock on the window. He looks up and smiles. He stumble-runs out of his beanbag, almost falling over, and flings the window open.

'Hey!'

I'm not in the mood for 'hey'.

'Get your dad's lighter.'

He doesn't ask why. He just says, 'Okay.'

He leaves and returns with the red lighter. His cheery mood is gone. He knows how I need him to be.

'Come on,' I say.

He climbs out the window and follows me. We walk in silence through the quiet streets, before coming to the main road. We run across between breaks in the traffic and make it to the railway lines. We run across them too, as the loud bells that warn of an oncoming train start to sound. We just get under the boom gates as they come down. Then, we're here, the park where I count the graves around the big tombstone. I think, right then, I accept there are no graves. This is, as Kay tried to tell me, just a memorial. A memory. It's just like the *History*. A lie. A stand-in. I wonder where all those men have gone.

I place the *History* at the base of the memorial. I open it up in the middle. I see now why Grandma's handwriting was familiar. It's the handwriting of the *History*. I touch it, thinking of her writing it. Not Henry, not a mischief. *Her*. Tears flow down my cheeks. Theodore touches my shoulder.

'I'm sorry,' his little voice comes.

What does he know? What does he have to be sorry for? He doesn't know anything.

'Give me the lighter.'

He hands it to me. I try four times before a flame shoots out. I hold it down to the *History*, right where the pages come together at the spine. The flame catches, and starts to eat through the paper. As the whole book is engulfed in fire, I stand back next to Theodore. He takes my hand, squeezes. I'm sobbing. It's shocking how it looks. It's just like Lou described. Its centre is black except for the red waves rolling through it. The edges, already burnt, crumble off. Flames and black smoke come off the top of it. It looks angry.

A train sounds its horn. I think I hear someone scream my name.

The fire jumps to the grass by the memorial. Theodore's grip tightens. I cry and cry. I feel so betrayed. This book gave me hope. It was full of sadness and tragedy but still managed to be fun and magical. I made my sad new life in this stupid old town magical through the mischief. Now it all feels like nothing.

Theodore glances behind me. Stephanie runs towards us. She screams something and shoves us away from the book. She whips off her cardigan and starts beating the flames. Red embers and ash fly off in every direction, but the flames don't die.

Then, the screech of tyres and a slamming car door. Kay.

'Jessie!'

She rushes towards me and grabs me up in a big hug. Then she notices the fire and lets me go, running to Stephanie's side. She tries to stamp on the flames with her boots. David's here too. He throws a bottle of water on the fire. Eventually, the three of them put it out. Nothing's said for a while. We all just stand there, staring at the blackened book and the burnt patches of grass.

'How could you?' Kay says.

I glance at her. She's in tears too.

'This was our history,' she says.

'It was all lies!' I shout.

Kay shakes her head. 'It wasn't though.'

Kay mumbles an apology to Stephanie. She tries to pick up the *History*, but it's still hot. David runs back to his car and returns with a green shopping bag. Kay snatches it from him and uses it like a glove to pick up the burnt remains of the *History*. Pages crumble and half the cover falls off. I don't know why she bothers.

She then grabs my hand and walks me home in silence. Her

breath shakes. She's trying not to cry.

I'm sent to my room. I slam the door as hard as I can. I sit down in front of my mirror, see the hair that's grown back. I almost look like my old self, before Mum and Dad died. I hate it. I take my scissors and cut off as much of my hair as I can. The scar becomes visible again. It's paler now, just a thin line. I feel betrayed even by that. My scar should be red and angry, like it was before.

It's really late when Kay knocks at my door. I ignore her, huddled in bed, but she comes in anyway with a plate of fish fingers and a jar of tartar sauce. She sees the piles of hair on the floor. She looks at me.

'You cut your hair,' she says.

I pull the doona over my head.

She puts the plate down on my desk. She then sits on my bed, way too close.

'I know you're angry,' she says. 'I am too.'

I move closer to the wall, pulling more of the covers over me.

'Grandma lied about a lot of stuff,' Kay says. 'I keep telling myself that she didn't mean anything bad. It was a different time … I dunno. But someone died because of her.'

*I DON'T CARE!* I want to yell at her.

As if she can hear my thoughts, she says, 'I know you don't care. You're angry about the *History*. But you need to realise something. It was real. It was the only way Grandma could tell Dad the truth. At its core, it was real. I can't believe you burnt it. It was the only thing you'd talk to me about. It was the only way we connected.'

I feel a little bad.

'I wish you could fix this. I wish I could fix this. I think Grandma does too.'

'She lied!' I shout through the covers.

'I know,' Kay says. Through the doona, she strokes my head,

really soft and gentle. Again, I feel bad. Guilty. 'But the *History* was real. The people were anyway. And they were good people, I think. They were part of *our* history.'

She strokes my doona-covered head again.

'Don't ever run away like that again. I called the police, Transperth, Stephanie. I was terrified.'

I nod under the blankets.

'Don't let your fish fingers get cold.'

I wait until I hear the door close. I get up and eat my dinner. I'm hungry. And guilty. I know Kay's right.

I can't sleep. At 2 am, I tiptoe to the study. I see the bookshelves in a new light. I wonder what else is hiding here that went into making the *History*. Then, I hear the sound of a vacuum cleaner.

Mrs Moran is out again. Cornelius grooms himself on the veranda as she vacuums up the sand in her driveway. This is my great-aunt, I realise. I stare at her through the lacy curtains, remembering the card that slipped out of her Sherlock Holmes book. Signed A. Mischief. I guess Mrs Moran never got over her sister's death. The mischief games they played around the lighthouse: she must've shared that with her husband and made a whole other *History*.

Then it sinks in. I destroyed the *History*. Mischief was something these sisters used to escape their grief. It was what Kay and I used too.

I promise Mrs Moran, right then and there, *I'll fix it*.


Monday comes around, but I already have a plan. I have to wait till Saturday, but I feel better, and go to school without causing a fuss. Theodore's waiting for me on the benches by the office.

'You okay?' he asks.

'Yeah,' I say.

'You get in trouble?'

'A little.'

'Dad took my iPod and iPad away. You can't come over for a while.'

'Sorry.'

'It's okay!' he says cheerfully.

I smile at him, at his chirpy tone that's just a little too loud.

'Theodore?'

'Yeah?'

I want to thank him for the way he follows me into stupid things without question. I want to thank him for not being angry at me, even when I'm mean or I get him in trouble. I want to thank him for being my friend, a true friend, the kind I don't deserve.

Instead, I say, 'You're cool.'

He smiles at me. 'You're cool too.'


Saturday comes. Kay leaves in the morning in her car. I go over to Mrs Moran's. We eat gingerbread from the bakery.

I tell her, 'Dragons like gingerbread.'

She says, 'Of course they do, dear.'

Kay returns within the hour. Grandma gets out of the car with her. Mrs Moran waves to them. Grandma just stares.

I run across the road and hug Grandma. She hugs me back.

'I'm so sorry about the *History*, Jessie,' she says.

'You have to make up for it, Grandma,' I say.

'I know.'

I take Grandma's hand and lead her across the road. The whole time, she stares at Mrs Moran with fear.

'I don't think this is a good idea,' she whispers to me.

'It's a great idea!' I say forcefully.

We make it to Mrs Moran's veranda. Cornelius is on her lap. She smiles at me.

'Who's this then, dear?' she asks.

'My grandma,' I say.

'I'd shake your hand, but, well, you can't disturb a cat now, can you?' she says, and pats the seat beside her to invite Grandma to sit down. Grandma keeps staring. A single tear rolls down her face.

'Whatever's the matter, dear?' Mrs Moran asks.

Grandma doesn't know what to do. Mrs Moran starts to frown.

'What's her name, Grandma?' I ask.

Grandma glances at me.

'Mrs Moran wasn't always Mrs Moran, was she?' I say.

Tears, a flood of them, roll down Grandma's cheeks.

'You called her something else once,' I say. 'What was it, Grandma?'

Her hand's shaking in mine.

'Pan,' she says.

Mrs Moran's face changes. The way she looks at Grandma shifts entirely. She stands up, ignoring Cornelius' meow of complaint.

'Lou,' she says.

It's not a question. She knows. She hugs Grandma, who cries. I go back to Kay, to *my* sister, the one who looks like Mum. We leave them to it. They talk for hours. I'm sneaky and watch them through the lace curtains in the study. Mrs Moran never lets go of Grandma's hand. There's no anger in her. *I* would be angry. I think Grandma expected her to be angry. But she isn't. She keeps touching Grandma's face, brushing away tears.

Kay brings me a Vegemite sandwich. We eat together, spying on the two old ladies across the street.

'They seem okay, yeah?' she says.

I nod.

'I told Grandma we were going for high tea. I don't think she believed me though. Still, pretty good mischiefs, you and I, hey?'

I smile. 'Yeah.'

'We should try and find Henry's family. Clear his name.'

I nod again. We finish our sandwiches and Kay takes the plates away. All these months, she's been Mum. Making food. Cleaning up. Reading to me. Doing everything. I wait for her to come back, but she doesn't. I go into the kitchen to find her. She's washing up. Earphones still in her ears. I wonder if there'll be a day when she doesn't need them.

'Kay?'

She tugs the earphones out. 'Yeah?'

'I'm sorry I burnt the *History*.'

She nods. 'I know.'

It's dark by the time Mrs Moran and Grandma finish chatting. Kay drives Grandma home.

That night, Kay returns with her own mischief. She says, 'You need to make up for burning it.' She says, maybe, we can write our own *History of Mischief*. We can turn all the special people in our lives, all the secrets and sadness and joy, into stories. Instantly, I imagine Theodore in an ancient war, singing and dancing his mischief across a battlefield, with Broom at his feet and paper cranes flying like real birds. I imagine Mrs Moran turning all the sand in her driveway into a castle of glass. I imagine Mum and Dad, both of them mischiefs, running through history with me and Kay. I decide we will live together in every century.

Tomorrow, I will go to the library.

# About the Author

Rebecca Higgie is a writer from Perth. Her whole life has been spent in the company of books, with careers in libraries and universities. Formerly an academic at Curtin University and Brunel University London, she has published research on satire and politics. She has worked in the stacks of the State Library of Western Australia and fostered childhood literacy as the Library Officer at Guildford Primary, Western Australia's oldest public school. Her creative work combines whimsy and play with extensive research and critical insights. Her stories and poems have appeared in publications such as *Westerly*, *Stories of Perth* and *Visible Ink*. Her novel *The History of Mischief* won the 2019 Fogarty Literary Award for an unpublished manuscript.

# Acknowledgements

*The History of Mischief* took twelve years, on and off, to write. I could fill another volume with the people who have helped me along this journey. Here, I thank those who have made the biggest impact.

This book is a testament to my love of libraries and books. I am grateful for local public libraries, particularly South Perth Library and Guildford Library, and the vital service of inter-library loan. I have also been lucky to be a part of the magic of school libraries. Thank you to the students, staff and parents of Guildford Primary School, who embraced me and my antics as their Library Officer. It was an immense and joyful privilege.

Thank you to Annie Fogarty and the Fogarty Foundation for funding the Fogarty Literary Award. It is wonderful that you have invested in such a fantastic prize for young WA writers. It was a dream come true to win the inaugural award.

Thank you to the amazing team at Fremantle Press, who have championed the book from day one. I would particularly like to thank my publisher Cate Sutherland. You made me excited about what the book could be. You made this book so much better.

I would like to acknowledge Deb Hunn and Ron Blaber, who supervised my PhD on satire and oversaw the Diogenes research that found its way into the book. I am also grateful for the early advice of Julienne van Loon who assessed the first chapter of the book as part of a manuscript assessment at the Katharine Susannah Prichard Writers' Centre in 2012.

Countless books were read in the process of researching every history. Thank you to all the authors, historians and academics whose works inspired me.

A very special thank you must go to my friends. To the Tugboats – Eva Bujalka, Erin Pearce, Mel Pearce and Elizabeth Tan – thank you for keeping me on track, for always supporting me, and for your invaluable advice on my manuscript. To Kelly Hill, thank you for reading my book and encouraging me to embrace the magical element of the story long ago.

Thank you to my family, especially my mum Linda who has read everything I have ever written, from my PhD to the fairy book I wrote when I was five. Back then, Mum, you never told me that I misspelt the word 'fairy' on every page. You just said it was wonderful. It made me want to write again.

My biggest thanks goes to my husband Yirga. This book would not be possible without your endless encouragement. Marye, thank you for believing in me and for reminding me that the story I needed to tell was more important than what I thought people wanted to hear. Every moment of love and joy in this book stems from you.

Lastly, to my son Tewodros, who swam in my belly as I finished the book. I cannot tell you how much I love you, Teddy. I hope you will be proud.

Rebecca Higgie, 2020

First published 2020 by
FREMANTLE PRESS
25 Quarry Street, Fremantle WA 6160
www.fremantlepress.com.au

Cover design and illustration by Rebecca Mills, www.rebeccamills.com.au
Printed by McPherson's Printing, Victoria, Australia

The History of Mischief
ISBN: 9781925816266

A catalogue record for this
book is available from the
National Library of Australia

Fremantle Press is supported by the State Government through
the Department of Local Government, Sport and Cultural Industries.

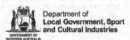